SALAMIS

SALAMIS

Harry Turtledove

CAEZIK
SF & FANTASY

ARC MANOR
ROCKVILLE, MARYLAND

✳

SHAHID MAHMUD
PUBLISHER

www.caeziksf.com

ISBN: 978-1-64710-007-0

First Edition. 1st Printing. November 2020
1 2 3 4 5 6 7 8 9 10

An imprint of Arc Manor LLC

www.CaezikSF.com

This one is for my publisher, Shahid Mahmud, who liked the Hellenistic traders well enough to want to see a new story about them.

Thanks, Shahid!

A NOTE ON WEIGHTS, MEASURES, AND MONEY

I have, as best I could, used in this novel the weights, measures, and coinages my characters would have used and encountered in their journey. Here are some approximate equivalents (precise values would have varied from city to city, further complicating things):

1 digit = ¾ inch	12 khalkoi = 1 obolos
4 digits = 1 palm	6 oboloi = 1 drakhma
6 palms = 1 cubit	100 drakhmai = 1 mina (about 1 pound)
1 cubit = 1 ½ feet	60 minai = 1 talent
1 plethron = 100 feet	
1 stadion = 600 feet	

As noted, these are all approximate. As a measure of how widely they could vary, the talent in Athens was about 57 pounds, while that of Aigina, less than thirty miles away, was about 83 pounds.

I

THE HELMET SAT HEAVY ON MENEDEMOS' HEAD. The cheekpieces covered his ears, too, so that he felt as if he had his fingers stuffed in them. Together, the cheekpieces and the nasal squeezed his vision. So did the upper rim of his big, round, bronze-faced hoplite's shield. The shield was also heavy; keeping it up so it warded the lower half of his face took work.

His right hand closed tighter on the spearshaft. The spear was as long as he was tall, and not a weapon he was used to using. He knew what to do with the sword on his belt, but in this kind of fighting, swords were for emergencies, when you'd lost or broken your spear.

"Come on, you cowardly cur!" his foe shouted, capering in front of him. The Cretan mercenary, equipped much like him, was a lean, tanned, leathery, much-scarred man with a mouthful of broken teeth. His Doric dialect was broader and harsher than the one Rhodians spoke.

"To the crows with you, Heragoras!" Menedemos answered, and thrust at him. The mercenary easily blocked the spear, and went low with his own. Menedemos thought the strike was aimed at his right leg, which was partly protected by a bronze greave. He swung his shield that way to make sure the blow didn't land home.

That was a mistake. Fast as a striking viper, Heragoras switched the direction of his thrust so the speartip smote Menedemos' unarmored left shin, not his right. Like Menedemos', that tip was a bundle of rags, bound on with a rawhide cord, but it still hit hard enough to hurt.

"*Papai!*" Menedemos exclaimed, more from anger at being bested than from the pain. He hated to lose at anything he did.

Heragoras' snaggle-toothed grin said he knew that. He was a professional fighting man, Menedemos very much an amateur. "You know how you buggered it up, right?" he asked.

Glumly, Menedemos dipped his head to show he did. "My shield—" he began.

"That's right." Heragoras dipped his head, too. "You've got that greave there for a reason. You don't have one on the other side 'cause your shield's supposed to cover that leg. Next time, let the greave do its proper job."

"It's an honor to have a panoply," Menedemos said, by which he meant, *My family is rich enough to let me kit myself out.* He wasn't even wearing his corselet. Even on cool spring days like this, you started baking in it after a quarter of an hour.

"It's an honor to *use* a panoply," Heragoras retorted. Gods only knew where he'd got his gear. Stolen it or taken it from men he'd killed, most likely. "So use it. Let's have another go."

They did. This time, Heragoras bruised Menedemos' spear arm. "In a phalanx, my side man's shield would have blocked that," Menedemos said, rubbing where he'd got hit.

"Maybe. More likely, you'd be screaming and bleeding." Heragoras sounded cold as a Phoenician reckoning accounts. That made him more frightening, not less. Letting some of his scorn show, he went on, "You Rhodians are soft. You haven't had to do any fighting for a while, so you forget how."

"We're learning again." Menedemos waved around the gymnasion. Hardly any of the men there were running or wrestling or working with weights, as they would have in less troubled times. They were throwing javelins or shooting arrows at targets fastened to bales of hay or hacking at one another with wooden swords. Menedemos' cousin Sostratos, who was tall but ungainly, had just taken a wooden blade in the ribs. Had it been iron, it would have let the air out of him for good.

2

"Fighting's not something you pick up when you think it might be handy," Heragoras said. "Not that you won't get better, but you won't get good enough. Fighting's a trade, like potter or stonecarver or anything else. You do it all the gods-cursed time, till you don't need to think while you're doing it."

"We're like that on the sea," Menedemos said. Skipper of his family's merchant galley in times of peace, he captained a Rhodian trihemiolia—a shark-swift pirate hunter—when he wasn't buying and selling or when danger threatened.

Heragoras raised his right eyebrow. A vertical scar bisected it; how he hadn't lost the eye to that wound, Menedemos had no idea. "Reckon you can keep the Demetrios from landing on your island here if he sets his mind to it?" he asked.

"We're at peace with the Antigonos and his son," Menedemos said stiffly. "We're at peace with the Ptolemaios down in Egypt, too. We're at peace with everyone."

"For now, y'are." The Cretan mercenary hawked and spat. "But Egypt is a kakodaimon of a long ways away. Demetrios and Antigonos, they can practically piss on you." He pointed northeast, across the strait separating Rhodes from the Anatolian mainland.

"Sostratos and I were in Athens last year, when Demetrios … restored the democracy." Menedemos heard the catch in his own voice. The democracy in Athens, once restored, fell all over itself allying with the young, handsome, personable Demetrios and his old, wily father and voting them ridiculously exaggerated honors.

Heragoras' leer said he knew all about that. "You figure Rhodes'll point its backside towards 'em the same way Athens did? I sure don't. You wouldn't be makin' ready for a scrap if you aimed to do that."

"We want to stay at peace," Menedemos repeated.

"Sure you do. Sisyphos wants to get that cursed stone all the way up the hill. Tantalos wants hisself"—yes, Heragoras' Doric drawl was thick, and getting thicker as he warmed to his subject—"a drink o' water and a bite to eat. What d'you suppose the chances are?"

"If you feel that way, O best one"—Menedemos hoped to make the polite formula sting—"why are you here? Why didn't you join up with old One-eye and Demetrios instead?"

Antigonos was less lucky than Heragoras here; he'd lost an eye in battle. People sometimes called him Cyclops, but not to his face. No matter how old he was (and he had to be past seventy), he remained large and powerful in lands, in armies and fleets, and in his person.

The Cretan spat again. "He's just another one o' them whoresons who want to tell everybody what to do. This here, this is a nice town. Things're looser here than they would be across the water. Not as loose as they are back home, mind you, but back home a fella can't hardly make hisself a living."

Menedemos dipped his head once more. A lot of mercenaries left Crete because the island had nothing for them. And a lot of Cretans who didn't sell their spears to one of Alexander the Great's squabbling successors or another turned pirate instead. To Menedemos, that was worse. Mercenaries followed their paymasters' orders … most of the time, anyhow. Pirates were at war with the world, and especially with Rhodes.

There were rumors Antigonos and Demetrios had been recruiting pirate ships and crews to pad out their naval forces. Menedemos didn't want to believe that; it was too likely to be aimed at his island and his polis. He sighed and made the two-fingered gesture used to turn aside the evil eye and other misfortunes not stoppable by natural means alone. "Maybe everything will turn out for the best," he said.

"Sure it will," Heragoras said. "But whose notion of the best really *is* the best?"

That was such a philosophical question, Menedemos would have looked for it from his cousin, not from this battered soldier of fortune. Since he had no good answer, he hefted his rag-tipped spearshaft again. "As long as I'm here, I should get some more work in," he said.

Sostratos walked across the courtyard that lay at the heart of his family's home. A red-headed Thracian slave woman poured water on the flowers and herbs in the little garden there. "Good day, Threissa," he said. The name she'd been born with sounded more like a sneeze than a word; the one he and his kin used for her just meant *the woman from Thrace*.

4

"Good day, young master." Threissa kept her head down and didn't look at him. Her accented Greek was soft and nervous. He'd taken her to bed a few times after the family bought her. She'd put up with it, as a slave woman had to, but she hadn't been delighted about it. Well, she hadn't delighted him, either. He didn't intend to sleep with her again unless his prong got a desperate itch. She couldn't know that, though, and tried her best to make herself invisible in plain sight.

He heard her low sigh of relief when he kept walking. Some men would have got angry at that. He just went on toward the strongroom. Things went better when you *didn't* make a pointless fuss. He thought so, anyhow, though plenty might have made a pointless fuss arguing with him.

The firm, in which his father and uncle were the head and he and Menedemos the arms, kept most of its merchandise in a warehouse down by the harbor. They paid a night watchman—an old soldier who limped because he'd lost three toes from his right foot—to keep thieves at bay. Alxiadas did a good job, too.

But things that were small, easy to carry, and very valuable stayed in the strongroom here or in the one at Philodemos' house. Sostratos fumbled in a pouch on his belt for the bronze key that would open the lock on the strongroom door.

As he pulled out the key, it slipped between his fingers and fell to the ground. He swore at himself as he bent to pick it up. He was not the most graceful young man in Rhodes, and had such small mishaps more often than he wished. As he straightened, the key now firmly in his grasp, he stole a glance back at Threissa to see if she was laughing at his clumsiness.

She was paying him no attention whatsoever. He tried to decided whether that was better or worse than laughter. Then he chuckled in wry amusement: both were pretty bad. And, whether Threissa laughed at him or not, he could laugh at himself.

He eased the key into the iron lock. The lock had worked fine the last time he used it, a couple of weeks before. His fingers felt how greasy it was; he and his father both smeared it with olive oil to hold rust at bay. Yet the lock didn't release now when he twisted the key. Maybe they hadn't greased it well enough.

He jiggled the key forward and back, trying to get it to set better. It didn't want to move ... and then it did. When he twisted it this time, a *snick!* inside said it had done its job.

"That's better," he muttered. He took the lock off the bar, pulled the bar from the brackets supporting it, and pushed the door open. When he stepped inside, the air smelled rich and pungent, almost perfumed—spices like pepper, cinnamon, and cloves were part of the firm's stock in trade.

But, aside from making certain that mice hadn't been nibbling at the pitched stoppers of the spice jars, he didn't worry about them. It seemed likely that he and Menedemos would take the *Aphrodite* down to Alexandria this sailing season. No profit in bringing spices to Egypt. Many of them were shipped from there to the Hellenese farther north after arriving from the distant, exotic lands that produced them.

Instead, after letting his eyes adjust to the gloom inside the strongroom, he picked up a wooden box that sat on a shelf against the far wall. Even the box was a curiosity: the wood was paler than pine, so pale as to be almost white. He'd never seen anything like the carvings—an odd mix of sinuous and clumsy—that ornamented the top and sides, either.

He took off the top. Nestled inside were the chunks of amber he'd bought from Himilkon the Phoenician the autumn before. Amber came to Hellas from the north. It wouldn't be common in Alexandria, which traded more with the lands to the south and east. He hoped he could get a good price for it there. He hoped he could get a very good price, in fact, because he'd paid Himilkon a good one.

One of the smaller chunks of amber in particular .... Yes, that one. Sostratos took it from the box and walked out of the strongroom and into the watery sunshine. Trapped inside the almost-transparent amber was some kind of insect, smaller than the nail on his little finger. How had it got there? How long had it been there? He could wonder—he *did* wonder—but he had no way to know.

A shadow fell on his hand. He looked up in surprise. "Oh. Father! Hail," he said foolishly.

"Hail, Sostratos." Lysistratos sounded more amused than annoyed. He made allowances for his absentminded, often single-minded son:

more allowances, certainly, than his brother Philodemos was in the habit of making for Menedemos. When he continued, "You're thinking about the trip to Egypt," it wasn't a question.

"That's right." Sostratos dipped his head. "I've got the feeling we have a chance to do some really excellent business, and—" He broke off, truly noticing for the first time the expression on Lysistratos' face. "Father! What's wrong?"

"Word's just reached the city—just reached me, anyhow—that the Demetrios is in Loryma and wants to come to Rhodes to address the Assembly." Lysistratos sounded as grim as he looked. Adding the article in front of Demetrios' name signaled how important he was.

Loryma was the closest city to Rhodes on the Anatolia mainland. And Lysistratos was prominent enough that the news would reach him very quickly. Sostratos puffed out his cheeks and exhaled through pursed lips. "Have you heard what he wants to talk to us about?" he asked, fearing he already knew.

"Not officially," his father said. "But it can be only one thing, don't you think? He'll want to squeeze us or scare us into an alliance with his father and him."

"We can't do that!" Sostratos exclaimed.

"I hope we won't have to. I hope we can convince him we're of more good to Antigonos as a real neutral." Lysistratos' mouth turned down further. "If we can't do that, I hope he doesn't decide to invade the island. He can draw on a lot more men and lands than we can."

"He's clever, too," Sostratos said. "The way he cleared Kassandros' men out of Athens …." His voice trailed away. He'd been there with Menedemos when Demetrios took the city. After a moment, he resumed, "He's not the kind of general I'd like to face."

"I understand that, son. Believe me, I do. Antigonos is the same way—maybe more so," Lysistratos said. "But if we're going to be a free and independent polis, if we're going to stay a free and independent polis, we may have to fight."

Free and independent poleis had been the ideal for as long as Hellenes could remember—for a few hundred years, in other words. They'd beaten back the invading Persians, and they'd also fought ferociously among themselves. Philip of Macedon, Alexander, and the generals who battled furiously over Alexander's empire had subjected most of them. Rhodes remained, still free, still independent, still democratic, preserved in time like that bug in amber.

For the moment, anyhow. "I hope it doesn't come to that," Sostratos said. "I pray it doesn't."

"So do I. So does everyone. But it may," his father said.

Menedemos and his father walked toward the agora to hear what Demetrios had to say to Rhodes. The day was raw, and on the chilly side. Philodemos hadn't gone out on a trading run in a double handful of years. Even so, like Menedemos he made do with just a tunic, no cloak, and went barefoot down the muddy street. He'd been a sailor; in his mind, at least, he still was.

They waved to men they knew. Every Rhodian citizen—every property-owning native son, in other words—who could get out of bed was on his way to the marketplace. Most of them looked as worried as Menedemos felt. Even if they hadn't met Demetrios and seen him in action, as Menedemos had, they knew of him by reputation.

Thinking along with him, his father said, "I don't suppose the city's ever faced worse danger."

"I hope it will be all right," Menedemos said. "He's ... more easy-going than his father, and takes his pleasures where he finds them."

"Yes, you'd think well of all that, wouldn't you?" Philodemos said. Menedemos bit down on the inside of his lower lip till he tasted blood. That let him swallow a sharp retort instead of coming out with it. His father's gibe stung all the more because it held some truth. Philodemos added, "And my stake in this is greater than yours. Baukis will have her baby later this year, remember. What kind of place for a woman with child is a city under siege? And if it falls ... *Oimoi!*" He clapped a hand to his forehead.

"Avert the evil omen!" Menedemos said, and spat—red—into the bosom of his tunic to help do that. Grunting in something as close to approval as he was likely to give his son, Philodemos imitated the gesture.

But Menedemos went right on gnawing at the inside of his lip. Yes, Baukis was pregnant. Menedemos had no idea whether he'd started the baby when his father's new wife was coming home after a religious festival or whether it was Philodemos' seed sprouting inside her. Philodemos had no idea how Menedemos felt about his step-mother ... and how she felt about him. It made life under the same roof with them harder than he'd dreamt anything could be.

"Look!" he said suddenly, pointing ahead. "There's Sostratos." More than a palm taller than most men, his cousin stood out in crowds. Relieved at finding something safe to talk about, he hurried on: "Uncle Lysistratos will be with him. Shall we catch them up?"

"Let's." His father quickened his pace. For a man in his fifties, he was in good trim. His teeth hadn't troubled him much, and he still exercised in the gymnasion. Lately, in fact, he'd been practicing with spear and sword and shield, as Menedemos had. Menedemos needed to step lively to stay up with him.

Sostratos was looking this way and that, as he usually did. Some-times he tripped over his own feet on account of it. Now he spotted Menedemos and his father. He waved, then turned back and spoke to Lysistratos. They slowed to let their kinsmen join them.

"Hail!" all four men said at the same time. Menedemos laughed. Laughing at anything felt good.

They'd run most of the merchants and traders out of the agora. Affairs of the city would cost them a day's business. That was their hard luck. A few sellers did work their way through the incoming citi-zens with trays of cheap wine in cheaper little cups, of grilled squid on wooden skewers, of dough wrapped around cheese and fried in olive oil.

It was as noisy as a usual day at the marketplace, but the timbre was different. No one shouted, no one chuckled. No women's voices lightened things, either. Well-to-do women stayed home and sent slaves to shop for them, but the poorer ones had to go out for them-selves. Menedemos missed their leavening, though he didn't say so for fear of another sharp comeback from his father.

Someone had run up a small platform near the northern edge of the agora, from which Demetrios would speak. Like Sostratos, he was tall enough that people would have been able to see him anyway. Still, the platform was a nice touch. Menedemos and his kinsfolk worked their way towards it. So did everyone else, of course. As men squeezed closer together, a few elbows found ribs and a few toes got stepped on. Menedemos tried to give better than he got.

"Hail, Philodemos! Hail, Lysistratos!" The plump, gray-haired man's well-trained voice showed he'd done his share of public speaking and more.

"Hail, Xanthos," Menedemos' father said with less enthusiasm than he might have shown for other acquaintances. Uncle Lysistratos just dipped his head in a bare minimum of politeness. Xanthos liked to hear himself talk ... and talk ... and talk.

He paid no attention to Menedemos or Sostratos. He looked down his nose at the younger generation when he noticed them at all. But he regaled their fathers with a preview of everything Demetrios would say—everything he thought Demetrios would say, anyhow. To Menedemos, he sounded more like a Rhodian man of business than a Macedonian warlord, but that didn't stop him. It didn't even slow him down.

Someone clambered up onto the platform: not Demetrios but a man named Komanos, one of the most prominent people in the city. He called for quiet, then called for it again. When he didn't get it, he gestured to two men behind the platform. The trumpeters blew a loud, discordant blast that startled everyone.

This time, the assembled citizens paid attention when Komanos asked them to settle down. "Thank you, O men of Rhodes!" Komanos said. Menedemos eyed Sostratos, wondering if his cousin would explain how *O andres Rhodioi* was modeled after Athens' *O andres Athenaioi*, as he did at about every other Assembly. Sostratos pined for Athens the way most young men pined for a gorgeous hetaira they couldn't begin to afford.

But Sostratos, like the other men in the agora, really was giving Komanos his attention. He could see the civic leader better than Menedemos could; Menedemos was a digit or two under average height. *At least I make the most of what I've got*, Menedemos thought.

"O men of Rhodes, our polis has been free and independent since it was built, almost a hundred years ago," Komanos said. "The three towns here before, Ialysos, Lindos, and Kamiros, were likewise free and independent poleis." *Demetrios won't like that* went through Menedemos' mind as Komanos continued, "We are gathered here now to decide whether the day of the free and independent polis is past in Hellas, whether all small states must seek the protection of one strong neighbor lest another strong neighbor destroy them altogether. Here to put to us terms for a possible alliance with himself and his illustrious father is the general and admiral, Demetrios son of Antigonos. I know we'll hear him with the serious attention his proposal deserves."

By the gods, don't start throwing cabbages or rocks at him! That was what Komanos had to mean. By the way one of Sostratos' eyebrows jumped toward his hairline, he was thinking the same thing.

Up onto the platform stepped Demetrios. Where Komanos had scrambled, he was big enough simply to step, and that despite the weight of greaves and a corselet polished till their bronze shone almost like gold. His face was handsome and ruddy, his hair halfway toward the blond sometimes found among Macedonians and more often in their barbarous neighbors to the north and west.

"Hail, O men of Rhodes!" Demetrios' big, deep voice effortlessly filled the marked square. He spoke an Attic-flavored Greek much like Sostratos', with only a vanishing trace of the broad vowels and odd consonant clusters he must have used as a little boy. "It is a pleasure and an honor to speak to the citizens of the free and independent polis of Rhodes."

Some of the men in the crowd made small approving noises, soaking in Demetrios' flattery like dry sponges soaking up water. Menedemos thought the Macedonian was being sardonic, in effect saying, *You believe you're free and independent, but I'm the one with the soldiers and the ships.* By the way Sostratos' eyebrow rose again, he heard the Macedonian's words the same way.

Demetrios went on, "In the old days, it was easy for a polis to stay free and independent. It was facing only other poleis, more or less the same size it was. But times have changed. I was fortunate enough to liberate Athens from Kassandros' oppression last year. Athens was a polis, with only the force a polis could draw on. Kassandros rules broad lands in Europe. He has great wealth, and many men to obey him. Without help from my father and me, Athens on her own couldn't have hoped to gain freedom and independence once more."

Again, some of the citizens of Rhodes dipped their heads in agreement and made approving noises. Menedemos had been in Athens. To him, what Demetrios called its newfound freedom and

11

independence looked a lot like a change of masters from Kassandros to Antigonos and his son. To Sostratos, too, by the set of Menedemos' cousin's mouth.

"Out in the east, Seleukos rules huge tracts of land, all full of barbarians," Demetrios said. "Hellenes are settling there, but they have no free and independent poleis. Seleukos doesn't let them, and the locals would swallow places like that if he did. Egypt is the same way. You know that's true, O men of Rhodes. Ptolemaios rules Egypt like the Persians before him, and like the Pharaohs before the Persians. He tells people what to do, and they do it. No free and independent poleis in Egypt, by the gods!" He threw his hands high, artfully scorning the very idea.

"He's sly," Sostratos murmured before Menedemos could. Demetrios was doing the most dangerous thing he could: telling the truth, but slanting it in his direction.

"Now my father, on the other hand, has plenty of free and independent poleis working alongside him as friends and allies," the Macedonian went on. "That's what we're looking for from Rhodes: friendship and alliance. That's all, by the gods! Join with my father and me in our struggle against the tyrant Ptolemaios, and everything will go back to the way it was as soon as the fight is over."

To Menedemos, he sounded like a man trying to talk a girl into bed. No mean seducer himself, Menedemos knew a smooth one when he heard him. He looked around. How many of his fellow citizens felt the same way? Did they think freedom and independence were worth holding on to in a world that had changed?

Then again, how many of them traded with Ptolemaios' Egypt? Joining Antigonos and Demetrios would put a crimp in that. Men tended to think about where their silver came from.

"We don't want trouble on our border," Demetrios said. "Next to my father's lands, Rhodes is only the size of a flea, but even fleabites are annoying. Friends, it's easier to go the way the wind already blows. Think about that when you make up your minds. If you try to sail the other way, the wave that's coming will swamp you. Good day." He hopped down from the platform. In the dead silence in the market square, Menedemos heard Demetrios' armor clatter about him, as if he were one of Homer's warriors going to his doom.

He also heard Sostratos mutter, "'My father's *lands,*'" to himself in thoughtful tones. He understood that; he'd noticed the odd phrasing himself. Since Alexander's half-witted half-brother and young posthumous son met their untimely demises, none of the generals who held chunks of his empire had declared himself a king. That day might be—likely was—coming, but it hadn't come yet.

Komanos got back up where the citizens could see him. He was smoother than he had been the first time, but he still didn't have Demetrios' size or grace to make the ascent seem easy. "Thank you, most excellent son of Antigonos, for being so plain about your views and those of your illustrious father. We shall now discuss your proposal and determine what the sense of the polis may be."

Everyone started shouting and waving his hand hand at once. In Homeric assemblies, only the man holding the scepter had the right to speak. Rhodian democracy was rowdier and more freewheeling than that. *Everyone thinks he's Agamemnon or Nestor,* Menedemos thought, *but a lot of these people would embarrass Thersites.*

Xanthos made his way up onto the platform. Menedemos and Sostratos exchanged glances. So did Philodemos and Lysistratos. If that wasn't a put-up job, none of them had ever seen one.

"Hear me, O men of Rhodes!" Xanthos said loudly. *And hear me, and hear me, and hear me some more* went through Menedemos' mind. Sure enough, his father's long-winded friend spent half an hour walking through the obvious: that Rhodes had long been free and independent, that the polis would probably stay safer if it didn't get caught up in its bigger neighbors' quarrels, and that many people in the polis did a lot of business with Egypt. Much later than he should have, he finished, "All this being so, that which is now most expedient to us is to continue the course we have always taken," and stood down.

The next speaker, a farmer named Polyaratos, proved a fiery partisan of Demetrios and Antigonos'. "They're what the future looks like," he declared. "They'll put Alexander's empire back together. Do we want to be on the outside looking in after they do that? I don't think so! They'll be kings with crowns, and they'll treat us the way kings always treat people who make 'em angry. We'd have to be mad to turn down what the Demetrios is offering us—mad, I tell you!"

"I wonder how much of Antigonos' silver he's got in his wallet," Sostratos said in a low voice. Menedemos dipped his head; it wasn't as if the same thought hadn't crossed his mind.

But others also spoke for the Macedonians. Most of them, like Polyaratos, were men with few ties outside the island. Then another merchant, Rhodokles son of Simos, got on the platform. He was a rival to Philodemos and Lysistratos' firm, but no one had ever called him a fool.

Blunt as usual, he said, "I've heard that Demetrios and Antigonos are paying pirates to join their fleet. If they do things like that, I don't care to go to war alongside 'em. It's about that simple." He jumped down again.

His blunt announcement seemed to take the wind from the sails of Demetrios' friends. Not a Rhodian breathed who didn't hate pirates. When Komanos called for the vote, a solid majority chose continued neutrality. Komanos invited Demetrios up. As the warlord scowled at the citizens who hadn't done his bidding, Komanos put the best face he could on things: "We are not your foes, O Demetrios. We wish only to remain friends with everyone."

"I shall take this news to my father. Hail!" Demetrios said, and not one word more. That ended the Assembly in unceremonious fashion.

"What do you think?" Menedemos asked Sostratos as they started home with their fathers.

"We may try hard to stay away from the wider world's affairs, but those affairs won't stay away from us," his cousin answered. Menedemos clicked his tongue between his teeth. That seemed only too likely to him, too.

II

DAMONAX TORE A CHUNK FROM A LOAF OF BARLEY bread and dipped it into a small bowl of olive oil. Then he held it out to Sostratos. "Here, O best one, try this."

"Thanks." Sostratos took the morsel from his brother-in-law with odd reluctance. He popped it into his mouth and chewed, smacking his lips once or twice as he judged the flavor.

"Tell me what you think. Be honest." Damonax's smile was crooked. "As if you could be any other way."

He's nervous of me, Sostratos realized with surprise. He was also nervous of Damonax. Any handsome, self-assured man could do that to him. Menedemos certainly did, and he and his cousin had known each other since before either could remember. He also resented Damonax for taking his sister Erinna, one of the few friends he'd had in the world, out of his house, and for caring more about himself than about the trading firm he'd married into.

But Sostratos *was* honest: relentlessly so, sometimes. He wouldn't—he couldn't—tell Damonax the oil was fit only for greasing capstans unless that were true. And it wasn't. "Good oil," he said after swallowing. "Nice and fruity—you can really taste the olive in it."

"Is it good enough to take off the island?" Damonax sounded anxious. And well he might; he was still paying down debts he'd had before he married Erinna. Before Sostratos could answer, his brother-in-law held up a hand. "Your father and I went round and round last summer while you and Menedemos were in Athens. He made me see why none of you wanted to ship the oil there. I still don't like it, but I understand it."

"All right." Sostratos left it at that. Lysistratos had told him he'd finally told Damonax he would sooner stick an amphora of his olive oil up his back passage than carry it to Athens. He'd also told Sostratos not to let on that he knew that, so he didn't.

Damonax continued, "But Alexandria isn't Athens. Olives don't grow there, so they have to bring in all their oil. You could get a good price for mine in Egypt."

"It *is* good oil." Of his own accord, Sostratos dipped another chunk of bread into the bowl and ate it. "We can probably take some. Trouble is, an akatos like the *Aphrodite* doesn't have the carrying space a sailing freighter does. We have to weigh value against bulk a lot more carefully than those ships do."

"How much do you suppose you can get for each amphora?" his brother-in-law asked. Yes, Damonax was anxious about silver.

Sostratos had a figure in mind, but named one only half as high. Damonax's face fell. "We'll try to do better, O marvelous one," Sostratos assured him. This way, if he did better than he said he could but not so well as he hoped, Damonax would stay happy. If he promised the high price but didn't deliver, he'd never hear the end of it. Few merchants' tricks were so basic, and few worked better.

"I shall have some jars ready to load before you sail away," Damonax said. "Try not to leave without them this time, all right?"

"We'll do our best." Sostratos matched dry with dry. The year before, he and Menedemos had had to feign deafness to keep Damonax's oil off the *Aphrodite* as she headed towards Athens.

Lysistratos walked into the dining room. He dipped his head to Damonax. "Will you excuse us, please? Someone is here with whom Sostratos and I need to consult in privacy."

"However you please, of course, my father-in-law," Damonax replied, though curiosity stuck out all over him like a hedgehog's prickles. No, not just curiosity, Sostratos judged: annoyance, too. Damonax would be wondering, *Why don't I get consulted, too?*

Because you aren't important enough, that's why, Sostratos thought, enjoying the other man's discomfiture even though he had no idea who his father's prominent guest might be. Damonax sulkily took his leave. When his sandals flapped on the stairs leading to his second-story room, Lysistratos also left the dining room. He returned a moment later with Komanos.

"Hail, best one!" Sostratos said in surprise. He clasped the Rhodian leader's hand.

"Hail," Komanos said. Threissa came in with wine, a mixing jar of water, and a tray of little cakes sweetened with honey and almond paste. He made small talk till the slave woman left the room. After pouring himself a little wine and watering it well, he resumed: "So you and Menedemos will be going across to Alexandria soon?"

"That's right, sir. As soon as the weather gives us a decent chance to cross safely," Sostratos said. "You'll know this from my father?"

Komanos dipped his head. "So I will," he agreed. "Do you think you might be able to get in to see the Ptolemaios and let him know what the Rhodian Assembly told Demetrios? He should hear as quickly as possible. Knowing what we've done will affect what he does."

"And knowing we haven't allied with Antigonos and Demetrios will make him better inclined towards us?" Sostratos asked.

Instead of answering, Komanos glanced at Lysistratos. "He knows things, he sees things, this one. And I see why you told me he talks about writing history. He should do it. He has the understanding."

Sostratos was nearly thirty. He couldn't remember ever feeling so flattered before. Hoping he wasn't blushing like the embers of a fire, he said, "Right at the moment, sir, aren't we just trying to live through history?"

"Everyone tries to live through history," his father put in. "No one's done it yet."

"Too true." Komanos gave his attention back to Sostratos. "*Can* you arrange an audience with Ptolemaios?"

"I ... think so," Sostratos said cautiously. "We met him when he was on Kos ... let me think ... three years ago now. He's the kind of man who remembers names. And you're right, sir—he will be curious about what Rhodes has been up to."

"This gods-cursed war! Alexander died"—Lysistratos counted on his fingers, reckoning it up—"seventeen years ago now, if I have it right, and his generals keep clawing away at each other like a big bowlful of crabs. If they'd just be happy with what they have …."

"Some people are, Father. Some always want more," Sostratos said. "I don't think you get to be a general unless you have that in you."

"That sounds right to me," Komanos said. His wealth argued that he wanted more, too, even if he was no warlord. "The gods brass you and protect you for doing the polis' business along with your own."

"About that, O best one …," Sostratos coughed discreetly. "we may need to spread some silver around to get to see Ptolemaios. We may need to sit in waiting rooms for days, too, instead of trading. Ptolemaios isn't officially a king any more than Antigonos is, but he lives in as much state as if he were."

Komanos laughed. "By the dog, son of Lysistratos, you see all kinds of things! On my oath, your business won't suffer because of what you do for Rhodes. There! Are you happy?"

"*Malista!* I should say so!" Sostratos did his best to sound grateful. He wished he had an actor's smiling mask to clap on. Oaths like Komanos' were all the better if written down. But to come out and say so would only offend the magnate.

A few years ago, I would *have asked him to put it in writing,* Sostratos thought. *And he* would *have got angry. One step at a time, I'm learning how to be a human being.*

Komanos turned back to Lysistratos. "I'll go over and talk to your brother and nephew now, let them know you're all right with the arrangements." He started for the front door, and held up a hand when Lysistratos moved to accompany him. "Don't bother, best one. I know the way. Hail!"

"Hail!" Sostratos' father echoed. When Komanos had gone, he scratched his head. "Isn't that interesting? I'd have guessed he'd already talked with Philodemos. I'm just the younger brother, after all. Maybe he thought we'd be easier to persuade. I'm not sure I like that."

"Maybe he thought we'd be the ones with the sense to see what the polis needs." Sostratos had been thinking about actors' masks a

18

moment before. Now he thought about the men who wore them. "Sometimes Menedemos can be as proud and vain as anyone who goes on the stage."

He said nothing about Philodemos. It was not his place to criticize a man a generation older. By the way Lysistratos chuckled, he didn't need to say anything. No one was more likely to know his uncle's flaws than his father.

Lysistratos asked, "Do you think you and Menedemos have enough diplomacy in you to serve the polis this way?"

"I hope so." Sostratos took the question seriously. He took most questions that way. Sometimes it annoyed Menedemos. He went on, "Dickering for Rhodes shouldn't be much different from dickering for the firm. And we know as much about what's going on as anyone is likely to."

"However much that is, or however little," his father said. "Do you know where the Demetrios went after he sailed back to the mainland?"

"No, Father." Sostratos tossed his head. "But fishing boats are going out farther from the harbor as the weather gets better, and our patrols against pirates will start putting to sea before long. We'll hear as soon as anyone else does."

"I hope we hear before you put to sea yourself," Lysistratos said. "That would be something else important you could pass on to the Ptolemaios."

"It would, yes." Sostratos hesitated. "Antigonos and Demetrios may not like it if Rhodians go telling tales to Ptolemaios. They may decide we like him better than we like them." He paused again, then finished, "Which we do, but we don't want to throw it in their faces."

"True enough," his father said. "Ptolemaios is less dangerous to our freedom and independence than Antigonos and Demetrios are. We'd make them a nice snack—at least they think so. And most of what Egypt ships to Hellas and Anatolia comes through Rhodes. We make a lot of silver from the lands the Ptolemaios holds."

"Antigonos will know that," Sostratos said. "I'm not sure how smart Demetrios is. He's not stupid, but I don't know if he's *that* smart. Antigonos, though … Antigonos has only the one eye, but I think he sees everything anyway."

"True again, however much I wish it weren't." Lysistratos set a hand on Sostratos' shoulder. "All we can do is all we can do. Gods grant it be enough."

Sostratos had his doubts about the gods, as many young men who'd studied a bit did. When his father's father was young, talking about doubts like that might have led to hemlock. It had for Sokrates. Things were looser now, but he didn't want to risk upsetting his father. And .... "The way things are, I'll take any help Rhodes can get."

"So will I, son," Lysistratos said. "The way things are, we'll need it." His father walked out of the dining room.

Sostratos stayed there a little longer, scratching at the edge of his mustache as he worried. Most young men these days shaved their whiskers, imitating Alexander's style, but he'd let his grow out in hopes of being taken for a philosopher. Maybe he'd let them grow in hopes of persuading himself he was a philosopher, not someone who worried more about the price of papyrus than the nature of the good.

He was harder to persuade than he had been when he first came home from Athens. Then he'd hated to return to a life he scorned. Now? *Now I make a pretty god merchant, maybe a better merchant than I would a historian.*

Should I cut off the beard, then? he wondered. But he tossed his head, rejecting the idea. Stylish or not, shaving every day was a cursed nuisance.

He walked into the courtyard. A lizard skittered away from him. That it was out and moving was another sign spring was on the way. Someone down the street shouted "*Exito!*"—Here it comes!—and dumped a slop jar out a second-story window. The splash was followed by curses from passersby who hadn't got out of the way fast enough. Sostratos laughed and sympathized at the same time. It wasn't as if he'd never got splattered.

Damonax came down the stairs and hurried up to him. "What did Komanos want with you?" he asked eagerly.

"Oh, this and that," Sostratos answered. He could have made a better liar, but he knew blabbing about the polis' business wasn't the smartest thing he could do.

His brother-in-law exhaled in annoyance. "Do you think I'll go spreading the news from Karia to Carthage?"

"No, I don't think so," Sostratos answered, more or less honestly. "But if … whatever it was *should* get about and Komanos asks me, 'You didn't tell anyone, did you?', I don't want to have to say, 'Well, only my brother-in-law.' Do you see what I'm saying?"

Damonax waved his hand, a gesture full of impatience and contempt. "You just tell him, 'No, of course I didn't,' and go on about your business."

Sostratos stared at him. They both used Greek, but they were speaking two different languages. "I don't think that would be a good idea, O marvelous one." He freighted the overblown honorific with as much scorn of his own as he could.

"Well, to the crows with you, then!" Damonax turned on his heel and stamped away. Had there been a small dog in the courtyard, he would have kicked it as he went.

Sostratos wanted to kick something—or someone—himself. He hoped his brother-in-law wouldn't take out his anger on Erinna. His sister would have understood that some things needed to be kept quiet; she had the same kind of good sense as Sostratos himself. But Damonax? No wonder he'd got into trouble over debt if he had no more self-control than he was showing.

Once the *Aphrodite* put to sea, it would be tempting to dump the olive oil overboard and claim the amphorai had somehow broken. Reluctantly, Sostratos tossed his head. The sailors would gossip, and it would cost the firm money. But it *was* tempting.

Sikon the cook tipped Menedemos a wink. "They've been selling fine squid the past few days. The agora is full of fishermen with wicker baskets. So many of 'em out now, I bet they're nice and cheap," he said.

"They'd better be," Menedemos answered. "If they aren't, my father's wife won't be happy with you."

Sikon shrugged. "She hasn't been so bad lately, young master. You and your father, the two of you managed to talk some sense into her. And she hasn't cared about food so much, anyway, since she started carrying the baby."

He took the kind of casual liberties a trusted slave with an important job could. He was about Menedemos' father's age, and had

21

been with the family longer than Menedemos had been alive. Born in Karia or Lykia or some other barbarous place, he'd got a Greek-sounding name when he was sold. Some sort of accent still flavored his speech, but he'd used the dual *you* to talk about Menedemos and Philodemos, something even native Hellenes were doing less and less often these days.

"Don't give her trouble, especially while she's pregnant," Menedemos said. Baukis tried to make Sikon spend less on food for the household than he wanted to. That was the mistress' prerogative, as trying to get around it was the slave's.

"If she had her way, we'd eat barley mush all the time, with salted olives for opson," Sikon said.

"Don't give her trouble, I told you." Menedemos spoke less sharply than he wanted to. He couldn't show half of what he felt about Baukis, not without landing in more trouble than anyone would want. *If only I knew whether the baby she's carrying is Father's or mine*, he thought.

"I heard you, young master." Like any cook worth his prawns, Sikon had a double chin. The flesh under there wobbled as he drew his head back in touchy pride. Yes, he thought the household revolved around him and the kitchen.

Sometimes he wasn't so far wrong, either. "Why don't you head for the market and come back with some of those squid?" Menedemos said. "As long as they're as cheap as you think they are, I mean."

"Of course, young master." Sikon could have posed for a statue of innocence personified—one more trick every sly slave knew. If he kept a few oboloi out of the seafood budget, who'd ever heard of a slave that wouldn't steal a bit? They only caused trouble when they got greedy.

Out the cook went, whistling a tune Menedemos had heard in a tavern in Athens the summer before. He didn't remember hearing it here in Rhodes, but Sikon must have. It was probably a tavern tune here, too. Some masters wouldn't have let their slaves have enough time or money to visit taverns. Some masters measured their slaves' rations every day, and made sure their men and women didn't get anything on top of what they were supposed to have.

Menedemos' father wasn't like that. Philodemos recognized that his slaves were human beings with human quirks and desires, not automata like the ones Homer had Hephaistos making. Menedemos' mouth twisted. His father was easier on the slaves than on him. He had quirks and desires, too, but his father didn't want to acknowledge them.

Since one of those desires was for his father's wife …. His mouth twisted again, as if it were full of the sourest vinegar. He hoped the *Aphrodite* would sail for Alexandria soon. Alexandria was thousands of stadia, hundreds of parasangs, from Rhodes. It wasn't as if he wouldn't think about—worry about—Baukis while at sea and down in Egypt. But, think and worry as he would, he wouldn't be able to do anything. And physical distance gave emotional distance. It might, anyhowat any rate.

The political side of things, too …. He'd hashed that out with his father—who was cool and sensible about such things—and with Sostratos and *his* father. They all agreed Rhodes would be better off truly free and independent than under the muscular thumbs of Antigonos and Demetrios. Uncle Lysistratos had said, "Between you and Sostratos, you just about make one diplomat." Menedemos rather liked that. He thought it might be true. He hoped it was.

His father stuck his head into the kitchen. "I just saw Sikon heading out," Philodemos said.

"That's right." Menedemos dipped his head. "He says there've been lots of squid in the agora lately, so he can get them for a good price."

"Whatever he really pays, he'll swear to us it was more," his father said. "The difference will go straight into his mouth." He mimed sticking an obolos between his cheek and his teeth, the way people did when they stowed away small change. Then he laughed—sourly, but he did. "I've never known a cook who didn't steal some. As long as it isn't too much …." He spread his hands.

"I was just thinking the same thing!" Menedemos exclaimed. "Isn't that funny?"

"Maybe you're growing up. Or maybe I'm slipping into my second childhood." Philodemos couldn't praise without adding a scorpion's sting in the tail of what he said to Menedemos. He rubbed his chin as he eyed his son. "I really ought to get you married off. High time I had grandchildren."

Maybe you do, or you will soon, Menedemos thought. Snow rarely fell on Rhodes, but ice walked up his back. He knew which woman he wanted to wed. He also knew how impossible that was. He rarely even got the chance to talk to Baukis, not about anything that mattered. You never could tell what a slave might overhear. Slaves were cursed nuisances in all kinds of ways. Living without them, though, meant doing all your own work. Life was easier with them.

Menedemos knew he didn't change expression when his father brought up marriage. It wasn't the first time, and he had practice holding his features still around the older man. After no more than a heartbeat's pause, he answered, "Most of the time, Father, I'd say we should do it soon, too. But with the political situation the way it is—"

That worked better than he'd dreamt it would. His father clapped a hand to his forehead. "The political situation! *Oimoi!* I hunted you down to tell you what I just heard, and then we started talking about other things and I forgot. Maybe I really *am* losing my wits."

"What did you hear?"

"When you take the *Aphrodite* to Egypt, I expect you plan to go by way of Cyprus. Am I right?"

"I meant to, certainly. It makes the passage across the Inner Sea as short as possible. Why? Are you saying I shouldn't?"

"I'm afraid I am. That's my news. Demetrios has a fleet in the waters there, and he's landed an army near Karpaseia, at the tip of the peninsula in the northeast. The poleis on Cyprus mostly back Ptolemaios, and Antigonos' son is attacking Menelaos, who's holed up in Salamis. Where else on the island he may go, I can't tell you."

"*Oimoi!* is right, then," Menedemos said. The last thing a trader wanted was to sail into the middle of a war. He'd done that in Sicily and southern Italy, and he never wanted to do it again. After a moment, he continued, "So you think we should go straight from Rhodes?"

"Don't you?" his father returned.

"Probably. But—" Menedemos muttered to himself and counted on his fingers. In that moment, full of thought and calculation, he might almost have been Sostratos, though Sostratos would have been offended to hear it. "It's … what? Something like three thousand stadia from here to Alexandria?"

"About that, yes," Philodemos said. "I don't know that anyone's reckoned it up exactly."

"I don't know how you would," Menedemos agreed. "But we'd cut a quarter or a third off the distance over open water if we could stop for food and water and a rest at Paphos or one of the other towns on the west coast of Cyprus."

"I know. You wouldn't get supplies if Demetrios' men are attacking those places, too, though. You'd get your ship seized, is what you'd get. And your whole crew would be sold into slavery or held for ransom—or as hostages to make Rhodes do whatever Antigonos and Demetrios tell us to."

"You're right, Father. I wish you were wrong, but you're right." Menedemos retreated into that brown study again. "Three thousand stadia ... with a good wind behind us, we could do it in three days. It'll take longer if we have to row most of the way. We won't man all the oars all the time—we'd kill the crew if we did. That will slow us down. Five or six days, I'd guess."

"That sounds about right," his father agreed. Neither one of them said a word about storms. Out in the middle of the vast Inner Sea, the *Aphrodite* would bounce like a toy boat made from a wood chip, a stick, and a bit of rag when boys threw stones into the rain puddle where it floated.

"All part of the business," Menedemos said, putting the best face he could on things. His father dipped his head. For once, they understood each other perfectly.

Damonax stood on the pier, watching the workmen he'd hired pass amphorai of olive oil down to the rowers who were stowing them in the *Aphrodite*. "Put them well back towards the stern," he said importantly. "Make sure they're well padded, too. Straw and whatever else you have."

Sostratos tossed his head. "No, they go forward," he said, his voice sharp and annoyed. "We have other cargo we'll need the stern space for." He rounded on his brother-in-law. "I don't tell you how to run your farm, O best one. I'm toikharkhos on this ship, and I'll thank you to remember it. Things go where *I* say they go, and nowhere else. Have you got that?"

Damonax stared at him. Sostratos was usually a mild-mannered man, one who might let himself be pushed around where most Hellenes wouldn't have. Not here, though. A nervous smile on his face, Damonax said, "I meant no harm, truly."

"Neither did Oidipous," Sostratos snapped. "Not a bit. How did that turn out?"

His brother-in-law flinched. Unlike Sostratos, Damonax was conventionally pious. He didn't take the old myths as parables or explanations; to him, they were *truth*. "My dear fellow!" he managed after a false start. "That's ... a bit much, don't you think?"

"And telling my men how to do their work on my ship isn't a bit much, you mean?" Sostratos was implacable as a Fury.

"I won't do it again." Damonax sounded like a small boy who meant, *Not while you can catch me, anyway*. After a moment of weighing the odds, he asked, "What *will* be stowed back towards the stern?"

None of your cursed business. That got as far as the tip of Sostratos' tongue, but no farther. You could always say things some other time. You couldn't call them back once said, and he guessed he'd given Damonax enough already. What he did say was, "Wine. Fine wine. Grapes don't do well in Egypt. The Egyptians make a brew out of dates—"

"Sounds disgusting!" Damonax broke in.

"I tried it a couple of years ago, when we went to the land of the Ioudaioi," Sostratos said. "It will get you drunk if you pour down enough, and it won't give you a flux of the bowels the way plain water can, but it's not what anyone would call good. So ordinary freighters bring lots of ordinary wine into Egypt for the soldiers and cooks and carpenters and masons and what have you. We'll bring some of the fine vintages, for the people who can afford them."

"Why do you want them there and not the oil?" Damonax asked.

"Because a metretes of wine is heavier than a metretes of oil," Sostratos said. A metretes was the amount a large amphora held. He went on, "The ship will handle better if we have more weight at the stern, not at the bow."

"I didn't know that," Damonax said, as if he blamed Sostratos for his own ignorance. Realizing how that had to sound, he added, "Your business is more complicated than it looks at first glance, isn't it?"

"Most things are," Sostratos replied, which made his brother-in-law wince again. "We'll get the oil aboard. We'll get it to Egypt and get the best price we can for it. We'll do the same with the wine, and with everything else we're carrying." He said not a word about the amber. The fewer people who knew of it, the better.

"What kind of wine will you carry?" Damonax asked.

Sostratos would have told him that—it wasn't a secret. In fact, he was a little surprised his brother-in-law didn't already know. But Damonax came up to the polis of Rhodes only when he had business here; he stayed on his farm most of the time. Before Sostratos could answer, though, a procession of bearers, each carrying a two-eared amphora, approached the *Aphrodite* from the direction of the family warehouse.

Pointing at them with his chin, he said, "Here they come now. Suppose you tell me where they're from."

Damonax scratched the side of his jaw as he considered. "Well, I recognize those jars the men in front have, the ones that are longer and skinnier and more conical than Rhodian ware. They're from Khios, aren't they?"

"*Euge!* Very good, best one!" Sostratos made as if to clap his hands. "That's not just any wine from Khios, either. That's Ariousian, from the northwestern part of the island. Some came into Rhodes last year, while we were in Athens, and my father and my uncle bought all they could."

"Ariousian!" Damonax's voice went dreamy. "The best wine in the world, people say."

"Some people say that," Sostratos allowed. "But what about the other amphorai, the ones that are fatter than those we make here?"

Those amphorai made his brother-in-law frown. At last, reluctantly, Damonax said, "I'm afraid they have me stumped."

"Well, you don't see them all that often in Rhodes." Sostratos could afford to sound tolerant. He knew at a glance the shape of amphorai from at least a score of different islands and poleis, perhaps twice that many. Menedemos likely recognized even more. Sostratos continued, "Thasos lies way to the north in the Aegean; it's off the European coast, just east of the fingers of land that come down from the Khalkidike. And Thasian wine …. Wine doesn't get much better, if it gets any better at all."

27

"Thasian! That's the one with the bouquet like apples!" Damonax exclaimed. "I've had some once or twice. It was so smooth, I didn't want to water it."

"No?" One of Sostratos' eyebrows slid upwards. "I didn't realize we'd brought a Macedonian into the family." Macedonians were notorious for drinking their wine neat, as if they were Thracians or other outright barbarians, not men who passed themselves off as Hellenes. From everything Sostratos had seen, they'd earned that notoriety.

"I hope you know me better than that, O best one," Damonax said. Sostratos had to dip his head, acknowledging that he did. His brother-in-law had his share of human flaws and foibles, but drunkenness wasn't one of them. Then Damonax turned the subject: "Is it true, what they're saying about the Demetrios?"

Sostratos spread his hands, palms up. "I don't know, my dear. What have you heard? I wouldn't give you an obolos for a thousand of the stupid stories that go through the market square."

"That the son of Antigonos is trying to take Cyprus away from Ptolemaios."

"Oh. That *is* true. Or at least I've heard it from people I believe."

"Like Komanos?" Damonax gibed. Sure as a daimon, being excluded from the meeting with the prominent politician still rankled.

"No," Sostratos said. *Not directly*, he added to himself. He didn't like to lie, but he didn't want to tell Damonax the whole truth, either. "I got the news from Uncle Philodemos, as a matter of fact. My guess is, Menedemos told him. Menedemos gets everywhere and hears everything—you know that."

Damonax sniffed. "Your cousin thinks he's a lot more clever than he really is."

It wasn't a thought Sostratos had never had, but he'd had it more often and much more strongly about Damonax than about Menedemos. All he said was, "You may be right."

"Will you sail straight across the Inner Sea, then?" Damonax asked. "How can you hope to find Alexandria if you do?"

"We'll manage," Sostratos said. "You go to sea often enough, you learn to steer pretty well by the sun and stars." He prided himself on how well he could do that. If pressed, he would have admitted he was no better than Menedemos and might have been worse than

Diokles. The oarmaster, of course, had started going to sea years before Sostratos was born.

Perhaps luckily, Damonax didn't press him. Instead, with a small shiver, he said, "I wouldn't care to get out of sight of land."

Good. Otherwise you'd come along and want to run things. Sostratos didn't say that, either. He said nothing at all. Around Damonax, nothing was often the best thing to say.

III

MENEDEMOS STOOD ON THE RAISED, PLANKED platform at the *Aphrodite*'s stern. One hand gripped the handle of each steering oar. From long use, the wood was smooth under his palms.

As had been true the past few years, part of him was anxious to escape from Rhodes and from the longing for his father's wife that he dared not show. Part of him was anxious for her, too. She'd have the baby, whether his or Philodemos', before he came back from Egypt. Childbearing was dangerous; his own mother, whom he barely re-membered, had died trying to bring forth a second child. The infant hadn't lived, either. If anything happened to Baukis ....

He made himself not think about that. Looking up to the sky, he gauged the breeze by the way a few small, puffy white clouds drifted from northwest to southeast. When one of them didn't glide in front of it, the sun shone brightly.

Dipping his head to Diokles, he said, "When we get out of the harbor, we'll raise the mast, set the sail, and let the wind do our work for a while."

The keleustes' grunt was what passed for laughter with him. "The rowers will think they're on a holiday cruise," he said. He'd been a rower himself till he advanced to setting the men at the oars their paces. His broad shoulders, powerful arms, and callused hands still showed his old trade. Though he had to be past fifty, he was no one Menedemos would have cared to wrestle. Years under the harsh sun of the Inner Sea had baked him brown as an Egyptian.

"Are we ready?" Sostratos called back from the much smaller platform at the akatos' bow.

"*Malista!*" Menedemos answered, and dipped his head. Sostratos waved to a dockside lounger who'd already got a couple of oboloi. The man undid the line that tied the trading galley's bow to a bollard on the pier and tossed his end of the rope into the *Aphrodite*. Sostratos coiled it with fussy precision; he wasn't a natural sailor, not to Menedemos' way of thinking, but attention to every detail made him a pretty good one.

Down the tarred planks walked the man. He undid the stern line and tossed it aboard the ship. The nearest rower made sure it didn't stay loose for long. As soon as everything was shipshape, Diokles asked Menedemos, "Are we ready to get going?"

"I expect we are," Menedemos answered. Irrationally, he expected the galley's motion to change now that she was no longer connected to the wharf. That didn't happen, of course; the *Aphrodite* had had next to no motion before—the water inside the harbor was almost as smooth as polished metal—and still had next to none now.

Triremes and other naval vessels used fluteplayers to give the men the stroke the keleustes ordered. The *Aphrodite*, a much smaller galley, couldn't afford extra men. Diokles had a hammer and a small brass gong. He clanged it once, to get the rowers' attention. They weren't worked in yet; some were still hurting from a last carouse the night before. He stroked the gong again, harder this time.

After a few heartbeats, they'd all set hands on their oars and were looking back toward him. "Thank you so much, my dears," he said. "Time to get your backs sore. Time to get your hands blistered. I know all your calluses have gone away over the winter—you're such sweet, soft fellows." Except for the sardonic rasp in his voice, he might have been a suitor courting a handsome youth in the gymnasion. But the rasp was there. "Try not to be too ragged. Try to remember what to do and how to do it together. So back oars, boys, at the gong—!"

31

He clanged once more. Not quite in unison, the rowers stroked. No one fouled anyone else, which was a good enough first stroke to satisfy Menedemos. Diokles hit the gong again. The akatos slowly moved away from the pier and out into the harbor. Diokles shifted the men to the usual forward stroke. He kept the rhythm lazy to let the twenty men on each side of the ship get used to pulling after a winter away from the water.

The rowers grunted and swore and complained before the akatos had gone even half a stadion. Menedemos grinned at them and let them grumble. Rowers always acted like that. He would have feared a sickness was running through them had they stayed quiet.

A tubby little fishing boat waddled over the water ahead of the *Aphrodite.* The boat could barely get out of its own way, and couldn't get out of the galley's, even if she was making less than half speed. Menedemos pulled the handle of the port steering oar toward himself and pushed the starboard oar handle out. The *Aphrodite* swung to port and glided past the boat. "Where you bound for in your sea-centipede?" one of the fishermen called.

"Lesbos," Menedemos answered. If one of Demetrios' warships met the boat, he didn't want the fellows in it to tell the Macedonians anything worth knowing.

The fisherman leered at him. "Want to get your prong sucked, do you?" he said; women from Lesbos had a name for that vice.

"To the crows with you, Pausias," Menedemos replied in mock anger—he knew most of the Rhodian men who went to sea. Pausias just laughed.

Moles narrowed the entrance to the Great Harbor and that to the naval harbor just to the north. They also let stout chains be stretched across the harbor mouths to keep invaders from landing soldiers inside. Menedemos had known that as long as he could remember. Now, eyeing the fortifications at the ends of the moles, he considered it much less hypothetically than he ever had before.

A big, beamy merchantman, probably full of grain or cheap wine or oil or stone, came into the harbor at a pace even more snaillike than the fishing boat's. Next to that big snail, Menedemos' ship was indeed a centipede, all legs and litheness. Like him, the merchant ship's skipper stood at the steering oars. He sketched a salute and called something in Aeolic dialect so thick Menedemos could hardly understand him. Chances were he really did hail from Lesbos, then.

"What's that you say?" Menedemos shouted back across half a stadion of water.

"Safe voyage!" the Lesbian yelled.

This time, Menedemos got it. He lifted his hand from the starboard steering oar to wave. "And to you, friend!" All Hellenes might not be brothers, but all seafarers were.

All except pirates and the whoresons in Demetrios' fleet, Menedemos thought. As any more or less honest skipper would, he hated pirates with a cold and deadly passion. Rhodes, which depended on free passage across the sea, hunted them like the vermin they were.

"Here we go, lads!" Diokles told the rowers, and upped the pace a little as the *Aphrodite* left the Great Harbor and headed out onto the Inner Sea.

Now the ship's motion changed. The water was still smooth by any reasonable standard, but it was choppier than it had been inside the protected harbor. "How do you hold, cousin?" Menedemos called toward the bow.

"I'm holding fine so far," Sostratos answered. Did he look a trifle green? Menedemos couldn't be sure, but he thought so. Sostratos' stomach tormented him every time they set out on a new trading run. Some men never got over seasickness, and were miserable whenever they had to put to sea. Sostratos wasn't like that, but he felt it the first few days he was on the water.

"Well, remember to lean over the rail far enough if you have to give back your morning bread and oil and wine," Menedemos said.

His cousin gave back not his breakfast but a filthy gesture. Menedemos laughed. Sostratos couldn't be feeling too dreadful if he was up to that. To starboard, the island of Rhodes slid past. The land was still spring-green. The sun would burn it brown and barren by the time the *Aphrodite* came home.

Gods grant summer's burning is all we have to fear, Menedemos thought.

The breeze hummed in the rigging. Sostratos noticed the noise only when he thought about it. The mast had gone into its socket in the keel and the big square sail had been unbrailed as soon as Menedemos decided the wind was likely to hold: not too long after they left the harbor, in other words.

Sostratos' stomach, though not altogether happy to be at sea, hadn't actively rebelled. He thanked the gods in whom he indifferently believed for that. His supper—bread, salted sprats, olives, and wine worse than what they planned to sell—seemed to be sitting all right. Now he had to keep the akatos running south and a little east through the night.

Twilight hadn't fully left the sky. Aphrodite's wandering star and Hermes' a little below it blazed through the paleness near the western horizon. In the east, the moon, a day past full, was just climbing out of the waves and drying itself off before it rose higher in the sky.

A handful of rowers stayed awake to tend the sail at need. Most slumbered at their benches, some as naked as when they'd rowed, others wearing chitons against the cooling night air. Snores rose here and there up and down the akatos' length.

Menedemos and Diokles lay on the stern platform, not far from Sostratos' feet. Menedemos had a tunic under him to soften the wood a little; Diokles didn't bother. The keleustes took life just as it came and never worried about anything till it happened. Sostratos admired the attitude without being able to imitate it.

More and more stars came out as night took hold. Lamps and smoke made it hard to see so many when in Rhodes. No smoke here, out on the sea. No smoke stench, either, nor reek of slops and rotting garbage and people who never washed enough. You didn't notice city stinks so much when you were in the middle of them all the time. You did notice once you'd got away from them, though.

The planets—the word meant "wanderers" in Greek—sank into the sea, first Hermes', then Aphrodite's. Sostratos imagined he ought to hear a hiss when their light was quenched, but of course he didn't. The moon's golden glow splashed from wavecrests. It seemed almost bright enough to read by, though from experience he knew it wasn't.

Steering south as he did, he had to look back over his shoulder to find the North Pole, which lay about halfway between the two brightest stars in the Little Bear. Eyeing that constellation and the Big Bear nearby, he wondered why they both had tails. So far as he knew, no actual earthly bears did. *If I ever meet an astronomer or an astrologer, I'll ask him about that*, he thought.

On through the night the *Aphrodite* went. Sostratos steered by the stars near the North Pole, by the moon, and by the slowly wheeling constellations. His navigation wouldn't be perfect—navigation on the open sea never was—but it would be good enough.

The men tending the sails woke up other rowers to replace them and got some rest themselves. Every now and then, someone would rouse and ease himself into the sea. Then he'd sit down on his bench and go back to sleep.

Sostratos came close to resenting the sailors when they stirred. They didn't say anything to him—no need—but they reminded him he wasn't all alone on the sea with his thoughts, as he wished he were.

After a while—three hours or so behind the moon, he thought, though he knew that was guesswork—Zeus' wandering star shouldered its way into the sky. It was brighter than Hermes', though less so than Aphrodite's. Unlike those two, Zeus' star didn't always stay close to the hem of the sun's robe. It went all around the sky, lingering about a year in each constellation of the Zodiac.

Babylonians and Phoenicians believed they could use the planets' motions through the heavens to foretell the future. Himilkon the merchant talked about horoscopes now and then. Over the year, quite a few Hellenes had come to believe in such things, too. Sostratos wondered if there was anything to it. How could you tell?

By the time Zeus' star was about halfway up from its rising to the meridian, Sostratos found himself yawning at the steering oars. It was midnight, or close enough.

Like most Hellenes, he usually rose and set with the sun. Everything was different at sea, though. He yawned again, hoping he'd be able to sleep past sunup. Then he bent down and touched Menedemos' shoulder. He made haste to get back to the steering oars; his cousin had a habit of waking quickly and completely, sometimes with a knife in his hand.

Now Menedemos looked around wildly for a moment, then relaxed as he realized where he was. In a low voice, he asked, "How's everything?"

"Seems all right," Sostratos said. "The breeze hasn't been very strong, but it's been steady. We've put some stadia behind us, sure enough."

"Good." Lithe as an Egyptian cat, Menedemos got to his feet. Sostratos envied his cousin's grace without being able to match it. Menedemos slowly turned through a whole circle, taking in the heavens and especially the positions of the moon and Zeus' wandering star. He dipped his head to Sostratos. "Fair enough. You've done your half of the night."

"Did you think I wouldn't?" Whispering, Sostratos couldn't sound as indignant as he wanted to.

Menedemos chuckled softly. "No, my dear. Everyone who knows you knows you're honest to a fault. But you do jump when somebody pokes you with a pin."

Sostratos seldom saw the sport in that; people who'd been the butt of too much of it rarely did. Menedemos' smile said he thought it was funny, and thought anyone who didn't think it funny was a bit of a drip. He hadn't gone through boyhood teased and tormented. And he would have laughed had Sostratos told him so.

Sighing, Sostratos said, "Take the steering oars, why don't you? I wouldn't mind shutting my eyes for a bit, and that's the truth."

"I'll do it." For a wonder, Menedemos left that there instead of teasing Sostratos about staying up past his bedtime. *He* was out by night quite often, drinking with friends or chasing women.

Sostratos stepped aside. His cousin took his place. Menedemos seemed made to conn a ship; it was almost as if he'd sprouted from the timbers under his bare feet. Sostratos lay down on the planking and twisted to try to find a comfortable way to sleep. Dogs curled up that way on the floor when they got tired. They ...

Next thing he knew, beams from the newly risen sun were poking him in the eye. The moon rode low in the west, as Aphrodite's wandering star and Hermes' had when he took over the steering oars. Yawning, he sat up and stretched and tried to rub feeling back into his left hand, which wanted to stay asleep after the rest of him had awakened.

Diokles was sitting, too. He dipped his head to Sostratos. Menedemos stood at the steering oars as if he hadn't moved a muscle since taking them back. "How do we hold?" Sostratos asked him.

36

"We're going along," his cousin answered. "We're out on the open sea. We're heading south. That's about as much as I can tell you."

"The open sea," Sostratos echoed as he got to his feet. Sure enough, all he could see in every direction was water and sky. He'd been out of sight of land before, crossing from Hellas to Italy and from Cyprus to the coast of Phoenicia. It always felt strange, though, and reminded him how tiny men and all their works were when weighed against nature.

Then one of the rowers said, "By Aphrodite's smooth-shaved piggy, I sure could use me some breakfast."

Sostratos laughed. No matter how small you were when measured against nature, you had to live as best you could. His belly told him he could use some breakfast, too.

Clink! Clink! Diokles beat out a rhythm for the rowers. The wind had palled, and the men needed to work to shove the ship forward. Menedemos had twelve sailors rowing on each side, so each man worked three parts out of five. Diokles didn't push the pace, either. If they got to Alexandria in the afternoon rather than the morning, what difference would it make? None Menedemos could see.

The sail was brailed up to the yard. If the breeze came back, Menedemos would order it set again. For now, he didn't need to worry about it. Neither did the rowers. Some of the men not at the oars dozed in the sun. Some rubbed olive oil on their bodies and especially their hands, which would have softened in a winter ashore. And some dropped hooks and lines into the wine-dark sea, using bits of salt fish as bait in the hope of catching something tastier.

Dark blue water below. Brighter blue sky above. That was the world, as it looked to Menedemos. Land somewhere, no doubt, but nowhere close, nowhere in sight. They were far enough out in the middle of the open sea that even gulls and terns and pelicans were scarce. The rowers exclaimed when a dolphin paced the *Aphrodite* for a while, every so often leaping out of the water and arrowing back in nose first with scarcely a splash.

"He's having more fun than we are," Sostratos remarked.

"If I could swim like that, I wouldn't use a ship, either," Menedemos answered.

"Not even if you wanted to carry cargo?" his cousin said in sly tones.

"Oh, I'd just strap it on my back and carry it along with me," Menedemos said blithely. Sostratos made a face at him.

Perhaps frightened by the dolphin, flying fish also took to the air. A couple of unlucky ones came down inside the akatos instead of back in the Inner Sea. Rowers who weren't at the oars grabbed and gutted them and took them forward to grill them on a little charcoal brazier near the bow. Having any fire on a ship always worried Menedemos, but it was too useful to do without. The grinning men gobbled their snacks, then licked their fingers clean.

The sun was nearing its noontime height. When it got there, he'd give the steering oars to Sostratos. After the first day out of Rhodes, he and his cousin had been splitting day and night between them. Diokles could also conn the galley at need—there wasn't much aboard ship he couldn't do, save possibly some fine work with the carpenter's tools—but, with the wind quiet, he was more useful giving the rowers the stroke.

"Come on, Leskhaios!" the keleustes barked to one of the men at the oars. "Put your back into it, my dear! You signed on as rower, not as a passenger. You aren't paying your way to Egypt. We're paying you—or we will if you work a bit."

"My hand is bleeding. I tore off a callus," Leskhaios said.

"Rub oil on it. Wrap it in a rag or a strip of leather. Your shift will be up pretty soon." Like most oarmasters, Diokles had heard it all before, and none of it impressed him. He added, "When you come off your oar, use wine or vinegar or turpentine if we have any instead of olive oil. That will toughen up your hide quicker than anything else I know."

"It'll hurt like I've got a weasel biting me, too," the rower said.

Diokles shrugged. "You can pay a little now, or you can pay more later because you didn't heal fast."

"Do you want to take him off the oars and put him on the sail till his hand heals up?" Menedemos asked—softly, so only Diokles would hear.

Shrugging, the keleustes said, "You're the skipper. If you tell me to, I will. But I don't think he's hurting all that much. I just think he's looking for a chance to get paid for being lazy."

"You may be right," Menedemos admitted—it wasn't as if he'd never run across rowers who did as little as they could get away with. "But take a look at his hand once his shift is up. If it really is bad, he can have some time away from pulling."

"Just as you say." Diokles put a hint of reproach in that, but only a hint. He'd sailed with Menedemos on several trading runs now. He put up with the skipper's easygoing, newfangled ways not least because Menedemos had them without flaunting them.

"Something else we might do tomorrow," Menedemos said, "is set everybody on the oars for a while so we can practice the kinds of maneuvers rowers on war-galleys have to know."

After so many years under the sun, Diokles usually squinted. Now his eyes narrowed further. "You reckon it will come to that?" he asked.

"I don't know, but it may." Menedemos waved north and east, in the general direction of Cyprus. "If Demetrios takes the island, we may run into his ships—or pirates he's hired—on the way home."

"Pirates!" Diokles spat on the planking. "That for pirates! As for proper naval ships, won't their crews know Rhodians are neutral and not to be interfered with?"

"I hope so, but you never can tell," Menedemos said. "And remember, if Antigonos goes to war with Rhodes while we're down in Egypt, we turn into fair game even though we may not even know the fighting's started. So I want us to be as ready as we can."

"Fair enough. That makes sense." The keleustes dipped his head. Then he eyed the rowers farther forward in the *Aphrodite.* "Some of the lads will have pulled in a trireme, sure enough. They'll help give the others the hang of it."

"I hope so." Menedemos lowered his voice again: "I hope they don't need to start rowing in triremes again, too. Antigonos has a lot more men behind him than we do."

"Truth. Too much truth. Antigonos is stronger than we are, but Furies take me if I care to bend the knee to any man. I'd sooner tie a boulder to my leg and jump off a pier," Diokles said.

"Spoken like a free Hellene!" Menedemos exclaimed. He felt the same way himself. He knew no citizens in Rhodes who didn't. A polis stayed free and independent as long as it could … and then, like as not, went down in a horror of fire and plunder and slavery.

He didn't want to think about that, not for Rhodes. But not thinking about it was much harder than not wanting to think about it.

He felt better after putting the crew through their paces the next morning. They sprinted for a couple of stadia; when they did, not even Diokles could grumble about how they towed. They practiced sharp turns to port and starboard. They sprinted some more, then one side would suddenly back oars while the other kept rowing straight ahead, which made the *Aphrodite* turn almost within her own length.

And they practiced lifting each side's oars out of the water, so the akatos' hull could smash an enemy ship's oars with its weight. Some of them had been aboard when the *Aphrodite* disabled a Roman trireme that way a few years before.

After the exercises finished, the men panted at their oars and passed around watered wine to ease their thirst. "What do you think?" Menedemos asked Diokles.

"They could be better—it's not like they practice all the cursed time," the keleustes said. "We should keep working them. But they could be worse, too. I may be spoiled judging them because I'm a Rhodian and I expect the best."

"We need the best from them," Menedemos said. "If we fight pirate pentekonters, we may get away with less. But against triremes or fours or fives, we're out of our weight. Either we have to be faster than they are or we have to be better."

"Or we're sunk," Diokles replied, and Menedemos knew he wasn't using a figure of speech.

Sostratos could tell they were nearing the Egyptian coast. Out on the open sea, pelicans and gulls had been scarce. Now they teemed again, as they did near Rhodes.

"What's that?" A rower pointed to something floating in the sea. "Looks like an overgrown feather duster."

"That's a palm tree. I saw them in Palestine," Sostratos said. "It must have washed out from the Delta. So we *are* getting close to land."

Menedemos saw the drowned palm tree, too, and called, "Two drakhmai to the man who first spies land!"

That set the men at the oars, who faced the akatos' stern, to looking over their shoulders. It almost fouled the stroke. "Pay heed to what you're supposed to be doing," Diokles growled, "or it'll cost you silver instead of making you any."

Instead of sighting land, someone shouted because he saw a boat out in the Inner Sea. Sostratos soon spotted it, too, and others a little farther away. Before long, the man who'd seen it first said, "That's the funniest-looking gods-cursed boat I ever set eyes on. What's it made of, anyway?"

"Papyrus," Sostratos answered. "Not the pith people use to write on, but whole stalks dried and woven together. It's not as strong as planking, but Egypt doesn't have many trees except for palms, and palm wood isn't very good, either."

Menedemos steered toward the nearest fishing boat. The four brown men—naked but for thigh-length skirts of dirty linen—who handled the nets looked scared, but realized they couldn't hope to flee the swiftly approaching galley.

"Do you speak Greek?" Sostratos shouted to them from his place at the bow. They all spread their hands and shook their heads, which barbarians did instead of tossing them like Hellenes. Sostratos tried again: "Do you know the Syrian speech?" He didn't speak Aramaic well himself, but he could just about get by in it.

Three of the Egyptians still looked blank. Intelligence kindled on one man's face, though. "Little bit," he called back. His own language flavored his speech, making it harder for Sostratos to follow. Since Sostratos' Aramaic had a heavy Greek accent, that was bound to work both ways.

"In which direction lies Alexandria? The city of Alexandria?" Sostratos said, adding, "We give silver for the truth."

"Not come to pirate us?" the Egyptian said.

"By the gods, no!" Sostratos said. "Traders us, not pirates. From Rhodes. Rhodes fights pirates."

The fisherman gabbled in Egyptian to his friends. One of them shrugged. Sostratos followed not a word, but he still had a good notion of what was going on. The men in the papyrus boat couldn't run and couldn't fight. What could they do but play along with the Hellenes?

"That way." The fellow who spoke Aramaic pointed south and west. "You go that way, you get there maybe sundown."

"Thank you," Sostratos said, pleased with the way he and Menedemos had picked their way across the Inner Sea. They hadn't been perfect—you couldn't hope to navigate perfectly out of sight of land—but they had been pretty good. He turned to Menedemos, who was at the steering oars, and called, "Bring us alongside and give me a couple of drakhmai to pay him."

"What did he say?" Menedemos asked.

Sostratos remembered he hadn't been speaking Greek. He explained to his cousin, then went back to the stern to get the coins. Menedemos guided the *Aphrodite* next to the fishing boat (which, like the akatos, had eyes painted at either side of the bow). The men on the galley's port side pulled in their oars so the ship could come close.

"Here you are!" Sostratos leaned out over the gunwale and stretched out his arm with the drakhmai in the palm of his hand. The Egyptian with whom he'd talked took them. He weighed them in his own palm, then smiled broadly. Sostratos said, "Safe travel! A good catch!"

"Safe travel you, too," the brown man replied. "Good trading."

They parted on friendly terms. Before long, Leskhaios spotted a low smudge of land on the southern horizon. By Menedemos' expression, he would rather have rewarded almost any other rower. But land it undeniably was. He gave Leskhaios the two drakhmai he'd promised.

The land looked unprepossessing: swampy and almost venomously green. Rain might not water it, but the Nile did. Before long, the *Aphrodite* encountered many more fishing boats. Some ignored the akatos; others spread sail to get away as best they could. When they came back to whatever village they'd started from, the fishermen could entertain their neighbors with tales of how they'd got away from sea raiders.

By the time the sun began to near the western horizon, they found themselves in the company of larger ships, first beamy merchantmen like the ones that came to and sailed from Rhodes wallowing along

42

as best they could with their sails spread to catch as much of the fitful breeze as they could, and then something altogether different: a five, a war galley with three banks of oars, two men on each oar in the top and middle banks and a single rower on the lower one. An officer with a red cloak flung back over his shoulders cupped both hands in front of his mouth to hail the akatos: "What ship are you?"

"We're the *Aphrodite*, out of Rhodes," Sostratos shouted back.

"Out of Rhodes, hey?" The officer's Doric accent was not too different from Menedemos'; he probably came from one of the Aegean islands himself. "You're the first we've seen that crossed the Inner Sea this spring. What's the news?"

"We'll put it first in the Ptolemaios' ear," Sostratos answered, hoping he wouldn't anger the man by declining to spill everything he knew. Some Hellenes would have; if talking too much and to too many people wasn't his folk's besetting vice, Sostratos couldn't imagine what would be.

For a wonder, the red-cloaked officer didn't lose his temper. "It must be important, then," he said. Sostratos had never been wooed as a boy, unlike his cousin—when Menedemos was fourteen, his name was written on half the walls in Rhodes, prefaced by *good* or *beautiful*. He'd never pursued boys after coming to manhood, either. All the same, at that moment he would gladly have kissed the naval officer.

He contented himself with dipping his head. "It is," he agreed.

"All right, then," the officer said briskly. "Stay with us into the harbor. We'll get your toy galley there tied up, and we'll send you to the palace. If they think your news is as big as you make it out to be, you can bet the Ptolemaios will hear you pretty cursed quick."

Toy galley made Sostratos' liking for the man flicker and blow out. "Thank you so much, O marvelous one," he said, as sardonically as he dared. Back at the steering oars, Menedemos bared his teeth at him. He realized he could have done better as a diplomat.

Luckily, the man on the five didn't notice. "We're going into the Great Harbor, the eastern one, and then to the Ptolemaios' own harbor, by the palace," he said. "Have you got that?"

Sostratos glanced at Menedemos. Menedemos dipped his head. "We have it," Sostratos said. Diokles upped the stroke a little. The *Aphrodite* followed the war galley towards Alexander's new city.

IV

ALEXANDRIA ASTONISHED MENEDEMOS IN EVERY way he could think of. He'd been to considerable poleis before. His beloved Rhodes was one. Athens and Syracuse were bigger still. But Alexandria dwarfed them all. Alexandria might have been as big as all three of them put together.

"It's not a polis. It's too big to be a polis," Menedemos said to Sostratos in the small palace room they'd been given to share. "It's a—It's a—" He broke off and threw his hands in the air. "I don't even know what to call it."

"It's a megalopolis, a great city, and no, I don't mean the polis in Arkadia," Sostratos replied.

"Megalopolis." Menedemos tasted the word, which he hadn't heard before except as the name for that polis. He dipped his head. "Yes, that's just what it is."

Sostratos hadn't finished. "The polis of Rhodes draws on the island of Rhodes for what it needs. Athens has Attica, Syracuse whatever chunk of Sicily it rules at any given time. Alexandria takes the wealth from all of Egypt, the way Babylon does in Mesopotamia. No wonder it can get bigger than any polis in Hellas or Great Hellas."

"I suppose so," Menedemos said. Egypt stretched south along the Nile for thousands of stadia—he had no idea how many thousands. "But Egypt is ancient. It's the oldest country in the world, isn't it?"

"I think so," Sostratos said cautiously. "The Babylonians may give it an argument, but I think so."

"But Alexandria's so new!" Menedemos exclaimed. "Most of it doesn't even seem finished. The palace here does, but this is the Ptolemaios' home." He lowered his voice to continue, "He may not be a king, but he lives like one, by the gods."

"Think of all the wealth of Egypt," Sostratos said again. "Now think of it concentrated not on one megalopolis but on one man."

Menedemos tried to do that. He felt himself failing. To the Egyptians, Ptolemaios wouldn't be a king if he put on a crown. He'd be a pharaoh, the next thing to a god. The whole country would belong to him, the whole country and all the myriads of people in it. Menedemos whistled softly.

By Sostratos' wry expression, he'd already done some thinking along those lines. "Yes, the palace is very fine, and the temples. That's what's been finished," he said. "The rest ...."

Alexandria had everything from homes that would have counted for palaces in Rhodes to shacks made out of whatever the builder could get his hands on. Sometimes one sat next to the other. Hellenes lived in one part of town, Egyptians in another, and Ioudaioi from Palestine in a third. Menedemos remembered from his trip to the Sacred Land two years before that the Ioudaioi claimed some kind of connection with Egypt. He couldn't come up with the details. *Have to ask Sostratos*, he thought. Sostratos soaked up facts the way a rag soaked up water.

Before he could ask, his cousin said, "Even Alexander's tomb is only half built."

"He just got here, like everybody else," Menedemos said. Sostratos chuckled, but Menedemos wasn't joking. There'd been only a little fishing village on the site of Alexandria till Alexander ordered the city built here after taking Egypt from the Persians. All the swarms of inhabitants, including Ptolemaios himself, had settled here since then.

As for the mortal remains of Alexander himself, his corpse had been on the way from Babylon to Aigai in Macedonia when

Ptolemaios' soldiers seized it at swordpoint and carried it off to Egypt instead. Till very recently, it had lain in Memphis, south of the Delta. But Ptolemaios ordered it here, as if Alexander's city needed to be adorned by what was left of him.

"The tomb will be impressive once it's finished. It—" Sostratos broke off because someone knocked on the door. If the knocker had listened beforehand, he would have heard Menedemos' cousin praising what the tomb would look like. *That's good*, Menedemos thought.

Sostratos was closer to the door than he was. His cousin stepped over and unlatched it. A burly Hellene—he looked like a paid-off soldier—in a chiton of incongruously fine linen stood there. "I'm Demodamas, the general's steward. The Ptolemaios will see the two of you," he said. No, not quite a Hellene: by his Greek, he was a Macedonian.

"Let's go," Menedemos said. Sostratos stood aside, then followed him into the hallway. Demodamas led them through the palace's twisting corridors till Menedemos longed for a skein of thread like the one Theseus had unrolled in King Minos' Labyrinth.

The man stopped not at the entrance to an audience chamber but at a door like any other. He tapped at it with his forefinger. "Come in, come in," someone on the other side said in impatient, Macedonian-accented Greek.

In they went. Ptolemaios and a young man—a secretary, Menedemos judged—sat behind a table strewn with sheets and rolls of papyrus. By their stances, the two bodyguards standing nearby had been bored to tears. Now, like watchdogs hearing strange footsteps, they perked up.

"Hail, sir," Menedemos said.

"Hail," Sostratos echoed.

"Hail, Rhodians," Ptolemaios said. He was about sixty, stocky and graying. His eyes had pouches under them, but they were very shrewd. He went on, "I know we've met before, but for the life of me I can't remember which of you is Sostratos and which Menedemos. If you'd dealt with as many people between then and now as I have, you wouldn't remember, either."

They straightened him out. Menedemos said, "You will have heard that we've brought news."

"Oh, yes. If you were just interested in selling me wine and oil, you'd be dealing with my cooks," Ptolemaios said. He'd had no trouble recalling the *Aphrodite*'s cargo. The secretary's finger had an inky blot on it. So did Ptolemaios'. He kept track of as many details as he could.

Taking turns, Menedemos and Sostratos told him about Demetrios' visit to Rhodes, and about the campaign Antigonos' son was now mounting against his brother in Cyprus. The ruler of Egypt questioned them closely about the size of Demetrios' army and navy.

"About fifteen thousand foot soldiers, I've heard, sir," Menedemos said, "and four hundred horsemen."

"More than a hundred ten triremes, and more than fifty heavier ships," Sostratos added, "plus the freighters and such to support the army and the warships."

"That's … not a small force, if what you hear has anything to do with what's true." Ptolemaios clicked his tongue between his teeth. "It's liable to be so, worse luck. Demetrios, Furies take him, doesn't do things by halves." He clicked his tongue again. "Menelaos holds Cyprus for me. You lads have met him, too, haven't you?"

"Yes, sir," Menedemos and Sostratos said, Menedemos half a beat ahead of his cousin. He had all he could do not to burst into applause. Ptolemaios really *did* note every detail.

Sostratos added, "It was the year after we met you, sir. We were trading in Phoenicia and Palestine. Rhodians want to be able to trade freely all over the world. That's why we turned down Demetrios' offer of alliance."

"When a mouse allies with a cat, the mouse doesn't give the orders. It takes them." Ptolemaios' voice was dry as Egypt away from the Nile.

"That's why we want to stay free and independent, sir," Sostratos said.

"Of course." Ptolemaios' tone remained dry as dry could be.

Menedemos remembered he'd started his career as a bodyguard of Alexander's, and had been a capable general all through the Macedonian king's whirlwind conquests. After Alexander died, Ptolemaios had held his own against the other squabbling Macedonian marshals. Not many men in the world had more power or more experience. Here, more than at their earlier meeting, Menedemos felt the weight of that power and experience.

Ptolemaios went on, "Rhodes thinks she can trust me—some—because I'm so far from her. If my land were just a long piss away, you'd be as nervous about me as you are about the Cyclops and his brat." He spoke about Antigonos and Demetrios with easy familiarity, half scornful, half affectionate. He would have been through a lot with Antigonos even before the conquests began, and would have watched Demetrios grow from baby to warlord.

After a brief pause, Sostratos said, "Perhaps so, sir, but things are as they are, not as they might have been. We have to deal with what is."

"Yes, I do remember you," the ruler of Egypt said. "You were the one who wanted to write history. Have you started that?"

"To my shame, no," Sostratos said, staring down at the floor mosaic: a hunting scene. "I keep looking for time, and life keeps getting in the way."

"A pestilence on that!" Ptolemaios said. "If you really want to do something, you cursed well *make* time for it, and do everything else around the chunk you've carved out."

"That's ... good advice, sir." Sostratos still didn't look up. Menedemos feared his cousin would be gloomy for days, wishing he were scribbling instead of selling things.

He asked Ptolemaios, "Do you have any idea, O best one, what you'll do about the attack on Cyprus?"

"I hope Menelaos can hold his own. But even if you've doubled what Demetrios has, it's plenty to be dangerous. If I need to lend my brother a hand, I will. Cyprus gives me eyes and ears and harbors near Anatolia. I want to hang on to it," Ptolemaios said.

"I think that's sensible, sir," Sostratos said.

"Thank you so much. I'm glad you approve," Ptolemaios rumbled. Sostratos blushed scarlet as the coals under a charcoal brazier. The audience ended a moment later.

Sostratos and Menedemos bought balls of mashed chickpeas fried in some oil that wasn't olive and rounds of flatbread to wrap them in. They'd got out of Ptolemaios' palace as soon as they could after the lord of Egypt dismissed them. Sostratos didn't want to talk about the audience where he might be overheard. When Menedemos started to, Sostratos contrived to step on his toe. His cousin, luckily, got the message and kept quiet till they were out in the bustling crowds of the city.

"By the gods!" Sostratos said when he bit into his snack. "This is better than I thought it would be."

"I was thinking the same thing," Menedemos replied with his mouth full. "Not like what we eat back home, but good."

"Frying improves anything," Sostratos said wisely, licking his fingers.

"That's true enough! Think how Demetrios would sizzle if you dropped him into a big tub of hot oil," Menedemos said.

"Heh!" Sostratos dipped his head in agreement. "Maybe Menelaos can take care of that for us."

"It would be nice. Then all we'd have to worry about would be Antigonos and his ordinary generals," his cousin said. "Oh, and Ptolemaios, too."

"Yes, and Ptolemaios, too." Sostratos dipped his head again. "He's no one's fool. And he said it himself: the only thing that makes him less dangerous to us than old One-eye is that he's farther away."

"He and Antigonos will have known each other longer than we've been alive—almost as long as our fathers have," Menedemos said slowly. "The other Macedonian warlords, too. It's not just a war with them. It's quarrels left over from the days when Philip was still king."

"Macedonian feuds are like that, I've heard. Only now they aren't squabbling with the clan a valley over. These wars stretch from Hellas all the way to India," Sostratos said. "Remember how Ptolemaios talked about hunting tigers when we sold him that skin?"

"I hope he'll remember that Rhodians gave him the news about Demetrios," Menedemos said.

"He'll remember. He remembers a lot. He remembered us, even if he didn't know which of us was which," Sostratos said. "Whether he'll care …. That will depend on whether he thinks caring will bring him any advantage."

"He has an eye for the main chance, all right," Menedemos replied.

"I thought I just said that," Sostratos remarked. His cousin stuck out his tongue at him. Ignoring it, he went on, "Look at how he grabbed Egypt after Alexander died. It's small compared to what

Antigonos and Seleukos hold, but it's rich. The wealth here is concentrated, the way bees concentrate nectar to make it into honey."

"The difference is, Antigonos and Seleukos want to grab everything and be Alexander," Menedemos said. "Ptolemaios doesn't care about that. He's happy with a chunk, as long as it's a good chunk."

Sostratos stopped in the street and sent him a speculative stare. "You'd better watch yourself, my dear. If you aren't careful, more people will realize you aren't always the fool you seem."

Menedemos stopped, too, to blow him a kiss. They both laughed—until a man behind them who was leading a donkey overloaded with sacks of barley or beans shouted in bad Greek for them to get out of his way. They did. The man—a sweating, sun-darkened Egyptian wearing only a linen skirt—and the poor, tired donkey plodded on.

Seeing the Egyptian's shaved head glisten like that made Sostratos rub the back of his arm across his forehead. He was sweating, too. "It can be warm in spring back on Rhodes, but not like this, and not this early," he said. "I wonder how bad it is here when full summer comes. I wouldn't be surprised if it's worse than Palestine."

"Neither would I," Menedemos said. "I wouldn't be surprised if some of those golden-haired, pink-skinned Macedonians fall over dead when it stays that hot for a couple of months, either. The Egyptians turn brown. We'd turn pretty brown if you left us under this sun for a year, too. But if you burn instead to baking ...." He tossed his head to show he wouldn't want to do that.

"Ptolemaios is colored about the way we are," Sostratos said thoughtfully—no, Menedemos was no fool, even if he sometimes enjoyed playing one. "But Alexander, they say, was very fair."

"His mother was a Molossian," Menedemos said. "They're as pale as Illyrians or Thracians, never mind Macedonians."

"I wonder if being so pink and going into all those hot places sped his end," Sostratos said. "It couldn't have helped."

"I can't begin to tell you. You're the one who fancies himself a physician," Menedemos replied. Sostratos' hot cheeks had nothing to do with the weather. He did what he could for sailors on the *Aphrodite* who hurt themselves or fell sick. Like any real physician from Hippokrates on down, the most he could hope for was doing more good than harm.

He changed the subject: "I wonder where we can find a jeweler who'll give us a proper price for our amber. I haven't wanted to ask in the palace—"

"I should hope not!" Menedemos broke in. "Whoever you talked to would blab to the customs inspectors, and we'd have to pay them a cut on the amber's value. The Ptolemaios doesn't miss any chances when it comes to raking in silver."

"Too right, he doesn't," Sostratos agreed ruefully. "We had to pay his duty on the wine and the oil. We couldn't very well sneak those in." He muttered to himself. "I ought to stick Damonax for all of the duty on the oil. That would teach him a thing or two."

"Why don't you? He deserves it," Menedemos said.

"Don't tempt me, my dear," Sostratos said with real regret. "The trouble is, if he ever finds out, he won't just make life miserable for me. He'll take it out on my sister. Things that bring in your family always get complicated in a hurry."

To his surprise, Menedemos winced as if someone had stuck a knife in his flank. Just for a moment, he looked as if he were about to weep. If Sostratos was any judge at all, his cousin needed a real effort of will to pull his face straight. "Well, O best one, you aren't wrong," he said at last.

When he didn't go on from there, "Sostratos asked, "Is there anything you want to tell me? Is there anything you *need* to tell me?"

Menedemos tossed his head. "Not a thing," he answered in a voice that sounded like a bright parody of his usual way of speaking. "Everyone has troubles. Everyone has worries. Everyone has family."

"Your father was that bad before we set out?" Sostratos guessed.

"You have no idea!" Menedemos said. But the way he seized on the question made Sostratos guess he was using it to cover whatever really ate at him rather than to show it.

"You know I don't spread gossip from Karia to Carthage," Sostratos said.

"Yes, I do know that. You wouldn't tell me your own name if I didn't already know it. But let it go anyway," Menedemos said in tones that brooked no argument.

Sostratos didn't care for getting pushed away like that. But he could see that charging straight ahead like a ram trying to knock down a wall with its horns would only infuriate his cousin. *A few years ago*, he thought, *I wouldn't have noticed that. I* would *have plowed on, and Menedemos* would *have started screaming at me, and I would have had no idea why.*

He wondered if he was growing up at last. Most people seemed to do it by the time they turned eighteen. He was more than ten years past that. *Better late than never*, he said to himself, and hoped it was true.

Menedemos said, "We'll find out where the people who advise Ptolemaios live, the ones who help him run Egypt and fight his wars for him. They're the men who can afford the best, and the men who sell it to them will have their shops close by."

He was trying to get away from whatever private woe gnawed at him. Sostratos could see that. But what he said made good sense. Sure enough, he was less silly than he sometimes liked to pretend.

"That's a fine plan!" Sostratos meant it and was acting—perhaps overacting—at the same time. *Have to steer the akatos of conversation away from the rocks*, he thought. "We'll do it! It will give us the excuse for more sightseeing, anyhow."

"As if you need an excuse," Menedemos gibed. His eyes were grateful. He went on, "I know you. I know you too well, in fact. First chance you get, you'll climb on a riverboat and go down the Nile to see the Sphinx and the whatever-you-call-'ems."

"The Pyramids," Sostratos supplied. "I'd like to. Wouldn't you? We're so close and they're so grand. Nothing else like them anywhere, not in the whole world. Be a shame to go back to Rhodes without looking at them if we can."

"And then you'll go a little farther down the Nile, and a little farther yet, and then I'll hear you're living in a mud hut with an Egyptian girl and raising a flock of brown babies," Menedemos said.

"If I ever live with a woman, I'll want one I can talk to," Sostratos said. "That will be hard enough if she speaks Greek."

His cousin snorted. "Talking is for men. Women are for babies and for running your household."

"If that were true, hetairai would go out of business," Sostratos said.

"Hetairai are different. I thought you were talking about *wives*," Menedemos said.

Sostratos didn't see the distinction. "Hetairai or wives, they're all women, aren't they? If you have a wife you can talk to, you don't need to go looking for a hetaira who'd never look at you if you didn't give her silver or perfume or fancy jewelry."

"You'd best be careful, my dear." Menedemos eyed him the way he'd inspected a lizard in Palestine whose like he'd never seen in Hellas. "You tell that to someone who isn't related to you and doesn't know you're a bit daft, he'll think you're a dangerous radical."

"Well, let him." Sostratos rather liked the idea. "If I tell it to women, by the gods, I bet it will draw them to me the way spilled wine draws ants." He rubbed his chin. He rather liked that idea, too.

Most of the servants in Ptolemaios' palace were Egyptians. Hellenes came to Egypt hoping to get rich and have slaves and servants working for them. They didn't come to sweep other people's floors or wash clothes or put fresh linen on beds. Menedemos understood that. If you were someone else's subordinate, were you truly a free man?

He had no trouble coaxing one of the little brown women into bed one morning after Sostratos went out looking for jewelers and wine merchants. He spoke not a word of Egyptian, while she knew only a little Greek, but a charming manner and some kisses and the promise of a drakhma proved persuasive enough. More than persuasive enough, in fact; the eagerness with which she nodded her head convinced Menedemos he'd overpaid.

When he took off her chlamys, he found she was as nicely made as he'd hoped. When he took off his own tunic ... she laughed in surprise and pointed at his phallos. "What wrong with it?" she asked. "I never did with Hellene before. All Hellenes like that?" She didn't seem to care for the notion.

"There's nothing wrong with it, and of course we're all like that. How else would we be?" Menedemos said in some annoyance. He'd wanted a good time, not a girl who mocked him for how he was made. But then he remembered some of the stories Sostratos had brought back from the land of the Ioudaioi. "Wait! Do Egyptian men circumcise?" Her blank look said she didn't follow. He tried again, with simpler words: "Do Egyptian men cut off their foreskins?" He used fingers to show what he meant, too.

She nodded so vigorously, it made her breasts bob. "Oh, yes. Men do. Not look—funny."

"I don't think I look funny. I think men with naked cockheads look funny," Menedemos said with dignity. He wasn't sure she followed him. She didn't get off the bed and run out of the chamber, though, so he went on, "No matter what it looks like, it works the same way once it's in there. Come on!"

Egyptians and Hellenes proved to differ even in their preferred postures. He would have bent her forward and gone in from behind. When she lay on her back and urged him atop her, though, he acquiesced. He wasn't fussy, and he expected it would be fine any which way.

And it was. Of course, it was almost always fine for a man. His partner also seemed happy enough. After he got off her, she squatted over the chamber pot and let his seed dribble out of her. "No baby," she said. "I hope no baby."

Menedemos dipped his head. He didn't want a little brownish bastard, either. "Did being the way I am make any difference?" he asked.

She shrugged. "Not much. Still funny-looking."

"Is this funny-looking?" He gave her a Rhodian drakhma with the head of Helios the sun god on one side and his polis' rose on the other.

She looked surprised and pleased. "I not even got to asking. You my first Hellene. All honest like you?"

"Don't count on it, sweet one!" Menedemos exclaimed. She understood his tone if not the words. He asked, "How does it happen that I'm your first Hellene?"

Bad grammar and small vocabulary made her need to back and fill several times before he got the story. Her uncle was a baker in the palace, and had just got her a position here. Plainly, though, she hadn't been a shy innocent in whatever Delta village she came from. She wasn't a maiden, and she knew what to do in bed.

As she put her tunic back on, she asked, "You want again, another time? And your friend here?"

Menedemos chuckled. "Dear, you love us for our silver alone! But we aren't the mines of Laureion in Attica." That flew straight over her head. She opened the door, blew him a kiss, and was gone.

After Sostratos got back from his ramble through the overgrown city, he told Menedemos, "Well, I've found a couple of men who seem to have the money and the interest to buy some of the amber, anyway."

"*Euge!*" Menedemos said, miming applause.

"And how was *your* morning?" Sostratos' tongue didn't really drip venom, but he enjoyed acting as if it did.

"Pretty good. Better than pretty good, in fact. She wasn't used to a sausage still in the skin, but that didn't keep her from enjoying it."

Sostratos stared at him. "A sausage still in the—? What *are* you going on about now?"

Menedemos told him exactly what he was going on about. He added, "She asked about you, too."

"Did she?" his cousin said. "Well, a drakhma's not a terrible price. I don't know how you feel about sharing a woman, though. Come to that, I don't know how I feel about it, either. We've never tried that before."

"She's only an Egyptian. It's not as though either one of us will fall in love with her or anything, She won't fall for us, either. She's as mercenary as one of those Cretans who sells his sling to whoever pays him most."

"I'll have a look at her, I suppose. If I like what I see, I'll try her," Sostratos said. "Then she can laugh at my prong, too, so you won't feel all alone. What's her name, anyhow?"

"Her—?" Menedemos' mouth fell open. He thumped his forehead with the heel of his hand. "By the gods, I'm an idiot! I never asked her!"

"That will make her easier for me to find, won't it? I'll shout, 'Hey you!' and she'll come running." Sostratos clicked his tongue between his teeth. "How can you screw somebody if you don't even know who she is?"

"My pole did the talking, my pole and her piggy," Menedemos said. Sostratos made that tongue-clicking noise again. They eyed each other in perfect mutual incomprehension.

In Greek letters, the palace girl's name was Seseset, or something close to that. It had a couple of the sneezing consonants Aramaic also used but Greek didn't. She gave herself to Sostratos as readily—maybe as

greedily—as she did to Menedemos. Now that she knew about foreskins, she seemed to take them in stride.

Sostratos also soon discovered his cousin was right. Seseset gave
what she gave cheerfully enough, but she cared little for either Hellene beyond the silver they paid her. She was honest about it, at least.
Sostratos preferred that to drama. A lot of things he enjoyed watching in a play at the theater were less enjoyable in real life.

So when he got the urge and he had a drakhma he didn't mind
parting with, he found Seseset and slaked his lust. Sometimes he
thought she enjoyed it; others, her attitude toward him put him in
mind of his when he petted a friendly dog. The creature was there.
It was amusing for a moment. Past that, it wasn't worth getting
excited about.

He could have had exactly what Seseset gave him, and clever
conversation with it, for much more money from any of the hetairai
who'd flocked to Alexandria. A city full of rich men naturally attract-
ed women who wanted some small share of riches for themselves.

Sostratos had no interest in visiting the fancy women. For one
thing, he was stingy; he didn't always care to part with even a single
drakhma. For another, he was shy. Holding up his end of the conversation with a hetaira might have strained him. So Seseset suited
him fine.

It was funny, in a way. As he'd told Menedemos, he hoped for a
wife with whom he'd be able to share all his thoughts. Once he got
to know herSeseset, he wouldn't—he might not—be shy around her.
And she wouldn't have the hard, bright, bitter edge of so many pro-
fessionally witty women.

Meanwhile …. Meanwhile, business went on. Finding wine
merchants was much easier than coming up with jewelers who'd pay
the price he wanted for his amber; neither of his leads the morning
Menedemos first bedded Seseset came to anything. The wine merchants didn't always want to buy, either.

A plump fellow named Dromeus peered closely at an amphora
a sweating sailor had lugged to his shop. "Everything *seems* to be in
good order, my dear fellow," he said in Greek that declared he came
from Athens. "The jar has the proper shape for Thasian vintages. The
stamps on the neck are as they should be. Your first price isn't too

outrageous, if the wine matches the container it comes in and I may be able to talk you down some. But, you see"—he spread his hands in regret—"I don't know you."

"By the dog, sir, you know the Ptolemaios, don't you?" Sostratos usually spoke an Attic-flavored Greek himself. When he got annoyed, as now, more of Rhodes' native dialect came now.

"I have met him, yes—I've had that privilege," Dromeus answered warily. "Why?"

"Suppose you ask him whether my cousin and I would pour swill into a Thasian amphora and pitch up the stopper again," Sostratos growled. "*He's* bought from us. He knows honest men when he meets them."

Dromeus' face fell: a good impersonation of well-bread dismay. "I assure you, my friend, I meant no such thing. I have no doubt your integrity is above reproach."

"Then you'll buy, of course," Sostratos said. The Alexandrian wine dealer stood mute. Sostratos had expected no more, or he would have got angry. Wearily, he said, "My cousin and I have a room in the palace. You can send someone there to find out if that's true and if we really have dealt with the Ptolemaios. Once you satisfy yourself, you can send a messenger back to me, and I'll dicker with you. But I promise my price will be ten drakhmai a jar higher because of the time you'll make me waste. That's the way of the world, you know."

Dromeus lost his air of gentility. He said something Aristophanes would have been proud of. Sostratos made himself remember it so he could tell it to Menedemos, who adored the Athenian comic poet.

To the wine merchant, he replied, "I love you, too, my dear."

Dromeus glared. "All right. *All right.* It's Thasian, and you're an honest shark—excuse me, an honest man. If we don't go through the rigmarole, you'll let me have it for an honest price, not a ridiculous one, yes?"

"It wouldn't be ridiculous," Sostratos said steadily—now he had his fish on the hook. "And I'm sure you'll make a nice profit off the wine no matter what you pay me. Alexandria is swimming in the cheap stuff, but it's a long way from where the good vintages grow."

Dromeus still glared, but in a different way now. "Why couldn't you be another stupid oaf who doesn't know what the daimon he's doing?"

"You say the sweetest things," Sostratos murmured, though the extremely backhanded compliment did warm him. "I've been doing this for a while know. I try to do it as well as I can."

"Faugh!" Dromeus made a disgusted noise. "For a while!" He had a double chin. His hair was retreating at the temples and starting to go gray. "Your mother hasn't even licked you dry yet."

They started the dicker on that cheery note. Sostratos got the price he wanted, and a few more drakhmai for the amphora besides. He left Dromeus' shop well pleased with himself. The rower who'd lugged the jar dozed outside in what little shade he could find. Sostratos gave him a drakhma for his hard labor. Grinning, the fellow headed for a tavern that sold cheap stuff.

V

MENEDEMOS GLANCED UP AT THE SKY WITH A certain apprehension. It was cloudless and bright, the sun beating down. A drop of sweat slid along his cheek. Rhodes got weather like this in midsummer. It wasn't even midspring yet. When Menedemos thought about midsummer here in Alexandria, he wanted to hide under a flat rock like a lizard.

The Egyptians on the streets took the weather in stride. They'd been born to it, so why wouldn't they? Quite a few Hellenes wore petasoi—broad-brimmed felt hats—or low, conical headgear woven from straw or rushes to keep the pitiless sun from baking their brains.

"Hail, friend!" Menedemos called to a thin-faced man with a straw hat. "Can you tell me where to buy one of those?"

"There's a fellow named Marempsemis who makes good ones," the Hellene replied. "His shop is … let me see … three blocks up and two blocks over from here." He pointed. "And my name is Diophantes. Tell him I sent you—he'll knock a bit off the price."

"Thanks. Marem …. Sounds like an Egyptian, however you say it. Does he speak Greek?"

"Enough to sell you a hat, stranger. Remember, tell him Diophantes sent you."

"I will." Menedemos had no idea whether using the thin-faced man's name would win him a discount. He suspected it would get Diophantes a rakeoff, though. Maybe he'd trot out the name, maybe not. He did give the man an obolos himself, even if Diophantes didn't have his hand out. Keeping people sweet went with being a trader.

He found Marempsemis' little shop between that of a man who sold little terra-cotta statuettes—"Servants for next world!" he called in accented Greek as Menedemos walked by—and an eatery run by a middle-aged woman who ladled beans out of a big kettle and into bowls.

When Menedemos paused to look at a couple of hats on display on poles, a little dog ran out of the shop and yapped at him. When it made as if to nip an ankle, he drew back his foot. That was plenty to send the dog away in a hurry, its stumpy tail down.

An Egyptian following the dog scooped it up and scratched it behind the ears. "Good you no kick," he said to Menedemos in bad but understandable Greek. "He no bite you. He better not bite you." He aimed a stream of crackling Egyptian syllables at the dog as he set it down. It scooted into the shop.

"Are you Marempsemis, by any chance?" Menedemos asked.

"That me." The Egyptian jabbed a thumb at his own chest. He was within a digit of Menedemos' height, and strikingly handsome. Had he been a Hellene, suitors would have misspelled his name scrawling it on walls when he was a youth. He had a thick head of jet-black hair, regular features, and a strong chin. His smile, though, showed a missing front tooth, lost in an accident, in a brawl, or to a dentist.

"A man named Diophantes told me you make fine hats." Menedemos decided to try the experiment.

Marempsemis nodded. "Ah. Him. Yes. He buy hat from me every year."

"Will you show me what you have?"

"I do." The hatmaker nodded again, then disappeared into his shop, which was also plainly his home. He came back with half a dozen hats. Some were of straw, some of rushes. Some were wide, others narrower. Two had cloth straps that could go under the chin to help hold them on if the wind blew hard; the rest didn't.

Menedemos took a wide one with a chinstrap. He put it on his head. "What do you think?" he asked the hatmaker.

Marempsemis winked at him. "I think I try sell you hat."

That made Menedemos chuckle. "I think you just sold me one, my dear. How much did you sell it to me for?"

"Usually four oboloi. Since you know Diophantes, for you three oboloi, four chalkoi. I take off half-obolos for friend of friend."

And maybe he did, and maybe the hat usually cost three oboloi and he'd give the extra bronze coins to the Hellene Menedemos had met on the street. Menedemos didn't worry about it for long. Even four oboloi wouldn't have been a bad price. A lot of skilled work went into weaving the straw into shape.

As Menedemos was paying the Egyptian, the little dog ran out again. A boy of about ten followed. He had a half-finished hat in his hands and looked just like Marempsemis, though he still owned all his front teeth. Marempsemis put an arm around his shoulder. "Son of my," he said.

Menedemos dipped his head to the boy. "Hail, sonny! Do you speak Greek?"

"Only a little bit," the hatmaker's son replied. He had a better accent than his father. Well, he'd started picking it up younger than Marempsemis had. With a shy smile for Menedemos, he grabbed the dog and went back in.

"I get old, he do after me," Marempsemis said, as any father might.

"Good," Menedemos said. Barbarians might only now be discovering the glories of Greek culture and the beauty and precision of the Greek language. If not for Alexander's conquests, they might have wallowed in squalid ignorance for centuries more. Ignorant or not, though, they were still recognizably people. Marempsemis' hope for his son would have made perfect sense to Philodemos back in Rhodes.

Menedemos paid the hatmaker four small silver coins. He got four broad bronze ones in return. Bronze coins, for amounts smaller than silver could easily deal with, were new in the world. No one had thought of them when the polis of Rhodes was first built. *That was only a hundred years ago, too*, Menedemos thought—change visible almost within the span of a lifetime. They certainly helped grease the capstan of commerce so it went round and round without squeaking.

After the Hellene set the hat on his head, he looked a question at Marempsemis. "You fine," the brown man assured him. "No cook over—ah, under—sun."

"Thanks," Menedemos said. He fiddled with the hat to get its brim just so. Along with shielding him from the remorseless fire in the sky, it also cut some of the glare. He liked that.

Well pleased with himself, he made his way back to the palace. By now, he was starting to be practiced at negotiating the maze of corridors that led to the room he and Sostratos shared. He tapped on the door and waited. If Sostratos and Seseset were in there together, he'd give them time to put on their clothes, even if he'd seen both of them naked.

But Sostratos' voice penetrated the wood: "Come in." Menedemos did. Sostratos pointed to his hat. "So you went and got one, did you?"

"Yes, I did. I'm tired of baking under this horrible sun."

"What did you pay and where did you get it? I think I'll do the same," Sostratos said. "I'm a bit darker than you, but not enough to keep from baking myself."

Menedemos told him what he needed to know, adding, "Tell Marempsemis that Diophantes sent you. He'll knock the price down a bit."

"Who's Diophantes?"

"A Hellene who had a hat. I met him on the street when I was sweating like a swine, so I asked him where he got it. He sent me to that hatmaker."

Sostratos looked at him in admiration. "I'd never have the nerve to do anything like that."

"It's easy enough," Menedemos said. So it was—for him. "You don't have any trouble doing business. What's so tough about talking to someone on the street?"

"Business is almost as full of ritual as sacrificing is," Sostratos said. "And I'm dealing with people I know, or at least with people who may want to do business with me. Just chatting up a stranger ...?" He tossed his head.

"Really, my dear? I never should have guessed," Menedemos said, and started to laugh. Sostratos swore at him. That only made him laugh harder. These days, he had to work to get under his cousin's skin. He'd done it this time, though.

Breakfast for guests in Ptolemaios' palace wasn't fancy, but breakfast anywhere Hellenes lived wasn't commonly fancy. Sostratos and Menedemos sat on low stools in front of a table that held good wheat bread, indifferent olive oil, and pitchers of wine and water. Both Rhodians watered their wine more than they would have at home; getting drunk or even giddy was the last thing they wanted to do here.

A couple of Egyptians from well up the Nile didn't worry about it, and poured down neat wine. They were involved in some kind of lawsuit whose appeals had finally gone all the way up to Ptolemaios himself. They knew enough Greek to get by, but talked to each other in their own language. Only when another Egyptian came in did they clam up. He also pretended they weren't there. Sostratos guessed he was involved in the lawsuit, too, but on the other side.

The hard-faced steward who looked as if he'd campaigned with Alexander walked up to the Rhodians and tapped each of them on the shoulder. "I am to bring you before the Ptolemaios," Demodamas said. "Come along with me, if you please."

They came. Sostratos gulped his cup empty; Menedemos ate one more big bite of bread and left the refectory still chewing. Sostratos didn't think the steward was leading them on the same route they'd used before.

He soon found he was right. Instead of going to a private chamber, they washed up in a waiting room to an audience chamber that would have been a throne room if only Ptolemaios called himself a king. None of Alexander's marshals had yet taken that step, though Sostratos kept thinking it couldn't be far away.

He planted himself on a stool no different from the ones in the refectory. A couple of other Hellenes already sat in the room, waiting to be summoned. They didn't speak to Sostratos or Menedemos, but chatted with each other in low voices so the Rhodians couldn't overhear.

Before Sostratos could decide whether he was insulted, someone new strode into the antechamber. The man was as tall as he was, or even a digit or two taller. There the resemblance ceased. The new-comer, who wore only an Egyptian-style linen skirt, was broad in the shoulders and thick through the chest, as Sostratos wished he were.

And he was far darker than the Egyptians, his skin a brown so dark it was nearly black. He had full lips, a rather low nose, and hair so curly it was almost crispy. He carried himself like a man of conse-quence; since he'd come to this more or less royal waiting room, no doubt he was.

Beside Sostratos, Menedemos was also doing his best not to stare. Out of the side of his mouth, he whispered, "I've heard some people were that color, but I never saw anybody who was before."

"Neither have I," Sostratos whispered back. The way the dark brown man's eyes swung toward them made the Rhodian wonder if the fellow understood Greek. "Excuse me, best one, but do you speak my language?" he asked, almost before realizing he'd done it. The idea of asking directions on the street could paralyze him with anxiety. This, though, this was pure intellectual curiosity. And intellectual cu-riosity was *important*.

"Enough to manage," the dark man said, his accent softer than the one with which Egyptians flavored their Greek. He bowed to the Rhodians. "I am Harsioteph son of Nasakhma, envoy of King Gatisen to the Ptolemaios. And you gentlemen are ...?"

Sostratos and Menedemos rose from their stools to introduce themselves. Harsioteph gravely clasped hands with each of them in turn. His hand was large and strong and hard; the skin on his palm was paler than the rest of his hide. Sostratos asked, "Is, uh, Gatisen king of Ethiopia?"

"Hellenes use this name sometimes," Harsioteph said. "We call our land Kus." The last sound was a hissed or sneezed consonant like the ones in Seseset's name, a sound for which the Greek alphabet had no letter. The dark brown man added, "King Gatisen's capital is Meroë."

"Meroë!" Sostratos felt himself caught up in history. "Herodotos wrote of it a century and a half ago!" To Harsioteph, he explained, "Herodotos was a man who wrote about the long-ago wars between the Hellenes and the Persians."

"We of Kus fought the Persians, too. We also fight Hellenes if we have to." Harsioteph sent him a measuring stare.

Ignoring it, Sostratos exclaimed, "Your wars were in the days of the Persian King Kambyses, weren't they? Herodotos talks about them."

Harsioteph shrugged. "Old Persian king a long time ago. Don't know if anyone in Kus remember—ah, remembers—his name."

Before he could say anything more, an attendant came out of the audience chamber and spoke to him: "The Ptolemaios will see you now. He asks me to ask you to give his respects to King Gatisen."

"I do that," Harsioteph replied, and followed the man inside. The Hellenes who'd got there before Sostratos and Menedemos scowled at his back.

In other circumstances, Sostratos might have done the same. He was too excited now. "An Ethiopian, straight out of Herodotos!" he said. "The old gossip knew what he was talking about after all—he mostly did. Pity Harsioteph didn't daub himself half with ash, half with vermilion, the way the historian says Ethiopians do when they go to war."

"He's not going to war. He's talking peacefully, which is more than you can say for Demetrios," Menedemos remarked. "If Alexandria thrives the way it looks like it's thriving, there'll be a colony of black people here before long, if there isn't one already. Money draws men the way honey draws flies."

"I hadn't thought of that, but you're likely right," Sostratos said.

"Those people are only good for the mines," one of the other Hellenes said. "If their dark hides don't mark them as the slaves by nature Aristoteles talks about, what ever could?"

"I don't think I'd care to try making a slave of that Harsioteph," Sostratos said. "He may be a barbarian, but he's a man."

"Chains and the lash would soften him up soon enough," the other man said.

"Or make him murder you as soon as you turn your back," Menedemos put in, which matched Sostratos' view of things.

The other Hellene and his friend argued with the Rhodians, more or less good-naturedly, till the attendant came out again and said, "The Ptolemaios will see Menedemos and Sostratos now." In they went. Sostratos didn't look over his shoulder, lest he see the other Hellenes glaring daggers at him.

He and Menedemos bowed before Ptolemaios. The general who ruled Egypt as a king in all but name frowned from his massive chair—no stool for him. "Well, men of Rhodes, I kept hoping you were wrong with your word of what old Cyclops' brat is up to, but you had the straight word," Ptolemaios said. "Between his army and his cursed fleet, he's been gobbling up the poleis in eastern Cyprus one by one, and he's laying siege to Salamis."

"Has he, sir? Is he? That's not good news. We heard that he was starting the campaign, but we left Rhodes before we got word of how it was going," Sostratos said.

"We wanted to make sure we got the news to you as soon as we could," Menedemos added. Sostratos had to work to keep from grimacing; he should have thought to put that in himself. Greasing the powerful never hurt.

"Not good news at all," Ptolemaios said heavily. "Who would have guessed the gods-cursed brat had a gift for laying siege to cities? But he does, pestilence take him. His old man is a good general, too—don't get me wrong. The brat will have it in the blood and in the training. But Antigonos is about as charming as a viper. Demetrios can talk anybody into anything, or so it seems."

"He didn't talk the Rhodian people into allying with him and his father against you," Menedemos said.

"Yes, the free and independent Rhodian people." To Sostratos' ear, Ptolemaios sounded sardonic, as Demetrios had in the agora. But Rhodes was more useful to the ruler of Egypt than to Demetrios and Antigonos—and Ptolemaios' power lay a long way from the island.

Sostratos said, "The Athenians certainly fell all over themselves voting honors to Demetrios and Antigonos after the polis fell to Demetrios and his men."

"I heard about that. It embarrassed me. Not the kind of thing you expect from free and independent people, even if the Athenians still claim that's what they are." Ptolemaios made as if to spit in disgust. Had he been with his fellow Macedonians, he likely would have. But he'd learned proper Greek manners, even if he sometimes wore them awkwardly.

"Rhodes isn't like that," Menedemos said.

"I hope Rhodes isn't like that," Sostratos said.

Ptolemaios eyed him. "You're made like an asparagus shoot, but not much gets past you, does it?" He was shaped more like a brick himself: these days, a brick with a potbelly.

"I try not to let it, sir," Sostratos said. "What do you plan to do about Cyprus, if you don't mind my asking?"

"I'm going to rescue it, that's what. I need it. And I'll get Menelaos out of whatever pickle he's in up there," Ptolemaios answered. Like Menedemos, Sostratos had no brothers. He'd seen how his father and Menedemos' could make a sport of tearing strips off each other, though. Evidently even the great and prominent weren't immune to that.

When Sostratos glanced over at Menedemos, he found his cousin looking back at him. They'd watched Demetrios swoop down on Athens. Could this aging warlord keep up with the rising generation?

"Building up my fleet and getting soldiers aboard will take a bit," Ptolemaios said, as if thinking out loud. "But when I hit Demetrios, by the gods, I'll hit him with a rock in my fist."

To that, Sostratos said nothing at all. Menedemos murmured, "Yes, sir." That was what you were supposed to say to a man who could order you thrown to the crocodiles. But Sostratos wondered whether Ptolemaios had paid any attention to what Alexander was doing when he campaigned with him. As much as anything else, Alexander had beaten the Persians with sheer speed.

"On your way, lads," the ruler of Egypt said. "I just wanted to let you know what I've heard. When you go back to Rhodes, you'll pass it along. I may even pay your polis a call myself, once I've given the puppy the kicking he deserves."

How did he mean that? Would he come with the fleet he was building up and the soldiers who'd travel in the ships? Sostratos feared he might prove as dangerous as Demetrios. When you were small, everyone large looked dangerous. An attendant appeared at his elbow. Another stood by Menedemos. The Rhodians bowed to Ptolemaios, who dipped his head to them as if he were Zeus in the *Iliad*. The attendants led them away.

Menedemos would have shushed Sostratos if he'd started talking about the audience while they were still inside the palace. Sostratos could be an innocent about such business (Menedemos conveniently forgot that his cousin had already shushed him once over the same thing). But Sostratos had the sense to keep quiet till they were out on the wide, noisy streets of Alexandria.

Two amphorai had fallen from an oxcart and smashed, spilling something sticky onto the street. Half a dozen Egyptian-looking men shouted at one another. A couple sounded angry enough to go for their knives, but they didn't. The ox, standing in the middle of the street and blocking traffic, lifted its tail to deliver its own commentary on the situation.

Both Menedemos and Sostratos started talking at the same time. Menedemos laughed. The two Hellenes must have each decided the commotion would cover whatever they had to say.

"So he *is* going to fight Demetrios on Cyprus!" Menedemos said. "That's important news."

"It is," his cousin agreed. "They need to know it on Rhodes. Now if only we had some way to tell them."

"If only," Menedemos echoed mournfully. "I wonder how many important affairs down through the years have smashed like a dropped amphora because the men in charge of them didn't get news they needed soon enough."

"Quite a few, I'm sure." Sostratos plucked at his beard as he thought. He did that often; it never failed to annoy Menedemos. "Xerxes might have conquered Hellas if he'd known what was going on with all his forces while it was happening instead of later. And the Athenians' attack on Syracuse might have gone better. It couldn't very well have gone worse."

"That came after the Persian War," Menedemos said.

Sostratos dipped his head. "Yes, a lifetime later. It would have been … let me think … about a hundred years ago. Somewhere not far from the time when the polis of Rhodes went up."

"How do you keep all that stuff straight in your head?" Menedemos asked.

"I never thought about how. I just do." Sostratos sounded surprised. "*You* can come out with whole books of Homer or all the filthiest bits from Aristophanes."

"But those are fun. Dates are just boring," Menedemos said.

"No, they aren't," Sostratos said. "Dates are the bones of history. Knowing when something happened tells you about the other things that caused it to happen, and about the things it influenced in turn. Without dates, everything would be chaos. 'Without form and void,' the Ioudaioi say."

"Do they?" Menedemos spoke without much interest. To him, the Ioudaioi were just another set of barbarians who got too excited about their religion to care about learning true civilization from the Hellenes. Sostratos' opinion of them was a little higher, but he spoke a bit of their language and had spent more time among them.

"They do, but that doesn't matter. What matters is getting word back to Rhodes. How can we do that?" Sostratos said.

"Quickest way would be to hop back into the *Aphrodite* and take her across the Inner Sea again." Menedemos laughed a laugh sour as vinegar. "With most of our cargo still unsold, of course. Our fathers would skin us and grind us for sausage stuffing. The news about the Ptolemaios' plans for Cyprus may be important, but it's not *that* important. Trading comes first."

"Which reminds me," Sostratos said. "I still hope I'll be able to sell the amber I brought for a good price here, but nobody in Alexandria wants Damonax's olive oil for anything close to what he thinks it should bring."

"Let me guess. The Egyptians think the stuff is nasty, and the Hellenes get theirs from the Phoenicians and the Ioudaioi," Menedemos said.

"Right both times." Sostratos smiled a twisted smile. "I'd tell him what I think of him, only I'm afraid he'd make my sister sorry if I did. Families are so enjoyable."

"Aren't they just?" Once more, Menedemos almost said more than he should have, but caught himself in time. Keeping Baukis' secret meant *keeping* it. He'd come close to spilling his guts before. This time, he went back to business so smoothly, he could hope his cousin didn't notice the hitch. "The wine is moving pretty well. After you finish your dealing with the amber, maybe you could hire a barge or a riverboat or whatever they use on the Nile and take some of the oil up the river to where people don't see it so often."

As he'd hoped it would, Sostratos' face lit up like a just-kindled torch. "Do you think so, my dear? If I took it down to Memphis, say, I might get to see the Pyramids after all. That would be wonderful!"

"Do what you have to first," Menedemos said. "After you've finished what you have to do, then you can have some fun."

His cousin laughed in his face. "You say that? You? The fellow who sleeps with every unhappy wife he meets in every polis we go to?"

Menedemos' cheeks heated. That was a hit, but he wouldn't admit it. He laughed, too, lightly, and replied, "Not *every* unhappy wife. Only the pretty ones." Sostratos stuck out his tongue at him. Menedemos laughed again. He'd distracted his cousin, anyhow.

Sure enough, Sostratos said, "Do you really think I could do that? I'd want to bring some rowers along, so the locals don't just knock the stranger over the head and walk off with everything he has."

"You should. All we're paying them for now is sitting around and whoring and eating their heads off. You may as well get some use out of them," Menedemos said.

"I'll have to find out how expensive a riverboat would be. I'll be paying Egyptian sailors along with ours—and yes, I know what ours cost. Keeping an akatos in business isn't cheap," Sostratos said.

"A good thing, too. More people would do it if it were easy." Menedemos paused a moment in thought. "I wonder if we could get the polis to pay some of the cost for our crew. We aren't just here for ourselves—we're doing Rhodes' business, too."

"That's pretty, but don't hold your breath. Ptolemaios is here, not down in Memphis. The people who run Rhodes will say there's no silver for side trips. They'll say we should be glad to help the polis, because it's our patriotic duty," Sostratos replied.

"You know what? You're probably right. You know what else? I'm going to submit the bill anyhow," Menedemos said cheerfully. "What's the worst they can do? They can tell me no. How am I worse off if they do?"

His cousin quirked an eyebrow. "When somebody tells me no, I want to slide into a crevice in a wall like a mouse getting away from a dog. And … no wonder you get so many women to bend over forward for you."

"No wonder at all." Menedemos knew he sounded smug. He didn't care. "You keep on trying. One yes makes up for a hundred noes."

"Not to me," Sostratos said, and then, "*Oimoi!*"

The Egyptians who'd been arguing with one another over the smashed amphorai went from shouting and wagging fingers under one another's noses to punching and kicking and wrestling in the dusty street. Other people, both Egyptians and Hellenes, either tried to break up the brawl or joined in.

Menedemos and Sostratos backed away from the melee. Sostratos was a peaceable chap most of the time. Menedemos' temper had a shorter lead, but he didn't jump into strangers' fights for the fun of it, the way some of the rowers might have.

Then someone shouted, "The watch! The watch!" Everyone who knew even a little Greek got out of the ruction and ran. A moment later, a squad of Macedonians rolled over the fighters who were still at it. A lot of the soldiers were older men or men who limped, but they wore linen corselets and bronze helmets and carried stout clubs a couple of cubits long. They left some of the Egyptians limp on the ground and dragged others off to question.

"My, my," Sostratos murmured. "Athens had Skythians policing it. Ptolemaios puts his old soldiers out to pasture here. I wonder how much those Egyptians' families will have to pay to get them turned loose."

Menedemos looked around before answering, then spoke quietly: "As much as they can afford, and then ten drakhmai more. You can bet the Ptolemaios will make sure of that." Sostratos dipped his head. They'd both seen that Egypt's lord and master missed no chance to enrich himself.

Sostratos walked west along Alexandria's main thoroughfare toward the Gate of the Moon. The Gate of the Sun was also on the boulevard, but at the eastern end of the city's perimeter. Sostratos cared little for the gates themselves, but the canal that led from Alexandria to the Nile ended near the Gate of the Moon. If he was going to hire a riverboat, that seemed the place to do it.

The sun beat down. It rose higher and higher in the sky as day followed day. Sostratos wished for a hat like the one Menedemos had bought, or even a Greek petasos. Wishing failed to provide one.

He sweated as he walked, and hoped he wouldn't keel over. *You should have gone to that Marempsemis' shop*, he told himself. *And you should have found out sooner that the fellow who said he wanted to buy your amber had more fancy talk than silver.*

He wished a covered colonnade gave shelter from glare and heat, as the Stoa did in Athens. Again, a wish didn't conjure one out of nothingness. Of course, it would have needed to be a *long* covered colonnade. This avenue was far longer and straighter than any in Athens. Athens' streets meandered every which way; back when the polis was a village, they'd probably been sheep tracks and dog runs.

Like Rhodes, Alexandria was built on a grid, but it dwarfed Sostratos' home polis. The avenue, for instance, had to be twenty stadia long, and at least sixty cubits broad. Four or five of the main streets in Rhodes could have cuddled side by side across this one. The sheer scale of the place could daunt someone used to smaller habitations.

Workmen used a creaking crane to hoist a block of granite onto what would become Ptolemaios' grand tomb for Alexander. More workmen on the structure waited for the block to arrive. Sostratos paused to watch for a moment. "Careful, you thickskulls!" called one of the men on the half-built tomb. "Don't squash us!"

"Who'd know the difference?" a man swinging the crane shouted back. They kept cursing each other till the block went safely into place. Then the workmen on the ground started tying up another big cube of stone. Sostratos went on his way.

An Egyptian who spoke enough Greek to get by grabbed his arm and tried to lead him to a brothel. "You try Egyptian girls, you don't never go back to Hellenes!" he said.

Sostratos shook him off. "Go away!" he said, and then, "Get lost!" The tout suddenly didn't understand Greek so well. He wouldn't go away. "To the crows with you, you abandoned rogue!" Sostratos shouted, and made as if to punch him.

Either the words or the gesture got through. The Egyptian skittered back. From a safe distance, he said, "You don't want no girls.

You just want to stick it up some boy's *prokton!*" He had plenty of vulgar vocabulary.

The gibe would have made Sostratos angrier had it held even an obolos' worth of truth. He'd been jealous that Menedemos was so much more admired than he was while they were youths, but not because he wanted to lie down with one of the admirers. He just longed for notice of any kind. Since becoming a man, he hadn't chased any handsome boys. He got his pleasure from women. He didn't want to spend money in whatever nasty crib the Egyptian worked for, though.

Before long, he got into the western part of the city. Farther from the palace and from Ptolemaios' eye, it held more empty lots and more little shacks built from whatever the people who lived in them could steal. He kept his hand on the hilt of his belt knife and wished he'd brought a couple of broad-shouldered rowers with him.

His nostrils twitched. He realized he had to be getting close to the canal: among all the other city stinks, the odor of stagnant water became the strongest note. Sure enough, booths and tents ahead sold things that came down the Nile to Alexandria.

Egyptians here assumed all Hellenes were rich. They swarmed toward Sostratos, trying to sell him duck eggs or flattish loaves of barley bread or linen cloth or amulets or whatever they happened to have. It was noisier, more frantic, more desperate commerce than any in a Greek polis.

Sostratos said "No!" and "Go away!" and "Leave me alone!" over and over. Then he said something filthy in Aramaic. Quite a few of the Egyptians got it. Several of them doubled over in laughter, startled that a Hellene should know any foreign language.

Piers jutted out into the canal. Sostratos had seen small boats on small rivers before. The rivercraft tied up here were anything but small. Well, the Nile was no small river, either. Some were made of papyrus like the ones the *Aphrodite* had met on the Inner Sea but vastly larger. Others—barges—put him in mind of giant floating boxes, though they could mount a mast at need. And workers were unloading more granite blocks, perhaps destined for Alexander's tomb, from a raft made of palm trunks lashed together. The raft could also raise a mast and sail at need.

A man standing on the pier was spouting a stream of quick orders in Egyptian to a gang hauling sacks of grain or beans out of a barge. Sostratos' heart beat faster; he still didn't like bearding strangers. But this was part of business, too. "Excuse me, O best one, but do you speak Greek?" he asked.

"Some," the man answered without looking at him. "What you want?"

"How much would it cost to hire your ... craft ... to haul amphorai of olive oil from here to Memphis?" Sostratos tried to speak slowly and clearly.

He got the Egyptian's attention. The man was close to forty, of about Menedemos' height but stockier. A scar seamed one cheek. "How many amphorai? When you want to go? When you got to get there? Not fast—we go against current." He used gestures to eke out his words.

Sostratos knew how much oil he had. The other questions had as much to do with the barge captain's convenience as with his own. He gathered that the Egyptian would see what other cargo he could pick up in Alexandria for the voyage south, though he made more bringing goods down the Nile to this new, brash boomtown.

He named a price Sostratos didn't find too outrageous. The Rhodian haggled anyhow; he didn't care to seem an easy mark. He said, "I want to bring some of my rowers along, too, to help me while I'm in Memphis."

The Egyptian, whose name was Pasos, grinned crookedly; the scar helped. "So I don't knock you on head, feed you to crocodiles?"

"*Malista.*" Sostratos dipped his head as coolly as he could. "That, too. Even friends should watch other friends."

"You maybe not come from the Two Lands, but you not so stupid, hey?" Pasos said. "Yes, you bring your mans—friend."

"Thank you so much—friend," Sostratos said. Pasos grinned again. So did the Hellene.

VI

OXCARTS HALF FULL OF STRAW WAITED AT THE
end of the wharf where the *Aphrodite* was tied up. Rowers—some of
them hauled out of wineshops and brothels, more than a few obvi-
ously the worse for wear—hauled jars of Damonax's olive oil from the
akatos to the carts and set them in the straw.

Menedemos tilted his hat back on his head and turned to his
cousin. "Are you sure you'll be all right without me?" he asked.

"Yes, my dear." Sostratos smiled patiently. "I made it to Jerusalem
and back on my own. I expect I can get to Memphis and back, too."

"But this is Egypt," Menedemos said. Sostratos brought out the
maternal in him. He always had, even when they were little boys.
Menedemos didn't understand it. He'd never felt that way about
anyone else.

"I'll be fine." Sostratos had enjoyed having a protector when he
was small. The idea pleased and amused him less these days, not least
because he towered over his cousin. Menedemos didn't care. No matter how large and clever his cousin was, he still had trouble coping
with that maddening tribe known as the human race. He needed a
helping hand. Menedemos would give him one—unless they happened to be squabbling, of course.

"Don't you think you should take more men along?" No, Menedemos didn't want to leave it alone.

"I'll be fine," Sostratos repeated. "A few men will help me. All the rowers we have won't save me if the Egyptians—or the Hellenes and Macedonians down in Memphis—decide they really want to get rid of me."

Menedemos knew he was right. Knowing didn't make him feel any easier about it. Like a duck with ducklings, he fussed over everything. "Be careful down there. Come back as soon as you can."

"The Egyptians would say 'up there,'" Sostratos answered imperturbably. "Memphis is up the Nile from Alexandria. This is Lower Egypt to them, even if it sits on top of what they call Upper Egypt."

"I don't give a curse what the Egyptians say," Menedemos told him, eyeing the men and the amphorai and the oxcarts. The carts were almost loaded. Pretty soon Sostratos would go off on this adventure. Menedemos unhappily recalled he'd encouraged his cousin to travel south if he got the chance. Sostratos would do well, or he'd do not so well. Whatever he'd do, he'd do it by himself. Menedemos was still unloading wine on fancy merchants.

"Everything will go fine," Sostratos assured him, which only made him worry more. Sostratos couldn't know that. Hearing him say it made Menedemos sure he would jinx it.

Menedemos eyed the men driving the oxcarts. Two were Egyptians, the other two Hellenes. They looked bored, as people who drove oxen often did. Oxen went at their own pace, even slower than walking. You couldn't hurry them. Such men seemed unlikely to turn on Sostratos and the rowers, but Menedemos worried about it anyhow.

And the rowers! Sostratos wished his cousin hadn't chosen Leskhaios for anything that might need more thought than pulling an oar. Not that Leskhaios couldn't think, but that he liked to argue to a degree unusual even in a Hellene. He put Menedemos in mind of Thersites in the *Iliad*: full of inopportune questions and unwilling to listen to sensible answers. Sometimes the only thing such men understood was a good clout. Could Sostratos see that?

"Are we ready?" Menedemos' cousin called. No one told him no. He waved to the drivers. Almost in unison, they flicked their whips above their beasts' backs. Not one actually touched his ox. The animals started forward anyhow, snorting as the weight of the cart and cargo resisted their work. Then the ungreased wheels squealed and the carts began to move.

"Safe journey! Gods go with you, you thickskull!" Menedemos said when Sostratos and his little band strode after the oxcarts.

"Thickskull? Me? You should talk!" Sostratos sounded more than confident enough.

Menedemos felt like a father watching his son march off to war. He wanted to call his cousin back. He had no reason to, but that didn't have anything to do with it. Sostratos looked over his shoulder after a dozen paces and waved. All Menedemos could do was wave back.

Once he was sure his cousin had got out of earshot, he turned to Diokles and asked, "Do you think he'll be all right?"

"He should be," the keleustes answered. "The Ptolemaios, he's got this place roped down pretty tight. Not much nasty business goes on unless he wants it to. Happens he likes us Rhodians just now. People here know it, too. Everything'll be fine, skipper."

"You have a good way of looking at things," Menedemos said gratefully. He'd wanted reassurance and he'd got some.

The oxcarts' wheels squealed more as they slewed round a corner and disappeared. A moment later, Sostratos and his rowers also vanished from Menedemos' ken. He fought down the urge to run after them. He had his own business to see to.

But Diokles also had things on his mind. Before Menedemos could leave the quay, the oarmaster set a hand on his arm and asked, "Do you have any notion how long we'll be tied up here, skipper?" He pointed with his chin in the direction of the *Aphrodite*.

Menedemos understood the question behind the question. When the akatos stayed in the sea without getting hauled up onto a beach or into a shipshed, her timbers soaked up waters like so many sponges. That made her heavy and slow. With regret, Menedemos tossed his head. "I'm sorry, but I've no idea. At least till Sostratos and the rowers come back, plainly."

Diokles clicked his tongue between his teeth: a discontented noise if ever there was one. "Any chance you might ask the Ptolemaios if we can use one of his sheds? We'll be heavier than I like by the time we get near Rhodes any which way with all those days at sea, but I don't want to make it any worse than I have to, know what I'm saying?"

"I'm afraid I do," Menedemos answered. If Demetrios quickly beat Menelaos and overran all of Cyprus, he might turn on Rhodes next. If he didn't quickly overrun Cyprus and Ptolemaios sailed north to oppose him, that fight might well involve the home island and home polis, too. Any which way, warships and pirate galleys might prowl in the waters around Rhodes. The *Aphrodite* could use every extra barleycorn of speed she could get.

"So will you ask him, then?"

"If he'll see me. If he won't see me, I'll talk to the harbormaster or one of his men. If they say no, well, I tried. If they say yes …. You're right. We'd be better off for it."

"Good. That's been on my mind." The oarmaster looked pleased. "Like you say, no sure bet they'll do what we want—gods-cursed Macedonians can be arrogant as all get-out. But if they will, it'll help. I keep seeing pentekonters chasing us like sharks after tunny."

"Heh," Menedemos said uneasily. Those long, lean fifty-oared galleys were pirates' favorite ships because of their speed. Even fresh and dry, the *Aphrodite* wasn't quite that fast. Because she carried cargo, she was beamier than a pentekonter. But, gods willing, they'd be near Rhodes if they had one of those encounters. That would help their chances of escape.

"Don't worry too much, skipper," Diokles said. "You've been doing this for a while now. Me, I've been doing it longer than you've been alive. Odds are you'll still be at it when you're old and gray like me." He chuckled. "I was going to say 'old and gray and ugly like me,' but I don't expect you'll ever get this ugly now matter how old you are."

Menedemos kalos, they'd written on walls when he was a youth. He hadn't let it swell his head, the way some boys did. He'd never heard it put quite like this before, though. He laughed, too, and batted his eyes at the crusty keleustes. "You say the sweetest things, my dear."

Diokles broke up. So did Menedemos. Laughing hard felt good. As when he lay down with Seseset, he had a little while when he didn't need to worry about his business … or about what might happen to Rhodes.

Pasos watched as Sostratos and his rowers stowed the last amphora of Damonax's olive oil on his barge. He also had jars of cheap wine from Phoenicia and bolts of woolen cloth for the Hellenes who'd settled along the Nile—Egyptians commonly preferred linen.

"Oil from those olive things? Really?" the barge captain said.

"Olive oil. That's right. Very fine olive oil," Sostratos said.

"I taste olive oil one time, here in Alexandria, just to see what is this stuff." Pasos screwed up his face and stuck out his tongue, as if he'd just choked down some nasty medicine. "Bad! Horrible! Have to be crazy to use. Even stinks when you burn in lamps."

"Hellenes are fond of it," Sostratos replied with dignity. His men, their work done for the moment, dipped their heads to show they thought he was right. A couple of them laughed at the Egyptian.

"Hellenes is daft. Well, I see this already." Pasos brushed a fly away from his face. The air around the stagnant canal was full of flies and gnats and midges and other buzzing, biting annoyances. After the sun went down, it would probably have more than its fair share of mosquitoes, too.

"It's all right, friend. We think Egyptians are the mad ones," Sostratos said. That made Pasos laugh in turn. He said something in his own language to his sailors. *Translating*, Sostratos realized. The barge crew laughed with their captain. By the way they pointed at Sostratos and his men, the Hellenes might have been so many monkeys with tails.

Men on the pier tossed the mooring lines into the barge. Pasos spoke to his crew again, his voice this time sharp with command. The men set sweeps—oars far longer and heavier than the ones the *Aphrodite* used—in the oarlocks (only loops of rope, but they served) and began to row, easing the big, ungainly craft out into the middle of the canal.

At first, Sostratos wasn't sure the handful of men straining so hard could move the heavily laden barge at all. But it did move—slow enough to make a turtle or even a snail chuckle, yet it did.

"That's not the kind of rowing we do, but those fellows know their trade," said one of the Hellenes, a fellow with a broken nose whose name was Arkesilas. "Cursed hard trade, too, looks like."

"It does, yes." Sostratos was thinking the same thing.

Pasos ambled over to him. "We set sail when we can," he said. "Take a while. Nothing on barge happen quick."

"I've had the same thought out on the sea," Sostratos replied. An akatos, though, was a much livelier craft than this ugly floating box. Waves and wind mattered more than they would on the Nile, too.

Once the barge was positioned as Pasos liked, the sailors raised the mast and set stays to secure it in place. The sail was a broad rectangle. "Look at that!" Arkesilas said. "They've got the brails on the back of the sail, not the front."

"Why, so they do!" Sostratos exclaimed. It wasn't a surprise. Just the opposite, in fact: he was noticing for the first time something he'd read about years before. Herodotos maintained that Egyptians did everything in the opposite way from most other folk, and how they placed their brails was one of his examples. Sostratos hadn't known he remembered that, but seeing it called the words up in his mind. And as for the sail itself …. "Are you catching the wind with papyrus, Pasos?"

"Papyrus." The Egyptian's head bobbed up and down. They shared that gesture with most other barbarians, no matter what Herodotos said. "You Hellenes, you like linen better, yes?"

"Yes. Papyrus doesn't grow in our land. You Egyptians, you have linen, too." Sostratos gestured toward Pasos' kilt. "Why don't you use it for sailcloth?"

With a shrug, Pasos answered, "For what our ships on river do, papyrus just as good. Cheaper, too."

He had a point. He wouldn't need to worry about waves or suddenly swinging winds or even the rain that might turn his sail all spongy and useless. "You'll sail down to Memphis and then let the current take you north again?" Sostratos asked.

The barge skipper nodded again. "This trip, keep going south of Memphis, too. Then come north like you say. That how we do it. This ship not fast, but just enough with wind to go against …." He gestured to show he meant *current*; he couldn't come up with the Greek word even though Sostratos had just used it.

Sostratos dipped his head to show he understood. He even sympathized—he had the same kind of lapses when he spoke Aramaic. He said, "You have a nice … steady life on the Nile." He almost said *an easy life*. Compared to sailing the sea and worrying about storms and pirates and generals who lusted after your polis, it was. But the sailors worked as hard as any sailors anywhere. Sostratos wouldn't have cared to pull one of those long, heavy sweeps for even a little while.

"Steady life, yes. But tough life. You Hellenes, you make to pay too many taxes," the Egyptian said.

Sostratos spread his hands. "I can't do anything about that. My ship has to pay them, too. I think we pay more of them here, because Rhodes is a foreign land. The Ptolemaios doesn't rule us, even if we're friendly to him."

"Too much wars. Too much fightings," Pasos said. Considering the times they lived in, Sostratos could hardly tell him he was wrong.

That big, wide sail filled with the breeze that blew off the Inner Sea. The mast groaned and creaked at the push, but the stays held. That happened on the *Aphrodite*, too. *It may not be just like the sailing I'm used to, but it's still sailing*, Sostratos thought.

The barge began to move down the canal. The motion was so slow, Sostratos wondered at first if he was imagining it. Little by little, doubt left him. They might have no better speed than the oxcarts had shown bringing the oil here, but eventually they'd get where they were going.

After a while, they got to the city wall. Sostratos had wondered if they would have to lower the mast and sail to pass under masonry with a portcullis that could be lowered to block access to Alexandria, but they didn't. There was simply a gap in the wall through which the canal passed. To Sostratos, that spoke of Alexander's confidence, and Ptolemaios', that the new city would stay safe and secure.

Thinking about the way the wider world worked, he was glad Rhodes' fortifications had no gaps.

The canal swung east and ran between the southern wall and Lake Mareotis, which lay south of Alexandria. The ground was low, muddy, marshy, and riotously green, far greener than anything Sostratos had ever seen anywhere else. Herons, black ibises, and little naked boys fished at the edge of the canal. Something large swimming beneath the surface made a sinuous ripple on it.

Sostratos pointed to the mark on the otherwise quiet water. "Is that the trace of a crocodile, O Pasos?" he called.

"Yes. Crocodile." The Egyptian grinned wickedly. "You maybe not go swimming right now, hey?"

"Water's too foul for swimming anyhow." Sostratos hoped he sounded calm enough. He did mean what he said. Rivers might bring fresh filth from upstream, but at least they carried downstream the filth that was right here. In the currentless canal, anything that got dumped stayed where it was and rotted.

That didn't seem to trouble the crocodile. There was a thrashing and a startled squawk near the bank. One ibis disappeared, while many more flew away. A couple of the fishing children nearest the attack moved back from the water. The rest kept on with what they were doing.

Shouting to one another in their own language, the sailors swung the yard slantwise so the sail could keep pushing them forward. Pasos and another Egyptian plied steering oars near the stern; the barge was too beamy for one man to handle both port and starboard. They chattered back and forth, plainly used to working with each other.

Sostratos soon got bored. He wasn't used to being a passenger; to him, passengers were as useless as cargo. But, since he and his men know not a word of Egyptian, they couldn't be of much use.

The canal swung south, then entered the lake. Little fishing boats scooted here and there, moving much faster than the barge. Pasos steered past low-lying islands. "Do those ever get flooded?" Sostratos asked.

The skipper nodded. As Sostratos had in the Sacred Land, he found himself getting used to the gesture. "Can happen," Pasos said. "High flood in Nile, plenty more water come down than most times. Lake fill full, islands go under." He made a face. "Big mess."

"I imagine it would be," Sostratos said. Some of the islands had houses on them. "What's it like farther up the river when the flood is high?"

"Bad," Pasos answered. "Big bad. Villages wash away. People drown. Animals, too. Have to dig out canals again when water go down. Big bad." The other steersman, who seemed to understand a bit of Greek but not speak it, said something in his own language. After nodding again, Pasos translated: "Flood bad, but drought worser. No water for fields, crops fail and people starve."

Hellenes thought of Egypt as a land of plenty. Ptolemaios certainly ruled Egypt as if it were a land of plenty. To the Egyptians, though, the land showed both kind and harsh faces. With enough water, it comfortably fed its swarms of people. With too much or too little ….

One of the branches of the Nile flowed into Lake Mareotis. Before they reached it, the sun began to set. At Pasos' order, the sailors dropped several anchors—heavy stones on ropes—into the shallow water. Egyptians and Hellenes ate together. Flat cakes of barley bread and a mush made from smashed beans were unexciting fare, but they filled the belly. Instead of wine, the Egyptians drank beer. Sostratos gamely downed a cup, but found it sour and unappetizing. "Wine is better," he told Pasos.

"Oh, yes," the skipper agreed. "Wine is better. Wine cost more, too. Can drink beer without—" He mimed an urgent squat.

"I understand." Sostratos dipped his head. Drink plain water anywhere and you asked for a flux of the bowels.

As the light faded, mosquitoes came out in buzzing clouds. Sostratos slapped whenever he felt one land. So did the other men on the barge. "We'll all look like raw meat tomorrow," a rower named Thersandros said mournfully. "The dogs will chew us up."

"They have cats here, too," Sostratos said. He'd seen some wandering the streets of Alexandria. He didn't know if they were wild or tame or somewhere in between. He wasn't sure the cats knew, either.

"I couldn't tell you what those furry things are good for," Thersandros said.

Pasos overheard him and came up to the Hellenes. "You smart, you no say such things here," he told the rowers. "Cats, they is gods in some parts Egypt. Someone understand you talk bad about them, you maybe get beat up, maybe get killed. Same with crocodiles. Same with lots other animals. You no want trouble, you watch mouth."

Thersandros didn't watch his mouth. He opened it, no doubt to tell the barge skipper he didn't care a khalkos for what a bunch of barbarians thought. Before he could, Sostratos contrived to kick him in the ankle and quickly spoke up himself: "Thank you, O Pasos. We will try to respect your customs here, the way we would expect foreigners"—he carefully didn't say *barbarians*—"to respect ours in Hellas."

The Egyptian weighed that, then nodded. "You speak good, Hellene." He went back to his own folk.

By the mutinous look on Thersandros' face, he didn't think Sostratos spoke well. In a low voice, he said, "Hellenes rule Egypt now. We tell these cat-worshiping savages what to do."

"Ptolemaios collects taxes from Egypt. He collects grain and papyrus and anything else he needs. He does that because he's got an army behind him," Sostratos answered, as patiently as he could. "The Persians did it before him, and the Egyptians themselves before that. But if you go into a tavern and start laughing at cats or crocodiles or monkeys or whatever they worship, do you think the Egyptians won't knock you over the head or stick a knife in your back?"

"And then the Hellenes will—" Thersandros began.

Sostratos cut him off with a sharp chopping motion. "The Hellenes will ask around. The Egyptians will say, 'We don't know what happened to him. He must have had an accident.' And they'll be happy, and you'll be dead. It's their country. There are a lot more of them than there are of us."

Had they been of the same status, Thersandros would have kept arguing. Sostratos saw it on his face. As things were, he subsided, if with ill grace. Maybe he would remember, maybe not.

As the sky darkened, stars came out one by one. Like any seafarer, Sostratos looked on them as old familiar friends. The two brightest stars in the Little Bear described small circles around the north celestial pole. They both lay noticeably lower in the sky here than they did back home.

The Egyptians curled up and went to sleep—all but one, who kept an eye on the barge's surroundings, and on the Hellenes. In a low voice, Sostratos said, "We'll do what they do. One man will stay awake all the time. I'll take first watch tonight. We'll trade off later in the voyage. Go to sleep now, men, and I'll rouse one of you when the time comes."

As the rowers began to snore, he tried to remember everything Herodotos had written about Egypt and the Egyptians. Plainly, the Father of History had seen this land himself, and talked as best he could with men who knew its past. Alexandria hadn't been here when he lived, of course, nor had the Macedonians. Egypt lay in

Persian hands then. But most of what he'd set down still seemed pretty accurate.

After a while, the Egyptian watchman noticed Sostratos was also awake. He waved. He might have waved several times before Sostratos noticed him. Sostratos waved back when he did. Good manners satisfied, the two men who didn't speak each other's languages went back to being alone together.

When Sostratos judged the time right, he shook Thersandros by the shoulder. He moved back quickly—Thersandros awoke with a knife in his hand. "Oh. It's you," the rower said, and the knife disappeared. Better to have a ready-for-aught along than not. Sostratos hoped so, anyhow.

He lay down and closed his eyes. Next thing he knew, the sun was prying them open. When he had to sleep aboard the akatos, he didn't usually do so well. Then again, Lake Mareotis was far calmer than the Inner Sea.

His men were awake, some of them breakfasting on more barley bread and beans. The Egyptians were eating, too. The Hellenes helped them haul up the anchor stones. Nothing complicated about that, as there was with the stays and rigging. Gestures sufficed to show what wanted doing.

At Pasos' order, the Egyptians spread the big square sail and got moving. Before long, they left the lake and entered one of the many Nile branches that formed the Delta. Little farming villages were everywhere, sometimes screened from easy view by reeds, sometimes not. The air was hot and wet. The more villages Sostratos saw, the more he realized how packed with people Egypt was. Hellas seemed a desert by comparison.

"O Pasos!" Sostratos called after a while. "What are those odd reeds with the tufts on top?" He pointed.

"Don't you know?" Pasos looked bemused. When Sostratos tossed his head, the skipper went on, "Is papyrus plant. Is what we get sail from, and for writing on."

"By the dog!" Sostratos exclaimed. The whole phrase was *By the dog of Egypt!*, but he swallowed the end of it, not wanting to chance offending Pasos. "When I think of papyrus, I think of the sheets we write on. I've seen boats made from the plants, but I don't think about those so much." He stared at them with fresh interest. They still looked like odd, tufted reeds.

The Nile's current fought the breeze filling the papyrus sail; the barge slowed from a lazy walk to a crawl. But it did keep making headway against the river. As the marshy land was full of people and villages, the Nile was just as full of boats and ships and rafts. Some were no more than skins stretched over a framework of sticks. Some were papyrus boats, like the ones the *Aphrodite* had met on the Inner Sea nearing Alexandria. Others, bigger, hauled this and that up and down the river. Without the Nile, Egypt would have ceased to exist. Sostratos had known that before: known it in his head. Now, seeing it, he felt it in his belly, too.

And Alexandria was the place where everything bound for the wider world went out, the place where everything Egypt got from the wider world came in. Alexander had known what he was doing when he founded the first of the many cities he'd named for himself. Ptolemaios, ruling there, could hardly help from becoming the richest man in the world … if he could keep it.

A sentry in the naval harbor scowled at Menedemos. "Who the daimon are you?" he growled in Macedonian-flavored Greek. "You've been skulking around here the past few days." He hefted a spear.

"I'm Menedemos son of Philodemos, a trader from Rhodes." Menedemos didn't think he'd been skulking. He'd been watching quite openly as Ptolemaios' men began to fit out their fleet for the counterattack on Cyprus. Contradicting an armed man seemed less a game and more a risk than it would have a few years earlier, though.

"That's what you say," the sentry answered. "How do I know you aren't spying for the gods-hated Cyclops and his pup?"

Menedemos could have asked how he was supposed to get word to Antigonos and Demetrios across the thousands of stadia of the Inner Sea. Instead, he pulled a sheet of papyrus from a pouch on his belt. "This is a letter from the Ptolemaios himself, giving me leave to come here."

He started to present it to the sentry, but the fellow waved it away. "You wait right here. Right here, you hear? I got to find me an officer.

You aren't here when I come back, I'll stick you if I ever see you again. You got that?"

"I'll wait." Menedemos was talking to the sentry's back. He chuckled to himself. In Rhodes, at least one man in three could read and write, and you didn't need to be part of the upper crust to know how. He'd seen things were different elsewhere in the Hellenic world. They certainly were here. The sentry seemed offended Menedemos should expect him to have his letters.

After a little while, the Macedonian came back. An officer with a red cape to show his rank strode behind him. "Let's see this letter," he said brusquely. He had a Macedonian accent, too, but one with an Attic overlay that made Menedemos think of Sostratos. Sure enough, anyone who talked like that would be able to read.

"Here you are." Menedemos gave him the square of papyrus. He held it out at arm's length; he was old enough for his sight to have started lengthening. But he could make sense of it—his lips moved as he sounded out the words.

When he finished, he gave the letter back to Menedemos. "He is who he says he is," he told the sentry. That was what Menedemos thought he said, anyhow. When he spoke to a countryman, he sounded much less like an Athenian and much more like a Macedonian.

"So he can go wherever he wants and see whatever he pleases?" The sentry sounded scandalized.

But the officer dipped his head. Macedonians might be half barbarous, but they weren't barbarous enough to nod. "That's right. The Rhodians aren't friends with old One-eye. They like us better—we make them money."

That mixed truth and scorn in almost equal measure. Menedemos wasn't inclined to complain. Neither was the sentry, who said, "Sorry I bothered you, O best one."

"It's all right. If you aren't sure what you need to do, you should always ask someone." The officer gave Menedemos the ghost of a wave. "Hail," he said, and walked off.

"Go on. You can do what you want," the sentry said. "I'm just glad Philippos there didn't break something over my head."

Whenever you had to get someone who could give you orders to do something, you ran the risk that he might take it out on you for interrupting whatever he was already up to. Menedemos faced that problem, among others, with his father.

He ambled along as if he had not a care in the world, seeing what he could see. He didn't seen any of Ptolemaios' war galleys, the fours and fives and even gibber ships that were all the rage with Alexander's jumped-up generals. He could see the sheds that housed them and kept them dry till they had to put to sea. Most of those were longer and quite a bit wider than the ones that sheltered Rhodes' triremes. He reminded himself to ask Ptolemaios to get the *Aphrodite* into a shed. Then he counted the sheds, but he didn't check to see how many actually had vessels inside them. Even with Ptolemaios' letter, that would have looked too much like spying.

No one put freighters in shipsheds. Freighters would always be slow. If they were a little slower with their planking waterlogged, so what? Menedemos took off his hat to scratch his head when he didn't see many tied up at the quays. Then he spied men carrying sacks and crates and jars into a shipshed. That made him pull his hat brim down lower over his eyes so he could pretend he didn't care what was going on there.

Ptolemaios would need supplies for his fleet and for his soldiers. Grain, beans, oil, wine …. Armies fed off the countryside as much as they could, but they needed some rations to supplement what they stole. If all those things didn't go aboard the usual freighters, where would they go? On galleys that could keep up with the rest of the fleet? If you had the rowers to power them, why not? It would make you fast, for sure.

He didn't see any meat animals or horses. That told him the fleet wouldn't sail right away. Cows and sheep and horses for the cavalry wouldn't board ship till the last minute. They'd be easier to care for while still on land.

Like the staples that fed warriors, weapons didn't need much care. Some workers carried sheaves of arrows for the archers and the larger, fatter bolts some catapults flung. Others had lumpy leather sacks: bigger catapults threw round stones about the size of a head at the works that protected poleis. If Demetrios had so quickly moved down from Karpaseia, where he'd landed, and besieged Salamis, he would have such artillery himself, and Ptolemaios had better not be behindhand.

Spears, helmets, shields, swords—an army also needed more than the ones the soldiers carried or wore. Some would get lost, some would get smashed, some would get thrown away when a man ran for his life. Centuries before, Arkhilokhos had written a lyric poem about that, telling how the Thracian who had his shield was welcome to it, and he'd get another, better, one when he found the chance.

Throwing away your armor to flee the faster was still a serious business. Back then, it had been a mark of complete cowardice and disgrace, a slave's brand on a reputation. It had till the poet laughed at it, anyhow. Arkhilokhos helped change the way the Greek-speaking world looked at such things.

A man with a stack of round shields for hoplites in his arms walked through a door in the back of a shipshed. Those shields, like everything else going into the ships, would get stacked somewhere aboard a four or a five that wasn't along to fight. Another man with shields followed the first, and another, and another yet. Soldiers had something to say about how the world looked at things, too.

VII

"HERE WE IS." PASOS' GREEK, THOUGH UNDERSTANDABLE, was far from perfect. The barge skipper pointed south. "We just about out from what Greeks call Delta. Last two big branches come together soon. After that, just ... Nile ... for ... long, long way." He threw his arms wide, as if to say that explaining *how* long the Nile was exceeded his powers.

"Memphis lies not far from the joining? And the Pyramids? And the Sphinx?" Sostratos thought he understood that, but wanted to reassure himself. Egypt wasn't just another land. Egypt was another world.

But, to his relief, Pasos nodded. "That right. You no worry—we gets there. Maybe not fast, but we do."

"I could swim faster than this tub crawls," Thersandros muttered. "It makes one of our freighters look like a pentekonter."

"It isn't the stadion sprint at the Olympic Games," Sostratos answered. "As long as we get there, just when doesn't matter much." There was more room on the barge than there had been with the *Aphrodite* crossing the Inner Sea, but he and the rowers had less to do. He was as bored as Thersandros, even if he tried not to let on.

Pasos mostly ignored the Hellenes when they talked among themselves. Maybe that was his notion of politeness. Or maybe his Greek wasn't up to following conversations not aimed at him.

A town called Kerkasoros lay at the place where the Nile went from two streams to one. Sôstratos didn't realize right away that that had happened, for a low-lying island in the middle of the river fooled him into thinking it was still divided. Once the barge fought past the island, though, he understood what had happened.

He whistled softly under his breath. He'd seen rivers before, of course. But the Nile might have been the mother of all rivers. How many stadia wide was that mighty, muddy stream?

And he saw a change in the landscape. In the Delta, everything had been lush and green and growing. Even mud bricks sometimes had weeds sprouting from them. Everything alongside the Nile's single channel was also green and lush … as far as the river's lifegiving water could be made to flow, and not a digit farther. Beyond that, it abruptly went a sun-blasted yellow-brown.

The Egyptians called everything west of the Nile Libya, everything east of it Arabia. Except for where they lay, Sostratos couldn't see any difference between the two sides. Desert and desolation were desert and desolation. Hellenes built poleis on the Libyan coast, a long way west of Alexandria. They sold silphium from them, a spice obtainable nowhere else in the world.

One of these days, he thought, *we ought to take the* Aphrodite *there and load up with as much as we can carry. We'd make a fortune.* That would have to wait till something more like peace came back to Rhodes, and perhaps to the whole of the Inner Sea, to the whole of the vastly extended Hellenic world, as well.

As they had on the Nile's branches in the Delta, fishing boats also bobbed in the single channel. Most ships pushed south by the wind stayed on the right hand of the river; most of those letting the current take them north used the other half. That improved traffic without perfecting it. Everyone still had to dodge the little fishing boats, which often didn't move at all. And crewmen on faster vessels shouted unpleasantries at slower ones while swinging wide to pass them.

Because it was so big and slow, the barge got passed a lot. And a lot of abuse rained down on Pasos and his Egyptians. After a while, the skipper came over to Sostratos and said, "Next time boat go by, maybe you and other Hellenes go to side with spears and show selves."

Sostratos grinned at him. "I think we can do that." He relayed the word to the rowers. They grinned, too, and dipped their heads.

Half an hour or so later, they got their chance. A river galley not much smaller than the *Aphrodite* glided past, using oars as well as sails to get more speed. Sostratos couldn't understand what the crew shouted at the bargemen, but he recognized the tone. He and his comrades took their places by the rail, spears shown in fine martial array.

Then Pasos and his men started yelling back. It was in Egyptian, of course, so Sostratos followed not a word of it. But, by the way the bargemen pointed at him and his fellow Hellenes, he guessed they were telling the galley's crew something like *You'd better not mess with us! We've got the new overlords of the Two Lands on our side!*

And the men in the river galley had to take it. They put on a burst of speed to get out of earshot of the barge as quickly as they could, but they didn't dare answer back. Egypt had been a conquered province for most of the past two centuries. Whatever pride the people here had had in long-gone days was as dead now as one of their mummified corpses.

Sostratos wondered what would have happened if Dareios or Xerxes had led the Persians to victory over Hellas. Would the freedom-loving, free-speaking folk he knew have turned servile like this under foreign domination? He didn't know—how could you *know* anything about something that didn't happen? But he didn't like the guesses he made.

Pasos' smile stretched from ear to ear as he clapped Sostratos on the back. "Ha! We show them wide-arsed sons of hippopotamoi a thing or three!" He had a decent—or rather, an indecent—grasp of Greek obscenity, but what he did to the irregular verb *to show* was a caution.

"Glad to help." Sostratos even mostly meant it. The rowers were laughing and smiling, too. They understood Pasos' joke. They'd mocked merchantmen as they glided past them on the Inner Sea. Most of the time, the sailors who manned them had to take the abuse. Today, Pasos had turned the tables on his tormentors.

The Egyptian said, "Pretty quick we come to Pyramids. Just before Memphis, you know. You want I should point for you?" He jabbed an index finger toward the Nile's western, or Libyan, bank.

"Please!" Sostratos knew he sounded eager. Nothing in Egypt could be more famous or more ancient than the Pyramids. Hellenes with all the silver and time they needed came here just to see them. Herodotos had done it. *Now I will, too*, Sostratos thought.

"I do, then," Pasos said. He saw the Pyramids every time he went up and down the Nile. They were just part of the landscape to him. He took them as much for granted as Sostratos did fried squid. Sostratos didn't know whether to pity or envy him.

For the first time in some little while, Sostratos noticed how very slowly the barge made headway against the titanic flow of the river on which it floated. An Egyptian peasant dipping water out of the Nile with a pot mounted on a pivoted pole might have been nailed in place. After a while, though, the barge did put him behind it. Sostratos laughed at himself. Having a goal just ahead made him notice the journey once more.

The sun had passed the zenith—this far south, almost literally—and was sliding down the western half of the sky when Pasos nudged him, pointed southwest, and said, "You look hard, you see them now."

Shading his eyes with his hand and wishing again he'd bought a hat like Menedemos', Sostratos did look hard. Sure enough, three pointed bumps sticking up from the desert could only be …. Looking at the desert and the fertile land between the Pyramids and him, Sostratos whistled softly. "By the gods, they're huge!" he murmured. Then he laughed again. How many travelers before him would have said the same thing?

"We keep going, they look more bigger," Pasos said.

"I'm sure they will. Memphis lies beyond them, is that right?"

"*Malista.*" Pasos used a Greek word and a barbarous nod.

"How far beyond?"

The Egyptian said something in his own language: a distance, presumably. Sostratos spread his hands to show he didn't know what that distance was. Pasos thought for a moment, then offered, "Two parasangs. Little less, maybe."

"Ah." Sostratos dipped his head. The parasang was a Persian measure. It meant how far someone could travel in an hour. It stretched or shrank depending on territory, but was usually about thirty stadia. So the Pyramids lay only a couple of hours' journey outside Memphis. "I'll have to visit them while I'm here."

"You take care. Take water or beer or wine with you," Pasos said. "You Hellenes, you not know how to live here. Sun bake you dead, you no watch out."

"Hellas isn't an oven," Sostratos said with dignity. Yes, Rhodes got hot weather as summer wore along, but not the kind of relentless heat Egypt saw. He tried to imagine how Pasos would react to snow. He'd seen it only two or three times himself, but he knew what it was. When he did his best to explain it to the Egyptian, he ran headlong into a wall of blank incomprehension.

"Water is ... water," Pasos said. "Not turn to flakes like gods got—" He brushed at his hair; Sostratos realized he meant *dandruff*. "You Hellenes, you tell funny stories. Or you tell lies, laugh when people believe."

Hellenes had that reputation among many different kinds of barbarians. Sostratos briefly wondered whether that reflected on them or on his own folk. Only briefly—he needed to answer, and he did: "By the gods, O best one, I'm telling the truth here. In northern lands, snow is real. Water can freeze there, too, the way liquid copper does when it cools. Frozen water—*ice*, it's called—is very cold. It's slippery to walk on. Sometimes, you can see through it. When the weather gets warmer, it turns back into ordinary water again. It *melts*, we say."

Pasos laughed at him. The Egyptian had never seen anything like that, so he didn't believe it could possibly be real. None of Sostratos' protests or oaths would persuade him. Neither did the way the rowers agreed with Sostratos. "You all Hellenes," Pasos insisted. "Of course you all say same thing."

After a while, Sostratos gave up. "Think whatever you want to think," he growled, and turned away. It was either quit or pitch Pasos into the Nile. That would have meant an all-out brawl between Hellenes and Egyptians, and the barge crew outnumbered his men. He wasn't even sure he *could* pitch the barge captain into the river. Pasos might be short, but he had a solid frame and didn't seem like someone who shrank from trouble.

Slowly, slowly, the barge crawled past the Pyramids and the ramp or causeway that led up to them from the Nile. The closer the look Sostratos got, the more tremendous they seemed. He couldn't see all of the famous Sphinx nearby, only the upper part. What he could see made him want to see more.

The sun was just about to set when they reached the riverside wharves at Memphis. The city was bigger than Sostratos had expected: not so big as Alexandria, but bigger than any polis in Hellas save possibly Athens. Temples of antiquity unimaginable stood not far from the Nile.

At Egyptian Thebes, farther south yet, the almost-historian Hekataios had told the priests he was sixteen generations removed from a god. They'd laughed at him and shown him the statues of 341 generations of high priest, each of purely human origin. Next to the Egyptians, what were Hellenes but a pack of noisy children?

The sun went down. Aphrodite's wandering star blazed in the western sky. Pasos said, "We unload with day tomorrow. You all right your cargo stay aboard this night?"

"I think so. That may even work out better for us." Sostratos did his best not to show how relieved he was. He didn't want to take the olive oil off the barge till he knew where he could store it.

None of the rowers complained. "Don't mind a good night's sleep before I go back to work," Thersandros said.

"Been sleeping aboard so much this trip, I may buy me a little fishing boat and live on her when we get back to Rhodes," Leskhaios added.

They had beer and cheap wine on the barge. They hadn't been aboard it so long, they felt an urgent need to go whoring. It was less comfortable than a bed ashore, but not much less. And they were used to living rough anyhow. If they hadn't been, they never would have signed on with the *Aphrodite*.

Sostratos had an easier life ashore than the other Hellenes did. Money shaded you from misfortune the way a roofed colonnade shaded you from the sun. As long as you had some silver and you kept your health, life looked good.

He curled up on the planking like an Egyptian cat, closed his eyes, and soon fell asleep. Even a straw pallet would have been softer, but he didn't worry about it. He had more room to toss and turn here than he did in the cramped confines of the akatos.

He was awakened in the night to do his turn as watchman. When it ended, he pissed into the Nile and slept again. Next thing he knew, twilight turned the eastern sky a red that soon brightened to gold. Some of the bargemen were already awake. One gave him a chunk of barley bread and a mug of beer. They had no words in common, but Sostratos let the fellow know he was glad to have breakfast.

When Pasos got up soon after, Sostratos asked him, "What god does that temple near the river serve?"

"Osiris," the barge skipper answered.

"Ah." Sostratos dipped his head. It wasn't just a name to him. He remembered from Herodotos that Osiris was for the Egyptians what Zeus was for Hellenes: the chief god, the most powerful one. Were they two names for the same deity, or were two different gods doing the same job in different parts of the world? He had no idea how to answer that. He also wondered whether the question meant enough to matter.

What did matter was getting the amphorai of oil out of the barge and onto the riverbank. Sostratos joined the rowers in taking them out of the barge. Menedemos probably would have let them do the work, and from him they probably would have accepted that. Sostratos had less of the air of the *kalos kagathos* about him; he couldn't play the nobleman the way his cousin did.

Egyptians and Hellenes gathered to watch the show. Nothing gave men so much pleasure as watching other men work. Sostratos took a couple of oboloi from his belt pouch. He pointed at a skinny little Hellene who looked like a tout. "Do you know the way to Psosneus' warehouse?" He'd got the name from Pasos.

"*Malista*, my master!" the man said.

"An obolos for you now, and another when you've taken me to him," Sostratos said.

"Such generosity," the Hellene said sourly. "Slow with your silver, aren't ye?" By his accent, he sprang from Thessaly or somewhere else in the north.

96

"I can always give the job to someone else," Sostratos said. Sure enough, two other Hellenes and an Egyptian who followed Greek were waving their hands.

"I'll take it," the skinny man said. "Gi' me the one, and then follow."

Follow Sostratos did. The warehouse lay only a couple of streets from the river, and three blocks north of the barge. Psosneus stood outside: a brown, bulky man chewing on roasted squash seeds. Husks under his feet said he'd already eaten quite a few. He spoke fair Greek. Sostratos used Pasos' name to make sure the skipper got whatever rakeoff he could from the warehouse owner. He paid the tout, who left.

"He good fellow. He send you, I give special price," Psosneus said.

"Special high or special low?" Sostratos asked, his voice dry. Psosneus laughed, for all the world as if he were joking. They haggled a little, then settled. Psosneus recommended an innkeeper, so he'd get himself a rakeoff, too.

Sostratos hoped to hire carts when he went back to the docks, but none was in sight. He and the rest of the Hellenes had to move the olive oil the hard way. Sostratos cursed Damonax as he lugged each jar. One way or another, he'd pay his brother-in-law back. So he vowed, swearing by his aching back.

"Oh, my dear fellow, I say, but you have some fine vintages there!" a wine merchant named Exakestos told Menedemos in an Attic accent so strong, the Rhodian guessed he was putting it on. "I'd dearly love to get some for the shop. Dearly! What are you asking?"

Menedemos told him. He flinched. "Sorry," the Rhodian trader said. "I have to turn a profit, too, you know."

"Yes, yes." The Hellene gnawed at his thumbnail. "Suppose I offer you a trade instead of sacks of tetradrakhms?"

"What kind of a trade?" Menedemos asked. If he sounded suspicious, that was only because he was.

"Stay right there. Don't move a muscle. Pretend the sight of Medusa's head has turned you stone." Exakestos disappeared into a back room behind the counter. Menedemos stood where he was, not petrified but not walking out, either.

Before too too very long, the wine merchant came forth again. He held both fists closed in front of him, like a conjuror about to make a drakhma appear from nowhere. Menedemos smiled at the drama. "All right, my friend, you've interested me. What have you got there?" he asked.

Exakestos opened his hands. One held some whitish globules, the other chunks of hard, resinous-looking stuff. "Go ahead and sniff," he answered. "Then you tell me. Or I'll tell you if you've not run across it before."

"If they're what I think they are …." Menedemos leaned forward across the counter. Exakestos brought his hands forward. Sniff Menedemos did, first the globules, then the resin. "Frankincense and myrrh," he said. "They're worth a good bit—no doubt about that. But how much do you have, and how much will you give me for a jar of Ariousian?"

"I have plenty, my dear. For one thing, I use them in the trade— myrrh especially helps keep wine from going to vinegar. And for another, Alexandria is practically swimming in them these days. The Arabs bring them up the coast…. You do know where Fortunate Arabia lies?"

"I've heard of it," Menedemos said cautiously. "South and east of here, isn't it?"

"Very good!" Exakestos beamed at him. "There's another sea, a narrow one, that splits Egypt from Fortunate Arabia. The Red Sea, they call it, though I don't think it really is red. Anyhow, the Arabs who bring the incenses up their coasts talk about the winged snakes that protect the myrrh and all, and how they have to drive them away to get any."

"Sounds like a story to keep the price high," Menedemos remarked.

"It could be, but when they have the stuff and you don't, what are you going to do?" Exakestos said. "They bring it up the coast till the coast stops, if you know what I mean. That's not *very* far from the Inner Sea. If someone could dig a canal …." He shrugged. "Some goes into Syria from there, and some comes here. Since the Alexander built Alexandria, more comes here."

"I can see how that would happen, yes," Menedemos said. Before Alexandria's creation, the coast of the Delta had been a sleepy backwater, with villages and small towns that lived off fishing and smuggling. Now the Delta had the greatest port on the Inner Sea. The Rhodian scratched his chin. Whiskers rasped under his fingers; he needed a shave. "So how much myrrh have you got, and how much frankincense? How much do you aim to give me for each amphora of Ariousian?"

"The incenses usually sell here for their weight in gold," Exakestos said.

"That incenses me!" Menedemos barely managed to turn his alarm into a joke. Silver was the usual monetary metal through the Greek world; gold staters were rare, and Persian darics seldom seen. But Egypt had been in Persian hands till a generation before. Thinking in terms of gold might remain common here.

"Let's do it like this, old chap," Exakestos said. "We'll work out the price of a jar in drakhmai. Then we'll turn that into staters or darics."

"Twenty drakhmai to the goldpiece?" Menedemos wanted to pin that down before he went any further. The usual rate of exchange between silver and gold was ten to one. Both the Greek stater and the daric weighed twice as much as the drakhma.

"Yes, twenty." Exakestos dipped his head. "There's been talk that the Ptolemaios will coin lighter drakhmai for the lands he rules, but it hasn't happened yet, and gods willing it won't."

"Why would he do that?" Menedemos answered his own question before the wine merchant could: "So he can make money changing money—why else? The Ptolemaios is a marvelous man, but he does like his silver."

"I won't try to tell you you're wrong," Exakestos answered. "It will set Egypt apart from other lands, too. Ptolemaios cares more about hanging on here than grabbing all of Alexander's empire like Antigonos or Seleukos."

That thought had crossed Menedemos' mind, too. It wasn't his worry, though, as it was the wineseller's. He said, "Remember, we're not just talking about Khian here. We're talking about Ariousian, the best wine Dionysos knows."

"There are those who would say wine from Thasos is just as good, or maybe even better. Don't know but what I lean that way myself," Exakestos said.

Menedemos bared his teeth at him in a predatory grin. "Of course you do. That lets you talk down the price of my wine. I'd sell you Thasian, but I've already disposed of most of what I brought."

"I'm not going to ask you what you got for it and say I'll pay the same for your Ariousian," Exakestos said. "That would give you an excuse to invent a price and ruin me."

"I'd never do such a thing!" Menedemos assumed a look of injured innocence.

"My *prokton*!" Just for a moment, Exakestos' actor's mask of Attic elegance slipped, Then he pulled it at least partly back in place. "I bloody well would, in your sandals."

"Not wearing sandals." Like other sailors, Menedemos went barefoot on land as well as at sea. In Alexandria's warm climate, doing without shoes just meant watching where you stepped. But he did it in winter at home in Rhodes, too. He also seldom threw a himation over his chlamys. Cloaks, as far as he was concerned, were for Thracians and Skythians, who needed them to keep from turning into blocks of ice during barbarous northern winters. That was one more nautical prejudice brought to land.

"You know what I mean, my dear fellow." Now the wine merchant might have just stepped out of the Parthenon after sacrificing. "Tell me what you *do* want for a jar of your fancy vintage, and we'll see how loudly I scream."

"Half a mina," Menedemos said easily. That was more than three times the price of an amphora of ordinary Khian, and something like ten times the price of the common stuff a cobbler or a potter might buy in a tavern.

Sure enough, Exakestos threw back his head and howled like a wolf. He did it so well, a little stray dog trotting down the street yipped in alarm. Then he dug a finger into his ear. "I'm sorry, but I seem to be going deaf," he said. "I imagined I heard you telling me you wanted fifty drakhmai for the jar. I must be getting old."

"I'll go up if you like." Menedemos sounded as helpful as he could.

That made the wineseller cough like a man choking on an olive pit. He waved Menedemos away when the Rhodian started around the counter to pound him on the back. "I'm lucky you didn't give me an apoplexy there," he said, glowering.

"Well, tell me what you aim to pay, then," Menedemos said. "After I'm done laughing, we can get down to the real dicker."

"It *is* better stuff than regular Khian," Exakestos said, with the air of a man making a great concession. "Regular Khian would go for fourteen, maybe fifteen, drakhmai the amphora. So, because I'm a generous bloke, I'll give you twenty. A stater's weight of frankincense or myrrh for a jar."

Menedemos did laugh then, raucously. "You must want my father to kill me when I get home," he said, and then bit down hard on the inside of his lower lip. If Baukis screamed out something while she was in labor with the baby, Philodemos might have a reason much more urgent than business to want to kill him.

It wasn't funny, but Menedemos laughed at himself anyhow. He wouldn't mind so much if his father murdered him on account of a botched business deal. But if his father killed him because he had, or might have, got his stepmother pregnant ....

That wouldn't just leave him in disgrace, worse luck. It would cast a black shadow of shame over the whole family. It wasn't quite what Sophokles wrote about in *Oidipous Tyrannos*, but it came too close for comfort.

Oidipous, of course, had killed his father and married his mother without knowing who they were. Fate struck him down regardless. Baukis wasn't Menedemos' mother by blood, but she was his father's wife. And he'd sported with her knowing exactly what he was doing. If the gods still looked down from Olympos, what did they think of that?

Exakestos had said something. Menedemos realized he had no idea what it was. "I'm sorry, best one. Try that again, please," he said. "The ridiculous price you offered left me struck all in a heap."

Exakestos snorted in annoyance. "I *said*, old chap, that I don't want you slain, by your father or anyone else. So I'll go up to twenty-four drakhmai the amphora without even being asked. So what a generous fellow I am?"

"If you aren't serious about the deal, tell me now. You don't seem serious, not when you haven't come close yet to what my family paid for the wine. Why are you playing dogs and robbers with me? You know what Ariousian is, and what it's worth. Maybe I should just go to another dealer."

"You won't get the precious incenses from another wineseller."

"Yes? And so? I'll get silver from him. Then, if I still want myrrh or frankincense, I'll go to a proper dealer, not someone who sells the stuff for a hobby," Menedemos said. "Do you want to trade, or just to waste my time?"

"I do want to trade. I don't much fancy beggaring myself to do it, though," Exakestos said.

Menedemos exhaled through his nose: to anyone who knew him, a sure sign of how irked he was. "You wouldn't. You know you wouldn't, too. You *are* wasting my time."

"If you think so, old man, you know what you can do about it."

"I'll do it. Hail!" Menedemos turned on his heel and stalked out of Exakestos' shop. As he went, he loosed a shot over his shoulder: "If you come to your senses, ask after me at the Ptolemaios' palace. That's where I'm staying."

"At … the Ptolemaios' palace?" Exakestos lost some of his hauteur. "How do you rate that?" His voice wobbled a little. *How much trouble can you land me in if you push it?* he had to be wondering.

"Since we aren't trading, that's none of your business." Out into the street Menedemos went.

He wondered if Exakestos would come chasing after him, but the wine dealer didn't. He had more pride or more spine than that. Menedemos shrugged and started back to the palace. If he spotted another wineseller's place, he'd stop in and see what he could unload. If not, maybe he'd curl up and nap during the noontime heat. A lot of Hellenes and Egyptians seemed to do that.

Two cats almost clawed his feet as they ran past, one chasing the other. Were they playing, or did they mean it? He didn't know cats well enough to guess. There were a few in Rhodes, but only a few. Most were the pampered pets of rich women; the fish they ate would have made a poor man, or maybe one not so poor, a nice opson to go with his bread at supper.

Then he wondered what he could get for cats if he brought some back in the *Aphrodite*. How much would people pay? Could he start a fad? The sales talk spun itself inside his head, like a spider's web taking shape in the early morning. *Yes, they're pets. They're friendly and smart. But they're more than pets, too. They catch mice and lizards and centipedes and other vermin. Get one now, before your friends buy them for their wives.*

That might not be so bad. He might even talk his way into some unwary fellow's women's quarters to show off a cat to the lady of the house. Something enjoyable might come of that. No guarantee, of course, but when did anything ever come with a guarantee?

His father would be angry at him for playing that game again, but it would be a relatively innocuous kind of anger, as opposed to the kind of anger caused by a relative. As far as Menedemos could tell, his father was always looking for reasons to be angry at him. If Philodemos couldn't find any, he'd invent one.

At the palace, Menedemos ducked into a refectory to cadge some barley bread and dates. He chatted with the cook or slave or whatever she was who kept an eye on things. She was an Egyptian but, like Seseset, she knew enough Greek to get by. Her smile said something might be arranged if he pushed it a little.

He thought about it. Then a yawn made him decide not to. Even with a hat, sallying forth in Alexandria's hot sun took it out of you. He went back to the chamber Ptolemaios had let him and Sostratos use, lay down on his bed, and dozed off.

A knock on the door brought him out of a dream where his father was accusing him of impregnating a swan—Leda's story turned upside down and inside out. Muttering, he went to see who it was. He hadn't slept as long as he'd wanted to.

When he found Demodamas standing in the hallway, he ran a quick hand through his rumpled hair. Ptolemaios' stone-faced steward let him finish the gesture, then asked, "What did you do to yank Exakestos' tail?"

"I told him I wouldn't sell him Ariousian at a price that would make me lose money." Menedemos' blurred wits suddenly started working faster. "And I told him I was staying here at the palace. So he's checking up on me, is he?"

"You might say so," Demodamas answered.

"What business of his is it where I'm—?" Menedemos broke off. Yes, his wits still needed a bit to get going. He scowled at the sturdy Macedonian. "So he's one of the people who tell the palace things, eh?"

"Don't be foolish. Palaces have no ears," Demodamas said. Menedemos snorted; that came closer to a joke than he'd expected from the steward. After a moment, the man went on, "You said that, remember. I didn't."

"Which means it's true but you don't want to admit it," Menedemos said. Demodamas just stood there. Menedemos waited to see if he would say anything. When he didn't, the Rhodian continued. "All right, fine. Along with selling wine, he spies for the Ptolemaios. Do you want to tell me who some of your other snoops are, so I can try not to have them bothering you, too?"

The Macedonian took his sarcasm literally. "No, I don't want to tell you that," he said.

"But you have them." Menedemos didn't make that a question.

Demodamas answered as if it were: "I don't want to tell you that, either." He looked unhappy. Menedemos judged he would have lied if he'd had the faintest hope of being believed. He turned abruptly and stamped away.

Menedemos watched him roll along like Sisyphos' boulder going downhill. Other people in the hall jumped out of his way. They saw he wouldn't move aside for them. Only after Demodamas turned a corner did Menedemos go back inside and close the door.

So Ptolemaios used spies to keep an eye on people, did he? It surprised Menedemos less than he wished it would have, but it saddened him. Ptolemaios had always struck him as a decent man for a warlord. If he stooped to such things, no doubt Antigonos and Demetrios, Seleukos, and all the other Macedonian generals battling over Alexander's empire did, too.

Till that moment, Menedemos hadn't thought a great deal about just what living in a free and independent polis meant. If it meant not having men spy on you for the rulers, that was plenty to make the Rhodian all for it.

VIII

PTOLEMAIOS' NOMARCH IN MEMPHIS WAS A grizzled Macedonian officer named Alexandros. He'd lost half an ear and the last joint of his right middle finger in one or another of Alexander the Great's battles. "Talk to my cooks, if you want to," he told Sostratos. "If they say your oil's worth buying, I'll buy it. And if they don't, many good-byes to you."

He had more than his share of Macedonian bluntness, plainly. "Do you want to sample it yourself, sir?" Sostratos asked. "Taste what you're getting?"

"Nah." Alexandros tossed his head. "All I know about food is, if it's there, I eat it. Once you've made a stew of dead donkey that's starting to go off—and been glad to have it, mind—you don't worry about this stuff. Nikodromos, take the Rhodian to the kitchens."

"Yes, your Excellency." Nikodromos was Alexandros' Greek secretary. He had two; the other was an Egyptian who also spoke decent Greek. The Hellene set down a waxed tablet and rose from his stool. To Sostratos, he said, "If you'll come with me, O best one …."

Sostratos came. So did Leskhaios, who carried the amphora full of Damonax's oil. The nomarch's residence was a maze King Minos might have envied. It had housed Persian provincial governors before Alexander took Egypt, and probably native Egyptian nomarchs before them. There'd been a lot of adding and rebuilding over the centuries.

As Alexandros had a Greek secretary and an Egyptian one, so he had both Hellenes and Egyptians in the kitchens. The most senior Greek cook was a plump, graying man named Rhodoios. "Are you from the island whose name is like yours?" Sostratos asked him, taking as much of the Attic overlay as he could from his speech.

"Bugger me blind if I'm not," the cook answered. "Born and raised in Ialysos, came to Alexandria, got work with Alexandros, and I've stayed with him going on fifteen years now."

Sostratos beamed. So did Rhodoios. Their accents were almost identical. And Sostratos had another reason to like the man from his own island. As far as he was concerned, any cook who stayed skinny on what he made himself was not to be relied on.

Also …. "From Ialysos, you say? Do you recall a fellow named Damonax? He would have lived on a farm outside of town, but his family had a place in Ialysos, too. He's about my age, a bit older, so he would have still been a youth when you came to Egypt."

Rhodoios screwed up his face in thought. "I just might. Good-looking, if he's the one I think he is. Liked himself pretty well, too."

"That's him," Sostratos agreed, trying not to giggle. Rhodoios had nailed Damonax down in a couple of sentences. "As it happens, he's my brother-in-law. I'm selling his oil here."

"Isn't that something?" Rhodoios whistled softly. "So this'd be oil like the oil I grew up with, is what you're saying."

"I'd think so. It *is* good oil, or I wouldn't have brought it to Egypt in an akatos. You can get plenty of the ordinary stuff here," Sostratos said.

"True enough, but that's not the same. I can get what they call good oil, too—I'm buying with Alexandros' silver, after all," Rhodoios said. "And it is good, or good enough. But it's not what I think of when I think of good olive oil. Different aroma, different savor on the tongue, even a different color. Can I have a taste of yours?"

"That's why I brought it to you," Sostratos answered. "The amphora's sealed, so it should be as fresh as when it went in last fall."

"I can take care of that, by the gods." Rhodoios cut away the pitch securing the stopper with a paring knife. After he pulled the stopper out, he bent over the opened jar to sniff the oil. A slow smile spread across his face. "Oh, doesn't that take me back, now? Doesn't it just?"

"Taste it, too," Sostratos urged. "I want you to be sure of what you're getting."

"I'll do that, and gladly," Rhodoios said. An Egyptian cook had just taken four loaves of bread from the oven and set them on a stone counter to cool. Rhodoios tore a chunk off the end of one. The other man shouted at him in Egyptian. He came back in the same language, with enough effect to make several Egyptians laugh. To Sostratos, he remarked, "I don't let these sons of crocodiles talk about me without knowing what they're saying."

"Good for you. I learned some Aramaic when I went to Phoenicia and Palestine a couple of years ago," Sostratos said.

"You're from Rhodes, all right. They don't grow too many stupid people there." Rhodoios poured a little of Damonax's oil into a bowl: a funny little bowl that stood on short legs and hippotamus feet. Then he blew on the chunk of bread—steam still rose from it—and dipped it in the oil. He took a bite, chewed, and swallowed.

"What do you think?" As any good trader would have, Sostratos tried to sound casual. If Rhodoios didn't like it, he would have to try to unload the olive oil on other Hellenes here, and the nomarch's headquarters seemed the best bet. Or he would have to go back to Rhodes and tell his brother-in-law he couldn't sell the oil. That didn't bear thinking about.

But Rhodoios smiled beatifically. "I taste that oil and I'm seventeen years old again and just finding out about girls." With what looked like a real effort, he brought himself back from long-ago Ialysos to Memphis. "Alexandros will like it, too. He goes for that new-oil taste—almost leafy, you know?"

"He talks about not caring what he eats," Sostratos said.

"That's till he wants to eat it," the cook replied. Sostratos grinned.

The Egyptian whose loaf Thodoios had torn turned out to know some Greek, too. "Is olive oil. Is nasty olive oil," he said. "You Hellenes is nasty people for liking it."

"If your arsehole were any wider, Khamouas, you'd fall right in," Rhodoios said without rancor. He added something in Egyptian that sounded just as polite. Khamouas said something back to him. They both chuckled. Rhodoios eyed Sostratos again. "So how much have you got, and how much do you want for it?"

Sostratos told him. He waited for Rhodoios to bubble and boil like a pot of beans forgotten over the fire. He thought he had the older man's measure, and felt sure he'd make a nasty haggler.

But Alexandros' cook hardly haggled at all, though he wanted only half the oil Sostratos had brought to Memphis. Oh, he made a show of dickering, for the benefit of the other men who were watching and listening to the bargain. But when he clasped Sostratos' hand, the price was still high enough to keep Damonax not just happy but overjoyed.

"You bastard!" Rhodoios said, though he sounded no angrier than he had with Khamouas. "It's good stuff, but you're making me shell out for it. Ah, well, the nomarch won't complain, not when he gets a taste of it."

When Sostratos heard that, it was as if the sun rose in his mind. Rhodoios would have fought harder if he'd had to spend his own silver. But how rich was Alexandros? Not so rich as his illustrious overlord, no doubt, but rich enough not to worry much about what the kitchens spent. Sostratos hadn't understood the kind of wealth Egypt yielded till he began to see it with his own eyes. He wasn't sure he did even now, but he certainly had a better notion than he'd had before crossing the Inner Sea.

He promised Rhodoios that he and the rowers would deliver the oil the next day. That satisfied the cook, who promised to have the drakhmai to pay for it. Then something else occurred to Sostratos. He asked Rhodoios, "Is there any chance of my getting a guide to take me out to see the Pyramids? I got a glimpse of them from the river, but I'd kick myself for the rest of my days if I came so close without taking a closer look."

Before Rhodoios could reply, Khamouas spoke up: "My brother-in-law's cousin, him do that. Take you there, bring you back …. You gots to pay, you know."

"The world runs on silver the way a fire runs on wood," Sostratos said. The Egyptian nodded. Sostratos went on, "Will you introduce me to—what's his name?"

"Him have name of Pakebkis," Khamouas said. Sostratos repeated the name several times under his breath so it would stay in his memory. Khamouas added, "You ever ride a camel?"

"No," Sostratos said.

"You ride camel with Pakebkis," Khamouas said. "Him trader, too. Take this across desert to oasis, bring back that. Him good fellow, Pakebkis, long as you watch he."

"I'll watch him." Sostratos would have even without the warning. If you didn't watch strangers, who knew what might happen to you? Nothing good—everyone knew that.

One of the other Egyptians said something in his own language. Sostratos looked a question at Rhodoios. The other Hellene translated: "Antas says camel hump baked with turnips and dates is a good festival meal." Sostratos wasn't dickering now, so his face must have shown what he thought, for Rhodoios added, "It isn't what I would've eaten back in Ialysos, either, but he's right. It's good. All that melting fat …." He smacked his lips.

"I'll take your word for it." All Sostratos knew about camels was that they were ugly and bad-tempered, and that horses couldn't stand their smell. If Pakebkis was going to put him on top of one, he had to hope the miserable creature wouldn't try to eat him instead of the other way around.

Menedemos found himself watching his tongue much more closely than he was used to doing. He'd been a free and independent Hellene from a free and independent polis all his days, and he'd taken freedom for granted till he came to Alexandria. Even what he'd seen in Athens the year before, when Demetrios Antigonos' son took the city from Demetrios of Phaleron and Kassandros, hadn't made him rein in.

Here, though …. How many people in Alexandria were spies and informers? How much did Ptolemaios or his Myrmidons know about all the Hellenes and Egyptians and Ioudaioi who lived here or came here on business? How much did they know about all the myriads up and down the Nile?

More to the point for Menedemos was how much Ptolemaios knew about *him*, and what he thought of what he knew. Did someone in the refectory report what he ate at breakfast every morning and how much opson he had with his supper bread every evening? Did Seseset tell someone what he said while they were making love and even which posture they used?

Once you started seeing spies, you saw them everywhere and you couldn't stop seeing them, whether they were really there or not. You had to act as if they were there, as if they were listening. He'd long since seen that Alexandria wasn't any kind of polis, much less a free and independent one. It was part of the realm Ptolemaios ruled as king in all but name.

Macedonians had always had kings, of course, some good, more not. They were used to running things that way. Hellenes, though, served under Ptolemaios as eagerly as their cousins from the north. A full belly and a nice house mattered more to them than freedom and independence.

But pausing to consider before saying what he thought griped Menedemos worse than bad fish in a stew. It was different from business politeness. Of course you wouldn't tell someone you were doing business with that he had bad breath or …. *Or that you've seduced his wife*, Menedemos thought, and chuckled to himself.

That was just common sense, though. Keeping your mouth shut about what you thought of a ruler because he might string you up by the thumbs if he heard about it? That was something else again. It made Menedemos wonder if the Macedonians and Hellenes, having overthrown the Persian Empire, had been conquered by Persian notions in their turn.

He wished Sostratos weren't down in Memphis. His cousin understood how states worked, even if he didn't always understand the people standing right in front of him. He'd quote Herodotos or Thoukydides or one of those brainy fellows, and everything would at least seem to make sense for a little while.

As things were, Menedemos acted like a happy fool when he walked down Alexandria's wide, brawling streets. He still haggled sharply, but he stopped saying anything about Ptolemaios, about the way Egypt was ruled, or about the way the wars of Alexander's generals were going.

An incense dealer—sure enough, there were such men—named Hermokrates, from whom he bought some frankincense, remarked, "You're a better bargainer than I thought you'd be. By the gods, O best one, not everyone squeezes that kind of price out of me."

"Isn't that interesting?" Menedemos kept a stupid smile on his face. But he couldn't resist a barb of his own: "You're named after the god of thieves. Does it bother you when you can't steal from someone?"

"To the crows with you!" Hermokrates said with a laugh. "I know what I have and I know what it's worth. So do you, and I wouldn't have looked for that from such a plain-seeming fellow."

"How about that?" Menedemos trotted out another phrase without much real meaning. If he acted stupid all the time, could he surprise other people the way he had with Hermokrates? Finding out might prove worthwhile.

On his way back to the palace, he bought some honeyed dates and raisins from a skinny woman who sold them off a tray. He didn't bargain hard with her; a glance told him she needed whatever she could get.

"Thank you," she said. By her looks, she could have been a Hellene; her tunic and her guttural accent said she was one of the Ioudaioi. She sent Menedemos a thoughtful glance. "You want to find somewhere quiet, spend some more money?"

"I'd love to, my dear, but I have to meet a friend very soon." Menedemos lied without compunction and hurried away. It wasn't as if he'd never paid for a woman—what else was he doing with Seseset? But this one stirred sorrow in him, not lust. He got away as fast as he could.

The next morning, he inveigled the serving girl into his room. "You not want me for a while," she said as she lay down beside him. "I think maybe you find somebody you like better or you pay less."

"Nothing like that. I've just been working hard." Menedemos did his best to persuade her without using any more words. He hoped he succeeded. He thought he did. But Seseset was here for silver, not—or not just—for pleasure. She might well act without wearing a mask.

111

"You work hard, yes," she said after they finished.

"What man wouldn't, with you?" he said. She liked that, and smiled back over her shoulder at him.

He smiled, too, hoping she couldn't see he was forcing it a little. The real reason he hadn't taken her to bed so often lately was that he trusted her less than he had before. He trusted everyone in Alexandria less than he had before: everyone who hadn't come with him from Rhodes, anyhow.

Drinking wine with Diokles in a little tavern not far from the palace, he spoke in a low voice: "You want to watch what you say in this town. You never can tell who's listening."

The keleustes spat an olive pit on the dirt floor. Brine-cured olives, dried and salted sprats—the bowls on the counter held cheap snacks designed to make a drinker thirstier. Tavernkeepers in Hellas played the same game. Then Diokles glanced around to make sure no one was listening just now. Also quietly, he said, "You noticed that, too, huh, skipper?"

Menedemos set a hand on his arm. "I might have known I didn't need to tell you."

"Being careful's never wasted." Diokles' hair was gray, almost white. His skin was dark and tough as leather. No one who went to sea got old unless he was careful.

"Do you think it's worthwhile to warn the rowers, too?" Menedemos asked.

"I wouldn't bother," Diokles said, tossing his head. "They don't know enough to get in trouble running their mouths. If you could tell them not to drink themselves blind and get into tavern brawls over whores …. By the dog, you can tell them till you're black in the face, but you can't make the thickskulls listen to you."

"Pretty much the same thing I was thinking," Menedemos said with a sigh. "Most rowers don't have much sense."

"No? I was a rower. I was a rower for years." Diokles set his cup on the table and opened his hands, palms up. He hadn't pulled an oar for a long time now, but still had ridges of callus running across his palms.

"I know. That's why I said *most*." Menedemos didn't care to anger a man he liked, respected, and needed. He was also sure that, when it came to tavern brawls, Diokles could still more than hold his own.

112

To make sure it didn't come to that, he soothed the keleustes' ruffled feathers and bought him another cup of wine.

Everything was fine after that ... till Menedemos started glancing around the tavern. Who in there could overhear him? How soon would word of whatever he said get back to Ptolemaios' henchmen, and perhaps to the lord of Egypt himself?

How soon before you start thinking everyone is spying on you, whether anyone is or not? Menedemos wondered. To keep himself from stewing over that, he got more wine for himself—and a fresh cup for Diokles, of course.

Sostratos and the rowers made their way toward the edge of Memphis as twilight brightened into day. By the way Khamouas led them, he was used to finding his way around in the middle of the night. "Leaving early better," he said. "Not too hot yet."

"Not too," Sostratos more or less agreed, watching the paling sky swallow another star. Then he stepped in something nasty, and realized he would do better to keep his eyes on the ground. He scuffed his foot in the dirt to clean it as best he could.

"Ha!" Khamouas said when the sun's red disc climbed up over the horizon. "Ra rises."

"We call the sun Helios," Sostratos said. "Usually, though, we name the sun god Apollo." He took the gods less seriously than men had even a couple of generations earlier, but the sun was impossible to ignore.

Several Egyptians waited on the northern outskirts of town along with the camels that would take them and the Hellenes to the Pyramids. Khamouas waved when he saw them. One of the Egyptians, a tall, lanky fellow, waved back. "Is Pakebkis," Khamouas said. "You can with he talk. Him speak Greek like me."

His Greek might not be perfect, but it was infinitely better than Sostratos' Egyptian, which didn't exist. "Thanks," Sostratos said, and gave the cook a thick silver didrakhm.

Khamouas spoke in crackling Egyptian to his brother-in-law's cousin. Pakebkis answered in the same language. "He say we do like we say before," Khamouas translated. "Three drakhmai a man, ten-and-eight all told."

"Yes." Sostratos dipped his head. Then he made himself nod, as he had sometimes in Palestine to make sure the locals understood. "I will give you half now, half when you've brought us back here."

"Is good," Pakebkis said—sure enough, his Greek was no more villainous than that of his kinsman by marriage. He held out his right hand, palm up. Sostratos paid him nine drakhmai. Pakebkis examined them, then stowed them in a belt pouch. "Is good," he said again. "You, me, friends of you, friends of me, we go together. All friends."

"All friends," Sostratos echoed, hoping it was true. The rowers and Egyptians eyed each other like two packs of dogs meeting in the street. All of them carried a spear or a sword or a club or a sturdy knife. One Hellene might vanish without a trace in a foreign land. Half a dozen Hellenes might still vanish, but not without putting up a fight.

One of the camels turned its large, ugly head toward Sostratos. Its jaw worked—not up and down, but from side to side. Then, with purpose (with malice, he would have sworn), it spat at him. He jerked aside just in time. The glob of saliva splashed the ground, not his face. The Egyptians thought it was hilarious. Sostratos found himself less amused.

"How do we get on those big, funny-looking critters?" asked a rower named Trityllos. "I didn't reckon they'd be so tall. They make horses look like donkeys beside 'em."

Pakebkis walked over to the camel that had spit. It tried to bite him. He smacked it on the nose. It let out a groan full of horrible indignation. The formalities complete, he tapped it on the back of a foreleg. It squatted on the sand. "You see?" Pakebkis said.

The saddle looked more like a padded bench made to fit on the camel's hump and strapped around its belly than anything else Sostratos could think of. Grinning, Pakebkis waved him forward. Gulping, he went. The rowers were grinning, too, at seeing him try it before they had to. If they laughed at him for showing fear, he'd never be able to lead them again. *Be what you wish to seem*, he thought, though philosophy didn't come easy then.

At Pakebkis' gesture, he got on the saddle. The camel sent him a yellowish stare full of ancient evil. Pakebkis tapped its foreleg again and said something in Egyptian. One piece at a time, the animal stood, jerking Sostratos this way and that as it did. He didn't drop the reins, but he came close.

He stared down from higher off the ground than he'd even been aboard a beast. "You all good?" Pakebkis asked. Sostratos started to dip his head, then managed a shaky nod. Pakebkis seemed used to people unsure of themselves on camelback. He got the other Hellenes mounted, too. A couple of the Egyptians knew what they were doing around camels. The others, plainly no more than hired toughs, gabbled and exclaimed like the rowers.

Pakebkis mounted last. Like most of the others, his camel made hideous noises at having to carry a man. He whacked it with an iron-tipped goad. It made different dreadful noises, then shut up. When he poked its sides with his heels, it started north at a surprisingly good clip. The other camels followed in a ragged line.

Sostratos had heard camels called the ships of the desert. He'd always thought that was because they could carry men and goods through wastes no other creatures could cross. Now he discovered they had a rocking, swaying motion very different from that of a donkey or a horse. The height at which he traveled magnified the effect.

He wasn't the only one who noticed. "Hope I don't get seasick!" Trityllos said. The rest of the rowers laughed. So did Pakebkis and a couple of other Egyptians who knew some Greek. Sostratos wished he thought it was funnier.

Sand lay thin over soil. They followed a trail even Sostratos could recognize. A lot of travelers over a lot of years had made their way north from Memphis to see the Pyramids. They'd scarred the land the way a mine slave's shackle came to scar his ankle.

Big vultures wheeled in the air high overhead. *You won't eat my flesh*, Sostratos thought, and then, *By the gods, I hope you won't.*

A jackal vanished into a hole: sharp-nosed like a fox, but with a different gait and bigger ears. Sostratos was the kind who classified things, partly because he was who he was and partly because he'd studied under Theophrastos the botanist in Athens. The rowers seemed more inclined to joke than classify. "Between the scavengers in the sky and the ones slinking on the sand, in two days won't be anything left of us if we keel over here," Thersandros said.

Pakebkis translated the gibe for his men who knew no Greek. They grinned and laughed. Sostratos smiled; people were people under the skin, whether Hellene or barbarian. An Egyptian looked up at the vultures, then caught the rowers' eyes and held up one finger, as if to say they'd be supper in only one day if they died here. When the Hellenes understood him, they laughed in turn.

A low rise in front of the Pyramids did a fair job of keeping Sostratos from getting as good a look at them as he would have liked. The sun shone off the white limestone that sheathed their outsides. It also beat down on the men traveling through the desert to view them.

Sweat dripped into Sostratos' beard. Jars of Egyptian beer were tied to each camel's saddle. "You gots to drink!" Pakebkis called. "You not wanting vultures eating at you, you gots to drink!" He matched action to word.

Sostratos dutifully imitated him. Used to wine, the Hellene still found beer thin, sour stuff. But he also noticed that this beer was cooler than it would have been had it come from a skin or a metal jug. He'd seen that before; as much as the greater cost of metal, it was a reason Hellenes commonly used pottery jugs for water and wine.

The rowers seemed to fancy beer even less then he did. Sostratos echoed Pakebkis' order: "Drink it like medicine if you don't want to drink it for fun," he said sternly. "The Egyptians know how to live here. Don't let yourselves cook because you hate beer."

"I'd sooner drink the muddy old Nile," Leskhaios said.

"And start shitting your guts out till you bleed from your *prokton?*" Sostratos said. "Nobody who can get anything else drinks water. It gives you a bloody flux too often. And foreign water's even worse than what we've got back home."

"Yes, Papa," the rower replied.

"To the crows with you!" Sostratos snapped. This was the thanks you got for trying to help people? Well, all too often it was.

Then the camels, sure-footed even when the going got rough, made it to the top of the little rise. The rowers stopped teasing Sostratos. Like him, they gaped at the spectacle laid out before them.

Two of the Pyramids were noticeably larger than the third, but even the smallest one dwarfed any construction Sostratos had ever seen before. The Egyptian Sphinx looked nothing like the sphinxes

116

of Greek myth and legend. It looked like a lion with a human head decked out with a headdress Sostratos had already seen on wall carvings of Egyptian pharaohs.

Off to the right, in the direction of the Nile, lay a village or small town. From Herodotos, Sostratos remembered it was called Bousiris. The ramp that ran from the river toward the Pyramids showed how the builders had got their stones where they needed them. If you had enough people and enough time, you could do almost anything.

Sostratos and the rowers weren't the only sightseers gawking at the grandiose monuments Egyptian kings had raised for themselves in ancient days. Nor was Pakebkis the only guide. Other Egyptians led curious men—and even a handful of women—mounted on camels or donkeys.

And people from Bousiris tried to sell them beer and wine and snacks and tiny terra-cotta Pyramids whitewashed to look as if they were clad in limestone and little painted figurines, also of burnt clay. Those last intrigued Sostratos. "Do you speak Greek?" he asked a man with a tray of them.

"*Malista!*" the Egyptian answered. "Talk Greek good."

"Tell me what your small statues are, then," Sostratos said.

"Them is *ousabti* figures." The Egyptian might not have much grammar, but he could make himself understood, all right. "Bury with you bunch of they. Them work in afterlife for you, so you don't got to nothing."

That tickled Sostratos' sense of whimsy enough to make him ask, "How much?"

"Four oboloi eaches," the *ousabti*-seller answered. "Maybe you buy one man, one woman, hey? Man, he do work things for you after you dead. You and woman, meantime—" He gestured lewdly.

"Cost too much." Sostratos kept things simple for the Egyptian. "I'll give you four oboloi for a man and a woman."

"You spit in my eye like camel you on!" the fellow exclaimed, clapping a hand to his forehead in badly acted despair. They haggled for a bit, and wound up splitting the difference. Sostratos gave the Egyptian a drakhma and got his *ousabti* figurines.

Mountebanks climbed all three Pyramids—no easy trick, not with their outer layers of smooth limestone. The acrobats, or whatever

117

the right name for them was, seemed to slide down once they reached the apex of a Pyramid. Sostratos got close enough to one of them to see that he had a leather patch sewn to the seat of his linen kilt, so evidently the sliding was real enough.

The Sphinx intrigued him even more than the Pyramids. No matter how enormous they were, they struck him as exercises in geometry. He imagined Pythagoras pacing along next to one, pointing with a stick and deducing theorems as he went. The Sphinx, now, the Sphinx had a touch of humanity to it.

As he came up close to it, he discovered he wasn't the only one who'd thought so down through the years. Graffiti marred its arms, some written on the stone, others scratched or carved into it. Some were in Greek, others in Aramaic or the hieratic script Egyptians used when they wrote hieroglyphics quickly.

One Greek scratching made him smile. *I, Xenopheles son of Xenon, wrote this*, read the first line. Below that, either Xenopheles or someone else had added, *So did I, Knife son of Nobody.*

Off at the edge of the desert, a couple of long-legged, long-necked birds at least as tall as a man stood watching for a little while, then ran away at least as fast as a galloping horse. Pointing at them, Sostratos asked Pakebkis, "What do you call those?"

"Them is *ostriches*," the Egyptian answered. "For you Hellenes, I hear you say *strouthos* for one."

"Do you?" Sostratos said drily. *Strouthos* was the Greek word for *sparrow*. Either Pakebkis had got it wrong, a Hellene was playing a joke on him, or someone was trying not to show how much a bird that size impressed him.

"Them hard to hunt, but good if you catch," Pakebkis said.

"Do they taste like chicken or duck?" Sostratos asked.

"No." The guide shook his head. "Red meat. Taste like cow. Maybe more better."

"Now I know something I never knew before," Sostratos said.

"Sometimes, some butchers in Memphis, they got," Pakebkis said. "Khamouas, he know where, when, I bet. He tell me the Ptolemaios like it."

Ptolemaios had hunted lions and tigers in the crumbling wreckage of the Persian Empire and in India. He'd fought against elephants

118

by the Indos River, and weren't there more elephants down in southernmost Egypt, or maybe beyond its southern border? And he'd eaten ostriches, too? What sort of marvels *hadn't* he known?

Pakebkis reached down and grabbed one of the jars of beer tied to his camel's odd saddle. He swigged from it. "Got to keep drinking. Drink, drink, drink," he said. "You no drink, Ra strike you dead." He pointed at the sun.

Thus encouraged, Sostratos drank more himself. The more he poured down, the more he sweated. He urged the rowers to drink again, too. He didn't want one of them falling off a camel from heatstroke. They chaffed him less than they had earlier in the morning, when the weather was cooler.

After a while, Pakebkis asked, "You see all things you to see want?"

"Yes, I think so. Thanks." Sostratos wished he had some way of making pictures so he wouldn't have to trust fading, unreliable memory for the rest of his life. But some things were simply too *big* to forget. "When I have grandchildren, I'll bore them silly with my story of how I came to Memphis and saw the Pyramids."

"They just there," the Egyptian said.

"They're just there if you're *here*. You are, so you can take them for granted," Sostratos said. "There's nothing like them in Hellas, believe me, or anywhere else in the world. If I crossed the sea to trade in Egypt, I wasn't going to miss them."

"The sea? Water all over everywhere till you no find land?" Pakebkis' eyes widened in wonder. "Maybe one day I go down Nile to Alexandria. I to see that want. Maybe." Everything was a marvel to someone who didn't know about it.

IX

SESESET HADN'T BEEN OUT OF MENEDEMOS' CHAMBER
in the palace for more than a few heartbeats when someone knocked
on the door. Guessing she was coming back because she'd forgotten
something, he thought about not bothering to put his tunic back on
before he opened up. He did, though.

And he was glad he did, because there in the hallway stood
not Seseset but Demodamas. "Come along with me," Ptolemaios'
tough-looking steward said.

Menedemos had the feeling the man would have said the same
thing if he had opened the door naked. "Lead on. I'll follow," he said.
The hard-faced Macedonian turned and walked away. After a glance
over his shoulder, he grudgingly gave Menedemos time to close and
latch the door—not much time, but enough.

He led Menedemos to a part of the palace where he'd never gone
before. Most of the men there had the look of soldiers: they were in
good shape for their age, they'd seen more sun and wind than most
men, and several of them bore nasty scars or had missing bits.

At last, Demodamas brought Menedemos into a room where
Ptolemaios was talking with a couple of men not far from his own
age. They were going back and forth in Macedonian. Menedemos

caught a word here and there, but not enough to follow what they were saying. Some people claimed Macedonian was a broad northern dialect of Greek; others said it was its own speech. Whatever it was, it was a long way from the language Menedemos used every day.

One of the other men pointed at Menedemos with his chin. Ptolemaios had to half-turn to see him. When he did, he switched at once to the almost-Attic he used with ordinary Hellenes: "Ah, the Rhodian! Hail, son of Philodemos! Tell Argaios and Kallikrates here what you told me when you got here."

"Of course, sir." Menedemos paused for a moment to gather his thoughts, then came as close as he could to delivering to the others the same report about Demetrios that he'd earlier given to Ptolemaios. He finished, "I expect you'll have more recent news than this."

"It's the same as what you've already heard," Ptolemaios said. "Demetrios holds eastern Cyprus, gods curse him. He still has my brother Menelaos holed up in Salamis, in the far southeast. Menelaos has a fair-sized fleet of his own, but he can't break out of the harbor. He has all he can do to keep Demetrios' ships from breaking in."

"I've tied up in that harbor," Menedemos said. "The opening is narrow. It would be hard to break into or break out of against opposition."

"That's about the size of it," one of Ptolemaios' officers said—Menedemos thought it was Argaios. A pale scar gulleyed one cheek and pulled up the corner of his mouth. Like Ptolemaios, he spoke Greek to Menedemos. Unlike his overlord, he still had a thick Macedonian accent.

"Menelaos can sneak small boats out under cover of darkness and get past Demetrios' scout ships," Ptolemaios said, "but it isn't easy for a small boat to get from Cyprus to Alexandria. So our news has been spotty."

"They'll be getting hungry in Salamis. Awful hungry." Argaios seemed a man who came out and said whatever was on his mind. By all accounts, such people were commoner in Macedonia than in Hellas.

"He's right," Ptolemaios said. "And that's a problem for us. You'll know, Rhodian, that the winds are mostly northerly on the stretch of sea between here and Cyprus at this time of year."

"It's worse yet farther north, up in the Aegean. You can count on the Etesian winds howling down from the north all the way through the autumnal equinox," Menedemos said. "But yes, you can't count on sailing north now."

"Which means that, if we're going to get help and supplies to Menelaos in time to do him any good, we'll have to take oared ships. Those tubby merchantmen would need gods can only guess how much time to get up to Cyprus."

"I can see that," Menedemos said. Sailing merchantmen were lumbering tubs even when a tailwind filled their big square sails to the fullest. Tacking against a steady headwind? Menedemos would have bet on garden tortoises to outpace them. He might have bet on the snails that came out at night to nibble holes in lettuce leaves. But he felt he had to ask, "Excuse me, sir—what has this got to do with me?"

By the way Ptolemaios looked at him, he knew he'd lost points. "You brought your galley here from Rhodes. It's not a big hull, but it's one more I can fill with grain and raisins and weapons and get them to my brother in Salamis while he can still use them. What will it cost me to hire the *Aphrodite* to do just that?"

Argaios spoke up once more: "Don't be shy, Rhodian. Everybody knows what a cheap prick the Ptolemaios is—"

"To the crows with you, Argaios!" Ptolemaios broke in without great heat.

The officer went on as if he hadn't spoken: "—but not when his brother's arse is on the line. Squeeze him. He'll pay." How long had the two men known each other, and how well, for Argaios to be able to say such things with Ptolemaios listening?

That question flickered through Menedemos' mind for a moment, then went out like a lamp flame in a strong wind. A much bigger worry loomed instead: "Forgive me, sir, but I don't think I can do that," he said to Ptolemaios. "My polis is neutral in your fight with Demetrios and Antigonos. If they got word I was helping you against Demetrios—"

"I can just seize your gods-cursed akatos," Ptolemaios said, and he might have poured snow down the neck hole of Menedemos' tunic. "You know I can, too. What could you do about it? Not even this!" He snapped his fingers. But then, a scowl on his heavy features, he went on, "*You* can't, no, but your detestable free and independent polis is liable to. You don't want to get Antigonos and Demetrios angry at you. I don't want Rhodes angry at me, or she might go over to old Cyclops, and that would be a nuisance."

"I'm glad to hear it, sir," Menedemos said, and he didn't think he'd ever told the truth more sincerely in all his life.

"I'll bet you are," Ptolemaios growled. "Look, I'm not asking you to lend a hand for nothing. Argaios is right, even if he is a loud-mouthed son of a whore who—"

"Listen to the *lakkoproktos*, why don't you?" the officer said. That was one of Aristophanes' choicer bits of obscenity. If someone who wasn't a bosom friend called you anything like that, you'd punch him in the nose and then kick him in the teeth.

Ptolemaios just laughed. "Never mind him. Tell me what you hoped to make on your trading run here. I know what all you brought. I even know about the amber—and some of my customs men are looking for work somewhere else because they missed it. Tell me, then, and I'll double it. By the gods, Rhodian, I will, and you have witnesses!" He waved to his officers. They solemnly dipped their heads.

"More than your little shit-stained galley's worth, too," Argaios said. "If we didn't need every hull that can keep up with the fleet ...."

Menedemos gulped. He believed the overlord of Egypt. Ptolemaios literally had more silver than he knew what to do with. He spent a talent the way an ordinary man spent an obolos, and thought no more about it. Fear of not getting his silver wasn't what made Menedemos stop and think. He had more than that to worry about.

After a long pause for thought, he said, "Sir, if I were just here working for the firm my father and uncle run, I'd say yes, I'd say thank you, and I'd spend the rest of my days singing your praises to the gods."

"I doubt it," Ptolemaios grunted. "Gratitude goes bad faster than octopus does."

Don't let him put you off, Menedemos told himself. Aloud, he went on, "I have to think of Rhodes, though. What good does your money do me if it makes Antigonos declare war on my polis? What good does it do me if Demetrios takes Rhodes the way he's taking the cities on Cyprus? He'll sell me into slavery or knock me over the head."

Ptolemaios' nostrils flared. His cheeks, already sun-browned, went darker still. He'd been playing a game before. Now he was really angry. "How much do you pay your rowers?" he said in a cold, deadly voice. "A drakhma and a half a day? Two drakhmai? How would you like to stay here in Alexandria till our campaign is over? Wouldn't it be a shame if that weren't till fall started and you'd risk going home in stormy weather? Wouldn't it be a shame if you had to overwinter here, owing them close to a mina of silver every day?"

A mina—a pound—of silver held a hundred drakhmai. Menedemos wouldn't owe his men quite that much every day, but they would easily soak up a talent's worth—sixty minai—of debt if they couldn't go back to Rhodes till next spring. And if Ptolemaios found or invented some fresh reason to delay them then ....

"You fight filthy!" Menedemos yelped.

Argaios, who seemed to do the talking for himself and Kallikrates both, guffawed. "You only just now noticed, pup of a Rhodian?" he said, and laughed some more.

"You've got yourself a choice, Menedemos," Ptolemaios said, ignoring his officer. "You can let me pay you twice as much as you think your cargo's worth and take your chances and your polis' chances on the Cyclops and his boy, or you can stand on your principles and see how much your father and uncle love you when I finally decide to let you go home. If I ever *do* decide to let you go home, I mean."

The kind of debt the firm could owe the rowers after months in Alexandria wouldn't break it, but wouldn't do it any good, either. Menedemos wanted to kick Ptolemaios in his plump belly. The overlord of Egypt looked insufferably smug, and well he might—he had all the power here. This wasn't anything like a dicker between equals, and Ptolemaios had just rubbed Menedemos' nose in that unpalatable fact.

What had Argaios called him? *Pup of a Rhodian*, that was it. Ptolemaios was treating him like a pup, all right, like a pup that had shat in the andron. The Macedonian was rubbing his nose in the turd. He was enjoying himself while he did it, too.

"Well, Rhodian? What's it going to be?" Ptolemaios asked genially.

"I think you talked me into it." Menedemos, by contrast, sounded as sullen as he had since he started shaving.

"You've decided to get rich instead of bleeding money. A merchant smart enough to do that will go a long way in this sorry old world," Ptolemaios said. That sent Argaios into another fit of laughter. Even Kallikrates chuckled once or twice.

"Joke all you please, sir. You aren't—" A few words too late, Menedemos broke off. Sure enough, he and Sostratos might add up to one diplomat. He certainly wasn't a diplomat all by himself.

"I'm not what? Not putting my land on the line?" Sure enough, Ptolemaios could divine what Menedemos hadn't swallowed soon enough. He'd mostly been playing at anger before, as a cat might play with a mouse. Now the mouse had nipped him, and he showed another spasm of real anger. The difference terrified Menedemos. "Furies take you if you're fool enough to think I'm not. I'll be in that fleet bound for Cyprus, you know. If Demetrios sinks my flagship, do you think a dolphin will carry me away like that one was supposed to do for Arion? Not fornicating likely! I'll rot on the bottom of the sea, and the crabs and the eels will quarrel over who gets my eyes for opson."

Menedemos stared at the floor between his feet. He hated being stupid. He hated getting called out for being stupid even more. "I'm sorry," he muttered, and meant it more than he was in the habit of doing.

"Likely tell! I *ought* to commandeer your gods-detested akatos, just for that crack. Even your father would say you deserved it," Ptolemaios told him. Did he know Philodemos? Whether he did or not, he was much too likely to be right. Contemptuously, he tossed his head. "Can't offend the other citizens of your free and independent pisspot, though—ah, polis. Is there any reason you can't drag your men away from our brothels and taverns and be ready to head north in a few days' time?"

"Yes, sir," Menedemos answered. Ptolemaios glowered at him. The vultures tearing at Prometheus' liver might have worn expressions like that. Menedemos quickly explained: "Sostratos and five rowers are down in Memphis, sir, trying to sell some of the olive oil we brought to Egypt."

"Oh." For a moment, a wordless rumble resounded, down deep in Ptolemaios' throat. "I don't give a fart about the rowers. "If you just need a handful of them, you can pick up others just as good right here from my fleet. But there are times when I think your cousin has enough in the way of brains to be worth noticing."

"I thank you for him, then," Menedemos said. Sostratos wasn't likely to win praise from a more discerning judge of men any time soon. Too bad he wasn't around to hear it in person.

"I will send up to Memphis to bring him and the rowers back here as soon as possible," Ptolemaios said. "The few days won't matter. We're still bringing soldiers into Alexandria, after all."

Argaios made a face at him. "You'll send *up* to Memphis to bring him back, Ptolemaios? You old Egyptian, you!"

Menedemos hadn't even noticed what Ptolemaios said till the officer spoke up. Sure enough, what Egyptians termed Upper Egypt lay below what they called Lower Egypt. They spoke in terms of the Nile, with farther up it being closer to its unknown source and farther down it being nearer to where it emptied into the Inner Sea. Hellenes didn't commonly think in those terms—not unless, Menedemos supposed, they'd lived in Egypt for a long time.

Clicking his tongue between his teeth, Ptolemaios said, "You know, Rhodian, this fool has been my friend longer than you've been alive. He's been taking advantage of it longer than you've been alive, too."

"That's what friends are for, sir," Menedemos said. "My cousin and I, we're the same way with each other."

"At least you have the bond of blood, the way I do with Menelaos," Ptolemaios said. "I'm just stuck with Argaios and Kallikrates."

"I thought you'd forgotten about me, the way you usually do." Kallikrates proved he could talk after all, and to wicked effect, too.

Ptolemaios snorted laughter. "This kind of rubbish is what you've got to look forward to, Rhodian. I do thank you one more time for lending your akatos' service to my fleet. Always glad to do business with a fellow who's so eager to help."

"Uh, yes, sir," Menedemos said. "Since I *am* helping, will you be kind enough to haul the *Aphrodite* up into a shipshed and let her planking dry out? If you want her keeping up with your fleet, that'll help."

"I'll give the order," Ptolemaios said at once. "That's fair enough. Anything else? No? Hail!" The dismissal couldn't have been any shorter or sharper.

Ears burning, Menedemos all but fled the chamber. Behind him, Ptolemaios and his officers went back to slanging one another in

Macedonian. Kallikrates had plenty to say in the tongue he'd grown up using, even if he didn't in Greek. Menedemos understood not a word of it.

Sostratos eyed the shop before he went inside. It was in a good-sized building, and one that had been well kept up. It also lay only a couple of blocks from the nomarch's sprawling residence, on a street as prominent as any in Memphis. All things considered, Rhodoios had probably done him a good turn by suggesting that he try to sell what was left of his olive oil here.

He turned to Thersandros, who was lugging an amphora of oil. "Shall we go in?"

"I'll go anywhere that gets me out of the sun for a while," Thersandros answered. Since Sostratos felt the same way, he ducked through the doorway (it was barely tall enough for someone of his height). His two-legged beast of burden came right behind him.

It was a little cooler and a lot dimmer inside. The smell of spices in the air tickled Sostratos' nose. He recognized the fragrances of cinnamon and pepper. A man a few years younger than he was stood behind the counter. "Hail!" he said. "Are you Zoïlos?"

The young man tossed his head. "No, that's my father. He's in back. My name is Psaphon. Do you need him, or can I help you with something?"

"Well, I don't know." Sostratos nodded toward the amphora of oil, whose pointed end Thersandros had promptly stuck into the smooth earth of the floor. "I have some fine olive oil from Rhodes, and Rhodoios the cook told me your shop might want to buy it."

"Oh, you're that fellow!" Psaphon said. "Father told me Rhodoios told him you might be coming by."

"Did he?" Sostratos said. He'd already given the cook a little silver for the tip. If Rhodoios wanted to earn a bit more from the shopkeeper … well, why not? You made money as you found the chance.

An older man who looked a lot like Psaphon except that he was going bald stuck his head out of the back room. "Hail," he said, and he sounded like his son, too. "Thought I heard voices out here. I'm Zoïlos son of Psaphon. What can I do for you?"

127

Like many Hellenes, he'd named his son for his father. "Hail," Sostratos said, and then summarized what he'd told Psaphon. "Would you like to try the oil, O best one? And your son, too, of course. If you care for it, we can talk about price. If not"—he shrugged—"I'll say good day and leave you at peace."

"If it's any good, I'll buy some," Zoïlos said. "Rhodoios got some for the nomarch, so it can't be too bad." He turned to his son. "Why don't you run get us some bread so we can see what we've got here?"

"All right, Father." Psaphon went into and likely through the back room. Zoïlos came all the way out to talk with Sostratos. The first thing he said was, "What's this I hear about Demetrios landing on Cyprus?"

"It's true," Sostratos replied, wondering how Zoïlos knew. He hadn't even told the nomarch here in Memphis. Had news already come up the river from Alexandria? Or were the rowers gossiping in the wineshops and brothels? He hadn't told them not to; that hadn't crossed his mind. But it was an odd state of affairs when a merchant knew something a provincial governor might well not.

Psaphon came back then with half a loaf on an earthenware plate. "Mother just finished baking, so it's fresh from the oven," he said.

Sostratos' nostrils twitched. "Nothing in all the world like the smell of new-baked bread," he said.

"That's the truth," Zoïlos agreed. "Let's see what we've got here, shall we?" He reached under the counter and pulled out a small bowl in the same style as the plate the bread lay on. "Pour in some of that oil and we'll all have ourselves a taste."

The weight of the full amphora made Sostratos grunt, but he got oil into the bowl without spilling it all over the counter, so he set the jar down well pleased with himself. Psaphon was the first to tear off a chunk of bread, dip it, and take a bite. He looked pleased "That *is* good oil!" he said with his mouth full.

His father let out a theatrical sigh. "Smooth going, boy! You just made the price go up." Then he tasted the oil, too. His verdict was more judicious: "I've had worse, I will say that."

Sostratos also ate some. It was Damonax's oil, still good, still fresh. "The bread's very fine," he said. "The flour tastes like it's half wheat, half barley."

"That's just what it is," Psaphon said. "Mother puts it through the mill once more than most do, to make it extra fine."

"I'll buy your oil," Zoïlos said to Sostratos. "Tell me what they gave you for it in the nomarch's kitchens." But when Sostratos did, he clapped a hand to his forehead in dismay. "*Papai!* You're making that up!"

"By the gods, best one, I'm doing no such thing," Sostratos answered. "Send your son to Rhodoios and ask him if you doubt me."

"Never mind. I believe you," Zoïlos said. "But you have to remember, the nomarch's cooks have a whole nome's worth of money to play with. I'm just a plain old merchant, so I don't."

Sostratos had thought the same thing when Rhodoios didn't dicker as hard as he might have. Since he didn't want to take any of his brother-in-law's oil back to Alexandria, he asked, "Well, what can you afford, then?" The price Zoïlos proposed made him toss his head. "You can do better than that, O marvelous one. Plenty of Hellenes in Memphis these days, and when's the next time anyone will bring oil this good this far up the river?"

"You must get laid a lot. If you sweet-talk the girls the way you're sweet-talking me, how can they tell you no?" Zoïlos said.

"If only it were so!" Sostratos said with real regret. Both men laughed. Sostratos went on, "Seriously, my dear, you can do better. You know you'll charge more than whatever you pay me."

"Of course I will, but I'll get it back a little at a time, and I'll have to pay you for all the oil at once," the Memphite merchant said.

"That's the way trade works," Sostratos said. "The time my cousin and I sailed to Italy and Sicily with a cargo that included peafowl …. *Oimoi!*" Even years later, that wasn't a pleasant memory, even if they'd made money on the voyage.

"Peafowl! I've heard of them, but I've never seen one," Zoïlos said. "Are the peacocks really as fancy as they say?"

"Fancier," Sostratos answered. "But they're also stupid and bad-tempered. Are they ever! Come up a bit and I'll tell you some stories."

Zoïlos did. Sostratos told a story. When he stopped, Zoïlos said, "That's only one."

"Well, you didn't come up very far."

Zoïlos came up a bit more. Sostratos spun out another tale of peafowl. He stopped again. Zoïlos came up again. After a while, they had a price that left neither man too unhappy, and clasped hands on it.

"I'll get some laughs with your stories. That may turn out to be worth money for me," Zoïlos said. "Somebody laughs with you, he doesn't haggle so hard." He cocked his head to one side. "What else have you got? Never can tell what I might buy, if I think I can make a profit off it."

I made you laugh with me, Sostratos thought. Aloud, he answered, "Well, I have some amber that I bought last year. That won't come cheap, though. I paid two minai of silver for it. But when will any Egyptian jewelers see amber again?"

"When I still lived in Corinth, I saw some," Zoïlos said. "One chunk had what looked like a piece of fern in it."

"One of the bits I bought has a bug in it," Sostratos said. "How does something like that get inside a piece of rock?"

"I have no idea. I wish I did," Zoïlos replied. "So tell me—did you bring your amber up the river from Alexandria?"

"Before I answer, tell me why you want to know," Sostratos said.

"Because you're right—that kind of stuff doesn't come to Egypt, and whatever the price I pay to you, I'll make more when I unload it. And if you like, I'll trade you something the likes of which you aren't likely to find in Hellas, either. So what do you say?"

"I'll be back in a quarter of an hour," Sostratos said. "Thersandros, you won't have to take the jar back to the warehouse—you're done for the day."

Zoïlos laughed under his breath. Sostratos made that sound himself when he had a customer on the hook, so he recognized it. He didn't fancy being on the receiving end, but what could he do about that?

He got the curious wooden box that held the amber out of the leather sack that held his worldly goods. It was wrapped in the chiton he wasn't wearing, which might have hidden it from a thief for an extra heartbeat—maybe even two heartbeats if the thief was a halfwit.

"Never seen work like this before, or even wood like this," Zoïlos remarked when Sostratos set the box on the counter. Psaphon dipped his head in agreement.

"I thought the same thing when I got it," Sostratos said, and opened the box.

Zoïlos took out the chunks of amber one by one. He paused when he found the one with the insect trapped inside. "Isn't that something?" he murmured, and seemed reluctant to set it down.

"Have you got something to show me, too?" Sostratos asked him.

"Oh, I might, Rhodian. Yes indeed, I just might." Smiling, Zoïlos reached under the counter and took out something wrapped in a large square of embroidered linen that had gone yellow with age. Sostratos had seen that before, but rarely. Most linen didn't last long enough to show its years.

Before Sostratos undid the cloth, he looked a question at Zoïlos, who waved for him to go ahead. He did, and then stopped. "Oh, my," he whispered.

The necklace was of gold and lapis lazuli and garnet. Along with beads, it had lotus flowers and, above them, the moon disc riding a boat—across the sky, Sostratos supposed. The moon was paler than the rest of the goldwork. He suspected it was of electrum. The Lydians in Anatolia had struck their first coins from the natural alloy of gold and silver.

"Where ... did you come by this?" he asked.

Zoïlos tipped him a wink. "I'll pretend I didn't hear you. Robbing rich Egyptian tombs has been against the law since the day after they made the first one, and hasn't stopped since. There's a lot of gold in Egypt, especially if you're a Hellene and you aren't used to it. But most of it gets used over and over, not just once."

"Isn't that interesting?" Sostratos reached toward the necklace, then paused till Zoïlos dipped his head again. He picked up the necklace then, hefting it with experienced hands. Close to half a mina of gold, he judged: the equivalent of four or four and a half minai of silver, about what he wanted to make for the amber.

The jewels would add some value, too, and the artistry in the piece was very fine even if it wasn't Greek. "Are you sure you want to make this bargain?" he asked. "I don't want you to think I've cheated you."

Zoïlos nodded toward the necklace. "I can get more pieces like that. They come around every so often," he answered. "Robbers find a new tomb, maybe—I don't know. I don't want to know. They sell at a discount, because it isn't stuff everybody will touch, you know what I'm saying?"

"I hear you." Sostratos realized he'd have to be extra careful with the necklace if he took it. If Ptolemaios' men found it on him, paying export duty would be the least of his worries. Like most traders, he didn't see smuggling as a crime. Getting caught smuggling would be an inconvenience, though.

"Your amber, now, that's something different here," Zoïlos said. "I know men who'll want it, and they'll pay plenty. I may even keep the piece with the bug for myself. So—have we got a deal?"

"I think we do," Sostratos said slowly. "And speaking of paying, if my men deliver the oil tomorrow, will you have the silver for it?"

"I'll have it." Zoïlos didn't fuss. Sostratos liked his calm self-assurance. And if he was a man who dealt in gold, even at cut prices because it wasn't legal gold, he would have plenty of silver around, or be able to lay hold of it in a hurry.

Sostratos hired a large, two-ox cart to carry the oil from the warehouse to Zoïlos' shop. He had the rowers come along anyhow. If Zoïlos meant to make trouble, Sostratos hoped to leave him on the receiving end of at least some.

But Zoïlos didn't. Like a lot of men on the fringes of the law, he was scrupulous about doing everything just so when he walked on the legitimate side of the street. He had Sostratos' silver waiting in three leather sacks. "You can count the drakhmai if you want," he said. "They won't all weight the same—they come from all over Hellas."

"Do you have a scale?" Sostratos asked. Zoïlos pulled a balance and a set of weights off a shelf on the wall behind the counter. Sostratos eyed the weights. He hefted a couple of them. They felt about right, anyhow. Zoïlos couldn't get away with cheating customers too openly. The local merchant grinned at him, seeing what was in his mind. With a shrug, Sostratos weighed each sack in turn. His lips moved as he added the three weights together. He dipped his head. "Close enough." If Damonax wasn't perfectly happy with the accounting he'd get, too bad.

"Pleasure doing business with you," Zoïlos said.

Sostratos gave each rower a drakhma above their daily wage. No, Damonax wouldn't miss the money. "Have yourselves a drink or three, boys," he said. That made them grin, too. A tavern lay a few doors down the street.

The first thing Sostratos did when he got back to his room was to take the necklace he'd traded for the day before and put in in the least full sack of coins, covering it over with silver. Coins were coins. He had several sacks of them here, and a robber might easily miss one. The necklace was something special. Anywhere else among his personal goods, it would surely draw notice.

Only a little while after he'd made his arrangements, someone knocked on the door. When he opened it, he found a Hellene he'd never seen before standing in the inn's narrow hallway. "Tell me your name," the stranger said.

"Sostratos son of Lysistratos," Sostratos answered automatically. Only then did he think to ask, "Who are you, and why do you want to know?"

"I am a messenger from the Ptolemaios, that's who," the man said. "You and the sailors who came to Memphis with you are ordered to return to Alexandria with me at once. I came by horse, but I have a boat waiting on the Nile."

"I'm not going anywhere on your say-so," Sostratos said. "For all I know, you'll cut my throat and toss my body in the river."

"Tempting," the man said, which left Sostratos with his mouth hanging open. The Hellene went on, "If the nomarch vouches for me, will that make you happy, O marvelous one?"

"Y-yes," Sostratos managed. He and the man went over to the nomarch's residence together. Sure enough, Alexandros affirmed that the newcomer, whose name Sostratos still didn't know, was in Ptolemaios' service. When Sostratos told Ptolemaios' official where his rowers were, the nomarch sent men to bring them back to the inn. Everything else went just as smoothly. Sostratos barely had time to clean out his chamber before he was on his way down to the riverbank.

Menedemos watched workmen load the *Aphrodite* with weapons of war. Now she lay in a shipshed, as he'd asked of Ptolemaios. The shed had been built for a trireme, the smallest kind of war galley in the

Egyptian navy. Even so, inside it the *Aphrodite* seemed like a puppy in a doghouse made for a big, mean Molossian hound.

Menedemos' mouth twisted in wry amusement. Nothing was too good for him or his ship as long as they were in Ptolemaios' service. Before, the akatos could have stayed tied up in the harbor till shipworms bored holes in her planking and she quietly sank.

Diokles waved from the steering platform at the stern. Ptolemaios' payment for use of the *Aphrodite* was stashed under the platform. That was the safest spot on the ship, but someone from her company always kept watch now. Otherwise, no telling what the men who brought aboard arrows and spears and swords and shields would walk off with.

These were sheaves of arrows coming aboard now, their iron heads glistening with oil so they wouldn't rust. Diokles ordered the men carrying them forward. With Sostratos gone, he was best suited to deciding how to stow her new, deadly cargo in ways that kept her trim and as seaworthy as possible.

Not three heartbeats after Menedemos thought of Sostratos, a familiar voice behind him said, "We've come up in the world a bit, I see."

Whirling, Menedemos embraced his cousin. "By the dog of Egypt!" he exclaimed—a fitting oath here. "The Ptolemaios told me he was going to bring you back from Memphis as fast as he could, but I didn't expect you for another couple of days."

"His agents are like the Persian couriers Herodotos wrote about. Neither snow nor rain nor heat nor gloom of night stays them from the swift completion of their appointed rounds," Sostratos said.

"Not likely they need to worry about snow or even rain here," Menedemos said with a snort. "Heat, now, heat's a different business."

"Worse in Memphis than it is here, too." Sostratos looked around to make sure no one could overhear, then lowered his voice anyhow. "And Ptolemaios' helpers may as well be his Eyes and Ears."

That was what people called the Persian kings' secret agents. In the old days, they'd been pointed to as proof of Persian oppression. Menedemos would have bet Ptolemaios wasn't the only Macedonian warlord using such Persian tricks these days, though. Once again, it made him wonder who'd really conquered whom.

"Did you see your precious Pyramids?" he asked.

He couldn't help but smile at the way his cousin's face lit up. "I did! I really did! And the Sphinx, too!" Sostratos said. "And they were …. You can't imagine how big they were. I couldn't imagine till I saw with my own eyes. Nothing human beings make has any business being that big."

"Maybe the Egyptian gods did it," Menedemos said slyly.

Sostratos tossed his head in indignation. "Oh, rubbish! There's a gigantic ramp, a causeway, whatever you want to call it, that leads from the Nile to where the Pyramids sit. Herodotos talks more about it than he does about them. The Egyptians quarried the stones farther south, floated them down the Nile till they got to the right place, and hauled them along the causeway so they could trim each one perfectly square and set it just where it went. If gods built the Pyramids, they wouldn't have gone to all that trouble. They'd have just plopped them down where they wanted them, wouldn't they?"

"Don't ask me, my dear. I'm no god," Menedemos said. "What did the rowers think of them?"

"They thought we were way the daimon out in the desert. They were keeping an eye on the fellow who owned the camels we rode on, and on his friends. We didn't have any trouble with them, so that worked out all right," Sostratos said.

"Good. And how was business?" To Menedemos, that was more important than Sostratos' sightseeing.

"Damonax's oil is gone, gods be praised, and at a decent price, too," his cousin answered. "The nomarch's kitchens bought some, and I unloaded the rest on a merchant in Memphis." He lowered his voice again. "I made a deal for the amber with him, too."

"Ah? And how did you do on that?"

"I'll show you when we go back to the room," Sostratos said. "How was your trading up here?"

"Just about all of the wine is gone," Menedemos said. "Prices were good—not great, but good. I bought some incenses, so not all the pay was in silver. We'll have something to sell when we get home. And the Ptolemaios is paying plenty to hire the *Aphrodite*, too. We'll make a nice profit on the trip—if we don't get sunk, I mean."

X

WHEN THEY DID GET BACK TO THE CHAMBER IN
Ptolemaios' palace, Menedemos watched in amusement as his cousin made a small production out of barring the door. Then Sostratos
rummaged in his large leather sack till he found a smaller one that
clinked nicely as he lifted it out.

He reached inside and rummaged through the drakhmai be-
fore lifting out something that wasn't silver. "This," he said softly but
proudly, "this is what I got for the amber I brought here."

"By the dog!" Menedemos exclaimed. He held out both hands
close together, palms up. "Let me have a better look at that." With
visible reluctance, Sostratos gave him the necklace. He felt the weight
of the gold and admired the workmanship. "You got value for value
and then some, I'd say," Menedemos agreed. "Do you have any idea
how old this is?"

"Old," Sostratos said. "That's as much as I can tell you. Five hundred years? A thousand? Five thousand? I couldn't begin to guess. If
I had to bet, I'd say it goes back to the days before the Trojan War."

"That's ri—" Menedemos broke off. It might not be ridiculous
after all. The Trojan War, people thought, had been fought about
nine hundred years before. Everyone knew Egypt was an ancient

land. They'd had goldsmiths and jewelers long before brilliant Akhilleus slew Hektor of the shining helm on the windy plains of Troy. Menedemos found a business question instead: "Will you break it up and sell the pieces or keep it together?"

"I'd like to leave it intact," his cousin answered. "It's stayed this way for all these centuries. I'd feel I was robbing the world of something precious and wonderful if I took it apart."

Menedemos suspected the firm might make more profit from selling off the bracelet piecemeal, but he didn't quarrel with Sostratos. For one thing, they still had to get the piece, and themselves, out of Egypt and back to Rhodes. For another, he understood what Sostratos was talking about. Selling the gold and ivory from the image of Athena in the Parthenon might net more than the statue would as a whole, but it would also be a dreadful desecration. Breaking up the necklace would make a smaller sin, but one of the same kind.

As gently as he could, he gave the necklace back to Sostratos. His cousin hid it under the silver he'd got for Damonax's oil. The coins had their own value, of course, but that whole sack probably didn't match the necklace.

"When will the fleet sail? Do you know?" Sostratos asked.

"Not to the day, but it won't be long," Menedemos said. "The Ptolemaios has been making ready since before you left for Memphis." He paused as a different thought struck him. "I wonder if my father's wife has had the baby yet."

"We'll find out when we get back." Sostratos had only a dim interest in Baukis' baby.

"I guess we will," Menedemos agreed tonelessly. He couldn't let on that his own interest was much greater than his cousin's. As far as Sostratos knew—as far as anyone but he and Baukis knew—the child surely sprouted from his father's seed. That was how things had to look to the outside world.

"Would you rather have a little boy or a little girl running around and getting into trouble?" his cousin asked.

"A boy," Menedemos answered at once. *A son!* he thought. "I'm glad the gods made me a man. I could teach him what he needs to know to get along in the world." *But not who is father is, or may be, curse it!*

"Well, I can see that. A sister isn't so bad, though," Sostratos said.

"If you say so. I played with Erinna a bit when we were all small, but I don't know much about little girls." Thinking a leer was called for, Menedemos duly produced one. "When they get bigger, though …."

"Yes, my dear. You don't have to remind me you're cockproud," Sostratos said. "I already know that. Maybe you should remind me which towns we can't trade in because they have outraged husbands who want to kill you."

Menedemos raised an eyebrow. "*You* must have eaten something sour on your way back to Alexandria."

"The whole thing was sour," Sostratos said. "I didn't even know why I was ordered out of Memphis till I walked into the palace here. If Ptolemaios' man did know why he had to fetch me, he didn't let on, not even a little bit. Are you sure hiring the *Aphrodite* to Ptolemaios was smart? If Antigonos and Demetrios get wind of it—"

"I thought about all that. You said it yourself—I'm not as stupid as I look," Menedemos replied. "I had two choices, O cousin of mine. I could take Ptolemaios' silver and let him hire the akatos, or I could watch him confiscate it without giving me even a khalkos. He may not call himself a king, but that doesn't mean he isn't one."

Sostratos opened his mouth, then closed it again. After a moment, he remarked, "Maybe I should just shut up."

"Maybe you should," Menedemos agreed. "When the lions fight, the mice get mauled by accident."

"Or not by accident. We're worth more to Ptolemaios the way we are, but Antigonos just itches to get his hands on our island and our polis and our people and our fleet," Sostratos said.

"I'd sooner see every trireme we own burn in its shipshed than let the Cyclops get hold of it," Menedemos said savagely.

"The really frightening thing is, he could be worse," Sostratos said. "Up in Macedonia, Kassandros is just a soldier. Antigonos is clever— you have to give him that."

"I'd like to give him a good swift kick, is what I'd like to give him." Menedemos lowered his voice. "I'd like to give the Ptolemaios another one, too, even harder."

"He's made you do something you didn't want to do, something that may prove bad for Rhodes," Sostratos said, also not much above a whisper.

"Too cursed right, he has," Menedemos said, sending Sostratos a grateful glance—his cousin knew what was gnawing at him, all right. "I'm a free Hellene, from a free and independent polis. He's got no right to treat me like a barbarian or a slave."

"Remember what the Alexander said on his deathbed when they asked him to whom his empire should go," Sostratos said.

"'To the strongest,'" Menedemos responded. Almost any Hellene from Sicily to the Indos could have done the same. "I don't care if Alexander did study with what's-his-name—"

"Aristoteles," Sostratos supplied.

"Aristoteles. Thanks. I don't care if Alexander studied with him or not. You know what veneer is?"

"Oh, yes." Sostratos dipped his head. "They glue thin strips of good wood over cheap stuff so a table will look more expensive than it is. Or they hope it will. Most of the time, you can see what they're up to."

"There you go. That's what I'm talking about, all right," Menedemos said. "Well, Aristoteles may have given Alexander the veneer of a Hellene, but down under it he was still a Macedonian. And so are his generals. They're used to having kings. Pretty soon, they'll get used to being kings and they won't care a fart about free and independent Hellenes."

"It hasn't happened yet," Sostratos said.

"To the crows with that! It happened to me!" Menedemos exclaimed.

"It hasn't happened to Rhodes, gods be thanked. If we stay lucky, it won't," his cousin said.

"That seems a bigger, harder *if* every day," Menedemos replied, and then, after a moment, "Do you suppose the Athenians still imagine they live in a free and independent polis?"

Sostratos needed only a moment of his own to answer that: "The stupid ones do."

Menedemos started laughing and discovered he didn't want to stop. If he stopped laughing, he would either shriek or weep, and he feared he also wouldn't be able to stop either one of those. So he laughed and laughed and laughed.

"Are you all right, my dear?" Sostratos asked after a while, real anxiety in his voice.

Wiping his eyes with the back of his arm, Menedemos tossed his head. "I'm afraid not, O marvelous one," he said, gasping a little as the spasm passed. "But I daresay it's for the best. In times like these, anyone who thinks he's all right has to have something wrong with him, doesn't he?" Sostratos didn't answer, which was probably just as well.

Leskhaios didn't look at Sostratos. The rower looked through him, at a point a couple of cubits behind his head. "No," Leskhaios said.

"But—" Sostratos began.

"No," Leskhaios said again, and by the way he said it he might have been Zeus pronouncing doom for some strong-greaved Akhaian in the *Iliad*. "I don't care when the *Aphrodite*'s going back to Rhodes. I'm not going back there with her."

"What will you do here?" Sostratos asked.

"I've been sniffing around, like," Leskhaios said. "There's a baker not far from this inn who needs himself a helper. He wants to take on a Hellene, not an Egyptian, so he'll be able to talk with him. He doesn't pay a whole lot, but it's better work than pulling an oar, and if you're in a bakery you'll never starve."

An angry flush heated Sostratos' face. "You pulled an oar from Rhodes to here, and since then you've collected your pay for lying around and doing nothing most of the time."

"That's how it goes. I didn't know we'd be stuck here so long when I climbed into your akatos," Leskhaios said. "You'd put slaves at the oars if you could trust 'em far enough—they'd cost you less. And have you got any notion of what a rower's life's like in winter when the ships stay in port? If I came around to your house to beg some oil 'cause I was flat, you'd set the dogs on me."

"To the crows with you if we would!" Sostratos snapped. "Sometimes men who've rowed on the *Aphrodite* do come in the wintertime, asking for money or food. My father and I always give—Menedemos' family, too. We know rowing's a trade for spring and summer."

"Mm, maybe. Your family doesn't have the bad name some shipowners do. I give you so much," Leskhaios said. "But that's not the point. The point is, if I stay in Alexandria, I won't have to worry about getting thin after the cranes fly south."

Sostratos doubted that. Leskhaios was the kind who did as little as he could to get by, or a bit less than that. Such men often failed to endear themselves to the people who paid them. Telling him so would only be a waste of breath; Sostratos knew as much. Instead, he asked, "What about your family in Rhodes?"

"What about 'em?" the rower said. "If I never see my father again, I'll thank the gods. He'll have to hit my mother some more, 'cause he won't have me to knock around. My brother didn't live past eight—lockjaw. Don't have a wife. Don't have a sweetheart. Maybe I'll find one here."

Again, Sostratos wondered. Why would anyone want anything to do with somebody like Leskhaios? "You're leaving us in the lurch," he said.

"Don't blame just me," Leskhaios answered. "You know as well as I do, I'm a long way from being the only one."

That made Sostratos' lips skin back from his teeth in what came closer to a snarl than a smile. Half a dozen rowers had decided they didn't want to go north with the *Aphrodite*. Like Leskhaios, the others thought they could do better for themselves here in Egypt, As with Leskhaios, Sostratos thought most of them were fooling themselves, but they didn't want to listen.

Trying to sound patient, Leskhaios went on, "So if you'll pay me what you still owe me, I'll be on my way."

Sostratos was tempted to tell him he could be on his way without his back pay. More than a few traders would have said just that. What could Leskhaios do about it? Nothing. Nothing legal, anyhow, though murder and arson might jump to mind. But Sostratos prided himself on scrupulous honesty. "I'll do it," he said. "It may be less than you hope. You've drawn silver while you were here and when you went up and down the Nile with me."

"Yes, yes," the rower said. "It'll keep me afloat a little while, anyway. The baker will be putting money in my hands before long."

"I think I know how much you're due. Let me talk to Menedemos and Diokles to make sure we all have about the same number in mind, and I'll give you your money this afternoon," Sostratos said.

"That's fair, I expect. Gods only know how you stay in business when you don't go out of your way to cheat people," Leskhaios said.

141

After Sostratos left the inn where most of the rowers were staying, he kicked at the dirt in the street. He wouldn't show Leskhaios his fury, but he couldn't hold it all in, either. When he got back to the palace, he knocked on the door to the room he shared with Menedemos.

His cousin opened it, then drew back a pace. "What's wrong? You look as though a mask-maker could do a Gorgon from your face."

"Do I? I'm not surprised. Leskhaios just told me he's staying in Alexandria," Sostratos said.

"Another one?" Menedemos swore. He went on, "Many good-byes to him! He didn't like to row. He just wanted to eat and complain."

"I know, but he still leaves another bench empty. Where will we get the bodies to fill them up? If we go where there's fighting, we'll want a man at every oar," Sostratos said.

"We could ask the Ptolemaios or his admirals for rowers," Menedemos said.

"I don't like doing that. It would be all right till we got to Cyprus, but what about when we go on to Rhodes? Men with families here won't care to do that," Sostratos said.

"I'll do it anyhow. Maybe we can give them back to Ptolemaios after he wins his sea-fight. We wouldn't need them so much then," Menedemos said.

Sostratos stepped into the room, closing the door behind him. When he spoke again, it was in a voice not much above a whisper: "But what if Ptolemaios loses?"

His cousin scowled at him. "That would spill the perfume into the soup, wouldn't it?" Menedemos also made sure no one outside the chamber could overhear. He sighed. "I'll ask around. Maybe some Rhodians here are willing to pull an oar to go home again. Maybe." He didn't sound as if he believed it.

Sostratos didn't, either. He changed the subject: "By your reckoning, what do we owe Leskhaios?"

"A good kick in the arse," Menedemos said. He startled a laugh out of Sostratos. Menedemos calculated on his fingers, then named a number not far from the one Sostratos had in mind.

Relieved, Sostratos said, "I want to check with Diokles, too— make sure we haven't forgotten anything."

"I forget things all the cursed time. I didn't think you ever did," Menedemos said, which made Sostratos' ears heat. Menedemos continued, "But ask Diokles, of course. If we did miss something, he'll catch it."

When Sostratos asked the keleustes what Leskhaios had coming to him, Diokles answered, "How about a sharp stake up his backside, the kind the Persians use to get rid of people they don't like?"

"Tempting, but I was thinking more along the lines of back pay," Sostratos said.

"Too bad," Diokles grunted. Then his face got a faraway look for a few heartbeats. When he came back to himself, he named a figure only a couple of drakhmai less than the ones Sostratos and Menedemos had worked out.

Determined to be as fair as he could, Sostratos paid Leskhaios the highest of the three calculations (his own). After counting the silver coins, the rower rolled his eyes up toward the heavens. "Well, I was afraid you'd give it to me by the back door in spite of all your fancy talk, and by the gods you did."

Whatever sympathy Sostratos might have felt for him went out as abruptly as a torch dropped in a rain puddle. "If you aren't happy with it, you can give it back," he said in a voice so cold and deadly, he had trouble recognizing it as his own.

It made Leskhaios flinch, too. "Never mind that," he said hastily. "I'm off to make my fortune." He left the rowers' inn at something not far short of a run, as if afraid Sostratos *would* kick him or take the money away if he lingered. He might not have been so far wrong, either.

The captain of one of Ptolemaios' fives was a Thasian named Blepyros. He might have been carved from the same block of dark wood that had produced Diokles. At the moment, he eyed Menedemos with all the warmth of a Thracian blizzard. "*How* many rowers are you after?" he demanded, his voice as frigid as the rest of his manner.

"Half a dozen, sir," Menedemos answered.

And Blepyros thawed as if by magic. "Is *that* all?" he exclaimed. "I thought you were trying to steal scores of 'em from me."

"My akatos only has forty oars," Menedemos said. "I'm just trying to get them all filled."

"Akatos?" Blepyros' bushy eyebrows jumped. "Oh. You're that fellow, the Rhodian. I heard about you."

"Did you?" Menedemos said tonelessly. How many of Ptolemaios' skippers had heard about him? How many of them were laughing at the way Ptolemaios had made him join their fleet?

"Sure did. The way the story goes, you held the big boss man for ransom, or near enough as makes no difference, before you finally threw in with him," Blepyros said. "Must be something to that 'free and independent' stuff after all, hey?"

"Well, we like to think so," Menedemos replied, all at once feeling better about the world. "The rowers need to know my ship will go on to Rhodes after the campaign off Cyprus is over. We won't come back to Alexandria."

"I understand. Do you suppose you can put them aboard one of the other ships in the fleet before you head off on your own?"

Menedemos puffed out his cheeks, then blew a stream of air through pursed lips. He'd done more thinking about that after talking with his cousin. "Part of me wants to say yes, O best one, but I don't dare promise. Gods only know what we'll run into in Rhodian waters. Maybe we'll have clear sailing. But if we find pirates or some of the Demetrios' war galleys, we'll want a backside on every bench."

"That makes sense. Your mother may not have licked you all the way dry yet, but you know your trade," Blepyros said. "Come back tomorrow morning and I'll line my men up outside the shed here. Tell 'em whatever you're going to tell 'em, and if five or six want to go with you, fine. I can pick up replacements easy enough." A certain hard glint in his eye suggested he might not be fussy about how he picked them up, either.

The next morning, the rowers looked like ... rowers: sun-tanned men with wide shoulders, thick arms, and horny hands. Most were Hellenes, though there were also a handful of Egyptians. "I need half a dozen men to pull a one-man oar on an akatos from here to Cyprus, and then on to Rhodes," Menedemos said. "Two drakhmai a day. We won't come back to Alexandria this year. You can settle in my polis if you like, or you can take passage on a ship sailing here next spring if things stay peaceful. What do you say?"

Three men, two Hellenes and an Egyptian, stepped forward right away. "I'm for it," one of the Hellenes said in the broad Doric of Crete. "A little fella like that, the work's bound to be easier than pulling a five along."

Blepyros waited to see whether more rowers would volunteer. When none did, he said, "All you men who aren't married, hold up a hand." Several unwary rowers did. Blepyros pointed at three of them. "You, you, and you. Yes, you, Kerdon. Go with the Rhodian and help him out."

Kerdon scowled. Then he took another look at Blepyros' face and thought better of arguing. "Looks like I'm your man, Rhodian," he said to Menedemos. By the way he talked, he might have sprung from the same Cretan village as the other rower. With more people than it had land for, Crete exported sailors and mercenaries. A lot of the men who stayed behind went to sea anyhow, as pirates. Hard as that life was, it was bound to be easier than trying to scratch out a living on a tiny, dusty, stony plot of ground.

Menedemos sketched a salute to Blepyros. "Much obliged, sir."

"Any time." Ptolemaios' captain turned to the rowers who were changing ships, some willingly, some less so. "Go on, lads. Chances are you can count yourselves lucky. That little toy boat won't get into any sea fights. You stay with me, who knows how much fun you'll have off Cyprus?"

Naval battles with fours and fives and sixes were a different business from those involving triremes. Triremes fought with lizard-quick maneuver; the ram at the bow was their main weapon, though they also carried a few archers. Along with the swarms of rowers, the bigger war galleys had far more marines on them. They would lay alongside an enemy ship, board it, overwhelm its fighters, and then slaughter the men at the oars. For all practical purposes, it was land warfare on the ocean.

Menedemos wanted no part of it. The *Aphrodite* would be at an even worse disadvantage against such seagoing monsters than a trireme would. Hoping his new recruits felt the same way, he said,

"Come along with me. You can meet the men you'll be rowing with." He eyed the Egyptian. "You do speak Greek, don't you?"

"Fornicating right, I do," the brown man answered.

"All right." Menedemos laughed. "Let's go, everybody." As he led the rowers toward the inn where the *Aphrodite*'s men were quartered, he wondered just where Blepyros would get his replacements. He guessed they'd come from the fishermen and merchant seamen who used the Harbor of Happy Return, on the other side of the long mole from the Great Harbor. Some of them would want to pull an oar for Ptolemaios, or at least for his silver. Others might prove less eager, which, Menedemos suspected, wouldn't matter one bit to the war galley's skipper.

As Menedemos and the akatos' new crewmen neared the inn, Sostratos came out the front door. Seeing the miniature procession, he stopped in glad surprise. "You got them!" he exclaimed.

"I figured I would," Menedemos answered. Then he spoke to the new rowers: "This is my cousin, Sostratos. He's toikharkhos on the *Aphrodite*." He remembered the title meant something different on a merchant ship from what it did aboard a naval vessel. "That means he's the supercargo and the purser, not a petty officer. He'll write down your names, and you'll draw your pay from him."

That made Sostratos the object of the new rowers' interested attention. He took from his belt pouch a stylus and a small, three-faced wooden tablet whose leaves were coated with wax. "I'll take your names now, if that's all right." When he got to the Egyptian, he asked, as Menedemos had, "You do speak Greek?"

"No, not me. Not a fornicating word of it, not even a little bit," the man answered.

Sostratos blinked. "He did the same thing to me," Menedemos told him.

"Did he?" Sostratos said, and then, to the Egyptian, "All right, tell me your name." He poised the sharp end of the stylus above the wax.

"I'm Attinos son of Thonis," the fellow said.

Sostratos asked him to repeat it, then set it down in Greek letters as best he could. "The real register is on papyrus, which isn't so easy to alter without leaving a trace," he said, holding the stylus with the blunt end, the end that rubbed out, uppermost to show what he meant. "I'll enter all of you properly as soon as I can, but I have what I need for now."

"Go on in. Meet our Rhodians—they've pretty much taken over the place since we got here," Menedemos told the new men. "They'll be glad to see you. Nobody wants to start a trip with empty benches."

In went the rowers. The inn had its own wineshop; Menedemos hoped no brawls would start right away. When things inside the place stayed quiet, he breathed easier. To Sostratos, he said, "They're warm bodies, anyhow, and at least they know what to do with an oar."

"My dear, I wasn't complaining—not a bit of it," his cousin answered. "I'm more impressed than I can tell you. I didn't think you'd be able to fother our leak so fast."

"Thank you!" Menedemos said, and then, "Thank you very much." Sostratos was more in the habit of calling him a thickskull than of singing his praises. That thought led to another: "Do you know what the Ptolemaios said about you while he was, ah, hiring the *Aphrodite*?"

"No. What?" Sostratos asked. Menedemos told him, imitating the lord of Egypt's gruff voice and manner as best he could. Sostratos dug his toes into the dirt in embarrassed pleasure, like a girl hearing someone say she's pretty for the first time. "Did he really say that? It won't be easy to live up to."

"Let's see if we can get back to Rhodes in one piece, and without Demetrios only half a bowshot behind us. If we manage that, you can worry about everything else later," Menedemos said.

"You say the sweetest things," Sostratos murmured. Menedemos laughed and stood on tiptoe to kiss his cousin's cheek. Yes, when you laughed you could pretend for a little while that the things you laughed about didn't really matter, and that they had no chance at all of happening.

Sostratos peered over the *Aphrodite's* rail, down into the muddy, filthy water of Ptolemaios' Harbor. The akatos had even less freeboard than usual; Ptolemaios' workers had filled it fuller with weapons than he and Menedemos did with merchandise.

They had another new rower, as one more man who'd come down from Rhodes decided at the last minute to stay in Alexandria instead of going home again. Like a couple of the other new fellows, Oku-menes was a Cretan. He took the akatos' oars so much for granted, Sostratos wondered if he'd rowed before in a piratical pentekonter. The way his eyes darted now here, now there also suggested he was looking for the chance to lift something.

Out at the opening in the moles that separated Ptolemaios' harbor from the larger Great Harbor, the lord of Egypt's fours and fives were going out one by one. The *Aphrodite* waited with the other ships that carried men and beasts and supplies. The war galleys—there had to be well over a hundred of them—were the teeth and claws of the fleet, the rest of the ships just the tail. Like any other tail, they came last.

People on the moles cheered and waved squares of colored cloth as the war galleys rowed past them. They made a brave show, one the men in the fours and fives would forget as soon as they got out of sight.

The oared transports followed the warships out of Ptolemaios' harbor. Sostratos took his place at the *Aphrodite*'s bow. Menedemos clasped the steering oars at the stern. Diokles stood in front of him on the stern platform, hammer and bronze triangle ready to give the rowers their rhythm. For the exit, every oar was manned. They wouldn't keep that up once they got out on the Inner Sea. Several days of it would leave the rowers on the fours and fives worn and useless in battle.

When the oars on the freight-haulers just ahead of the akatos began churning the water to foam, Menedemos dipped his head to Diokles. "Come on, boys!" the keleustes said. "We may be little, but by the gods we'll show 'em what we can do!" He smote the triangle with the hammer, at the same time calling, "*Rhyppapai!*" Another clang. Another "*Rhyppapai!*" Clang! "*Rhyppapai!*"

The *Aphrodite*'s oars dug into the dirty water, a little more rag-gedly than Sostratos would have liked. The rowers grunted and swore. They hadn't worked for quite a while; they hadn't got hardened by go-ing from one polis to another the way they did on most trading runs.

Slowly, slowly, the akatos began to move. The bigger galleys in the fleet's supply tail weren't setting the sea on fire with their speed, either; the *Aphrodite* had no trouble keeping up. She might have left Ptolemaios' harbor last of all, but Sostratos thought she did so in some style.

By the time she glided out through the opening between the moles, most of Ptolemaios' cheering claque had given up and gone home. War galleys were exciting, ships laden with sheep or horses or catapult stones much less so. But one of the men still standing there pointed at the *Aphrodite* not just with his chin but with his index finger and shouted, "Look at the toy boat with all the big ones!"

Sostratos wasn't about the let anyone sneer at his ship that way. He leaned out over the rail and stared at the man on the mole, widening his eyes as much as he could. As someone who did his best to stay rational, he—mostly—thought the evil eye was so much nonsense. But he knew other people (foolish people, as far as he was concerned) felt otherwise. If this fellow did ….

Sure enough, the Alexandrian noticed his gaze and flinched away from it as he would have from a clenched fist. He thrust out his own fist at Sostratos, thumb thrusting forth between index and middle fingers: a protective gesture. Sostratos just kept on staring. "Don't you cast a spell on me! Don't you dare!" the man cried shrilly. "By the gods, I'll murder you if you do!"

Out into the Great Harbor glided the *Aphrodite*. Sostratos kept staring till he got too far from the man on the mole to see the point anymore. Then he walked back to the stern platform. As he passed Attinos, the Egyptian rower asked, "You really have the fornicating evil eye?"

"If you think I do, maybe I do," Sostratos answered, and paused to see what Attinos made of that.

He might be a barbarian who flavored his Greek with obscenities the way a rich man's cook flavored his cheese casseroles with pepper, but no one would ever call him a fool. With a sly little chuckle, he said, "Like that, huh?" He kept the stroke perfectly while he talked; he'd done enough rowing so he didn't need to think about it.

"Just like that, my dear," Sostratos answered, liking him very much in the moment.

"You had the shit-talking lardhead so scared, he futtering near fell in the water," Attinos said, and laughed some more.

"I was hoping he would, but it didn't quite happen." Sostratos went on back to the stern.

"What were you talking about with the new fellow?" Menedemos asked when Sostratos took his place next to Diokles. He explained. "Oh, is *that* what you were up to?" his cousin said. "I saw you looking at the fellow and I saw him hopping around as though he'd just come out of a brothel full of fleas, but I didn't know what was going on. *Euge!* You gave him something to remember you by."

"If you really did have the evil eye, you should've aimed it at the *Demetrios*," Diokles said.

"Or at some of the abandoned rogues who've cheated us or made us do things that might turn out bad for the polis." Menedemos named no names, but looked ahead toward Ptolemaios' gaudily ornamented flagship. By his expression, he wouldn't have minded owning the evil eye himself at that moment.

More Alexandrians stood on the low, sandy island connected to the mainland by the mole called the Heptastadion: it was seven stadia long. They also cheered the departing war galleys. Because they were farther away, their cries had the strange, attenuated quality voices over water often took on.

Sostratos didn't think he'd ever left a harbor to applause before. Of course, Rhodes remained a free and independent polis. It had no ruler who would order people to cheer him; it had no people who cared to curry favor with that kind of ruler. If the gods knew mercy, it never would.

If. Still hindmost in Ptolemaios' fleet, the *Aphrodite* centipeded out of the Great Harbor and onto the rougher waters of the Inner Sea.

XI

"HOW ARE YOU DOING?" MENEDEMOS ASKED HIS cousin, trying to sound sympathetic rather than scornful.

"Not ... too bad." Sostratos' greenish pallor gave his words the lie. He'd leaned over the rail and emptied himself a couple of times since the *Aphrodite* left Alexandria.

"You had an easier time on the trip down to Egypt," Menedemos said. "You kept everything down then."

"I know," Sostratos said dolefully. "Don't remind me. The waves were mostly with us when we sailed south, Now they're hitting us bow-on. The motion's different, and so ...."

Menedemos thought he'd feed the fish again, but he didn't quite. Before too long, Sostratos would be all right again. But he'd been on land long enough to lose his sea legs, and his sea stomach. He wasn't wrong; traveling against the waves instead of with them did change the way the akatos pitched. To Menedemos, though, the difference was only a difference, not a disaster.

At the moment, he had every other oar manned. Putting a rower on them all was for show, as when leaving the harbor at Alexandria, or for an emergency. Ptolemaios' skippers had also eased back as soon as they got out of sight of the Alexandrians. The *Aphrodite* had no trouble keeping up with the lord of Egypt's fleet, even at the relatively slow stroke Diokles was beating out.

Up ahead, in the war galleys, the rowers would be thanking their oarmasters for whatever respite they could get. When they fought Demetrios' fleet, they'd need every bit of strength and energy they could find. Menedemos hoped—he prayed, in fact—the men on the akatos' oars wouldn't need to worry about battle.

The sun sank toward the western horizon. Italy and Sicily and Carthage lay in that direction. Rhodes was farther west than Cyprus, too, though not nearly *that* far. Menedemos wondered whether the *Aphrodite* could slip away from the fleet under cover of darkness and make for home instead of Cyprus.

Regretfully, he decided that was a bad idea. He didn't want to turn Ptolemaios into a deadly enemy by deserting. That could have consequences for years to come, if not for generations. It would hurt the family firm, and might hurt the polis, too.

Of course, if one of Demetrios' sailors happened to recognize the *Aphrodite* …. Menedemos didn't want to make deadly foes of the young warlord and his fearsome father, either.

"We're cursed no matter what we do," he muttered.

"What's that?" Sostratos asked. Menedemos explained. His cousin dipped his head. "All we can do is all we can do, and hope everything comes out well for us."

"I know. And I hate having to depend on hope. It's what came out of Pandora's box last, remember. There's a reason for that, too."

Menedemos waited for Sostratos to mock the myth as, well, nothing but a myth. Sostratos often enjoyed poking at old beliefs for the fun of poking. So it seemed to Menedemos, anyhow. But his cousin just came back to where he stood and set a hand on his shoulder for a moment. "Believe me, my dear, I know the feeling," he said quietly.

As light drained from the sky, sailors in Ptolemaios' ships set burning torches in iron sconces mounted on their sternposts. That let the vessels behind follow those ahead more easily than they might have, especially when the early hours of the night would be moonless.

Aphrodite's wandering star blazed low in the west. That was always the brightest star in the sky. *Like the love the goddess stands for*, Menedemos thought. He wondered how Baukis fared and, again, whether she'd had her baby—his baby?—yet. She might be in labor right now, groaning and shrieking up in the women's quarters, attended by the midwife and a house slave or two. Better, he supposed, to be far away than to have to listen to that for however long it went on.

The sky darkened with his mood. High in the south, Zeus' wandering star appeared soon after Aphrodite's. Ares', about halfway between Zeus' and Aphrodite's, took longer to come out. It could rival Zeus', but shone far fainter at the moment. So did Kronos', which hung in the southeast.

Even though Ptolemaios' ships had their stern lights and replaced the torches as needed, they also slowed to less than half speed as night took over. Ptolemaios sensibly rested his rowers as he could. Diokles also pulled more men off the *Aphrodite's* oars.

"When will you want me to take over for you?" Sostratos asked.

"The moon should rise in an hour or so. That will do," Menedemos said. "Keep the steering oars till it gets close to due south, then wake me. We'll give one of the older, more sensible rowers the hammer and triangle then, too. Diokles is also flesh and blood, even if he tries to make out that he isn't."

"I'm doing fine, skipper—bugger me blind if I'm not," the keleustes said.

"So am I ... right now," Menedemos said. "But we'll all wear down to nubs if we don't get some rest. It'll be a lazy stroke through the night, and Sostratos can keep the rower at the right pace if he gets ahead of himself."

"I suppose so." Diokles didn't sound as if he believed it. He truly trusted no man's skill and knowledge but his own. Since he came closer with Sostratos than with most people, though, he subsided with no more than a low-voiced grumble in the back of his throat.

Up came the moon out of the sea, a fat gold daric up there in the heavens, its eastern edge gnawed away: it was a couple of days past full. "Go on, my dear. Find somewhere to curl up," Sostratos said. "Nothing's likely to happen while you sleep."

"That doesn't mean it won't." Menedemos felt at least as leery about letting someone else do his job for him as Diokles did. And anyone who made his living by going to sea put no faith in wind and wave.

Still, only Talos the bronze man could go on and on without sleep or food. Menedemos stepped back from the steering oars and let his cousin take his place. Diokles woke a rower named Nikagoras, who'd made several voyages in the *Aphrodite* and hadn't shown himself to be conspicuously stupid. When the keleustes explained what he needed, Nikagoras dipped his head and said, "I'll take care of it."

Diokles sat at the bench Nikagoras had vacated to go aft. As an ex-rower, he was used to leaning against the rail and falling asleep when at sea. He did it again tonight. Menedemos lay down abaft of the steering oars, where the platform narrowed toward the sternpost. He'd slept soft in Ptolemaios' palace, but he could sleep rough, too. Closing his eyes, he proved it.

Next thing he knew, someone's hand was on his shoulder. His eyes snapped open. His right hand darted for the knife on his belt. He found he had no belt, nor any other clothing. He remembered where he was, and who had likely shaken him awake. Sure enough, there stood Sostratos in the bright moonlight. Diokles held the steering oars for the moment, so the *Aphrodite* ran steady.

"Hail," Menedemos said, and yawned. Around the yawn, he continued, "How do we fare?"

"We're still with the Ptolemaios' fleet." Sostratos didn't sound altogether happy about that, either. He went on, "Nikagoras made a good keleustes, good enough so I gave him three oboloi for duty above his station."

"*Euge!*" Menedemos said, and then raised his voice so Diokles could hear: "I guess that will let us put the old stallion here out to pasture. He's pretty long in the tooth these days."

"Old stallion? Long in the tooth? By the gods, this old stallion'll graze on your grave, and shit on it, too," Diokles retorted. Then he laughed, which relieved Menedemos. He wanted to be sure the keleustes knew he was joking.

He took the steering oars from Diokles, who in turn reclaimed the keleustes' tools from Nikagoras. The rower went up to his bench. Menedemos looked back over his right shoulder. The moon showed Sostratos had given him a little more sleep than he'd asked for.

"Grab some rest, my dear," he told his cousin. "I've got the ship for now." His mouth twisted, though in the moonlight Sostratos might not be able to see that. "I don't exactly know what I'll do with her, but I've got her."

Sostratos' stomach troubled him all the way north from Alexandria. He didn't heave after the first day at sea, but often felt queasy. Hard bread and salted sprats and olives weren't the kind of fare he would have recommended to someone with sour guts were he playing physician, but they and rough red wine were what the *Aphrodite* carried. He grabbed a flying fish that landed in the akatos and grilled it over the little brazier on the bow platform. It tasted better than anything else he ate on the journey to Cyprus, but it was a morsel, not a meal.

Always having Ptolemaios' fleet on the northern horizon made this voyage different from the one between Rhodes and Alexandria. Then the *Aphrodite*, solitary in the middle of the Inner Sea, might have been the only ship, the only man-made object, in all the world. Sostratos had rather liked that, though it made some of the rowers anxious. Now they could have no doubt that the rest of the world was very much with them.

But, while part of the world was there, news from outside the fleet wasn't. Sostratos wondered what Ptolemaios would do if Demetrios held all of Cyprus when this expedition arrived. Up ahead in his gaudy galley, the lord of Egypt was bound to be wondering the same thing. One could say a great many things about Ptolemaios, but he was nothing if not forethoughtful. The way he'd seized and held Egypt showed that.

Fluffy clouds glided across the sky from north to south. Every so often, one of them would pass in front of the sun and give the men on the *Aphrodite* a brief respite from its glare. But then the shadow would pass on. If Sostratos looked astern instead of ahead, he could watch it darken a receding stretch of ocean behind the akatos.

"Cousin!" Menedemos called from his place at the steering oars. "Come back here, will you?"

"Of course! Do you want me to spell you for a while?" Sostratos said.

"No, not yet." Menedemos tossed his head. "We need to talk, though."

Sostratos made his way back to the stern platform. About half the oars were in the water. The other rowers dozed or rested or played knucklebones on the benches. Up the three oaken steps Sostratos went. "What's bothering you?" he asked.

"What do we do if things go wrong off Cyprus?" Menedemos said, and then, a heartbeat later, "Why are you laughing?"

"Because I was thinking about the same thing just a moment ago, that's why," Sostratos said.

"Oh, you were, were you? Well, what were you thinking? I want to know—you're good at it."

"What if I am? That and a few oboloi will get me enough sardines for a decent opson."

"If the Ptolemaios thinks well of your wits, my dear, you'd best not play them down yourself," Menedemos said. "So what brave thoughts did Athena goddess of wisdom send you?"

Sostratos didn't think his wisdom, what there was of it, came from Athena. He thought it came from Athens, where he'd studied till his family called him back to Rhodes. But no point talking about that. "My thoughts aren't brave. I was wondering more how we'd get away," he said.

"I wonder why!" Menedemos took his right hand off the steering oar for a moment to wave at the akatos and then at Ptolemaios' much bigger ships ahead. The *Aphrodite* had ruined a trireme once. Ptolemaios' ships, and Demetrios', too, dwarfed even triremes by comparison.

"If we do have to run for it, chucking all the arrows and bolts and whatnot we're carrying into the sea will lighten the ship a good deal and help us go faster," Sostratos said.

"I know it will, but I don't want to do it unless I really have to," Menedemos said.

"Really?" One of Sostratos' eyebrows lifted. "Why not?"

"Because as things are, if we have to run we'll bring Rhodes a shipload of arms the polis can use against Demetrios, that's why." Menedemos sounded as bleak as Sostratos had ever heard him.

He also made more sense than Sostratos wished he did. "Do you truly think it will come to that?" he asked.

"*Malista.* Don't you?" Menedemos returned. "Sooner or later—probably sooner—we'll have to fight. I hope we can do it. We've lived at peace for a long time. We've forgotten what war is all about. In the gymnasion, one of those Cretan soldiers of fortune would have carved gobbets off me as if I were a sacrificial sheep with its throat cut. Demetrios has thousands of men like that—tens of thousands, for all I know. If they get over the wall and into the city ...." He spat into the bosom of his chiton to turn aside the evil omen.

That was nothing but superstition. The rational part of Sostratos' mind insisted as much. He imitated the gesture anyhow. *It may not help, but it can't hurt*, he told himself. Even as he did, he knew he was rationalizing, not rational.

He said, "If we go under, that's pretty much the end of the free and independent polis in Hellas. A few left in Italy and Sicily, but Italy and Sicily are the back of beyond." He didn't even notice his own condescension, though it would have infuriated Italiote Hellenes.

"Of course they are," Menedemos agreed. He waved at the fleet again, and then more broadly to take in Cyprus. "If things go wrong .... If things go wrong, we flee if we can and fight if we have to. I keep trying to make firmer plans, but I can't. I hoped you could."

"It would be nice, wouldn't it?" Sostratos said, that being the smoothest way of admitting he didn't know what to do next, either. He continued, "I have a different question for you, though."

"What is it? I'd be glad for anything that takes my mind off the main worry for a little while."

"As you've watched our course by day and especially by night, doesn't it seem to you that we're bearing a bit too far west of north to put in at Salamis?"

Before Menedemos could answer, Diokles spoke up: "It does to me. I was wondering if I was the only one who noticed, and I was wondering whether I was losing my wits, too."

Menedemos eyed the sun. He eyed the ships ahead of the *Aphrodite*. Rubbing his chin, he said, "Harder to gauge exactly by day than by night, but it seems to me you aren't wrong. What do you want to do? Hustle up to the Ptolemaios' galley and tell him his admirals and navigators don't know what the daimon they're doing?"

"He's a general, not an admiral. As far as I know, he did all his fighting for Alexander on land, not at sea. If the men who should know *are* making a mistake, he won't recognize it himself," Sostratos said.

"He'd better not be making for Rhodes," Diokles growled, but he tossed his head a moment later. "We haven't swung *that* far west. I don't reckon we have, anyway. But I'll be watching the course and the stars tonight—you'd best believe I will."

"So will I," Menedemos said. "But even if we think they're going astray, we can't be sure. They may have a plan of their own. And it's not as if we can put down cords and measure angles, the way they do when they lay out a new street. All we've got are—" He opened and closed his eyes three or four times.

"I know. Once you get out of sight of land, navigation isn't much better than a guess and a prayer," Sostratos said.

"Too right, it isn't!" his cousin said with feeling. "Let me see a stretch of coast and I'll tell you where we are. One stretch of ocean, though, looks too much like another."

"If we could fly like Daidalos, we could glide high above the ships and see the coast from a long way away," Sostratos said.

"Or have our wings come undone and crash into the sea like Ikaros," Menedemos said. "The way things are going on this voyage ....We have all the silver, but what good does it do us if we can't bring it home? I told Ptolemaios the same. He said my other choice was getting the *Aphrodite* stolen out from under me, so here we are."

"Here we are," Sostratos echoed mournfully. The leather sacks full of coins under the stern platform didn't reassure him, either.

Menedemos knew the fleet was nearing land before any came up over the horizon. Gulls and terns and pelicans lived on land and went out to sea to get food, the way fishermen did. Over the waters halfway between Alexandria and Cyprus, the skies were almost bare of them; he'd noticed the same thing sailing south. When they returned, he knew Cyprus was drawing nigh. Floating branches and, once, a plank told the same story.

He wished the mast were up. He would have sent a small, skinny sailor up to the top to see what he could see: not Daidalos' wings, but as much as he could do. Then he shrugged, standing there at the steering oars. Sostratos was back on the stern platform, and sent him a quizzical look. Menedemos ignored it. Unless he meant to skedaddle, spying land sooner wouldn't matter anyway.

The grin that spread over his face caught him by surprise. "Skedaddle!" he exclaimed.

"What's that?" his cousin asked.

"Skedaddle," Menedemos repeated happily. The look Sostratos gave him this time suggested that the knots in his rigging had come undone. He said the word again, relishing the silly sound: "Skedaddle."

"Skedaddle." By the way Sostratos said it, it wasn't, or shouldn't have been, a Greek word at all. "What *are* you babbling about, my dear?"

"I'm not babbling at all," Menedemos replied with dignity. "It's the opening scene in Aristophanes' *Knights*. Don't you know it?"

Sostratos tossed his head. "If I did, I wouldn't be wondering whether you've gone out of your mind. Well, I might not be, anyway."

Taking no notice of him, Menedemos went on, "Nikias and Demosthenes—you know, the Athenian generals—"

"I didn't think you meant Demosthenes the orator," Sostratos broke in. "Aristophanes was dead long before he came along."

"True. Anyway, they're complaining that Kleon's lies have confused the Athenian people and led them astray, and so they want to get away."

"Athens would have been better off if Nikias *had* got away before he led the expedition to Sicily," Sostratos said.

"Yes, yes. But you wanted to know what I was talking about," Menedemos said. "See, Nikias tells Demosthenes to say 'Daddle.' So Demosthenes goes ...."

" 'Daddle.' " Yes, Sostratos still sounded like someone humoring a maniac.

"Splendid, O best one!" Menedemos made as if to applaud without quite lifting his hands from the steering oars. "Then Nikias says that Demosthenes should say 'Let's ske.' And Demosthenes says ...."

" 'Let's ske,' " Sostratos repeated obediently. Then he tossed his head. "So what?"

"Say them over and over again, slowly at first but then quicker, as if you're playing with yourself in bed," Menedemos said, adding, "I'm quoting the playwright there, too."

"You would be," his cousin muttered, but he continued, "Dad-dle …. Let's ske. Daddle—let's ske. Daddle. Let's ske daddle! Oh! I see where this is going!"

"That's right—straight over the hill," Menedemos agreed.

"And this came into your mind, such as it is, just how?" Sostratos asked.

"About the way you'd expect. I was thinking some more about what we might do when we got to Cyprus," Menedemos said.

"From what you said before, you didn't plan on skedaddling." Sostratos rolled his eyes. "That word again!"

"If we make landfall at Paphos, though, or somewhere else near the western end of the island, we're a lot closer to Rhodes than we would be at Salamis," Menedemos said.

"Still dangerous," Sostratos said. "We've been over this ground. If we run, we make Ptolemaios angry at us—and at Rhodes. Would he sit on his hands if Demetrios and Antigonos attack the polis after we do that?"

Menedemos gnawed on the inside of his lower lip, the way he did when he worried about how Baukis was doing. "I don't *think* he would," he said slowly. "With men like him, reasons of state count for more than grudges."

"You hope they do," Sostratos returned. Menedemos opened his mouth, then closed it again. He had no good answer for that. His cousin, an uncommonly sensible man, made all too much sense here.

Then he stopped worrying about it, because sailors from Ptole-maios' ships ahead of the *Aphrodite* started shouting "Land ho!" and pointing northward. Menedemos peered ahead. Was that a smudge on the northern horizon? Maybe it was, but he couldn't yet make out what kind of smudge it was.

"Take the steering oars, my dear," he told Sostratos. "I'm going up to the bow to get the best look I can."

Once he got a decent look at the shoreline ahead, he would know where the fleet was. He'd gone all around Cyprus on one trad-ing journey or another. Landscapes he'd seen once, he remembered. He carried much of the coastline of the eastern regions of the Inner Sea around inside his head, as if on papyrus book-rolls. Most skip-pers he knew had their own inner libraries like that. Recognizing a stretch of coast from a bare glimpse was a tool of his trade, as an oven was for a baker.

For a while, he called down Aristophanean curses on the big, awkward galleys ahead of the *Aphrodite*. Their bulk kept him from viewing the coastline as clearly as he wanted to. But, little by little as land drew closer, he saw what he needed to see.

He hurried back to the stern platform. As he reclaimed the steering oars from Sostratos, he said, "You're a better navigator than the buffoons the Ptolemaios uses. We're a little east of Paphos, a long way west from Salamis."

"Yes, that's about where I put us, too," his cousin replied, and Menedemos realized, perhaps later than he should have, that skippers weren't the only ones who knew their way along the coast. His eyes slid to Diokles. The keleustes had seen more coastline than he had. Did he remember it the same way? By how knowingly he dipped his head, that seemed certain.

Menedemos gave his attention back to Sostratos. "All right. You're Ptolemaios. We wind up here, not off Salamis. What do we do now?"

"It depends," Sostratos said judiciously. "Did we come to Paphos because the navigators are bad or because they're good? If we go into the harbor for rest and refit, that would be good. If Demetrios has moved west and put a garrison in the town …." He didn't go on, or need to.

"I didn't even think about skullduggery like that. See? I bring you along for a reason," Menedemos said, which made his cousin stick out his tongue at him. "From what I'd heard, I just assumed Demetrios was staying in the east to finish Salamis off."

"If he landed near Karpaseia, he may not have bothered with the cities down here, that's true. We'll find out soon enough." Sostratos pointed north, at the rest of the fleet. "Look! They're swinging west, towards Paphos. Either they're going to fight for it or they think they'll get a friendly welcome. I wonder which."

"You said it. We'll find out soon enough," Menedemos answered.

New Paphos, with its harbor, was a much more recent foundation even than Rhodes. King Nikokles had moved most of the town, though not its temples, from its older inland site, over the last few years of his reign. The Paphians did nothing to keep Ptolemaios' fleet from filling the harbor—filling it to overflowing, in fact.

Despite their acquiescence, Sostratos said, "I hope the Ptolemaios keeps a tight lookout on the town."

"That might be smart, yes," Menedemos replied. King Nikokles had been Ptolemaios' ally ... till he started intriguing with Antigonos. When Ptolemaios found out about that, two of his henchmen made Nikokles kill himself. His whole family followed suit, in spectacularly horrid style. How the Paphians felt about that ... would be something the lord of Egypt needed to wonder about.

Sostratos knew the story. Five or six years before, it had been on everyone's lips. He turned out to know it better than his cousin did, in fact, for when he went on, "Yes, I wonder just how much hatred Kallikrates and Argaios sowed here when—" he found he had to stop. Menedemos' eyes were almost bugging out of his head.

"Wait! Who?" he said.

"Kallikrates and Argaios. You know, the two Macedonians who took care of Nikokles."

"Oh, by the gods!" His cousin clapped a hand to his forehead. "By the gods! I'd forgotten their names. I met the two of them in the palace, when Ptolemaios commandeered this ship. I just took them for old drinking buddies of his, not, not ...."

"His hired murderers?" Sostratos suggested.

"Something like that, yes." Menedemos looked and sounded shaken to the core.

It might have been just as well that four men chose that moment to row a boat toward the akatos. "Ahoy, the *Aphrodite!*" called a red-caped officer at the bow.

Menedemos pulled himself together with commendable speed. "I'm the skipper," he said. "What do you need?"

"Captains' conference aboard the Ptolemaios' ship at the end of the first hour tomorrow morning," the man said. "You and your toikharkhos are bidden to attend."

"Well!" Sostratos exclaimed in glad surprise. That the invitation included him had to mean it came straight from Ptolemaios. Giving the would-be historian a chance to sit in on history in the raw, was he?

Meanwhile, Menedemos said, "Tell him we'll be there." The officer waved in reply. As the boat swung back toward Ptolemaios' galley, Sostratos' cousin elbowed him in the ribs and murmured, "Teacher's pet!"

"Ah, to the crows with you," Sostratos answered. Menedemos laughed—shakily, but he did. Then Sostratos added, "I hope our boat doesn't leak."

"That would be good," Menedemos said. "We'll find out, I expect."

Lots of boats were in the water an hour after sunrise the next day. Men aboard several had to bail with dried gourds on sticks or with long-handled pots. Rather to Sostratos' surprise, the planking on the *Aphrodite*'s little rowboat seemed sound.

He and Menedemos both wore their better chitons. Past that, they didn't—they couldn't—dress up for the occasion. Even the captains from the larger transports seemed far more glorious than they did. As for the exalted commanders of Ptolemaios' war galleys ….

As they neared Ptolemaios' five, Sostratos said, "I don't think I'd want my flagship all tricked out in scarlet and gold like this. Wouldn't every enemy galley try to sink it?"

"When you're a warlord, you have to let people know you're a warlord. Otherwise, why would they take orders from you?" Menedemos said. Sostratos grunted thoughtfully; the answer was more to the point than he'd looked for.

Being a five, with three decks of rowers, the flagship had more freeboard than the *Aphrodite*. Sostratos and Menedemos had just stepped over the rail and down into the rowboat. They couldn't get up again the same way here. But Ptolemaios' men had thoughtfully hung nets from the sides of the ship. Those made coming aboard easy enough.

A long fighting platform ran between the rowers' benches, a little higher than the heads of the rowers on the upper, or thranite, row would have been. A bolt-throwing catapult was mounted near the bow. Normally, the platform would have been full of fighting men: some archers, others armed with spear and sword to board and seize enemy vessels.

Normally, but not this morning. Ptolemaios' skippers took their place today. Sostratos' height let him glimpse the ruler of Egypt himself. He was talking with a couple of men who, if they weren't admirals, could have played them on the stage even without masks.

Ptolemaios kept looking toward the sun every so often. After a bit, he must have decided that the first hour had indeed ended, for he raised his voice to a roar that would have carried far across any of the many battlefields he'd fought on: "Listen to me, O best ones! Listen, curse it! Anyone who hasn't shown up yet, a pestilence take him! He can get the word from one of you, that's all."

Even as he spoke, an embarrassed-looking skipper scrambled up the nets and aboard the flagship. The officers who'd come in good time laughed at the newcomer.

"*So* good of you to join us, Euphemides," Ptolemaios growled. He *would* be one to recognize the tardy captain. After a moment to let Euphemides hang his head in shame, Ptolemaios went on, "All right, we're on Cyprus, even if we're a good ways west of Salamis. Last night, I sent horsemen east to let Menelaos know help is on the way."

Sostratos wondered whether Ptolemaios' messengers would be able to get through the siege lines around Salamis, but that wasn't his worry. Meanwhile, Ptolemaios went on, "We'll stay here for a few days to see how many other ships come in from the Cypriot cities the enemy doesn't hold. Then we'll head east to deal with the Cyclops' mangy puppy. We'll give him what he deserves, we'll take back the whole island and tighten things up here, and we'll sail home to Alexandria. Any questions?"

Several skippers said "*Euge!*" at the same time—almost as a chorus, in fact. No one seemed to want to ask the lord of Egypt anything. Almost before Sostratos realized he'd done it, he stuck a hand in the air. Menedemos contrived to step on his toes, but too late: Ptolemaios had already seen him.

"Who's that?" Alexander's marshal rumbled. "Stand aside, you men, so I can see who I'm talking to."

There wasn't much room on the fighting platform for the officers to stand aside, but they did their best. More than a few of them stared at Sostratos as if sure he'd lost his wits. His very plain tunic might also have inclined them to that view.

Ptolemaios continued, "Go on, tall fellow. Ask away." A moment later, on a falling note, he added, "Oh, it's you, son of Lysistratos. Well, what do you want to know?"

"Thank you, sir. I just wondered, are we wise to linger in Paphos?" Sostratos said. "If you can send riders to Menelaos, men who don't like you so well can send them to Demetrios, too."

"We won't catch him by surprise any which way. He'll know or guess we're coming, and he'll have some of his piratical friends scouting for him," Ptolemaios said. "Fours and fives can't outrun those cursed pentenkonters, however much I wish they could."

Trihemioliai can, Sostratos thought. But Egypt's navy was built for power, not speed. Ptolemaios didn't worry about pirates nearly so much as Rhodes did.

The lord of Egypt hadn't finished yet, either. "If any ships do come in, I'll be glad to have them, too. From what I've heard, Demetrios' fleet is bigger than mine, though he'll need to leave some of it behind to try to keep my brother's galleys shut up in Salamis' harbor." He set his hands on his hips. "Are you answered?" Every line of his body warned, *You'd better be!*

"Yes, sir," Sostratos said, and not another word. He might have replied differently had Ptolemaios asked him whether he was satisfied.

"Did you really think you'd get him to change his mind?" Menedemos asked when they were safely off the flagship and in the rowboat on the way back to the *Aphrodite.*

"Did I think so? No. But it wasn't impossible, not quite, so I tried," Sostratos said.

"And now all his skippers think you're daft," his cousin observed.

"As if I care! They've forgotten what dealing with free Hellenes is like. High time they got reminded," Sostratos said. Laughing softly, Menedemos clapped him on the back.

XII

PTOLEMAIOS LINGERED AT PAPHOS UNTIL THE moon was a skinny nail-paring of a crescent, rising just before the sun came up. A few ships dribbled in from nearby poleis, but only a few. Menedemos found himself agreeing with Sostratos: the boost Ptolemaios' forces got wasn't worth the delay in going off to fight Demetrios.

"Maybe you should hop into the boat again, head over to the flagship, and talk some sense into him," he told his cousin.

Sostratos looked at him. "I didn't know you wanted me dead so badly."

"He wouldn't kill you. He'd just curse you up one side and down the other for wasting his time," Menedemos said. "You might hear some things even Diokles doesn't know."

The keleustes was gnawing on a chunk of hard-baked bread. He looked up long enough to say, "To the crows with you, skipper," and then went back to eating.

"When the Ptolemaios really got rolling, he'd probably fall back into Macedonian, so I wouldn't understand him anyway," Sostratos said.

"There is that," Menedemos allowed. "When he and his cronies talked to each other, I couldn't follow more than maybe one word in five."

Not long after sunrise, a boat came out to the akatos. It was the first time the Rhodian ship had been so honored since the summons to the captains' conference. This boat didn't draw any too near, as if afraid the *Aphrodite* carried a dangerous contagious disease. *We do, too*, Menedemos thought. *Sostratos named it—freedom.*

From a safe distance, the officer in the rowboat called, "Ahoy, the trading galley! Do you hear me?"

"I'm the captain. I hear you," Menedemos said. "What's the word?"

"We move east at noon," the man replied. "Make sure you're ready to accompany us."

Menedemos waved to him. "We'll be along," he said. Ptolemaios' officer grudgingly dipped his head, then spoke to the men at the oars. They backed water, turned around, and rowed away.

Quietly, Sostratos said, "What was that Aristophanes you were spouting? Daddle—Let's ske—Daddle—Let's ske—"

"Much as I'd love to, we can't right now," Menedemos said with real regret. "Sticking with the fleet is best for Rhodes right now. Antigonos and Demetrios already have plenty of reasons to want to grab the polis. I don't dare give the Ptolemaios a new one to leave us stranded. If you think he doesn't have an eye on the *Aphrodite*, you're daft."

"I understand that," Sostratos said. "But there's a big sea-fight coming. If Ptolemaios wins, *euge!* for him. If he loses, we're liable to get sunk. We're liable to get killed. If we live, we're liable to get enslaved."

"If you're going to whine about every little thing …" Menedemos said. His cousin stared at him, then burst out laughing. Menedemos laughed, too. So did Diokles, who stood on the stern platform with them. Something about the oarmaster's face, though, said he was laughing to keep from giving way to despair. Since Menedemos felt the same way, he didn't remark on it.

Horns blared across the harbor, ordering the fleet into motion at the appointed hour. "Noon," Sostratos grumbled. "Why couldn't he have picked a cooler time of day to set out? What does he think he is, a genuine Egyptian or something?"

"Not likely," Menedemos replied. "As far as I can tell, he speaks as much Egyptian as we do, and we don't speak any."

Ptolemaios' warships left the harbor before the transports and freighters, and formed up in a protective arc ahead of them: the same formation the fleet had used coming north from Alexandria. Now, though, the ships raised their masts and spread their broad sails slantwise to take advantage of the wind. They couldn't use it when it was dead against them, but took advantage of it when it blew at the quarter.

"Our rowers will be fresher this way," Sostratos observed.

"So they will," Menedemos answered. "Say, did you notice the catapults all the fours and fives carry? Nothing like getting a bolt through the brisket from a couple of stadia away!"

"Back when the catapult was newer—it would have been around the time the Alexander was born, I think—someone took a bolt to Sparta. King Arkhidamos looked at it and said, 'O Herakles! The valor of man is extinguished!'" Sostratos said.

"Did he? He wasn't so far wrong," Menedemos said. "If the river keeps flowing the way it runs now, one of these days we'll have the automata Homer says Hephaistos made doing our fighting for us, and the only way anybody will ever win a battle is if something goes wrong with one of them."

"Only half a century since Alexander was born," his cousin said in musing tones. "He would have been younger than Ptolemaios— much younger than Antigonos. He became king of Macedonia about the time *we* were born. The Persian Empire was still going strong. A few changes since."

"Just a few," Menedemos agreed. "When we were boys, every time a ship came in to Rhodes it would bring news that he'd conquered some other place a daimon of a long way away. I'd never heard of half of them before."

"Neither had I." Sostratos sounded angry at his own long-ago ignorance. He hated not knowing things; Menedemos had known that as long as he'd known him. His cousin went on, "Hearing all those strange names may have been what made me want to understand how the pieces of the world fit together, one next to another and through time."

"It made me want to go out and see some of those places," Menedemos said. "And I have seen ... well, some of them, anyhow. I don't know that I'll ever get to Persia or India."

"I suppose not," Sostratos said. "There are Hellenes in those parts now, though. Who would have dreamt of that fifty years ago?"

"Nobody. Not a soul," Menedemos said, and then, loudly, to the sailors tending the lines, "Shorten the sail by a brail's worth. We'll ram one of the scows ahead of us if we don't slow down." He hoped his voice carried over the water to the skippers commanding Ptolemaios' transports. They weren't really scows, but also weren't as sleek in the water as the *Aphrodite*.

Nearing Kourion, the fleet swung south to round the islet off Cyprus' southern coast instead of trying to slide through the channel separating it from the mainland. Menedemos dipped his head in approval as the akatos followed. The channel was shallow and treacherously full of ever-shifting sandbars. Better to stay safe. Someone advising Ptolemaios really did know these waters.

Diokles must have had the same thought, for he remarked, "One of these days, that passage is going to silt up and tie the little island to Cyprus for good."

"I'm just glad Demetrios didn't post any scout ships this far west," Sostratos said.

"Didn't post any we know about, anyway," Menedemos said. "Ptolemaios' fours and fives wouldn't chase a pentekonter. He said so himself, remember? That would just wear out the rowers, and they wouldn't catch it."

"For all we know, Demetrios has watchers on the beach, or on the high ground a little ways inland," Diokles added. "We aren't out of sight of land on this leg, so the land isn't out of sight of us. And as soon as somebody spots us, he gets a leg-up onto his horse and gallops off to give Demetrios the news."

Menedemos' laugh was sharp as pepper, sour as vinegar. "I wonder how many horsemen, Demetrios' and Ptolemaios', are galloping across southern Cyprus from west to east right now. Enough to make the chariot races at the Olympic Games seem like nothing next to them, I'd bet."

"They don't have rowing contests at Olympia. They don't have them at any of the great Games, not that I know of," Sostratos said. "But we'll see one of those contests when our fleet finally runs into Demetrios'."

"The winners won't get crowns of laurel leaves and fancy amphorai full of olive oil, either," Menedemos said. "They'll get something better yet—they'll get to stay alive."

Kition, near the eastern end of Cyprus' south coast, was only a couple of hundred stadia from Salamis … if one went by land. Ptolemaios' fleet would have to round Cape Pedalion to reach the besieged city, which would make its journey at least twice as long.

The ships paused a day at Kition to take on water and wine and bread. Ptolemaios didn't call another council, but gossip came out to the galleys along with the supplies. One of the men handing jars of wine up to the *Aphrodite* told Sostratos, " 'Tis said the Ptolemaios hath commanded his brother to send Salamis' sixty warships hith-er forthwith, but that shall not come to pass, for Demetrios hath blocked the channel with his own galleys."

Like most Cypriots, the fellow spoke such old-fashioned Greek that Sostratos had to hide a smile. It wasn't quite like hearing a rhapsode recite Homer for coins at a fair, but it wasn't far removed from that.

However odd the local sounded, his news was important. "We'd be better off with those sixty ships than without them," Sostratos said.

"Yea, verily. But the admiral Antisthenes yet stoppeth the harbor's outlet, as a dose of poppy juice will plug the bowels," the Cypriot replied.

When Sostratos passed on to Menedemos what he'd heard, his cousin dipped his head. "Forsooth," he said. "I've heard the same."

Sostratos grinned. "You must have heard it from a Cypriot, too, by the gods."

"They do talk funny, don't they?" Menedemos smiled, too. "You can follow them, but it's as if the rest of the world has moved on while they stayed the way they were."

"When you do that, the rest of the world will break in whether you like it or not," Sostratos said. "Or how else would Ptolemaios and Demetrios be fighting a thunderous big war here?"

"Too true, too true. All I ever wanted to do here was buy and sell, but that's all I want to do most places," Menedemos said.

"The ones where you don't run across any women who catch your eye, you mean," Sostratos said with a different kind of grin.

Menedemos should have grinned back and returned something bawdy, either from his own wit or from Aristophanes'. Instead, just for a moment, his face went so hard and cold, he looked twenty years older than he really was. In that instant, Sostratos would have believed he was looking at stern Uncle Philodemos, not Philodemos' fun-loving son.

And Menedemos must have realized from Sostratos' expression that he was alarming him, for he did smile then, if crookedly. "I'm sorry, my dear," he murmured, "but I have other things besides loose women on my mind right now."

"Are you well? Let me take your pulse!" Sostratos made as if to grab Menedemos' forearm.

His cousin jerked it away, but he laughed with something that sounded like real amusement. "I'll last till we get back to Rhodes. After that .... After that, we're all too likely to have other things to worry about," he said.

"Something's gnawing at you. You haven't been right since we set out, maybe even since before we did," Sostratos said. "If I can do anything to help, you know I will."

"Yes, yes." But Menedemos seemed like a man with an impatient small boy tugging at his tunic. "Nothing anyone can do, I'm afraid. I've told you that before."

"I thought something might have changed since then," Sostratos said.

"Something might have. Nothing has." Menedemos looked old and bleak again. This time, he didn't seem to care. Sostratos thought he was talking more than half to himself as he went on, "By the gods, though, I'll be glad when we get back to Rhodes."

Sostratos almost asked, *Why?* He would have, had he thought he would get an answer that meant anything. Since he didn't, he kept quiet.

By the way his cousin eyed him, Menedemos was looking for him to ask, and had readied some sort of comeback that would pierce him the way a catapult bolt could pin a rider to his horse. Sostratos smiled his most innocent smile. All he did ask was, "What do you think of Ptolemaios' chances against Demetrios?"

Menedemos visibly relaxed, as if the oversized bow that propelled a catapult's bolt were uncocked. For a couple of heartbeats, he looked grateful—not an expression Sostratos often saw on his face. With a shrug, he answered, "You never can tell ahead of time. That's why you roll the knucklebones: to see who takes home the drakhmai."

"But knucklebones are all luck. There's skill involved in this," Sostratos said.

"Yes, but I don't know who has the better admirals or the better sailors," Menedemos said. "We've come all this way across the Inner Sea, but I don't think our rowers are too worn to give a good account of themselves."

"No, neither do I," Sostratos said. Menedemos could talk coolly about a sea-fight in which he was liable to get killed. It didn't bother him nearly so much as the thing he wouldn't talk about at all, whatever that might be. Again, Sostratos was tempted to ask. Again, he thought better of it. He went on, "Whatever happens, it will happen soon now."

"Be a relief to get it over with," Menedemos said. "I feel as if Ptolemaios tied a fat bag of silver to each of my good sense's ankles and then threw it into the sea to drown."

"What else could you have done but what you did? He would have stolen the *Aphrodite* out from under you if you hadn't come along, stolen her, and left us stuck in Alexandria," Sostratos said.

"I understand that, my dear. Believe me, I do," Menedemos replied. "And do you know what else? We might have been better off stuck down there than we are up here." Sostratos found no answer at all for that.

Suitably refreshed, Ptolemaios' fleet left Kition the next morning. Sostratos' belly tightened as the harbor shrank behind the *Aphrodite*'s sternpost and then disappeared. Not much save fire happened quickly on the sea, but the meeting with Demetrios' naval forces couldn't lie far away.

But for Cape Pedalion projecting out to the southeast, the meeting would have been closer yet. As soon as the ships rounded the cape and swung north toward besieged Salamis, they lowered their masts and went to oar power. That was partly because the wind lay against them once more, partly because galleys never trusted the world's fickle breezes in battle.

"We're the last juggler in this parade," Menedemos said as the akatos finally passed the cape. "All kinds of things may be going on up ahead of us without our knowing."

"Sooner or later, we'll find out." Sostratos remembered thinking how useful a way of directly communicating between Alexandria and Cyprus would have been. A way for the front part of a fleet to communicate directly with the back part would have been just as useful, since the one and the other were separated by a good many stadia.

"Sooner or later. Sooner, I think." Menedemos sounded as if he looked forward to it. Maybe he did. If he was in the middle, or even at the back, of desperate action, he wouldn't have time to brood about … whatever he was brooding about. This wasn't the time to ask. Sostratos suspected there was no time to ask.

Somebody at the stern of the nearest transport shouted something back toward the *Aphrodite*. Whatever it was, distance turned it meaningless, at least to Sostratos' ear.

To Menedemos', too, for he called to the rowers, "Did anyone make out what he was saying?" When no one admitted it, Menedemos said, "Up the stroke, Diokles, so we can get closer and hear him. Sostratos, go forward and shout for him to give us whatever that was again."

"I'll take care of it," Sostratos said.

As he hurried up toward the little bow platform, Diokles clanged harder than usual and started calling "*Rhyppapai!*" to draw the rowers' notice to the quickened tempo. Sostratos could feel the akatos moving faster over the sea.

The man at the stern of the galley ahead also noticed the *Aphrodite* coming closer. He stayed where he was instead of going back to whatever he'd been doing before. As the gap narrowed, Sostratos cupped his hands in front of his mouth and bawled, "Tell us your news over again!"

"We've been spotted," Ptolemaios' man shouted back. When the *Aphrodite* got closer yet, he added, "One of those polluted seagoing cockroaches with fifty oars. We tried, but we couldn't catch it."

"Too bad," Sostratos said, and then, "Thanks!" He turned and waved to Menedemos and Diokles, a signal that he had what he needed and they could let the rowers fall back to their usual pace. Sure enough, the stroke slowed. Sostratos walked back to the stern platform.

"Well?" Menedemos asked when he got there, as his cousin hadn't been able to make out what the sailor on the bigger transport was saying.

Sostratos relayed the message, finishing, "As soon as that gods-cursed pentekonter gets back to Salamis, Demetrios will come after us."

"Or as soon as it gets back to his fleet," Menedemos said. "He knew we were at Paphos. He's bound to know we were at Kition, too. He knows which way we have to come—we're not going to descend on him from the north. He may have his fleet waiting out there just over the horizon." He pointed in the direction they were going.

"You're right. He may." Sostratos hated feeling outthought, but he did at that moment. Demetrios was only too likely to try to force the action. He'd done that in Athens, and here on Cyprus ever since invading the island. Menedemos had seen as much. Sostratos hadn't, not till his cousin pointed it out to him.

"Chances are we won't even know the sea-fight's started till a galley catches fire and we spy the smoke from the pyre," Menedemos said. "I can't see Ptolemaios' warships from here, only the transports. Can you?"

"No." Sostratos tossed his head. "But the forward transports will be able to see them. When we see the ships ahead of us speeding up or changing formation, we'll know what we need to do."

"No, we'll just know what's going on. It's not the same thing," Menedemos said. "We won't know what to do unless we have to run from a five or try to fight one, and that will mean the perfume's gone into the soup."

"Too right it will!" Sostratos spat into the bosom of his tunic. He told himself again and again that he didn't really believe the apotropaic gesture would turn aside ill-fortune. If the gods were there at all, if they deigned to pay any attention whatever to poor, miserable mankind, surely they had too many other things to do to alter fate every time someone entreated them.

That all made perfect logical, reasonable sense. It didn't keep him from spitting into the bosom of his chiton every now and again. The gesture couldn't hurt anything, and it might just possibly do some good, so ....

Sostratos frowned and cupped a hand to his ear. "What is it?" Menedemos asked sharply.

"Horn calls ahead ... I think," Sostratos answered. "Ptolemaios' war galleys are signaling back and forth, unless I miss my guess."

"Makes sense," his cousin said: a two-word epitaph that might go on Sostratos' grave monument. "Trumpets carry a long way, and with luck the foe won't know what your calls mean." After a moment, Menedemos added, "Your ears are good. I can't hear them."

"Better you leave your hands *on* the steering oars," Sostratos said.

"There is that," Menedemos said, and then, "What are they doing? Can you tell?"

Now Sostratos used his hand to shade his eyes, though he faced away from the sun. He stared for a little while, but ended up tossing his head. "Whatever it is, they're too far ahead for me to make it out. But they haven't signaled like that before. If I had to guess, I'd say they're likely shaking themselves out into the line of battle, but I can't prove it."

"Which means Demetrios *will* have sailed out to meet us. Happy day!" Menedemos whistled tunelessly between his teeth. "Which means that, by the time the sun goes down, we'll have answers to the questions we've been asking since before we left Alexandria."

Shadows told Sostratos it was a little past noon. The sun told him the same when he turned to glance at it. They'd got an early start from Kition. And, evidently, Demetrios had got an early start from Salamis.

"Here's hoping Menelaos breaks out of the harbor," Sostratos said. "Sixty ships coming to give Demetrios one up the *prokton* would hand him something new to worry about."

"That would be marvelous!" Menedemos said. "Do you think he can?"

"I wish I did. How about you?" Sostratos said. Menedemos' expression told him everything he needed to know.

"Well," his cousin said, "we'll do the best we can even without him. Keeping him jugged up in there is costing the Demetrios some ships, at least, ships he won't be able to throw at Ptolemaios."

"True enough." Sostratos couldn't help noticing that he and Menedemos had both tagged the enemy warlord with the *the* of respect, but not their own fleet's commander. Maybe that just meant they were more familiar with Ptolemaios. Or maybe it meant they both thought Demetrios stood a better chance of winning.

Sostratos didn't want to believe that. Your chances when you lost a battle ranged from bad to worse. Captured and held for ransom? Captured and sold into slavery? Maimed? Speared? Drowned? He tried not to think of any of those and wound up thinking about them all, in turn and together. Cursing his runaway imagination, he waited to see what the afternoon would bring.

Part of Menedemos wanted Ptolemaios' transports to close up on his war galleys. That would give the transports' skippers, himself among them, a better notion of how the fight ahead of them was going. But part of him wanted to stay as far away from the sea-fight as he could. If Demetrios beat Ptolemaios, the longer the start on enemy pursuit he had, the better his chances of getting away clean.

For now, all he could do was peer northwards, try to make out the distant horn calls, and worry. *Maybe I should have let Ptolemaios take the* Aphrodite *away from me*, ran through his head more than once. He and Sostratos and the rest of the crew could have waited out the war in Alexandria.

But Ptolemaios had paid, and paid extravagantly. This would be a profitable voyage … if it brought them back to Rhodes, anyhow. Menedemos wished he hadn't thought of Rhodes. Thinking of Rhodes made him think of Baukis, of the baby that might be his, of her screaming in childbed the way women did, and of his own father listening to those screams. Next to thoughts like that, brooding about a mere sea-battle seemed a pleasure.

It did, at any rate, till Diokles pointed to the new plume of smoke rising a bit west of due north. "Something's on fire," the keleustes said.

"So it is." Menedemos did some more tuneless whistling. "Isn't that delightful? We just have to hope it's something that belongs to Demetrios."

Something. If you thought of a war galley on fire, you could pretend to yourself that it carried no rowers or naval officers or marines or catapult crewmen. Only a thing of rope and wood and cloth and metal was burning, not a small town's worth of young men. No, those weren't men roasting there like a sacrifice on an altar, or jumping into the sea to drown so they wouldn't roast … jumping into the sea to drown with tunics already blazing or with flesh already blazing.

Yes, that was only a ship. Didn't you have to think of war as being about things, not about men? How could you fight it if you thought about the *men* on the other side you were going to maim or kill, or about the men on your own side the enemy would slaughter? How could you fight if you thought about the enemy slaughtering *you*?

Diokles' voice brought Menedemos back to himself: "Skipper, the transports ahead of us have stopped rowing. By your leave, I'll do the same. We don't want to get too close to the war galleys till we know what's going on up there."

"Yes, do it," Menedemos said.

"Easy oars!" Diokles bawled, and emphasized the order by clanging away with hammer and triangle.

The *Aphrodite* glided to a stop as the rowers rested at their oars. Then she began to bob on the Inner Sea like a toy boat on a rain puddle. The motion felt odd to Menedemos: a galley on the open sea should be going somewhere, doing something. He looked forward to his cousin to see how Sostratos was taking it. To his relief, Sostratos seemed all right. Menedemos didn't call out to him, lest he remind him things were out of the ordinary.

Part of the skipper still wanted to go north so he could find out how the sea-battle fared. But if he found out it was going badly, that would be worse than staying back and staying ignorant. Good news could wait.

He wasn't the only one fretting. "Wish I knew what was happening," Diokles muttered.

"What do you think? Shall we go up and get a better notion?" Yes, that part of Menedemos still wanted to.

"I'd like to, but …." Diokles tossed his head. "To a five, we'd be no more'n a fried sprat. Wouldn't even bother chewing, just swallow us whole."

"That's how it looks to me, too," Menedemos said, not without regret. It had also looked that way to his cousin. Diokles' notion of good sense was very different from Sostratos'. When the two of them coincided, going—or, here, not going—in the direction they both indicated seemed a good idea.

Time went by. The sun crawled toward the western horizon. Somewhere not very far ahead, horrible things were happening to men who probably hadn't done anything in particular to deserve them. If those things didn't go the way Ptolemaios hoped, before long those horrible things might start happening to the transports, too.

Or to me, Menedemos thought uneasily. He spat down his tunic front to turn aside the omen. Superstition came easy out at sea, and he was less skeptical to begin with than his cousin.

Not very much later, Diokles said, "Looks to me like the fighting is curling towards us, not away."

"I was thinking the same thing. I kept hoping I was wrong," Menedemos said.

Then came an unmistakable sign: almost in unison, the crews manning the transport galleys ahead of the *Aphrodite* started rowing again, and rowing as if their lives depended on it. And, no doubt, their lives did. They straightaway lost the order they'd kept so long. Some sped south; others wheeled in the water and hurried back toward the west.

Sostratos trotted aft from his station at the bow platform. Before he even got to the stern, he started calling, "Daddle! Let's ske! Daddle! Let's ske!"

In spite of everything, Menedemos laughed. Then he said to Diokles, "It's gone bad. The Ptolemaios can't blame us if we head for Rhodes now. I'll bet he's trying to save his own hide, if he still can."

As if to underscore that, someone aboard a transport heading west shouted "Fly, you fools! It's all up with the war galleys!" to the akatos.

Diokles said something pungent. Then he beat on his triangle. "Port oars forward, starboard oars back!" he shouted to the rowers. "Get ready, boys! We're heading home, if we can get there. On the stroke!"

Aided by the steering oars, the *Aphrodite* turned almost in her own length. "O Sostratos!" Menedemos said sharply. "Come on up here and keep watch astern of us. If any of Demetrios' ships get on our tail, I want to hear about it."

"I'll do it," Sostratos said, and did. Standing on the stern platform, he could see a little farther. If the mast were up, if someone small could scamper to the top of it, that would be better yet. But the mast would stay down for now.

Menedemos kept wanting to look back over his shoulder himself. And he yielded to temptation every so often. He could afford such glimpses. He told himself he could, anyway. Sostratos might have had something sharp to say about the way he rationalized, but Sostratos didn't know he was sneaking those looks. Menedemos' dutiful cousin kept his eyes on the water behind the akatos and didn't check to see what anyone ahead of him was doing.

Then, just when Menedemos was feeling proud of himself at not checking for a while, Sostratos sang out, "I think someone's chasing us!"

"Oh, a pestilence!" Menedemos blurted. He did look back then. Sure enough, a beamy galley, a six or maybe even a seven, was churning up the Inner Sea as it came after the *Aphrodite*. To Diokles, Menedemos said, "Have the boys give it all they have. Maybe we'll be able to run away from that overgrown seagoing catamite."

Diokles grunted laughter. "I like the way you talk, skipper. The way you think, too." He raised his voice to a shout so all the rowers could hear him: "Put your backs into it, lads, unless you reckon going up on a slaver's block is the best thing that can happen to you."

He upped the stroke again. The men at the oars couldn't hold that kind of sprint for long. With luck, the rowers aboard their pursuer couldn't, either. "Let me know if she's gaining," Menedemos told Sostratos.

"She is," his cousin answered: not what he wanted to hear.

XIII

SOSTRATOS WISHED HE HAD SOMEWHERE NICE and safe to run to. That failing, he wished he could show how afraid he was. Well, he could, but not if he wanted to be a man among men in Rhodes ever again. Sokrates' *Be what you wish to seem*, ran through his head once more.

Sokrates had been brave in battle. Alkibiades talked about it in Platon's *Symposion*. The philosopher might have been scared green inside, but he hadn't shown it. And Sostratos did his best to look relaxed as he gripped the *Aphrodite*'s sternpost with one hand and shaded his eyes with the other.

Demetrios' gods-cursed war galley kept looking bigger, which meant it kept getting closer. Why weren't its rowers exhausted? They'd fought in the sea-battle against Ptolemaios' fleet. And pulling big oars like that, even with two or three men on them, had to be wearing … didn't it?

By the signs, no. As a wave trough showed the war galley's ram, Sostratos got a glimpse of its three-flanged bronze ram. He imagined that ram crunching into the *Aphrodite*'s stern or flank. He'd always prided himself on how vivid his imagination was. Just this once, he could have done with less of it.

Like Ptolemaios' warships, this one mounted a catapult at the bow. Its crew seemed busy. Sure enough, its crew *was* busy. A bolt flew from the catapult and splashed into the sea no more than thirty 30 cubits astern of the akatos.

"O Menedemos!" Sostratos said sharply. "They're shooting at us!"

"They should get a catapult bolt up their pink piggy!" his cousin replied. Then he raised his voice to a roar all the rowers could hear: "If you've got anything left in you, boys, now's the time to spend it. We won't have much fun if they catch up to us."

Back on Demetrios' galley, the catapult crew loaded a new bolt in the groove and drew back the bow with the windlass, then shot again. To Sostratos' relief, this missile also fell short. By a little less than the first? Or by a little more? For the life of him—which might be literally true—he couldn't tell.

Archers also stood on the fighting platform that ran from the war galley's bow to stern. They didn't waste time or arrows shooting at the *Aphrodite*. If the catapult couldn't reach her, their arrows surely wouldn't.

They wore crested helms and bronze corselets, as if they were fighting on land. Sostratos wouldn't have cared to do that. A stumble could send you into the drink, and then you'd surely drown. But you'd want such protection if you had to worry about other galleys full of archers and slingers and spearmen. A big ship like that turned a seafight into a pankratiasts' brawl where brute force usually prevailed over skill.

The catapult let fly once more. This bolt definitely fell farther behind the fleeing *Aphrodite* than the first two had. Demetrios' ship looked a hair smaller, too, the eyes at its bow less fierce and menacing.

"We gain!" Sostratos told his cousin.

"Good! Those turds *are* worn down, then," Menedemos said, and raised his voice for the rowers again: "Come on! *Come* on, my dears! We can't outfight that big, ugly tub, but by the gods we can outrun her!"

If only Olympia had lain by the sea so rowing could be a competition there, the *Aphrodite*'s oarsmen would have been crowned with laurel. They put more and more distance between the akatos and the pursuing war galley. Demetrios' catapult men quit shooting, not wanting to waste any more bolts.

If we can stay ahead till the sun sets, we've won, Sostratos thought. *They'll never find us in the dark. They won't try very hard, either.* No sooner had that gone through his mind than one of the portside rowers passed out, overwhelmed by the hard work he'd put in.

Without wasting a heartbeat, Diokles set his hammer and triangle on the stern platform and dashed forward. Over his shoulder, he said, "You're keleustes now, O son of Lysistratos! Reckon I can still pull for a bit." He dragged the unconscious rower from his bench and took the man's place. The rowers ahead of and behind that bench hadn't lost more than a couple of strokes before the oar was served once more.

Menedemos took his hand off the port steering oar and stood aside to let Sostratos get to the tools of the keleustes' trade. "Next one who goes down, *you* grab an oar," Menedemos said.

"I will," Sostratos answered. He knew how to row, as most Rhodian men did. Unlike Diokles', though, his hands were soft, as befit a gentleman. He'd tear his palms to pieces if he had to ply an oar for long. Well, that was as nothing next to the things that would happen to him if he were sold into slavery. He'd pull his lungs out, and worry about bloody blisters later.

For a little while, he set himself so he could see both the rowers and Demetrios' galley. Then Menedemos said, "Pay attention to the stroke. I'll tell you when you need to speed up or slow down."

"As you say." When his cousin spoke as captain, Sostratos gave him full of obedience. And he found he *was* steadier with the rhythm when he didn't look up to see how the war galley was doing.

When the sun lay only a couple of its own diameters above the western horizon, Menedemos said, "I think they're giving up. We've gained a lot of ground—well, of water—on them, and they have to realize they can't overhaul us before the light goes."

"Gods be praised!" Sostratos said. "If we make it home safe to Rhodes, I'll give Poseidon a sheep." He might not be sure Zeus' brother ruled the seas, but he also wasn't altogether sure the god didn't. Better to take no chances, then.

"As long as that wide-arsed bugger is still in sight of us, I'm going to keep going south as well as west, even if we could round Cape Pedalion now," Menedemos said.

"Why?" Sostratos asked, as he was no doubt meant to do.

"Because, my dear, I want Demetrios' captain there to think the *Aphrodite* is a natural part of Ptolemaios' fleet, and that we're trying to get home safe to Alexandria," Menedemos replied. "The less that ties us to Rhodes, the happier I'll be."

"Oh." Sostratos chewed on that for a moment, then dipped his head. "Well, when you're right, you're right. The fewer reasons Demetrios and Antigonos have to hold a grudge against us, the better off the polis will be."

"*May* be," his cousin amended bleakly. "The Demetrios will take all of Cyprus now. Once he's done that, he'll look around and see only one polis in the neighborhood that doesn't bend the knee to his father and him."

"Rhodes," Sostratos said.

"Rhodes," Menedemos agreed. "He and Antigonos may decide to swallow us just to tidy things up, you might say."

"I wish I could tell you you were wrong," Sostratos said, "but I'm afraid you're right again." Menedemos had made much more sense than usual on this voyage. Maybe he truly was growing up at last.

"One good thing," he said now. "The moon's as near new as makes no difference, so it won't be rising till just before sunrise. That gives us plenty of time to get away from the war galley with her skipper none the wiser."

After the sun sank in the sea, twilight lingered longer than Sostratos wished it would. Or maybe that was only his imagination, stretching time finer than it really went. As night's onset cooled the air, the rower Diokles had replaced came to his senses.

"Get out of there, old man!" he told the keleustes. "I'll take back my oar."

"Drink some wine. East some bread and oil," Diokles said. "Get your strength back. You won't be working tonight. I'm fine here."

"He's right, Rhinias," Sostratos said. "We should be safe now, but you don't want to push hard and pass out again."

"Or drop dead," Diokles said.

"I wouldn't do that!" Rhinias said.

"You won't get the chance," Sostratos said firmly. "If you're all right tomorrow, maybe we'll put you back to work. Till then, you're a passenger, only we pay you instead of your paying us." Since he doubled as the *Aphrodite*'s physician, his words carried weight.

They also made Rhinias smile. "Since you put it that way, why can't the rest of you abandoned troglodytes row faster?" he said. Everyone laughed then. Laughing let Sostratos forget for a little while what a disaster Rhodes' most important friend had just suffered. Was Ptolemaios still alive? If he was, was he still free or Demetrios' prisoner? Not knowing, all Sostratos could do was worry.

Menedemos looked over his shoulder as the sun rose behind him. Since it rose north of due east at this summery season, the akatos was still heading southwest. The ship had left Cape Pedalion behind early in the night. She was out of sight of land. That bothered him less than it would have before he crossed the Inner Sea to go to Alexandria. Even if he couldn't see Cyprus, he had a good notion of where it lay.

More to the point at the moment, he couldn't see Demetrios' war galley, either. The *Aphrodite* had made a clean getaway during the hours of darkness. If no piratical pentekonter came shooting out from behind a little headland, the *Aphrodite* had a clear track to Rhodes … and to bringing Rhodes what news she had of Ptolemaios' defeat.

Menedemos swung the ship to starboard, pulling the tiller in his right hand toward him and pushing the one in his left away by about the same distance. When he'd turned her through about a quarter of a circle, he asked Sostratos, "How are you holding?"

"I'm tired," answered his cousin, who'd beaten out the stroke for the rowers all through the night. "I can keep going a while longer if I have to, though."

"Can you conn the ship till you spy land? It shouldn't be more than a couple of hours, but I'm so worn I feel as though daimons have been beating on me with mallets. You can give Diokles back his toys. We don't need every single oar manned now."

"Toys?" Diokles called from the rowing bench he'd taken, his voice full of gruff—and false—indignation.

"What else would you call them?" Sostratos returned. Diokles' answer made Menedemos snicker—it came straight out of *Lysistrata*, whether the keleustes knew it or not. Diokles came back to reclaim the hammer and triangle. Sostratos took the steering oars from Menedemos. Menedemos curled up on the stern platform like an Alexandrian cat in the sun.

Cats, he thought. *I was going to bring some cats back to Rhodes. Have to do that some other year.* He closed his eyes and thought no more.

Next thing he knew, a hand on his shoulder shook him awake. "Diokles has the helm," Sostratos said. "We're in sight of land."

"Oh." Menedemos sat up, knuckling sand from his eyes. He could have used another couple of days' sleep, or at least another couple of hours'. He remembered he wasn't the only one. Everybody aboard the *Aphrodite* had to be weary down to the very marrow. "Do you and the oarmaster want some rest? Nikagoras can set the stroke for a while. No one's on our tail, gods be praised."

"If you'd be so kind," Sostratos said. Even Diokles didn't claim he was fine, which proved how tired he had to be.

Once more, Menedemos' hands molded themselves around the steering-oar tillers. He wondered whether, if he lived to be an old man, they would take that curved shape of themselves. Plenty of men who did the same thing over and over for years found it marking their bodies.

His chances of living into old age seemed better now than they had when Demetrios' war galley came after the akatos. Those big ships might carry swarms of marines, but they weren't as fast or as agile as this one.

He'd been thinking about the news he would bring to Rhodes. Now he wondered once more what kind of news Rhodes would have for him. Did he have a half-brother, or perhaps a son? Baukis would have had the baby by now, surely. Was she all right? Remembering the fate of his own mother, his father's first wife, he knew there was no guarantee. No guarantee the baby would survive, either. So many newborns didn't.

How many times had he chased those fears round and round inside the cavern of his skull? More than he could count. They felt different now, more real, more urgent. Now he was almost home. Soon he wouldn't fear anymore. Soon he would know, and knowing might be worse.

How would his father greet him, at the quay or at the family house? As a son come home safe after a dangerous but profitable voyage? Or as an adulterer who'd debauched and impregnated his stepmother? If Baukis had called out the wrong name—or rather, the right one—while in the torment of labor ....

The tragedians Sostratos loved so well wrote plays about stories like that, though theirs had gods in them. When such things happened in real life, what then? Menedemos saw only one thing. If he escaped without bloodshed, what could he do but flee Rhodes, change his name, and make a new life in some inland town that had no traffic with the sea?

Sostratos had promised Poseidon a sheep for delivering the akatos from Demetrios' war galley. A sheep was not a small offering, but .... "Aphrodite, if you keep Baukis' good name safe, and mine, I'll give you a bullock," Menedemos murmured.

For a moment, the sound of the sea seemed the sound of laughter. Menedemos imagined it was the goddess laughing at him. He wasn't asking her to turn the future. He wanted her to change the past if that past hadn't turned out the way he wanted it to. Even if the goddess were inclined to grant such a prayer, wouldn't the Fates prevent it?

Of course they would. If the gods started granting retrospective prayers, the past would turn into something like the wax on a writing tablet's panel. Endlessly scribbled on, rubbed out, and then scribbled on again with something new. That wasn't answered prayer. That was chaos.

Still holding the steering-oar tillers, Menedemos shrugged. If everything turned out all right, he'd still give Aphrodite her bullock. You didn't want to cheat the gods, even when you'd asked one for something she couldn't possibly give.

Four or five rowers not at their oars rested on the small bow platform. Two stretched out in slumber. The rest were sitting up, talking and looking out over the sea. Suddenly one of the loungers pointed to port and bawled, "There's a ship out there!"

Ice ran through Menedemos, even under the hot sun. He couldn't worry about what would happen when he came to Rhodes if he never got there. His eye followed the rower's finger. Sure enough, there was a bump on the southern horizon.

That shout also roused Sostratos, who sat up. "What are you go-ing to do?" he asked around a yawn.

There was the question, all right. Menedemos needed only a few heartbeats to come up with an answer. "As long as that ship doesn't turn towards us, I'm not going to do a gods-cursed thing," he said. "If she does come at us, either we'll run or we'll serve out some of the weapons the Ptolemaios saddled us with and give the whoresons the best fight we can. Or if you have a better scheme, give forth. I'd love to hear it."

His cousin tossed his head. "Not me. Those seem about the best choices we have."

"Good." Menedemos meant it. Sostratos was a modern Odys-seus, always full of clever plans. If he saw nothing that improved on Menedemos' idea, chances were there was nothing to be seen.

Chances were … Menedemos worried the inside of his lower lip with his teeth, almost as if he were fretting about Baukis. The weight of command pressed on his shoulders as the weight of the world must have pressed on Atlas'. Sostratos could suggest whatever popped into his head. Menedemos had to decide, and afterwards to live with what he'd decided.

Or to die with it. That chance was what made command such a weight. Make a mistake and you might lose your ship, your freedom, or your life. So might all the men who followed your mistaken order. It wasn't a game you played for yourself alone. Everyone aboard the *Aphrodite* relied on you to be right. So did your family back in Rhodes.

Thinking of his family in Rhodes brought Menedemos back to Baukis. Everything did, sooner or later. He kicked at the planking under his feet. Suppose he came home safely. Suppose she'd had her baby. Suppose it was his, and a boy. Then what?

That was one more thing he hadn't cared to dwell on, and still didn't. Even if everything went as well as it could for him and for the woman he loved, she'd still be his father's wife. After she recovered from childbirth, she'd go back to his father's bed. She wouldn't warm his. The most they could hope for was rare, frantic couplings like the one that might have got her with child to begin with. Most of the time, they'd have to pretend they were nothing but stepmother and stepson. What kind of life was that?

No kind of life at all. The one good thing he could see about it was that it looked better than any other possibility. That didn't seem enough, but what else was there?

Nearly everyone aboard the *Aphrodite* was craning his neck to port, doing his best to make out what the strange ship was. One of the rowers said, "I think it's a gods-cursed pentekonter!"

That was the last thing Menedemos wanted to hear. A pentekonter, whether attached to Demetrios' fleet or a pirate ship prowling alone, was fast enough to overhaul the akatos and carried enough men to overwhelm the Rhodians. His own fear grew, for the stranger was surely a galley, showing no mast or sail. Yet it had not turned toward his ship.

Sostratos had good eyes. Menedemos didn't know how he did, since he stared at scrolls so much, but he did. "No, it's *not* a pentekonter," he said now. "Not enough oars. I think it's another akatos, maybe bound from Paphos to Kition."

"Gods, I hope you're right," Menedemos said.

"We'll know pretty soon," his cousin replied.

The stranger on the sea wanted no more of the *Aphrodite* than Menedemos wanted anything to do with her. Instead of approaching, her rowers put more distance between her and the Rhodian vessel. As she turned away, Menedemos started to laugh.

"What's so funny?" asked Diokles, who was also awake now.

"Not a pentekonter. Not even an akatos," Menedemos answered. "A fornicating akation, that's all, with maybe six or eight oars on each side. Her skipper's really got something to be scared of from us. But we ….We saw a cat walking down an alleyway in Alexandria at night, and we thought it was a lion."

"Cats are bad enough," Diokles said. Menedemos was glad he hadn't talked with the keleustes about bringing some back to Rhodes. Not everybody liked them, plainly.

"Many good-byes to that cursed baby galley," Sostratos said. "I hope her rowers all fall over dead from apoplexy. Getting a scare like that after we made it out of the sea-fight whole was too much."

"If you think I'll argue with you, you're daft," Menedemos replied. "We'll be pissing ourselves every time we see anything on the ocean bigger than a fishing boat."

"I wondered whether the polis has our fleet out on patrol," Sostratos said. "Or are we keeping the triremes in the shipsheds so we don't give Demetrios and Antigonos any excuse to fight us?"

"There's an interesting question!" Menedemos said. "The only good thing is, Rhodians will recognize the *Aphrodite* when they get close. They won't try to sink us on sight."

"We hope they won't. They're going to be edgy, too. Everyone in the eastern half of the Inner Sea is edgy right now. By the gods, for all I know the Carthaginians are edgy out west, too," Sostratos said. "We just have to pray our skippers don't try to ram first and figure out what they're ramming afterwards."

"Thank you, my dear. You always know how to cheer me up," Menedemos said.

"My pleasure, O best one," Sostratos answered with courtesy he didn't usually show: sardonic courtesy, if Menedemos was any judge … and, after a lifetime with his cousin, he was. "Any little thing I can do to ease your mind, you have but to ask."

Something else occurred to Menedemos, though it was nothing that eased his mind. "I wonder what Menelaos will do back in the town of Salamis. Ptolemaios isn't going to rescue him, or bring him reinforcements and fresh supplies."

"The other interesting question is, what will Demetrios do to Menelaos if he takes Salamis by storm or if Menelaos has to surrender to him?" Sostratos said. "Menelaos is probably mighty interested in that question now."

"I would be, in his sandals," Menedemos said. War was a hard business when you lost. Victors commonly sold defeated soldiers into slavery. Alexander hadn't done things like that when he overran Persia, and Demetrios prided himself on matching Alexander in generalship as well as looks (though Alexander was said to have been short, while Demetrios stood well above 4 cubits high—he was even taller than Sostratos). How much could Menelaos rely on his magnanimity, though?

"For all we know, the Ptolemaios is dead or captured himself," Sostratos said. "If Demetrios and Antigonos have Ptolemaios and Menelaos, doesn't that mean they have Egypt, too? And if they have Egypt, too, who's going to stop them from grabbing the rest of Alexander's domain?"

"Seleukos may," Menedemos said. His cousin sent him a look, and he understood why. Seleukos' strength lay far to the east. If Egypt fell to Antigonos and Demetrios, who would stop them from gobbling up Rhodes next? No one Menedemos could see.

"We have to act as though Ptolemaios is still free and running Egypt till we know for certain that he isn't, because—" Sostratos began.

"Because if he's not, we may as well cut our own throats now and save ourselves the trouble later," Menedemos broke in. Sostratos was thinking along with him much too well. If Demetrios had Ptolemaios, if Demetrios and Antigonos had Egypt, the game in the eastern half of the Inner Sea was as good as over.

"What do you think the people who run things in Rhodes will do when we bring back news like this?" Sostratos asked.

"People like our fathers, you mean?" Menedemos gibed.

His cousin dipped his head. "People like them, yes, and people who can buy and sell them."

There weren't many people like that in Rhodes, as Menedemos knew. But there were some, and their weight in shaping the polis' relations with the outside world was inversely proportional to their scanty numbers. Slowly, Menedemos answered, "Either they'll stick their heads into their shells like so many tortoises and not want to come out at all or they'll run in crazy circles, as if they were hens that met the chopper but didn't die right away. Whichever road they choose, they won't be happy about it."

"No." Sostratos left things right there, which was probably just as well. Messengers who brought bad news weren't loved for it, and all of Rhodes had relied on Ptolemaios as a counterweight against Demetrios and his father. For the time being, at least, the counterweight was gone. Menedemos and Sostratos would have to tell that to the polis' great men.

That wasn't quite so terrifying a prospect as having Demetrios' war galley chasing the *Aphrodite* after Ptolemaios' line of ships got shattered, but it wasn't far behind, either. Menedemos swore under his breath. The akatos was bringing home not only bag after bag of silver but also the military supplies Ptolemaios had commandeered her to carry. And what kind of thanks would her captain and crew get for that? Not much, not if Menedemos was any judge.

Sostratos wasn't surprised when Menedemos put in at Kourion, well short of Paphos, on the voyage west. People in Paphos would remember the *Aphrodite* had stopped there with Ptolemaios' fleet. They'd ask questions without convenient answers. Best to skirt that if at all possible.

In Kourion, they knew Ptolemaios' fleet had sailed east to meet Demetrios', but that was all they knew. Menedemos didn't tell them anything more. "I sailed from Alexandria myself, a few days after the Ptolemaios left," he said to people who called questions from the piers. "I aim to stay out of trouble, not get into it."

"You lie like a Cretan," Sostratos told him—quietly, so none of the locals would overhear.

"The daimon I do," his cousin answered. "I aim to stay out of trouble, but sometimes I miss."

Sostratos burst out laughing. When it came to bare-faced effrontery, Menedemos could play with anyone. But Menedemos wasn't in this game alone. "How do we keep the rowers from blabbing?" Sostratos said. "I know we're only here for the night, but—"

"Promise them an extra day's pay if no one gets diarrhea of the mouth," Menedemos said at once. "With silver on the line, they'll watch each other like falcons, and we've got more of it than we know what to do with, almost."

"My dear, I think you just rolled a triple six!" Sostratos sketched a salute. Then he went up the rowing benches, passing the word on to the oarsmen. The ploy worked as well as his cousin had hoped it would. The men loudly and profanely agreed to keep their mouths shut, and to pound to gravel anyone who slipped up.

With a few rowers, Sostratos went down the pier to the shops near the base. He bought fried fish and fresh bread, enough for everyone to enjoy a good supper. They brought the food back to the akatos and handed it out.

"*Euge!*" the sailors cried. Some of them raised cups full of rough shipboard wine in salute.

One of them went further, spilling out a small libation and calling, "This for Sostratos the beautiful!" The rest of the men whooped and cheered.

"Oh, by the gods!" Sostratos exclaimed, which only made the rowers whoop some more. His face felt on fire; he hoped they wouldn't notice his blushes. No one had ever called him beautiful when he was a youth. He knew too well he hadn't been beautiful—that kind of praise always went to Menedemos. To hear it now, although it wasn't serious, flustered him more than he cared to admit, even to himself.

His cousin grinned and said, "They'll be scrawling your name on the walls next thing you know."

"Oh, to the crows with you!" Sostratos said. The rowers were teasing him for the fun of it. Menedemos really had had that kind of popularity, admiration, whatever the perfect word was. Sostratos knew how acutely he'd felt the lack of it when he was fourteen or fifteen.

That was half a lifetime ago now, of course. If he chose to, he could fill the role of erastes now, not eromenos: the lover, not the beloved. He was a man, not a youth. But the youth lived just under the man's skin, and always would. The pain the youth had known then could still stab the man.

For a wonder, Menedemos seemed to hear whatever had been in his voice. He let it go instead of pushing it the way he often did. That let Sostratos simmer down. It didn't let him forget. No one ever forgot being ignored and unwanted. You could, if you were lucky enough and wise enough, perhaps find a way to live without letting it trouble you too much. But it never went away.

The *Aphrodite* slipped out of Kourion even before the sun climbed up over the eastern horizon. "Rosy-fingered dawn," Sostratos murmured as the sky lightened toward real morning.

"Really, my dear?" Menedemos said. "I'm the one who quotes Homer most of the time. And when I do, you tell me Sokrates or Platon or Theophrastos show how the poet was talking rubbish."

"Funny. When I talk about Sokrates, you throw Aristophanes' *Clouds* at me," Sostratos said. "I wonder how often people who thought they were funny shouted bits of it at him when he walked down the street. I wonder why he didn't punch them in the nose, too. By the gods, I would have." Of themselves, his hands balled into fists.

192

His cousin sent him a quizzical look. "What's got into you today?"

"Nothing," Sostratos said, and not a word more.

"You sound like Odysseus telling Polyphemos the Cyclops his name was Nobody," Menedemos remarked.

"Nodysseus would come closer," Sostratos said. Sure enough, *outis*, the Greek word for *nobody*, sounded very much like the resourceful hero's name.

"That's pretty bad," Menedemos said, but he sounded more admiring than not.

"Don't blame me. Blame Homer," Sostratos said.

"You're here. He isn't," Menedemos answered. He looked around. "And we're out of the harbor, and I don't think anyone in Kourion has any idea we were part of Ptolemaios' fleet."

Sostratos cupped his hands in front of his mouth and called, "We did what we needed to do! A day's bonus for all the rowers aboard!"

The men pulling the oars raised a cheer. Menedemos cocked an eyebrow. "You might have waited till we got farther away. Now the Kourians may be wondering why we're so happy to leave their worthless little town."

"Huh!" Sostratos sniffed. "If you had to live out your days in that miserable place, wouldn't you want to get away as fast as you could if only you had the chance?"

"As a matter of fact, yes," Menedemos said. "There's no place in the world so grand as Rhodes—well, except Alexandria and Athens, I suppose."

"Alexandria's big. I don't know how grand it is, though I expect it will be once it's had the time to finish baking," Sostratos said, which made his cousin chuckle. But his voice turned serious as he went on, "Athens, now … Athens isn't just a polis. Even after everything that's happened to it the past hundred years, Athens is the world. Rhodes is a fine place—don't get me wrong, O best one. But the first time I went into Athens, I felt as though I'd come from a little farming village somewhere, with dung still on my feet."

"And I'll bet the Athenians made you feel that way, too." Menedemos was a couple of palms shorter than Sostratos, but by tilting his head back somehow contrived to look down his nose at him.

The sun rose as Sostratos laughed. "They can be like that, yes—you've seen it for yourself," he said. His cousin dipped his head. Sostratos continued, "But it's not just the people. It's the buildings and the art and the knowledge and the past. Hellas is what it is, for better and for worse, because Athens is what it is."

"These days, Athens is Demetrios' lapdog. We saw it happen."

"I know. But it's more than that, too, or he wouldn't have wanted it," Sostratos said. To his relief, Menedemos didn't argue. The *Aphrodite* went on toward Rhodes.

XIV

"OH, THE GODS BE PRAISED!" MENEDEMOS EXCLAIMED when his home polis came into sight ahead.

Diokles looked over his shoulder. "We knew things were all right when we talked to those fishermen off the coast."

"We knew things were all right when we saw Demetrios' friends weren't burning every farmhouse and village on the island so they could lay siege to the polis," Sostratos added.

"There's a difference between hearing things or reasoning about things and finding out with your own eyes," Menedemos insisted. "It's like the difference between hearing about love and being in love."

"Trust you to come up with a comparison like that," Sostratos said. Diokles laughed. Menedemos lifted one hand from the steering oar to aim a filthy gesture at them both. Diokles laughed harder. Sostratos hadn't been laughing, but he started.

"There are the harbor forts," Menedemos said, pointing. "People look to be working on the seawalls, too. That's good. We'll be … as ready as we can be, anyhow."

The keleustes and his cousin stopped laughing then. The news they were bringing back to their home city wasn't good, and nothing could make it good. Even if Ptolemaios had escaped from the battle off Salamis, he wouldn't be able to send, or want to send, another fleet north from Egypt for some time to come. Rhodes was on her own.

Menedemos sighed. "All we can do is all we can do. Diokles, get rowers on all the oars, will you? We may as well look good when we come into the harbor, eh?"

"Right you are, skipper." Diokles bawled orders to the men. Soon every bench was full. He picked up the stroke, too, even before Menedemos asked him to. The oars dipped into the water and rose from it in smooth unison. The rowers wanted to show off, too.

I wonder if any admirals or trireme captains will be watching us come in, Menedemos thought, and then, *I wonder how many of our crew will be rowing for the polis before long.* The answer to that seemed much too clear. Unless Rhodes changed course and yielded to Antigonos and Demetrios, she would have to fight, on the sea as well as on land.

As the *Aphrodite* neared the moles that protected the Great Harbor from storms at sea and the forts on the moles protected it from seaborne attack, men in the forts who recognized the akatos and knew where she'd gone began shouting for news.

Menedemos shouted back at them: "I'll tell it when I'm tied up at a pier—not a heartbeat before!"

The Rhodian soldiers swore at him. Like any other Hellenes, they wanted to hear the latest before anyone else could. They'd score points then for passing it on. Only they wouldn't today, because Menedemos didn't aim to tell it more than once, and then to people who needed to know it for reasons better than getting a leg up on gossip.

Two graybeards eating bread and drinking wine on a rowboat in the harbor, out for an afternoon wasting time in the sun, also called for news as the *Aphrodite* stroked past. They seemed even more offended than the soldiers when they didn't get it.

"Here we go! Here we go! Easy! Easy!" Diokles glided up to a pier. "Now back oars—stroke! Once more!" He eyed the planks and the pilings. "Good. We're home, by the gods!"

"We're home, by the gods!" Menedemos echoed to Sostratos.

His cousin dipped his head. "We are. We're home with a handsome profit, too—if we can keep it."

"If," Menedemos agreed.

A couple of dockside loungers made the *Aphrodite* fast to bollards on the pier. Menedemos hoped she could get hauled up into a ship-shed soon; she'd spent a long time at sea, and her timbers were bound to be waterlogged. But that would have to wait.

More men came down the pier to see what the merchant galley was carrying—and, again, to sweep up as much news as they could. That wasn't much. Sailors ran the gangplank from the ship to the pier. Menedemos crossed it. After so much time asea, planking that didn't shift under his feet felt strange, even unnatural, to him.

He pointed at three loungers he knew. "Two oboloi for each of you—one now, the second when you bring someone back here. Are you with me?" When none of them said no, he went on, "Karneades, go to my father's house and fetch him here. Athanippos, do the same for Lysistratos, my uncle. He lives across the street from my father. And Simias, you bring Komanos."

Every man collected a small silver coin and hurried away. One of the loungers Menedemos hadn't hired was peering into the *Aphrodite*. He asked, "How come your ship's all full of shields and arrows and things?"

"I'll tell the whole story once," Menedemos said. "Just once. You can wait and listen, or you can go play with it."

To his disappointment, the man hung around. A small crowd, and then a crowd not so small, gathered on the pier and on the dry land at its base. Half of Rhodes would know the *Aphrodite* had gone to Egypt, and all of Rhodes would know Antigonos' son was fighting Ptolemaios' brother on Cyprus. If Menedemos had news about any of that, people wanted to hear it.

They wouldn't want to hear what Menedemos told them. He knew that too well. One more reason to want to tell it just the once.

Someone on the pier made as if to go down into the akatos to see what all she carried. Menedemos said, "By the gods, friend, I'll shove you into the drink if you take one more step." He sounded as if he looked forward to it. He did.

"Who the daimon are you?" the fellow asked.

"The skipper."

The man didn't take the step. "I can't swim," he said.

Menedemos smiled, the way Medusa might have when she was turning someone to stone. "Good."

All at once, the Rhodian decided he wasn't so curious after all. He drew back, and nobody seemed eager to take his place. A commotion broke out at the back of the crowd. There was Karneades trying to push his way forward, with Philodemos doing his best to help.

"Let my father through!" Menedemos shouted in a voice that could have reached from the *Aphrodite's* stern to bow in the middle of a roaring gale. Sailors would have done whatever he told them without even thinking about it. Landlubbers were less used to taking orders. That always annoyed Menedemos, never more than today.

At last, Philodemos and his guide stood in front of Menedemos. After giving Karneades the second obolos, he clasped his father's hand. "Hail," he said.

"Hail, son. It's good to see you home," Philodemos said.

"It's good to be home," Menedemos said, and meant it. "Things have been … lively."

"They often are, where you're involved." Even at the moment of return, Philodemos couldn't resist a gibe. He did add, "They've been lively here, too, I will say."

"Ah?" Menedemos did his best not to seem too eager for news of Rhodes.

"That's right. You have a new half-brother. I've named him Diodoros, for he is Zeus' gift to the family," Philodemos said.

"Congratulations, Father. I hope your wife came through the birth well." Menedemos made himself sound calm and detached over something he cared about more than anything else in the world. If anything had happened to Baukis ….

She can't be dead, Menedemos told himself. His father's hair wasn't cropped short, as it would have been if he were mourning. But birth was as hard on women as battle was on men. Baukis might be suffering from fever, might be … Menedemos didn't know what all she might be. He'd never needed to worry about it, not in detail.

But Philodemos dipped his head. "She's as well as can be expected, gods be praised. And the little fellow looks much the way you did when you were a baby. He looks a lot like me, in other words. I must have strong seed." He sounded pleased with himself, even smug.

Menedemos wondered whether Diodoros looked like him because they both had the same father or because he *was* the baby's father. Odds were Baukis wasn't sure herself, in which case no one would ever know for certain. In law, Diodoros was Philodemos' son.

Then Menedemos got distracted, perhaps mercifully: the escorts leading Lysistratos and Komanos came to the harbor at about the same time. They and the men they'd brought fought their way through the crowd. Menedemos paid off the other two loungers. He greeted his uncle and the powerful civic leader. Then he held both hands in the air to get the crowd's attention.

Little by little, the men who'd been gabbling quieted down. "Hear me, O gentlemen of Rhodes," Menedemos said, as if he were speaking before the Assembly. That started them chattering again. He'd known it would. "Hear me!" he repeated, louder this time. He finally got something close enough to silence to suit him.

"The Ptolemaios and the Demetrios fought a great battle on the sea off Cypriot Salamis," he told the crowd. "I was there in the *Aphrodite*, which Ptolemaios had hired to help carry his military supplies."

His father, his uncle, Komanos, and others in the crowd who understood how things worked looked startled and alarmed. Rhodes was supposed to stay neutral in the wars among Alexander's generals. The political leader said, "Why did you go with Ptolemaios' fleet?"

"Because, O most excellent one, my other choice was having my ship confiscated and getting interned in Alexandria," Menedemos answered bleakly. "This way, at least we got some silver for having the *Aphrodite* used. The Demetrios won the battle, I'm afraid. Most of Ptolemaios' fleet is lost. I don't know if he lives, or whether he's free if he does. Not many of his ships got away. We were one of the lucky ones."

That set everyone exclaiming, as he'd once more known it would. Well, almost everyone. Komanos opened his mouth, then closed it again without saying anything. Menedemos' father also held his peace. His expression went thoughtful rather than shocked. Menedemos dared take that for a good sign. Uncle Lysistratos said, "So all these tools for murder in the *Aphrodite* would have gone to Ptolemaios' soldiers if they'd managed to land near Salamis?"

"That's right, sir. I don't think any of them managed to, or even to escape Demetrios' fleet. We had to outrun a big war galley ourselves. Believe me, I thought about throwing all that stuff into the drink so we could go faster," Menedemos said.

"Why didn't you?" Komanos asked.

"Well, O best one, for one thing, we managed to stay ahead of that big beamy whoreson without doing it," Menedemos replied. "And, for another, I thought Rhodes could use every sword, every arrow, every shield we were carrying. Just in case, if you know what I mean."

Komanos somberly dipped his head. "I know much too well. The polis may be in your debt."

"I live here, too, sir. I want to go on living in a free and independent polis if I can." Belatedly, Menedemos realized he and Sostratos might have sold the warlike gear to the city for a good bit of silver. He shrugged. Sometimes profit came at too high a price. He hadn't been joking. Rhodes could use every weapon she could lay her hands on. And she could use every drakhma in her coffers, for weapons or work on the walls or ships or grain or … anything.

Sostratos' father said, "You don't even know if the Ptolemaios got away safe?"

"No, sir. I have no idea," Menedemos answered. "I wish I did, but I don't. We were back with the transports, you understand, behind the warships, and at the rear of the transports at that. When the transport skippers realized Demetrios' war galleys had beaten Ptolemaios', we all scattered, every ship on its own."

"It will be as it is." Komanos' voice still sounded uncommonly heavy, as well it might. "Before long, we'll find out what did happen to Ptolemaios, and we'll go on from there."

"Yes, sir. But if he's sunk and drowned, or mewed up in chains on Demetrios' flagship—" Menedemos broke off. He saw no way to go on.

Komanos did. "If we have to make the best terms we can with Demetrios and his father, then we do that, and hope the future repeats the past."

Rhodes had briefly had a Macedonian garrison while Alexander was alive, but got free of it shortly after he died. Menedemos had been a youth then, not involved in the polis' affairs. Things were different now.

Underscoring that, Komanos said, "As I told you, the polis is in your debt for bringing us the news as quickly as you did, and for bringing these ... other things as well." His eyes flicked to the armaments stowed under most of the rowing benches and everywhere else there was room on the ship. "We do try to remember what we owe."

"We're citizens, sir. We try to remember that, too," Menedemos said. "If you'd care to tell off some men to carry the weapons to the armory ...."

"I will do that very thing." Komanos' voice rose as he addressed the men who'd been watching and listening. "Who'll fetch and carry for his polis? Three oboloi to any man who bears a bundle to the armory." A few hands went up, but only a few. Komanos chuckled. "Everything costs more than you wish it would. All right, O gentlemen of Rhodes—I'll not play the niggard today. A drakhma for every bundle. Now who's game?"

Doubling the wage produced many more willing workers. That surprised Menedemos not at all. Sostratos got the sailors to start handing sheaves of catapult bolts, stacks of shields, and other military gear up the gangplank to the loungers, which had the added benefit of keeping would-be thieves off the akatos. Sostratos had let Menedemos do the talking; that wasn't his strength. But when it came to making sure things ran smoothly, he was hard to beat.

As the last of the weapons headed into the polis, Menedemos came up onto the pier and spoke to his father and Sostratos': "We have silver aboard, too, and some other things that will want securing."

"I hoped you might," Philodemos said. Lysistratos dipped his head.

Sostratos spoke up then: "I'll need some of that silver to pay off the rowers. They had easy times in Alexandria, but gods know they worked hard taking us there and back. And they all pulled like heroes when we were getting away from Demetrios' monster of a galley."

"True. Too true!" Menedemos said. "I felt like a sprat with a tuna after me. But we *did* get away."

"Fine. I'll get some people we can count on to bring those things back to our house and Lysistratos'," his father said. "And Sostratos can bring the rest of the silver back with him when he finishes paying the men. I'll send a couple of beefy fellows to walk back with him, too, so no one knocks him over the head between here and the houses."

"Thanks, Uncle Philodemos," Sostratos said. Menedemos wondered if his father would have done the same for him had he been the one doling out drakhmai to the rowers. Probably, he admitted to himself. The silver was important, even if his own carcass wasn't.

He was back in Rhodes. He let himself believe it. He had a baby half-brother—or maybe a baby son. And the woman he loved, the woman with whom he might have fathered the baby, had come through the birth, and hadn't given him away. Taken all in all, life might have been much worse in spite of what Demetrios did to Ptolemaios.

"Tonight," he said, "I'm going to get drunk." No one, not even his father, tried to tell him no.

The sun was setting in the west, over the far side of the polis of Rhodes. Sostratos sat on the *Aphrodite's* steps leading up to the stern platform. He had a leather sack of drakhmai to his right and his notes on which man was owed how much to his left. He'd paid off the rowers one by one. Some of them grumbled a little at what they got. But he had the written records, and they didn't. Nobody kicked up a big fuss.

Last in line came Attinos. The Egyptian who spoke profane Greek didn't complain about his pay. Sostratos said, "I'm sorry, but I have no idea when you'll be able to go back to Alexandria."

"Me, neither. Ahh, futter it," Attinos said with a shrug. "You know where maybe I find some work here?"

"Let me think." Sostratos plucked at his beard. He switched languages to ask, "Do you speak Aramaic?"

"Little fucking bit," Attinos said in that language. What he knew, he must have learned from the kind of people from whom he'd picked up his Greek. Or maybe he spoke Egyptian the same way, too. Some men cursed as readily as they breathed. He went on, "Talk Greek better."

"All right. Even a little will help you," Sostratos said. "I don't know a whole lot myself. But there's a Phoenician merchant named Himilkon who might take you on. His warehouses are that way, three piers down and one street inland." He pointed. "Tell him he can ask me about you."

Attinos grinned crookedly. "So you tell him what a big son of a whore I is?"

Sostratos laughed. "If I thought you were, I wouldn't give you his name. It's starting to get dark, so I don't know if he's still there now, but he will be in the morning."

"I try him," Attinos said. "Most Hellenes, they wide-arses who don't even think Egyptians and other foreigners is people. You, you different. How come you is?"

As usual, Sostratos took the question seriously. "I don't know. I've done business with Hellenes and with barbarians, and I haven't seen a whole lot of differences. Good men and bad, honest men and thieves? Some everywhere."

"Truth. Fornicating truth." Attinos stowed his pay in a belt pouch. He sketched Sostratos a salute, then went up the gangplank, down the pier, and off toward Himilkon's warehouse.

Sostratos still had a few coins in his hand. He slid them back into the leather sack from which they'd come and tied it shut with a rawhide thong. After carefully noting that he'd paid the last rower, he turned to the pair of bruisers Uncle Philodemos had hired; they were lolling on the stern platform, waiting for him to finish his business.

"Very good, best ones," he said. "If you'll be kind enough to escort me back to my father's house ...."

They climbed to their feet. One was taller, the other wider. "Right you are, sir," the wider man said. "You just come with us."

As soon as they got off the pier, the taller one ducked into a tavern and came out with a sputtering torch. "Getting dark," he remarked. "This'll maybe keep us from stepping in something nasty." He and his friend wore sandals. Sostratos, as usual, went barefoot. He held his peace.

No one did step in anything too vile. The guard's torch was guttering by the time they got to Lysistratos' house. When his father let him in, Sostratos brought the man a fresh light. He also gave him and his friend a couple of oboloi apiece.

"You don't have to do that, sir," the torchbearer said. "Philodemos, he already paid us."

"I know. You're a good man for saying so, though," Sostratos replied. "This isn't from my uncle. This is from me."

Across the street, the squalls of a baby floated out from Philodemos' house. The tough fellow who didn't have a torch made a face. "You'll have fun sleeping tonight with a brat so close and all," he said.

"I won't mind too much. I hope not, anyhow. That's my new little first cousin," Sostratos said.

"That's Philodemos' son?" asked the man with the torch. Sostratos dipped his head. The guard went on, "How about that? Philodemos, he's not too young, but I guess he's not too old, neither."

Lysistratos stuck his head out into the street. "He's my brother. My *older* brother, mind you. I'll tell him you said that."

Everyone laughed. The guards headed off to their own homes, or maybe to a wineshop. After Sostratos went back inside, his father closed and barred the door. "Is anything left to eat?" Sostratos asked. "It's been a long time since breakfast."

"Go on into the andron," Lysistratos replied. "Threissa will bring you some supper."

Lamps already lit the men's room. A jar of wine, one of water, a dipper, and some cups sat on a small table by Sostratos' usual couch. His father came in with him. "Will you drink wine with me, sir?" Sostratos asked him. "How strong would you like it?"

"A little less than half wine, I think," Lysistratos said. "You're coming home tonight—we can have it stronger than usual."

"I was hoping you'd say that." Sostratos watered the wine for his father and himself. He raised his cup. "Your health!"

"And yours," Lysistratos answered. They both poured libations on the floor.

Threissa carried in a wooden tray with a loaf of barley bread, a small bowl of olive oil, a larger bowl of olives, and a platter of fried smelts—fried just now, Sostratos' nose told him, not sitting on a counter in the kitchen since the rest of the family ate.

"Thank you, my dear," Sostratos told the slave. "You've saved my life with this."

"Is not'ing," she said in her accented Greek. Like a lot of barbarians—and, indeed, like some Ionians—she had trouble with aspirated consonants. And she looked as if she wanted to hide while standing in plain sight. She was not enamored of Sostratos, but if he told her to come up to bed with him she had to go. He hadn't told her that for a long time, but it didn't mean he wouldn't, especially when he was just back from a long stretch at sea.

At the moment, he had other appetites that wanted slaking. He tore off a chunk of bread, dipped it in the oil, and popped it into his mouth. "That's good oil!" he exclaimed.

"It's Damonax's," his father replied. "The same kind of stuff you were flogging in Egypt. You must have got rid of it, too. I didn't see our work gang hauling any back here."

"I sold a lot of it to the fellow who cooks for Ptolemaios' nomarch in Memphis. He's a Rhodian himself, from the same village as Damonax's family. It tasted like old times to him, so he bought quite a bit," Sostratos said.

"*Euge!*" Lysistratos said. "Did you get a good price?"

"Father, I got a terrific price. He was playing with the nomarch's silver, after all, not his own. He didn't care how much he spent."

"Egypt is as rich as they say, then?"

"Richer!" Sostratos paused to sip wine, eat a couple of olives, and pop first one smelt and then another into his mouth. As he chewed, he went on, "No one who hasn't been there can imagine how rich it is. No one in Hellas, no one even in old Sybaris or in Syracuse, lives the way that nomarch does. And he was just a nomarch! Ptolemaios' place in Alexandria …." He tossed his head in disbelief, then took more smelts from the platter. After he ate them, he said, "I can't finish all of this, Father. I'll burst if I try. Have some with me, please."

"Maybe one or two," Lysistratos said. Then he held the platter out to Threissa. "Would you like some?" Sostratos wished he'd thought to do that.

"T'ank you, Master!" she said, and ate. The family didn't keep its slaves hungry, but they seldom got anything so nice.

"Get yourself a cup and have a little wine, too," Sostratos said, trying to make amends. She scurried away, returning a moment later with a cup like his and his father's. Sostratos watered her wine the same as he had for himself and Lysistratos. She made a face at him. Like Egyptians and many other barbarians, Thracians drank neat wine when in their native land.

But she smiled as she poured it down. "Is tasty!" she said.

"Good," Sostratos replied. He poured more for his father, then more for himself. Before long, the slave woman's cup was empty, too. Thracians had a name for drunkenness; Hellenes said Macedonians had learned their bad habits from them.

When he offered her a refill, though, she shook her head. Then she remembered to toss it like a Hellene. "No, young master, t'ank you," she said. "I will fall down taking t'ings back to the kitc'en for was'ing."

He shrugged. "However you please." Had he been thinking that, if she got tiddly, she might put up with him better? He knew perfectly well that he had.

His father asked, "Do I need to know anything your cousin didn't tell people at the harbor?"

"Only that we made a lot of silver down in Egypt, sir. If you're a Hellene, you have to work hard not to make silver in Egypt, I think," Sostratos replied. "The question is whether we'll be able to keep it."

"The polis has been strengthening the walls and the forts ever since Demetrios called on us this spring," his father said. "Our men are training with weapons, too—you know about that."

"Yes, sir. I was training myself, before the *Aphrodite* sailed."

"Everyone's doing it. Even oldsters like your uncle and I have been practicing with spear and shield and sword."

Sostratos smiled. "How much good do you think you'd do against a veteran mercenary half your age?"

"Probably not a lot." Sostratos' father was almost as thoroughgoing a realist as he was himself. But Lysistratos continued, "I'll have a better chance than if I hadn't practiced, though. So will Philodemos. And fighting is like dicing. Every once in a while, you roll a triple six. Maybe we'll be lucky."

"May the gods hear you!" Sostratos said.

"Thanks. Maybe we won't have to fight at all," Lysistratos said. "We won't do Antigonos and Demetrios any harm if they let us stay free and independent. They have to be able to see that … don't they?" The falling note in his voice said he was trying to convince himself.

"Let's hope the Ptolemaios got back to Alexandria. If he did, we still have a counterweight of sorts against Antigonos and his son. If he didn't." If Ptolemaios was captured or dead … Sostratos poured more wine, and watered it less than he had before. No, he didn't want to think about that at all.

Neither did his father. "Let me have another cup, too, if you please," Lysistratos said. Sostratos poured out another strong draught. After taking it with a murmur of thanks, his father asked Threissa, "Would you care for more, my dear?" He spoke to her with as much courtesy as if she were a high-born lady he happened to meet on a trading voyage. Sostratos admired the effect while knowing he couldn't hope to imitate it.

She'd turned him down. For his father, she dipped her head. "If you please, Master. T'ank you very muc'."

Sostratos did the honors. Again, he mixed the slave's wine as he had for himself and his father. She noticed the difference; she looked sharply at him after her first sip. But then she smiled. It might not have been the neat wine Thracians were said to crave so much, but it came closer to that than what she usually got.

Lysistratos drained his cup fast. After finishing it, he looked a bit glassy-eyed—or maybe it was only reflections from the lamps. He let out a long sigh. "We're sprats. You know that, son? Nothing but sprats. And the days when anchovies can make a living—can live at all—are just about gone. Pretty soon, the sea will hold nothing but tunny and sharks."

"Menedemos and I talked about the same thing. I hope you're wrong," Sostratos said, fearing his father was right.

"So do I, but I wouldn't bet on it. Only I am, aren't I, with my life and everything I care about?" The older man got to his feet. "And I've drunk myself stupid, or at least tired. I'm going up to bed. Good night, both of you." Stepping slowly and carefully, he left the andron.

"Will you come up to my room with me?" Sostratos asked Threissa as soon his his he heard his father's footsteps on the stairs.

She bit her lip. "Do I have to, young master?"

He tossed his head. "No. I won't make you. But if you can put up with me ...." He could have beaten her, or just spent the next year making her life miserable in ways small and large. He knew he wouldn't do anything like that. He hoped Threissa knew him well enough so she also understood he wouldn't. The way he'd said what he'd just said should have told her he didn't expect miracles of passion.

She thought for longer than he wished she would have. In the flickering lamplight, he had trouble reading her face. At last, she shrugged. "We can do. Why not? You don't try to hurt me or anyt'ing." By her tone, she understood how lucky a slave woman was to be able to say even so much.

"Come on, then." Part of Sostratos knew he should have felt shame, but desire swamped it. He got up and walked toward the stairs, picking up a lamp to light the way. Threissa followed.

He closed and barred the door to his room, then set the lamp on a stool near the bed. He pulled his tunic off over his head. A moment later, Threissa did the same with her longer one. Even the small lampflame showed her skin milk-pale where the sun didn't touch her. Unlike Greek or Egyptian women, she didn't pluck or shave her bush.

They lay down together. His hands roamed her. He kissed her mouth, and kissed and caressed her breasts. He wanted to make her happy if he could. He knew he hadn't when he'd taken her before. Pleasing her felt like a challenge.

He put her on elbows and knees and went into her from behind, as he would have done if she were a Hellene. His pleasure built and built and overflowed ... and if she felt any at all, she hid it very well.

When he slid out, she squatted over the chamber pot and got rid of as much of his seed as she could. Women who didn't want to conceive commonly did that. Maybe it helped, maybe not. They thought so. Sostratos had no idea, though he was sure it couldn't hurt.

She picked up her tunic and put it on. Sostratos had thought about a second round, but it wasn't urgent enough for him to say anything. He gave her a drakhma instead. "For your patience," he said.

"T'ank you," she said, and then, "Women got to be patient with men. We get in too much trouble when we not."

Any number of stories from history and tragedy sprang into Sostratos' mind. "I believe you," he said. "Good night." She opened the door and slid out. He pissed in the pot himself, then blew out the lamp, lay down, and fell asleep almost as fast as if he'd been clubbed.

XV

MENEDEMOS YAWNED AS HE ATE BREAD AND OIL and drank watered wine at breakfast. His father was yawning, too. "I'd forgotten what a racket you used to make all night long," Philodemos said.

"Diodoros takes after me, all right," Menedemos answered, and then quickly raised his cup to his mouth so his father couldn't see his face. *Careful, fool!* he told himself. He didn't know whether the baby was his or his father's. He never would. But he knew his father would want to kill him for lying with Baukis whether he'd got her with child or not.

Philodemos chuckled. "I expect I did the same thing when I was tiny. Everyone does."

"Tiny is right!" Menedemos could safely say that. "He fit in the crook of my elbow when I held him last night. And he doesn't seem to weigh anything at all."

"You have to be careful to keep something under their heads for the first few months," his father said. "They aren't strong enough to hold them up for themselves at first."

"Yes, Father. Your wife told me the same thing before she let me pick him up," Menedemos said. The way Baukis looked had shocked him. She seemed to have aged five years, and to have worked through those five years in the mines. They didn't call it labor for nothing. And she hadn't given the smallest sign of remembering the passion they'd shared. Everything centered on Diodoros to her.

"I'm glad to see what a good mother she makes. And she's come through childbirth as well as a woman can—better than your mother did after she had you." Philodemos stared down into his own cup of wine. He still mourned his first wife, while Menedemos hardly remembered her or the sister she'd died birthing.

As if in one of Aristophanes' comedies, Diodoros chose that moment to start crying again. Philodemos rolled his eyes. He'd been going through this since the baby came into the world. Menedemos said, "He has good lungs, that's for sure. Gods grant he stay healthy, and the lady your wife, too."

"I've prayed. I've sacrificed. I've done everything a man can do," his father said. "The midwife and the physician both think she's doing as well as anyone could hope—and your brother, too."

"May it be so!" Menedemos exclaimed.

"Yes. Losing a wee one is hard. You know you shouldn't love them—they're so fragile when they're small—but you can't help yourself," his father said. He would know what he was talking about, too.

Menedemos emptied his morning cup and thought about pouring himself another, this one with less water in it. That might make his heart beat faster. But people joked about men who started drinking hard as soon as they rolled out of bed. He knew a couple of men like that, and he joked about them … when they weren't around to hear him, anyway.

His father also cast a longing glance at the amphora and at the mixing krater, but he didn't fill his cup again, either. His father was a sensible man—not annoyingly sensible like, say, Sostratos, but sensible all the same. Philodemos slid off his couch and stood up. "Do you want to come upstairs with me and have another look at Diodoros?" he asked.

"I'll do that." Menedemos also rose. A house slave could clean up what they'd left—and likely eat some of the bread and oil. The household had never been one that fed its two-legged property barely enough to stay alive. You got runaways when you did that, and even the slaves who wouldn't flee also wouldn't work hard or take any pains at what they did.

And seeing his half-brother (if Diodoros wasn't his son) would also let him see Baukis. She wouldn't care, not the way she was right now, but he would. He followed his father to the stairs.

As they went up, the older man remarked, "I have to give you credit, son. You show more interest in the baby than I thought you would. My guess was, you'd just complain all the time about how much noise he made."

That made Menedemos miss a step. He grabbed at the handrail to keep from falling on his face. Then he said, "He's part of the family, too, sir. Depending on how things work out for Sostratos and me, he may end up running the business one of these years."

"You *are* growing up. It's taken you longer than it should have, but you are." Philodemos hardly ever gave a compliment without dipping it in vinegar first.

Philodemos knocked on the door to the women's quarters instead of just going in, as he had the right to do. He'd knocked the evening before, too, maybe because he'd also had Menedemos along them, maybe as a courtesy to the new mother inside.

A slave woman opened the door. She dipped her head to Philodemos. "Good day, Master." She dipped it again to Menedemos, not quite so deeply. "And good day to you, young master."

"Good day, Xanthe," Menedemos and his father answered together. The slave's hair was more light brown than yellow, but they called her Blondie anyhow.

"You wish to see the mistress and your son, sir?" she asked. Then she glanced at Menedemos. "Your little son, I mean."

"I understood you." Philodemos smiled. He seemed happier than he had before the *Aphrodite* sailed for Alexandria. And why not? He had that new son (or at least thought Diodoros was his), and Baukis had come through childbirth as well as could be expected. He went on, "We heard the baby crying when we were eating breakfast downstairs—and if he's awake, Baukis will be, too."

Xanthe also smiled. "That's right. She's nursing him now. Let me tell her the two of you are here." As a Hellene would have, she used the dual, not the plural, to show that Philodemos and Menedemos formed a natural pair. She'd grown up speaking Greek; her mother had been a slave before her.

She ducked back into the mistress' bedroom. Except a few times with his father after Philodemos remarried, Menedemos hadn't gone in there since the days when he was a little boy with his own mother. He wondered how he would have been different had she lived longer, but shrugged a tiny shrug. How could you hope to know such a thing?

Sticking her head out the door, Xanthe said, "She's ready for you, masters."

Menedemos stayed a step behind his father as they went inside. He was here on Philodemos' sufferance. Had Philodemos known how he felt about Baukis, had he known they'd lain together ....

No. That didn't bear thinking about. And Father didn't know any of those things. Gods willing, he never would.

The bedroom smelled a bit of human waste, but any room with a chamber pot in it was liable to. The odor here didn't seem much stronger than usual.

Baukis sat at the edge of the bed. A shawl draped over her shoulder and over the baby let her preserve her modesty while the baby nursed. Diodoros made little grunting and sucking noises, the way a puppy or a lamb might have.

"Good day, my husband," Baukis said. "I should be finished here soon. He drank the other breast dry—he won't want much at this one."

"All right. I'm always glad to hear he's eating well." Philodemos wore that almost-foolish smile again. He might be immune to all the ploys Menedemos used to soften him, but just by existing Diodoros had him wrapped around his finger.

"Good day," Menedemos said to Baukis. "How do you hold?"

"How do I hold?" Her mouth twisted into a wry smile. "I'm *tired*, son of my husband. I don't go anywhere—I hardly leave this room. I don't do anything but nurse the baby and take care of the baby, and that's plenty to leave me so tired, I can hardly see."

Menedemos noticed the way she said *son of my husband*. Diodoros also was, or might be, the son of her husband. Was she thinking about how things that worked to the baby's advantage might work against Menedemos, and the other way round? If she was, what could he do about it? Not much he could see.

Diodoros wiggled under the shawl. Baukis said, "See? I knew he was just about done. Turn your backs, both of you, while I set myself to rights."

Along with his father, Menedemos turned and looked at the door through which he'd come in. He didn't try to sneak a glance at his stepmother while she rearranged her clothes. He knew better than to blunder into such a simple trap.

"All right. You can turn around again," she said.

He did, along with his father. Her chiton covered her the way it should once more. She'd folded the shawl and put it on her left shoulder. Diodoros' head—still a bit misshapen after his passage through the birth canal—lay on it. She held him nearly upright with her left arm, using the crook of her elbow to support his backside. She patted—almost drummed—his back with the palm of her right hand.

Diodoros soon let out a surprisingly loud, surprisingly deep belch. Laughing in surprise, Menedemos exclaimed, "Brekekekex! Koax! Koax!"

His father chuckled, too. Baukis just blinked—she knew no Aristophanes. She asked, "Did he spit up any?"

"Not this time," Philodemos said.

"Good," she said. "I'm going to try to get him back to sleep." She slid Diodoros from almost upright to flat, making sure she supported his floppy little head all the while. Then she rocked him in her arms as if they made a cradle. Philodemos slipped out of the bedchamber, Menedemos half a step behind.

Menedemos didn't throw himself over the handrail and down into the courtyard headfirst. Why he didn't, he couldn't have said just then, but he didn't. He walked down the stairs behind his father instead.

Sostratos took to hanging around the harbor for news so much, anyone who didn't know him as a prominent merchant's son and as a rising merchant himself would have taken him for one of the odd-jobs men who made their oboloi running errands and hauling bundles from ship to storeroom or from storeroom to ship.

A skipper just in from Corinth did mistake him for one of those men, and gave him three oboloi to tell Himilkon the Phoenician his ship had arrived. Keeping a straight face, Sostratos took the little silver coins and stowed them between his gum and his cheek; he didn't happen to have a pouch on his belt.

One of the real dockside loungers told the Corinthian, "You silly fool, don't you know that's Lysistratos' son?"

"It's all right, Epinikos," Sostratos said easily. "I know where Himilkon's warehouse is, and I need to talk with him anyhow."

"I crave your pardon, O best one," said the Corinthian, who'd plainly heard of Sostratos' father. "I meant no offense."

"I took none. And it's fair pay for the job," Sostratos replied over his shoulder. "I'll be back with him before long."

Himilkon came back to the piers readily enough. "Mikkiades has some marble I hope to buy. I've got a sculptor asking after it," he said.

"It's all right with me," Sostratos answered in Aramaic. Talking with Himilkon helped him stay in practice. "Did you hire that Egyptian I sent you?"

"Yes, and thank you," Himilkon answered in the same language. "I'm glad you did. He works hard, and he's smart. May I ask you something else, if you would be so kind?"

"Ask, my master," Sostratos said. Aramaic had more flowery politeness built into it than his own language did.

Perhaps to make sure he'd be understood, the Phoenician fell back into Greek: "If Antigonos and Demetrios attack Rhodes, what will the polis do with resident aliens like me?"

"I don't think anything has been decided. If it has, I don't know about it. But I might not, since I'm just back from Alexandria," Sostratos said carefully. "Are you willing to fight for the polis?"

"Willing, yes. But I am no warrior," Himilkon said. Sure enough, he was middle-aged, potbellied, and soft-handed.

"If you're on top of the wall and trying to keep enemies from getting up there with you, that may not matter so much. Siege warfare is different from a battle on the plains."

"I suppose so." Himilkon seemed unconvinced.

"That drakhma has two sides," Sostratos went on. "If Demetrios besieges Rhodes—which the gods prevent!—he may just try to starve us into submission. How much room will we have for men who eat up our food but don't want to help us defend ourselves?"

Himilkon pulled a sour face. "There is that, yes. Would the citizens truly be hard-hearted enough to cast aliens out of the polis so the slave dealers who follow any army can seize them?"

"If it comes to a choice between that and falling prey to slavers themselves, they're liable to," Sostratos answered. "That's what will happen to us, and to our wives and children, if Rhodes falls. Maybe you should go to the gymnasion and learn what you can."

"I am not a Hellene. I do not care to show the world my naked body," Himilkon said with dignity, setting one hand on his paunch.

"We try to have bodies worth looking at. We don't always manage, but we do try," Sostratos said. "You could wear a chiton while you train, I suppose."

"Maybe. Unlike you folk, I think it's indecent for other people to watch my pecker flapping when I run or dodge."

"How do you feel about taking a spear in the belly because you didn't know which way to dodge?"

The Phoenician didn't answer that. Instead, he picked up his pace so he could get to the pier faster. The Corinthian merchant skipper might haggle about how much he wanted for his block of marble, but he wouldn't ask such inconvenient questions.

Sostratos didn't push him, either. When he was younger, he would have. Now ... *I don't* know *that the Assembly would throw aliens out of the polis*, he told himself. *And Himilkon is a free man, even if he isn't a Hellene. He'll have to choose for himself.*

Himilkon kept walking fast. At the moment, he seemed eager to be rid of Sostratos. The Rhodian peeled off and let him finish the trip to the harbor by himself. Sostratos paused in a tavern to buy himself a cup of wine. As he drank it—unwatered, as if he were a Macedonian or a barbarian—he thought about Sokrates, whom the Athenians had executed almost a century earlier.

Only people who studied philosophy read Platon's accounts of Sokrates' teaching and his defense against the charges the Athenians threw at him. Naturally, people who cared enough about philosophy to read those dialogues and the *Apology* sympathized with Sokrates.

For the first time, Sokrates wondered what living in a polis with Sokrates roaming the agora would have been like. How many people enjoyed the company of a man who went around asking those inconvenient questions all the time? One or two from Sostratos had been plenty to make Himilkon want to get away as fast as he could.

Sokrates had called himself a gadfly. What did you do, though, when a gadfly bit you again and again? Either you went mad with pain and irritation or you tried to squash it. Suddenly, Sostratos understood from the inside out what the grandfathers and great-grandfathers of today's Athenians had been up against.

He went to the gymnasion the next morning to start exercising again. He was intrigued to find Himilkon there before him; and Hyssaldomos, the Phoenician's Karian slave and right-hand man; and Attinos as well. The merchant and the slave still wore their chitons. The Egyptian, who'd rowed as naked as any of the Hellenes on the *Aphrodite*, stripped off in the gymnasion, too.

With an oarsman's powerful arms, a flat belly, and strong legs, he had a body fit to be seen. He had most of a body fit to be seen, anyhow. A Hellene shouted at him: "Hey! What's the matter with your prong?"

Like Ioudaioi, Egyptian men had their foreskins cut off when they were babies. To Hellenes, that seemed a mutilation. As Pindar said, though, custom was king of all. Attinos thought he was the normal one. "Nothing wrong with my prick, you cistern-arsed son of an ugly dog," he answered. "You want I should stick it up that fat *prokton* of yours?"

"You can't talk to me like that!" the Hellene shouted. "I'll murder you!" He charged the Egyptian, arms flailing.

People said that if you hit a barbarian in the stomach, he'd cover it up, so then you could punch him in the nose. People who said that had never seen Attinos. He ducked under the Hellene's wild punches, tripped him, jumped on him, and began hitting him in the face again and again.

"How you like my prick now, you hyena turd?" he said, and landed yet another punch.

Sostratos grabbed his shoulder. "Enough! Enough, by the gods! If you kill him, you'll get in trouble with the law and you'll have a blood feud with his whole family."

"All right," Attinos said, agreeably enough. As he got to his feet, he rubbed his bruised knuckles against the outsides of his thighs.

216

The Hellene was much slower rising, and none too steady on his pins when at last he did. He already had a mouse under his left eye and a bruise on one cheek. His nose leaned to the right; blood ran from both nostrils. He had a cut lip, too. When he spat, he spat out more blood and a couple of broken teeth.

"By the gods, I'll sue you for everything you'll ever have, you stinking barbarian!" he said, his voice mushy from the pounding his mouth had taken—and maybe because he still wasn't thinking any too straight, either.

"Futter your mother," Attinos replied, direct as usual.

"You're a fool if you go to law," Sostratos told the Hellene. "You insulted him first, and you tried to hit him first, too. Plenty of witnesses here will say so."

The man spat out more blood. "What are you doing, taking a barbarian's part against a Hellene?"

"What were *you* doing, picking a fight with someone who came to the gymnasion to exercise so he'd do a better job fighting for Rhodes if it comes to that?" Sostratos returned. "We need all the help we can find, and you want to laugh at somebody's prong? To the crows with you!"

When the other Hellene looked around, he saw no sympathy on the faces of nearby men. As he staggered away, someone held out a bowl of water. He dipped some up with both hands to wash off his battered face. When he saw how much blood he was rinsing off, he cursed some more.

Himilkon stared at Attinos as if he'd just grown a second head. "I should sack the man who guards my warehouse and pay you to do that!"

"Whatever you want, boss," the Egyptian said.

He proved less than expert with sword and spear, though. That plainly came from lack of practice, but it eased Sostratos' mind. He'd wondered whether he'd brought a new Herakles back to Rhodes.

He doggedly went through his own exercises. No one would ever mistake him for a demigod returned to earth. All he hoped for was a better chance to stay alive if war came to his island and his polis.

Sostratos was scraping off the oil with which he'd rubbed himself when a man hurried in saying, "Menelaos has surrendered his army—

217

twelve thousand foot soldiers and twelve hundred horsemen—and Salamis to Demetrios."

That saddened Sostratos without surprising him. Someone else beat him to the question he most wanted to ask: "What will Demetrios do with Ptolemaios' brother?"

"He's already set him free without any ransom. Same with the soldiers," replied the fellow with the news.

Sostratos whistled softly. Demetrios had acted very generously indeed, far more so than Hellenes and Macedonians usually did. As if reading his mind, the man who'd asked the question said, "He's asking for trouble."

"Maybe, but maybe not," the informant said. "I heard he's keeping the soldiers' armor. He's sending something like twelve hundred panoplies to Athens."

That impressed most of the men in the gymnasion, but not Sostratos. He'd seen how wealthy Egypt was. Most places would have trouble replacing an army's worth of armor. All Ptolemaios had to do was give the order and set the smiths in villages and towns up and down the Nile to work.

Ptolemaios … Sostratos asked the newcomer, "Did the Demetrios catch the lord of Egypt, or did he manage to get away?"

The man spread his hands. "I didn't hear one way or the other. I don't think anyone in Rhodes knows yet."

"All right. Thanks," Sostratos said. He'd wondered whether Demetrios had freed Menelaos because he still held the more important brother. Now he'd have to keep wondering till Demetrios paraded Ptolemaios before Antigonos, or till word came from Egypt that Ptolemaios had made it back to Alexandria.

"Before long, every bit of Cyprus will lie in Demetrios' hands," Himilkon said as he walked back toward his warehouse with his men and Sostratos. "That can't be good for Rhodes."

"Nothing that's happened lately has been good for Rhodes," Sostratos said. "We're like a sick man. If the fever breaks, we'll get better. If it doesn't …." He let his voice trail off, not wanting to speak words of evil omen.

Himilkon replied, "Well, I'm not sorry I'm starting to learn the warrior's trade after all." He patted that ample belly. "I have a bit more training to do, I think."

"If the gods are kind, all of this nonsense will have been for nothing," Sostratos said. Himilkon, Hyssaldomos, and Attinos walked along in a silence suggesting they didn't think it would be. Since Sostratos didn't, either, he could hardly blame them for that.

He said his farewells at the warehouse, then went back to his home, where he gave his father the news. "Demetrios must really want to be Alexander's successor," Lysistratos said. "Alexander might have done something like that. I can't think of any other Macedonian who would—and I'm including Demetrios' father."

"Antigonos? No. He always has his eye on the main chance," Sostratos agreed. He rubbed his chin. "But Demetrios .... That's interesting, what you said. I hadn't looked at it just that way before. He's as handsome as everyone says the Alexander was."

"I only saw him the once, in the Assembly, and we weren't that close to him," his father said. "I mostly know him from a bust or two and from coins. Those always make you look better than you really do."

"True enough." Sostratos dipped his head. "You did see he was tall, though—taller than I am, and not many are. Alexander was supposed to be a little fellow, wasn't he? Demetrios could make himself out to be the improved version, you might say."

"Improved how?" his father asked. "Alexander went out and conquered the Persian Empire and went on into India. All Demetrios has ever done is fight other Hellenes and Macedonians. Even if he went after Carthage or the barbarians in Italy, that wouldn't come close to matching what Alexander did."

"You're not wrong, sir," Sostratos said. "But before he does any of that, he'll try to take Rhodes."

He wished his father would have told him he was being foolish. But Lysistratos just said, "Yes, I think so, too." After that, the conversation flagged. Neither of them seemed to see much point in saying more.

Menedemos spent as much of his waking time as he could away from the house where he'd grown up. He worked out in the gymnasion with a ferocity even the hardened Cretan mercenaries who schooled Rhodians in the art of fighting on foot noticed.

One of them rubbed his shoulder after a blow from Menedemos' wooden sword got home. "You could hire yourself out to any warlord from Sicily to the Indos River," the veteran said. "I'll be sore for the next two moon quarters, bugger me blind if I won't. Most Rhodians, they still reckon this is a game. You, though, you want to kill things."

"Do I?" Menedemos thought about it. He shrugged. "Well, what if I do?"

"Not everybody's got that, not even every soldier." The mercenary twisted his neck. "It's turning black already, where you nailed me. Lucky you weren't using iron. I'd've bled to death by now."

His modest triumph pleased Menedemos not at all. After he scraped off his sweat and put his chiton back on, he went to a tavern. Someone who'd started pouring it down even earlier in the day had already drunk himself mean. For whatever reason, he chose Menedemos to swing at. Menedemos jerked his head to one side and kicked the brawler in the crotch. The man went down with a shriek. He rolled on the dirt floor, clutching at himself. Menedemos emptied his own cup, set it on the counter, and kicked the man in the ribs as he walked out.

"You could have killed him!" the taverner called after him.

"Too bad," Menedemos said over his shoulder. "Maybe he'll remember what I gave him before he tries to knock some other stranger's teeth out." He kept walking. He hoped somebody would come after him, but no one did.

Then he went down to the harbor. He wasn't surprised to spot Sostratos' gangly form there. They were both after news. Since he didn't feel like talking with his cousin, he stayed several piers away from him.

An akation rowed into the harbor. Menedemos shaded his eyes with one hand, wondering if it was the same one that had given him such a fright off the south coast of Cyprus. He didn't think so. This one seemed larger—not quite a triakonter, with fifteen rowers on each side, but not far short of that.

He didn't remember ever seeing the ship before. That was odd; he thought he knew most honest vessels of that size, vessels likely to bring goods to Rhodes. Pirates were different, but pirates didn't put in at this harbor.

The akation made for an open berthing space at the pier next to the one by whose base he stood. Casually, as if he had nothing much to do and all the time in the world to do it in, he ambled over to the newcomer. He wasn't the only man who did, of course, but in spite of his seeming laziness he got there in time to catch a rope one of the crewmen tossed him and to secure it to a bollard.

"You've been to sea a time or two, I reckon," the man said. "That's a proper square knot, by the gods."

"Oh, I may have," Menedemos answered. "What ship are you? You're new here, I think."

"We may be. This is the *Tykhe*, out of Alexandria."

"Lady Luck, are you? What's your cargo? If you don't mind my asking, I mean." Menedemos did his best to hide a sudden surge of interest. Some of the other Rhodians on the pier exclaimed, in surprise or excitement. A ship from Alexandria, now ....

Tykhe's skipper must have heard Menedemos' question. He answered it from the stern platform: "What we bring here is news, important news. I am pleased to inform the people of Rhodes that the great and glorious Ptolemaios, the lord of Egypt, is by the gods' kindness returned safe and hale to Alexandria."

Everyone in earshot shouted then, Menedemos no less than anybody else. When he could make himself heard over the hubbub, he said, "That's important news, sure enough, and the best of news for Rhodes. Will you tell it again, at my father's house?" He got away from the house whenever he could, yes. But this was the polis' business, not a family entanglement.

"Who are you, and who is your father?" By the way the *Tykhe*'s captain said it, he wouldn't visit just anyone. Well, who could blame him?

"I'm Menedemos son of Philodemos." Either the Alexandrian would know his name or not.

He did. "*Are* you?" he exclaimed, eyebrows rising. "Yes, I'll come with you, then. One of the things the Ptolemaios charged me to do while I was here was learn whether you'd made it back. He'll be pleased when I tell him you and your cousin have."

Menedemos was a little less than pleased the skipper had mentioned his cousin, too, though he knew Ptolemaios thought well of Sostratos. "Come along, then," he said shortly. But he unbent enough to add, "Tell me your name, O best one, so the slaves can use it to bring our polis' leaders to the house."

"I'm Areton son of Aretakles," the man said. As soon as his men ran the gangplank to the pier, he went up it and joined Menedemos. He was about forty, lean and fit and burnt brown by the sun.

Sostratos had been making his way toward the *Tykhe*—he was curious about the strange ship, too. He tagged along with Menedemos and Areton on their way to the house, then went into his own across the street to bring his father over. Philodemos was upstairs with Baukis and Diodoros when Menedemos brought Areton inside, but quickly came down. Sostratos and Lysistratos got back to the house almost at once. Menedemos' father sent slaves to fetch Komanos, Xanthos, and other civic leaders. In the meantime, he offered Areton bread and oil and raisins and olives and wine.

"You're very kind, sir," the skipper said.

"You are my guest-friend," Philodemos replied with dignity. To an old-fashioned man like him, that said everything that needed saying.

The dignitaries arrived even sooner than Menedemos had thought they would. They wanted news from Alexandria, all right. As soon as they got it, Xanthos started to launch into an oration of praise and gratitude. Komanos cut him off, asking, "Will the Ptolemaios be able to help us if Demetrios and Antigonos try to seize the island and the polis?"

"With supplies, possibly. With a naval force?" Areton tossed his head. "Not soon. Menedemos here will have told you what a beating the fleet took. Ptolemaios will be some time rebuilding and recruiting, I'm afraid."

"We're on our own, then." Philodemos brought it out like a physician giving a bad prognosis.

Areton didn't try to tell him he was wrong. "I am sorry, but that's how things hold right now."

"Well, it isn't anything we weren't expecting," Menedemos' father said. "Now we know the worst." Again, neither Areton nor anyone else contradicted him.

XVI

SOSTRATOS WATCHED THE *TYKHE* LEAVE THE harbor and head back towards Egypt. Good news and bad: good that Ptolemaios wasn't dead or loaded down with chains, bad that Rhodes was on its own.

One of the harborside regulars turned to him and said, "You were just down there, weren't you? What's it like?"

"It's like ..." Sostratos thought for a moment, then spread his hands in despair. "Egypt isn't *like* anything. Alexandria wasn't there at all when we were born, and now it's bigger than Rhodes. Bigger than Athens or Syracuse, too." Those were the biggest Greek cities he could think of. He went on, "And the rest of the country is as ancient as Alexandria is new. The Pyramids, the Sphinx, the temples .... They were all old a thousand years before Akhilleus fought Hektor on the plains outside of Troy."

"I didn't think anything could be older than that," the man said.

"It's true anyway. That's why Egyptians laugh at Hellenes the way grown men laugh at children. We *are* children to them, children or just-sprouted weeds," Sostratos said, remembering his Herodotos.

"Huh!" the other man said. He was unlikely ever to go to Egypt. Rowing or even being a crewman on a sailing ship would seem too

223

much like work to him. He had plenty of opinions about things he'd never seen, though. "We may be weeds, but we're weeds who tell the barbarians there what to do."

"That's …. Oh, never mind." Sostratos knew he couldn't explain it in a way that made sense to an ignorant, untraveled man. Ptolemaios and his nomarchs *did* tell the Egyptians what to do, at least to the extent of collecting the country's wealth. But they did it as the Great Kings of Persia had before them: by acting as if they were Pharaohs in their own right. Whether they could actually change the way the Egyptians thought …. Maybe they were wiser not to try. What would they spawn but rebellion?

"You see?" the dockside lounger said triumphantly. He thought he'd won the argument Sostratos didn't want to have. In the *Apology*, Sokrates talked about men who knew a lot about a little and thought that meant they knew a lot about a lot. This fellow was even worse. He didn't know anything about anything, but thought he knew everything about everything. And how many more just like him were there? Myriads upon myriads.

Sostratos wanted to shove him into the sea. He walked away instead. The man might go to law against him. Or he might not be able to swim and drown. Arrogant stupidity wasn't a capital crime. If it were, not many people would be left in the world.

On his way to nowhere in particular, Sostratos bought some sprats from a man who sold them off a tray. A few were still twitching, so he knew they were fresh. He took them to a tavern. For one obolos more, the man behind the counter plopped them into a kettle of hot olive oil. The sizzle and the smell made Sostratos' mouth water.

He bought some wine to wash down the fried fish. It wasn't a big midday meal, but often he went without any. The sprats were fine, crispy and delicious, the wine no better than it had to be. Sostratos shrugged. You didn't go into a place like this for fine wine. A man snoring on his stool at a table by the wall, his cup on its side in front of him with flies humming around the wine that had spilled from it, showed why people did go in.

When Sostratos left, he headed back to the harbor. But he'd drunk enough wine for nature to assert itself. He could have just hiked up his chiton and eased himself against the nearest wall, as men often did, but found himself only a couple of doors away from a dyer's shop. The man who ran it had rammed the pointed end of an amphora into the ground by his doorway. He used urine in his trade, and made it easy for men to give him some. Sostratos took care of what he needed to do right there.

As he let the front of his tunic drop back into place, he thought about one of the characters Theophrastos (under whom he'd studied in his brief spell in Athens) had described. A mark of the abominable man, Theophrastos said, was that he'd lift his chiton in the agora and wag his prong at women walking by.

Men who did such things thought they were hilarious. Sostratos had heard them laugh while they put themselves on display. The women they exposed themselves to didn't usually think it was so funny. Sostratos agreed with his old mentor: men who did such things *were* abominable.

Before long, he found himself back at the docks again. He seemed to spend time there every day. Whenever a ship from some foreign place came in, he would try to find out whatever news the skipper and sailors were carrying. Menedemos had beaten him to the *Tykhe*, but Sostratos heard things more often than his cousin did.

Ptolemaios' being safe was the most important news that had yet reached Rhodes from the sea-fight near Salamis. Menelaos and his soldiers would be going back to Egypt soon, presumably along with whatever sailors of Ptolemaios' Demetrios' men had fished from the sea.

And yes, Cyprus would belong to Demetrios and his formidable father. That had been plain from the moment the *Aphrodite* had to flee Demetrios' triumphant fleet. It wasn't good news for Rhodes, but Sostratos knew too well his polis couldn't do anything about it.

But what else would Demetrios and Antigonos do with their victory? It was the hardest blow one of Alexander's marshals (here, acting through his son) had dealt another since the great Macedonian conqueror died. Sostratos once more remembered what Alexander had said about who should take his empire while on his deathbed. Right this minute, Antigonos had good reason to claim he was the strongest would-be successor.

A fishing boat Sostratos didn't recognize was tying up at a pier. He would have bet he knew every fishing boat that put out from the polis of Rhodes, though not every boat from the island of Rhodes' smaller settlements.

Boats from the Anatolian mainland or from Cyprus might also visit here. Those from the mainland could be full of fishermen, or they could be full of spies: Antigonos ruled Asia Minor, after all. Sostratos realized the same also held true for Cyprus now that Demetrios had brought it under his father's sway.

But even spies would have fish in their boat's hold to disguise their real business. And even spies, however anxious they were to pick up local news, would also carry some from their home port. So Sostratos drifted over to the new-come boat.

As soon as he heard the fishermen talking, he knew they were Cypriots. Hardly anyone from anywhere else in the Hellenic world spoke that kind of Greek. He remembered thinking how listening to them made him feel as if he'd fallen back through time to Homer's day when Ptolemaios' ill-fated fleet anchored in the harbor at Paphos.

"In good sooth, a king is risen once more in the land," one of the men in the boat was telling the Rhodians who'd already gathered on the pier by the boat.

"Nay, a pair of kings," said another man, older than the first. Only a Cypriot was likely to come out with the dual form of a word like *basileus*, which came from an uncommon class of nouns. This fellow sounded as if he trotted it out every day. For all Sostratos knew, he did. The older man continued, "The Demetrios dispatched to his father a lackey, to tell him of the victories he'd won, on account of which the Antigonos was proclaimed king. And he forthwith sent his victorious son a matching diadem, so they may conjointly rule their realm."

That was as much as Sostratos needed to hear. It was, in fact, what he'd been waiting to hear, that or something very much like it. As the Cypriot had said, there were kings in the land once again.

Sostratos suspected there would soon be more of them, too. If Antigonos and Demetrios wore crowns, how could Ptolemaios not match them? Off in the east, Seleukos would surely do the same; he already behaved in a nearly royal fashion. The lesser players in Europe, Lysimakhos and Kassandros, likely wouldn't be far behind.

Full of such musings, Sostratos got almost to his house on instinct: he certainly didn't pay much attention to where he was going.

In fact, he nearly ran into Menedemos, who was coming down the street while he was going up.

"Good thing you weren't driving a cart, my dear," Menedemos said. "You would have run me down and killed me—and then, once you noticed you'd done it, you would have been surprised." Sostratos stammered apologies. His cousin waved them aside. "Never mind that. What did you hear that made you forget the outside world?"

"You know me too well," Sostratos said. "There's a boat from Cyprus in the harbor. We can bow before King Antigonos and King Demetrios."

"Can we, now?" Menedemos said. Sostratos dipped his head. Menedemos went on, "I only wish I were more surprised."

"I was thinking the same thing," Sostratos said. "I wanted to tell my father the news first, but you've got it ahead of him."

"I'll go back to the house and tell my father." Menedemos made a face. "I will unless you pretend you haven't seen me after all. Then you or Uncle Lysistratos can do it. I'll act properly amazed when he lets me know, I promise."

"Whatever you want, of course. But are you quarreling with your father again?" Since Sostratos rarely quarreled with *his* father, he saw no reason for anyone else to do anything so foolish.

Menedemos looked at him—looked through him, really—with eyes so perfectly opaque, they might have been made from Egyptian glass. "If you'll do me the favor, I'll thank you for it. But past that ….. Past that, my dear, it's really no business of yours how I run my life."

"I'll do it," Sostratos said, and not another word. Ears burning, he went into his own house to give his father the news.

As Menedemos had said he would, he artfully acted astonished when his father told him Antigonos and Demetrios were now crowned kings. The affairs of princes worried him because those princes cast hungry glances at his polis. If they hadn't, he wouldn't have given a fig for them.

The affairs of his own household counted a great deal more, as such affairs are apt to. That Baukis had come through childbirth safe and that the midwife had delivered her of a son (of *his* son?) delighted him.

That he couldn't speak to her in private for even a moment threatened to drive him mad.

Talking with her in private had always been a risky business. You never could tell when a slave might overhear whatever you were about to say that could least bear overhearing. It was no coincidence that slaves who snooped and slaves who accidentally heard things they shouldn't were staples of comic drama. In comedy, they made the audience guffaw. In real life ....

In real life, Menedemos found himself even more frustrated than he had been before Baukis learned she was with child. Before, at least she'd walked through the whole house. She'd had some memorable squabbles with Sikon when the cook spent more on opson than she thought he should have.

Now, with Diodoros to look after, Baukis hardly left the women's quarters at all. When she did, she always had a slave woman or two fluttering around here. They were even worse in the quarters, as Menedemos saw whenever he went in with his father. He couldn't visit by himself, not in propriety.

Days were often hottest when the sun was sliding down the ecliptic toward the autumnal equinox. One of those days was hot enough to drive Baukis and Diodoros out of the rooms where they spent so much time and to the shady part of the courtyard.

"If we spend another minute up there, we'll bake, and Sikon can pour melted cheese over us and serve us up for opson tonight," she said.

"It's hot, sure enough," Menedemos agreed. He had to stick to commonplaces—a slave woman stood behind Baukis, fanning her mistress and the baby and now and then herself with a fan made from woven straw.

"This gives Diodoros something different to look at, too," Baukis went on. She glanced at the herbs and flowers in the small garden at the center of the courtyard and clucked sadly. "This heat is killing most of the plants. The slaves don't see to watering them the way I did."

"Well, what can you expect from slaves?" Like Baukis, Menedemos spoke as if the woman with the fan weren't there. Unless they were talking about something their animate property shouldn't hear (what they felt for each other, for instance), they, like any Hellenes rich enough to own slaves, took them largely for granted.

Sure enough, Baukis answered, "I wish they weren't so lazy." This time, Menedemos did briefly wonder how energetic he'd be if he had to work for someone else all the time without ever getting paid. He didn't worry about slavery as an institution; he worried about getting sold into it if Demetrios and Antigonos conquered Rhodes.

To keep from thinking about that, he eyed Diodoros. His half-brother or his son? He'd wonder for the rest of his life. Undeniably, the baby looked like him. But he also took after his father, so that proved nothing.

He noted the way the baby was studying the courtyard. "He seems more alert—no, that's not right: more connected to the rest of the world—than he did the last time I saw him," he remarked. Talking about Diodoros was safe.

And, of course, at the moment Baukis' son was her favorite subject. She dipped her head. "He does!" she said. "Every day, he turns more and more into … into a person. I think he'll be smart, like you."

If I'm so smart, why did I fall in love with my stepmother? Menedemos knew that had no good answer, unless you thought *Because Aphrodite willed you should* was one. He was pious enough, in a conventional way, but he didn't think that. As far as he could see, love like his was a kind of madness. If it struck you, you couldn't hope to fight it. The most you could hope for was that it wouldn't harm you too badly.

"What brains I have, I got from my father." Menedemos would have said something else if the slave woman weren't listening, but she was. He might be mad with love, but he wasn't raving mad. He went on, "And it's not as if you're a fool. The way you manage the household …. A banker would be proud to do so well."

"Sikon will tell you a different story," Baukis said, her mouth twisting in annoyance.

"He's a cook. Cooks always think they're entitled to every obolos ever minted," Menedemos said. "And he's a good cook, so he thinks he gives extra value for what he spends. He's a good enough cook, I sometimes think he's right."

"You would," she said. Menedemos laughed, but she wasn't joking, or not very much. And she had good reason not to be in a joking mood, for she asked, "Will Demetrios and Antigonos attack us? Your father seems to think so."

"They're the only ones who know for certain, but I'm afraid I think so, too," Menedemos answered. "Why wouldn't they? We're rich, and the Ptolemaios can't help us for a while. No one can. Whatever we do, we've got to do for ourselves."

"What happens if … if a polis falls?"

"Nothing good." Menedemos left it there. The best a woman could hope for was to be sold into slavery, and have to come to her master's bed whenever he summoned her. If she was very lucky, she might get to raise Diodoros … as a slave himself. More likely, the soldiers who caught her would smash the baby's head against a wall. If they'd already taken a lot of captives, they might not bother with one more to sell, just cut her throat after they'd had their fun with her.

Menedemos knew he'd die before he let any such thing happen to her. But if Demetrios' soldiers got into Rhodes, death or slavery was all he had to look forward to himself.

The woman with the fan—they called her Lyke because she came from Lykia (and also because it was a joke of sorts: it meant "she-wolf")—spoke up for the first time: "Being a slave is never good. How bad it is depends on who owns you." She knew what happened when a city fell, all right, probably from experience.

Menedemos asked the question he couldn't very well avoid: "How does the family measure up?"

She shrugged. "There's always enough to eat. There's a lot of work, but not a *terrible* lot of work most of the time, if you know what I mean. You and your father don't treat slave women like we're nothing but piggies with legs." She brought out the Greek obscenity as matter-of-factly as if she were talking about the weather.

"Are things different other places?" Baukis, who got out less than Menedemos did, seemed more curious.

Lyke nodded, as someone born a barbarian would. "Oh, yes, Mistress! Some of the things you hear …," She rolled her eyes.

"Where do you hear them?" Menedemos asked—*that* kind of thing interested him.

"Oh, you know, sir. When I'm getting water at the fountain two streets over, I'll talk with some of the other women filling hydriai.

I chat with slaves at the shops, too, or when I have time off for a festival."

"All right," he said. He didn't know in detail how slaves lived their lives when their masters' eyes weren't on them, but what Lyke said sounded likely enough. It also sounded like the bits of business modern comic poets put in their plays. Either they drew from life or they were good at making things up.

Diodoros started to fuss. Baukis sighed. "He's hungry again. He's always hungry. Turn your back for a moment, Menedemos." He obeyed. He wasn't foolish enough to sneak a glance at what he shouldn't see, not with Lyke there. He didn't turn back till his father's wife told him he could. By then, she'd arranged things so the baby's head and her breast were decently covered.

His son or half-brother nursed noisily. "He's really slurping it up there, isn't he?" Menedemos said.

"He's sucking in too much air," Baukis said. "When I burp him, he's liable to spit up."

"Ah," Menedemos said, as if in wisdom. Nursing babies was as much a mystery to him as the picture-writing the Egyptians used. More of a mystery, perhaps: he had a chance at figuring out what some of the pictures meant. He asked, "How do you make him not do that?"

"If I knew, I'd do it," she said. He shut up.

As the baby slowed, Lyke said, "Let me get you a rag, Mistress. If he does spit up, it won't get all over your chiton then. Or it may not, anyhow."

"*It may not* is right" Baukis said. "But yes, go do that, please. Thanks for thinking of it."

As Lyke came back with a raggedy scrap of wool, she remarked, "In some houses, they never say *please* or *thank you* to a slave. Some people think a slave is a brute beast like a sheep, or even a tool like a mallet or a chisel. Living in places like that must be hard."

An uneasy silence followed. Menedemos would have told anyone he'd always believed in freedom and democracy: freedom for men who owned enough in the way of property, and courses chosen for the polis by the votes of an assembly of those property-owning men, who in their decrees called themselves the people of Rhodes.

Freedom for the people of Rhodes, whether the phrase meant those prosperous men who ran things—men like his father and uncle and cousin, men like himself—or the polis' whole population, looked less likely to go on than it had a little while before. And of course it seemed sweeter when it also seemed more likely to be taken away.

Diodoros punctuated his uneasy thoughts with another one of those burps that seemed too loud and too deep for the baby producing them. And he didn't just make noise. "You see?" Baukis exclaimed. "I knew he'd give back some of what he ate there."

"You were right," Menedemos said.

Lyke used the rag to wipe off the baby's face—and Baukis' shoulder, since the cloth hadn't perfectly protected her. "I wonder if this is even worth rinsing out one more time," she said. "It will smell like sour milk forever."

"The baby can go into the cheese-making business," Menedemos said—the rag was covered with what looked like curds. Lyke laughed. Baukis glared at him.

Then something noisy and unpleasant happened at Diodoros' other end. Plenty of things to say about that would have occurred to Menedemos even if he hadn't adored Aristophanes. The comic poet offered him more—and filthier—choices, though.

He opened his mouth, but then closed it again without saying anything. Sometimes whatever you came out with would only land you in more trouble. He wished he'd remembered that a little more often—or a lot more often—when talking to his father. But, while he loved the older man as a dutiful son should (when he wasn't sick-jealous of him for lying with Baukis whenever he pleased, anyhow), he wasn't in love with him. That made all the difference.

When he kept quiet, he saw something on Baukis' face he'd never found there before—never aimed at him, at any rate. He had too-brief proof she wanted him the way he longed for her, and worried about him because of that. This was different. It was quiet gratitude mixed with equally quiet approval. It was the kind of look one adult was apt to give another.

Sostratos had talked about growing up as he neared thirty. Menedemos hadn't felt like listening to him. Menedemos rarely felt like listening to anybody. Skippering the *Aphrodite* meant he didn't have to listen to anybody very often. But, while he didn't like listening, he didn't forget what he heard. Sostratos had a point. His cousin often did, however little he cared to admit it.

If I do grow up, will I turn into my father? he wondered. Then he thought, *If Diodoros or whatever other son I may have drives me as mad as I've driven him, who could blame me if I do?*

He chuckled. "What's funny?" Baukis asked.

"Nothing, really." He didn't care to tell that one to her—and to Lyke—even if he left Diodoros out of it. But he chuckled again.

Clouds rolled by overhead, traveling from northwest to southeast. Sostratos eyed them with mingled suspicion and relief: they were bigger and thicker and darker than the puffy little white ones that drifted across the sky at high summer. The rainy season wasn't here yet, but he literally could see it coming. Like every other sailor ever born, he prided himself on reading the weather.

Before very long, the rain *would* come. The wind *would* blow up storms. Sailing would probably shut down for the winter, though fishing boats would keep going out. Sostratos looked north. The Anatolian mainland wasn't far away at all. A bold man, an intrepid man—a man like, say, Demetrios son of Antigonos—might chance leading a fleet across that narrow stretch of sea and catching the Rhodians off guard.

He might, yes. But Sostratos didn't think he would. The risk seemed larger than the reward he might gain from it.

Every day the peace held between Rhodes on the one hand and Demetrios and Antigonos on the other felt like a day won, almost a day stolen. The walls were in better shape now than they ever had been in the century-long history of the polis. They'd been raised, they'd been strengthened, all the brush had been cleared away from their bases, and the ditch outside them had been deepened and studded with pointed stakes. More of that kind of work could go on through the winter.

Men who'd never had to play the hoplite could go on training, too. Sostratos practiced in his cuirass and helmet these days. He was starting to get used to the extra weight and the way the helmet's cheek pieces and nasal cut down his vision. He was getting used to the feel of a spearshaft and a sword—at least a wooden practice sword—in his hand, too.

Every once in a while, he would do something that made one of the Cretans who trained the locals look at him thoughtfully. His cousin had bragged about that kind of thing. He understood why, too. A couple of times, he got home with rag-tipped spear or oaken blade when the man he was working against didn't think he could.

"*Papai!*" one of them exclaimed, opening and closing his hand to make sure it wasn't broken after Sostratos rapped him smartly on the knuckles. "You dirty son of a mad dog, you think left-handed!"

"Thank you!" Sostratos said. The mercenary, who hadn't meant it as praise, swore at him some more. Sostratos went on, "Won't it help me stay alive if the foe doesn't know ahead of time what I'm likely to do?"

"Not if I get my hands around your neck." The Cretan stared down at his hand. "Bugger me! That's swelling up like a puff adder just before it strikes."

"Soaking it in cold water may help a bit." Yes, Sostratos did fancy himself as at least something of a physician.

"Thanks a lot, Asklepios!" the mercenary jeered. Ears afire, Sostratos mumbled some kind of farewell and went off to shed his kit and scrape away the sweat and oil on his body. He knew he'd never practice with that particular soldier again. He wondered if he'd practice at all after this. Getting killed later seemed better than getting humiliated now.

That made no sense. The rational part of him understood as much. But the rational part of him was also coming to recognize that it didn't rule all the time. Philosophers insisted that it should. Maybe it did for some of them. Sostratos wished it would for him. He couldn't make it do any such thing, though, try as he would.

And, the older he got, the more he suspected it didn't even for others who called themselves lovers of wisdom. Philosophers quarreled with one another no less than ordinary men did—they were just more eloquent about it.

They fell in love—and out of it—no less than ordinary men did, too. Even Sokrates, probably the wisest of them all, had stayed married to Xanthippe till the Athenians made him drink hemlock. She'd also cared for him in her own fashion. As he waited to take the poison, she'd wailed, "I don't want you killed for something you didn't even do!"

To which he'd replied, "Would you want me killed if I had done it?"

Neither Platon, Xenophon, nor anyone else had recorded her response to that. Sostratos imagined a comic playwright's crack: something like, *The only time a man ever got the last word!*

He put on his chiton and left the gymnasion with his kit in his arms. That was the kind of thing Menedemos should come up with. Menedemos didn't even pretend to be rational all the time.

As if thinking of his cousin conjured up the man himself, Sostratos ran into him before he got halfway home. "Hail!" Menedemos said. "What have you been up to?"

Sostratos hefted his corselet and helm. "What you'd expect—working out in the gymnasion, trying to learn how not to get killed."

"How not to get killed? There's a noble ambition! How did you do?"

Sostratos let out a horrible noise, one that would do for a death rattle, and made as if to slump to the ground. Straightening, he said, "Not too well, I'm afraid."

His joke worked better than he dreamt it would. Menedemos laughed till tears ran down his face, laughed and laughed and had trouble stopping. At last, wiping his face with his forearm, he choked out, "Oh, my dear, you've gone and flattened me. You should tell stories in the taverns, the way some men who fancy themselves for their wits do. You'd run them all out of business, and make more money than you do on trading runs."

"Did you bring home some poppy juice from Egypt?" Sostratos asked, less rhetorically than he'd intended. "You sound like a man who's taken too much of it—you're all full of hallucinations and phantasms."

"I don't think so," his cousin said. "I've never laughed so hard for them as I did for you just now."

Sostratos didn't think tavern comics were funny, either—certainly not so funny as they thought they were. "Have you made some kind of special comparison lately?" he enquired.

Menedemos tossed his head. "Not me. I haven't laughed much about anything lately. There doesn't seem to be much to laugh at, for Rhodes or for the family. Or there didn't, till you slew me just now." He started giggling again.

"We made a fine profit coming back from Alexandria, even without selling Ptolemaios' weapons to the polis," Sostratos said. "As long as Rhodes does all right, the family should, too."

Only a moment before, he'd wondered how to get Menedemos to quit laughing. Now he'd gone and done it, without even knowing just what he'd done. His cousin suddenly seemed as serious, even as somber, as if someone had jammed a stopper into the amphora that held his mirth. In a voice like winter, he replied, "Well, you don't know everything there is to know, do you?"

"Plainly not, O best one," Sostratos said, bewildered at the sudden mood swing. "How can I, though, if you won't tell me anything?"

"There's nothing to tell," Menedemos said: such an obvious lie that Sostratos just looked at him. Even under his seafarer's tan, Menedemos flushed. "There isn't, curse it!" he insisted.

"There may not be anything you care to tell," Sostratos said, "but that's not the same thing, is it?"

Menedemos stalked away. Sostratos took a step after him, then stopped. He could—sometimes—tell when something wouldn't do any good. This was one of those times.

XVII

MENEDEMOS HAD JUST BOUGHT SOME BREAD with fried cheese on it in the agora when a man strolling by told his companion, "Well, he's gone and done it."

"Who's gone and done what?" the second man asked, which saved Menedemos the trouble.

"The Ptolemaios. He's gone and put a crown on his own noggin now that Antigonos and Demetrios have started wearing them."

"How do you know that?" The news-bearer's friend couldn't have done a better job of asking Menedemos' questions for him if he'd rehearsed for a month.

"I heard it from someone who heard it from a ship just in from Paphos."

"Oh." The friend considered that. After a moment, he said, "I suppose the Demetrios doesn't have such a tight hold on the southwest of Cyprus, even after Salamis has fallen." He might have been a stage magician, only he was picking thoughts out of Menedemos' head instead of drakhmai from his ear.

Cutting short his own wanderings through the market square, Menedemos hurried home. When he walked in, his father was talking about a fine-looking piece of tuna with Sikon the cook. Menedemos said, "You'll never guess what I just heard."

"What? That Ptolemaios has named himself king, too?" his father said. "Pretty soon, the only Macedonian who isn't wearing a crown will be some knacker who carves up dead farm animals in the hills back of Pella."

"I just heard it now," Menedemos said in annoyance. "How did the news get here ahead of me?"

"I heard it in the fish market, young master, and brought it back myself," Sikon said smugly.

"Ah," Menedemos said. The fish market, naturally, lay next to the harbor. Any news from the sea would get there before it reached the agora.

"Everyone knew it was coming—more a matter of when than of if," his father said. "Ptolemaios wouldn't let Antigonos and Demetrios outrank him for long. And I hear that out in the east, Seleukos has been calling himself a king for a while now when he deals with barbarians—though he hasn't had the crust to do it with Hellenes."

"He will from now on," Menedemos predicted.

"No doubt you're right. He wouldn't want to seem a mere general among all those ancient monarchs. They might not let him sit at the same table with their glorious selves when they all gather for supper." Philodemos could be as sardonic about the great and powerful as he could about his own son.

Menedemos sent him an odd look. "That's almost the kind of thing I'd look to hear from Sostratos, not from you."

"I could do worse. Your cousin's a clever youngster. Even the Ptolemaios—I beg your pardon, even his Magnificent Majesty, King Ptolemaios—thinks so," Philodemos replied, still in that dry mood. "I could do worse than imitate him. And so could you."

"I doubt it. If I tried, I'd think myself to death inside a month. And now, sir, if you'll excuse me—" Menedemos didn't wait to learn whether his father would excuse him or not. He turned on his heel and strode out of the kitchen.

As he made for the front door, he heard Sikon say, "Do you have to twit him like that?"

"Bah!" his father said. "He takes everything the wrong way. Why, he—"

What mistakes he'd made now, Menedemos didn't wait to hear. He opened the door, then quietly closed it behind him, cutting off the voices from inside the house. He wanted to slam the door. He'd done that often enough, after one run-in or another with his father. But he held back this time, for fear of frightening Diodoros.

No, he'd never know if the baby was his. *Bound to be just as well*, he told himself, not for the first time. If he did know, he might throw it in his father's face in a fit of fury. It wasn't as if he didn't have them, gods knew. When the two men clashed, they struck sparks off each other, as stones sometimes did.

Even Baukis couldn't name Diodoros' sire. That bothered Menedemos, too, in a different way. He didn't want to look at the tiny boy—or at her—and imagine his father caressing her, imagine his father penetrating her. Of course his father did just that; he was Baukis' husband, after all. But imagining it made Menedemos want to behave like one of the characters in the tragedies that Sostratos admired more than he did.

When he was away at sea, none of that mattered, or not so much. Hundreds or thousands of stadia from Rhodes, he didn't think about it … except when he did. Whether he thought about it or not, he couldn't do anything about it then. Maybe he wasn't so clever or rational as his clever, rational cousin, but he was smart enough to get that.

But when he was home again, under the same roof as his father and Baukis …. That had been bad every winter since he'd found himself drawn to his stepmother. It had been worse last winter, when he took her as she was coming home from her women's festival and when she found she was going to have a baby. Now the baby was here. Menedemos wanted Baukis more than ever, and she had no time even to think of him.

He drank more than he'd been in the habit of doing. He didn't drink as much as he wanted to. As he'd feared what Baukis might blurt out in the pangs of labor, he feared what he might say if Dionysos seized his tongue in an unguarded instant. He did his best not to leave himself open to unguarded instants.

When he headed for the door late in the afternoon a couple of days later, his father asked, "Where are you off to now?"

"To Simaristos," he answered truthfully. Simaristos ran far and away the grandest brothel in Rhodes.

Philodemos frowned. "Do you think we're made of silver, the way Talos was made of bronze in the myth?"

Menedemos had been sure his father would say something like that. He was ready for it. Dipping his head, he said, "By the gods, sir, I do. After everything Sostratos and I brought back from Egypt, we've got plenty to let me have a good time if I fancy one. And you know it as well as I do, too."

He didn't sound defiant: more like a man stating facts so obvious, they shouldn't really need stating. His father opened his mouth, but closed it without saying anything. After a couple of heartbeats, he tried again. "Well, enjoy yourself, then," he managed.

No matter how gruff and grudging he sounded, that was more than Menedemos had looked for from him. "Thank you, Father," he answered, and left the house whistling.

"Philodemos' son! This is an unexpected pleasure!" Simaristos said when Menedemos walked in. The brothelkeeper rubbed his hands together, anticipating profit.

"That's what I'm after—unexpected pleasure," Menedemos said. Simaristos laughed; anything a client said was funny.

Octopus stewed in garlic sauce wasn't exactly an unexpected pleasure, but was a savory one. So was Thasian as sweet and smooth as any that had ever traveled on the *Aphrodite*. Simaristos showed Menedemos the amphora before broaching it (but after making sure he could pay the price). "You will know such things, and know I'm not playing tricks on you," he said.

"That amphora's from Thasos, sure enough," Menedemos agreed.

When he drank a cup's worth neat, Simaristos clapped his hands, either in admiration or, more likely, in the hope of getting many more coins out of him once he was drunk. "I didn't know you were Macedonian!" the brothelkeeper exclaimed.

"Please!" Menedemos tossed his head. "Anything but that! I had a bellyful of Macedonians this last trip. A bellyful and a half."

"However you please, O best one," Simaristos replied. "Let's say you're drinking like a Kelt, then—one of those new barbarians coming down into the lands north of where the Thracians live. They have a name for pouring it down as though there's no tomorrow."

"I've heard of the Keltoi, yes," Menedemos said with owlish seriousness; the potent Thasian was hitting him hard. He might make vows against getting sozzled, but Dionysos had a will of his own, and gods were always stronger than men when they wanted to be.

"Would you like to see one? Would you like to futter one?" Suddenly, Simaristos was greasy as pork fat. "We have a new girl here, one of those Keltoi. We call her Khryse."

" 'The Golden One?' All right," Menedemos said. Slaves got names like that, and Keltoi were said to be fair.

"Her tribe is the Tolistobogioi—I think I'm saying that right," Simaristos told him. "To the crows with me, though, if I want to try to call her Tolistobogia, or to make my customers have to say that. Shall I bring her out for you? She's something special when it comes to women. Even Aphrodite might be jealous."

"Well, you've interested me, anyhow. Why not? Let me see what you're talking up." Even with the Thasian dancing through his veins, Menedemos felt sure the brothelkeeper was stretching things.

But when Simaristos brought the girl out of a back room, Menedemos saw he'd told nothing but the truth. She was a couple of digits taller than he was, with wavy golden hair falling down past her shoulders, sky-blue eyes, and skin pale as milk. Even her nipples were only a delicate pink.

Women among the Hellenes were in the habit of shaving or plucking their pubic hair; Menedemos remembered being intrigued to learn Egyptian women did the same. Khryse didn't. As her bush was only a shade darker than the hair on her head, it seemed more intriguing than barbarous.

"What do you think?" Simaristos asked.

"She's quite something," Menedemos asked. To Khryse, he added, "You're beautiful."

"I do thank you," she said quietly. Her Greek had an odd, almost musical, accent.

"What do you want for as much of the night as I feel like spending with her?" Menedemos asked the brothelkeeper.

"Six drakhmai will do it—eight if you want her to ride you like a racehorse," Simaristos replied. Putting the woman on top and making her do the work always cost more.

Menedemos gave the man two fat silver tetradrakhms. "I may ask for change, and I may not. We'll just see what happens," he said.

Simaristos bowed, slick and polite as a Phoenician. "You always were a *kalos kagathos*, son of Philodemos. Khryse, take him to the blue room. Nothing but the best for him, now."

"This way, O best one, if you please." Khryse started up the stairs. Menedemos followed. She was as lovely from behind as from in front.

Sure enough, the blue room's walls were painted that color. The bed was large and comfortable. Menedemos closed the door. It latched, but had no bar. In case a brawl broke out, Simaristos or a bouncer might need to get in there in a hurry. He shrugged. He didn't plan on brawling with Khryse.

He took off his chiton and lay down on the bed. He felt the wine, but not enough to keep from rising to the occasion. Khryse got down beside him. "And what might you want, now?" she asked.

He shrugged again. "I don't know. We'll do things, and then we'll do some other things." She wasn't Baukis, but she was very beautiful.

After a while, he found it worked the other way round: she was very beautiful, but she wasn't Baukis. She was also skilled; she gave him great pleasure. When it was over, though, he felt as if it might as well not have happened at all.

By then, it was getting dark. She looked at him in the gathering gloom. "Who did you wish I was, there?"

"I'm sorry," he said, dully embarrassed. "I didn't realize it showed."

"Well, it did. You're, after all, paying enough for me. Shouldn't you get the joy you paid for? Will you try again?" Even slaves who were whores had their pride. Khryse was miffed he hadn't enjoyed her more.

"Give me a bit," he said; he didn't rise to the occasion again so soon as he had a few years earlier. "Shall I get some wine for us in the meantime?"

"I won't say no," she answered.

If he was spending money, he'd *spend* money. He got a cup of Thasian for each of them. He knew he'd feel it in the morning, but the morning still lay most of a night away.

As he drank, he wondered why he hadn't felt this way in Alexandria. He supposed it was that he hadn't seen Baukis for a while then, and he was across the sea from her. Now she was only a few streets away, doing whatever she was doing with Diodoros ... or with Menedemos' father. Menedemos didn't want to think about that, so he drank some more.

Khryse poured it down with an ease a tavern tosspot might have envied. Simaristos hadn't lied when he said Keltoi drank like Macedonians. She reached for him with practiced fingers. "Let's see if it's better this time."

It felt wonderful while it was going on. If you were a man, it always did. Afterwards, the only woman in Menedemos' mind was Baukis.

Khryse's sigh mingled resignation and annoyance. "If you cared for the girl you were with as much as you do for the one you haven't got, you'd be a lover to remember."

He'd been in the habit of doing that. He'd acquired a reputation for it, in towns around the Inner Sea. Now .... Now he wanted to burst into tears. Telling himself that was the wine, he made himself hold them in. He said, "Sometimes you just can't get around what's inside your head."

She stayed silent some little while. Then, in a low voice, she answered, "Well, it's plain you've never been a slave. Or a woman."

"You shame me."

"How can I be doing that? What am I, now? Only a chunk of meat with a pleasing shape. Ask the master if you doubt me."

Menedemos had no doubt about what Simaristos would say. "I hope you find some way to get free and do whatever it is you want to do," he said. He fumbled on the floor till he found his belt pouch, which he'd discarded with his tunic. By feel, he got out a didrakhm. "Here. You don't have to tell the vulture I gave you this."

"I thank you. He'll likely find some way to steal it from me, but I thank you even so. A kind thought, it is," Khryse said. "If I had my way, I'd go home to my own folk. But I'd only be enslaved again if I left Rhodes, and maybe in a place worse than this. I've seen some." She sighed. "And even if I did come back to my clan, they'd hate me and scorn me me for giving myself to every passing man, as though I do it by choice."

Try as he would, Menedemos found nothing to say to that. If he told her he'd swear off visiting brothels, she wouldn't believe him. Even he would know he was lying. He'd always thanked the gods he was neither woman nor slave. Now he did it once more, with special fervor.

He picked up his tunic. "I'd better go."

"Come again if you care to. I'd soon take you than a good many others," Khryse said. With that faint praise in his ears, Menedemos went downstairs. For a couple of oboloi, Simaristos gave him a tough-looking torchbearer to light his way home and scare off robbers lurking in the darkness. He tipped that slave, too, and hoped the fellow got to keep his silver.

Though the season was drawing on, Sostratos kept regularly visiting the harbor in hopes of picking up news. The weather stayed good, but fewer and fewer ships came from Cyprus. The local rulers, having yielded to Demetrios in preference to being stormed or besieged and sacked, might have thought commerce with Rhodes seemed too disloyal to encourage.

In their sandals, Sostratos supposed he might have felt the same way. Few towns on Cyprus boasted works to match the ones Menelaos had defended at Salamis. Those hadn't prevailed, so how could any others? And Demetrios and Antigonos, while implacable foes, didn't make the worst overlords.

So he told himself, while continuing to practice with spear and shield. Rhodes was a nut with a shell tough to crack. Tough enough? All he could do was hope ... and go on practicing.

He also suspected Antigonos and Demetrios didn't care for their new Cypriot subjects trading with men who wouldn't bend the knee to them. No skippers who did come to Rhodes wanted to admit any such thing. They acted as prickly about independence and respect as any other Hellenes. Wherever Greek was spoken, men were touchy about letting others subject them.

He didn't ask any Cypriots, then, about whether their cities belonged to the new-crowned kings. He asked questions like, "Have you heard whether Antigonos and Demetrios aim to move against Rhodes?" No one could mind a question like that. What else was likely to be uppermost in a Rhodian's mind these days?

None of the men from Cyprus said that he'd heard about or seen an expeditionary force fitting out or sailing this way. And then one day the captain of a fishing boat out of Paphos laughed out loud at his question. "Thou hast not learned, then?" he asked.

As always, his old-fashioned dialect made Sostratos want to smile. He carefully kept his face straight, though. "Learned what?" he said. "Not much news from overseas here since the Macedonians all started putting diadems on their heads."

"Why, man, thou and thy polis'll be the olives served after a great feast of tunny and mullet and eel," the fisherman said. "Art thou ignorant, then, of the two kings' movement against the one?"

"This is the first I've heard of it, by the gods!" Sostratos exclaimed. "The first anyone here has, I'm sure. Tell me what you know, if you'd be so kind."

The Cypriot just stood there on the deck of his boat. He had black, prominent eyebrows: all the more so when he raised one, as he did now. Sostratos could take a hint. He tossed the fellow a drakhma. Deft as a monkey, the fisherman caught it out of the air. "I am in thy debt," he said. " 'Tis true—they move on Egypt by both land and sea, the elder king commanding the army setting out across the desert Nilewards, the younger leading the fleet accompanying."

"If they can do that …." Sostratos' voice trailed away. This was the time to try, sure enough. With Ptolemaios weakened by the sea-fight off Salamis, Egypt might fall into Antigonos and Demetrios' hands like a ripe fruit. And the Cypriot was right—next to Egypt, Rhodes, rich as it was, would be only a snack.

"Verily, thou seest whither bloweth the wind," the Cypriot said.

"I do. And I thank you." Sostratos carefully didn't say anything like *Forsooth* or *thee*. He didn't mock people for their accents—not to their faces, anyhow. He hadn't liked it a bit when the Athenians snickered at the Doric drawl he'd had when he came to study at the center of Greek learning and wisdom, and had sense enough to see other people were unlikely to care for what he didn't. He added, "Men here who are more important than I am will need to hear this. Can you come with me and tell them whatever you know about it?"

"Will they pay me more, so I waste not my time? Otherwise, belike I'd make better use of selling the mackerel in my hold."

He cared nothing for Rhodes except for the money he could get here. Why should he? It wasn't his polis. Most Hellenes had always brought that attitude to their dealings with their neighbors. It was their besetting flaw. Because of it, the Great Kings of Persia had almost conquered Hellas, and the kings of Macedonia had. The ancient Greek homeland was a backwater these days.

Except for Rhodes, Sostratos thought, not without a certain parochial pride of his own. *Except for Rhodes*.

He realized the fishing-boat captain was still waiting for an answer. "You'll be paid, O best one. By the gods, I'll pay you myself if no one else does."

"Thy speech shows thee a true *kalos kagathos*. I'll come with thee," the skipper said. Before he did, though, he briefed the three men with him on what he wanted to make from the catch. They were all young, two clean-shaven and one with a soft, thin, fuzzy beard, and they all looked a bit like him. "My sons, and a nephew," he told Sostratos as he gained the pier with a gangplank.

"Likely lads," the Rhodian said politely. "Come this way, if you'd be so kind." For calling him a *kalos kagathos*, Sostratos would have forgiven his new acquaintance almost anything. The praise would have mattered more had he got it younger, but he didn't despise it even now.

They walked past the gymnasion on the way to Komanos' home. The Cypriot eyed the men there training in warlike arts. "Thy polis hath no trust in kings," he remarked.

"Would you?" Sostratos returned, and then, "Tell me your name, if you would, so I can give it to my leaders."

"I hight Paramonos, the son of Khairemon. And thou art …?"

Sostratos gave his name. A block farther on, he stopped in front of Komanos' house and knocked at the door. The old Lykian who was Komanos' man of affairs opened it. "Hail, son of Lysistratos," he said, his Greek almost without accent after many years of slavery. Dipping his head to Paramonos, he added, "And hail to you as well, best one."

"For which I thank thee," Paramonos said.

"Is your master in, Lydos?" Sostratos asked.

"He is, sir," the old man replied. "Come into the andron. I'll have refreshments brought for you and your friend, and tell the master you wish to speak with him."

The men's chamber was larger and grander than the one in Sostratos' home, or Menedemos'. They were far from poor, but Komanos was rich. Another slave brought in wine and olives and figs candied in honey; Lydos didn't lower himself to such a menial task.

After a short pause to let his guests eat and drink, Komanos walked into the andron. He clasped hands with Sostratos and, after Paramonos was introduced to him, with the Cypriot as well. Sostratos said, "I met Paramonos at the harbor. As soon as I heard his news, I brought him straight to you."

"Did you? You're still a young man, but not one to get excited over nothing. I've seen that before," Komanos said. Sostratos stared down at the mosaic tiles under his feet, embarrassed and pleased at the same time. Menedemos wouldn't have been flustered; he would have strutted. Komanos turned to the fisherman. "And what is this news, sir?"

Paramonos told of Antigonos and Demetrios' move against Egypt. He gave details Sostratos hadn't heard before: that Antigonos, with 80,000 men, was advancing on the Nile from Gaza, while Demetrios had accompanied his father down the coasts of Syria, Phoenicia, and Palestine with a fleet of 150 warships and some large number of transports.

"And they seize Egypt and put the Ptolemaios to the sword, they'll swallow Rhodes for a sweet," Paramonos finished. "An they fail there, haply they'll have thy polis in place of the supper they ate not."

Komanos sighed. "I wish I could tell you you were mistaken, my friend, but I fear you see all too clearly." He dug in his belt pouch, found a pair of massy silver tetradrakhms, and put them in Paramonos' callused palm. "This for your grace in telling us what you've learned."

"I thank thee for thy kindness," the Cypriot said. "Sostratos here assured me I'd not find thee lacking, and I see he spoke but the truth."

"Will you stay for supper with me?" Komanos asked. "And you, too, Sostratos, of course?"

Paramonos tossed his head. "Again I thank thee, but I needs must say thee nay. I'd best hie me back to the harbor, to make sure my spawn and my brother's son make all they can from what we brought to sell."

"You will know your own business best, of course," Komanos said smoothly, and then, in a louder voice, "Lydos! Show the gentleman to the door, if you'd be so kind."

By the speed with which Lydos appeared, he'd been standing just out of sight of the doorway. "Come with me, sir, if you would," he said to Paramonos. "Will you need help finding your way back to the harbor?" He didn't pretend he hadn't overheard.

"Nay, though thou'rt good to enquire." Paramonos smiled the kind of smile Sostratos had also aimed at landlubbers. "Sun and shadows will guide me back as well as any man might."

"As you please, of course," Lydos answered, and led him to the front door. How else could a slave respond to a free man?

After the door closed again and the bar thudded into place, Komanos used his fingers as if they were scissors blades to mime cutting a mourning lock from his gray hair. "I don't see how we can hope to stave off war now when spring comes round again," he said to Sostratos. "Shall we cheer for Antigonos and Demetrios in the present fight, or for Ptolemaios?"

"For Ptolemaios," Sostratos said at once. "If he wins, it will weaken the two kings. Also, we'll still have an ally then, even if not such a strong one as we'd like."

"That's very plain once you say it." Komanos dipped his head. "And we buy a fair bit of our grain from Egypt. I wouldn't want Antigonos and Demetrios to pinch us with hunger that way. Yes, you're a sensible chap, all right."

You could have seen it for yourself if you'd thought for a moment instead of just talking, Sostratos thought. There would have been a day, and it wouldn't have been so long before, when he would have come right out with that. Little by little, he was learning you didn't always help yourself with the full and exact truth.

Sokrates never did learn that. Men would remember Sokrates for centuries to come; Sostratos had the sorry certainty men wouldn't remember *him* the same way. But, in the end, what had the full and exact truth got Sokrates? Hemlock. Having watched a man die from it, Sostratos knew Platon hadn't told the full and exact truth about what a nasty way to go it was.

Komanos said something—Sostratos realized he had no idea what. "I'm sorry, O best one. I was woolgathering," he said sheepishly.

"Thinking those fine, clever thoughts of yours, I'm sure," the civic leader said with a smile. He knew how to keep men sweet, sure enough. To Sostratos, perhaps because he had so much trouble getting along with people, that seemed a more important talent than being clever. Komanos continued, "What I said was, if Antigonos and Demetrios do take Egypt from Ptolemaios, we may have to acknowledge them whether we want to or not."

"Demetrios freed Athens last year. He says he did, anyway. So do the Athenians. But he has soldiers in the polis, and I think I'd sooner die than lick a man's arse the way the Athenian Assembly did with him. I was there, sir, with my cousin. We saw it."

"I understand. Believe me, I want Rhodes to stay truly free and independent, too. But when the choice is between submitting and actually dying, it gets harder. The Alexander had a garrison here for a little while when you were a boy. We got rid of it. We could do that again."

"I remember, sir."

"Yes, you would have been the kind of boy who took note of such things, I'm sure. I am no god. I don't know what the future holds. I don't want to close off any choices, though."

"That's ... bound to be wise," Sostratos said with reluctant respect. "Maybe I could stand for Macedonian pikemen swaggering through the streets. But Antigonos and Demetrios pad out their fleet with pirates. The idea of those stinking jackals coming into our harbor ...." He made a fist.

"Spoken like a trading man. You won't be alone in feeling that way, either. It's the kind of thing we can dicker about if worse comes to worst. The kings will want our fleet to sail alongside them, too. I can hope they'll be reasonable."

"They'll be reasonable—as long as we do whatever they command," Sostratos said. "Flattering them till they glow with all the grease we've smeared on them won't hurt, either. Demetrios laps up praise the way a Molossian hound laps up water."

"I've heard the same thing," Komanos replied. "Antigonos, though, is supposed to be harder to charm that way. The old Cyclops has a jaundiced view through the eye he's got left, people say."

"I've heard the same thing. I don't know how true it is." Sostratos left it there, not caring to quarrel with Komanos. He did know Antigonos hadn't declined any of the ridiculous honors Athens had conferred on Demetrios and him. But he could have kept quiet about them because his son enjoyed them, not because he did himself.

Sostratos had also heard the old man doted on Demetrios, all the more so now that Philippos, his other son, had died. There was a story that he'd gone to visit Demetrios and got to his room just as an uncommonly beautiful hetaira was coming out. Later, Demetrios told him he'd been in bed with a fever, at which Antigonos chuckled and replied, "Yes, I saw her leaving a little while ago."

That little tale sparked a thought in Sostratos. He said, "Sir, if the polis boasts something uncommonly lively in the female line and we make Demetrios a present of her, that might make him think better of us. After he and Antigonos come back from their fight in Egypt, I mean, of course."

Komanos pursed his lips, considering. "That's not the worst notion I ever heard, by Aphrodite's sacred piggy," he said. "I don't go to the brothels as often as I used to, so I don't know whether we've got anyone special enough or not. I'll ask Simaristos, though. If he doesn't have a girl like that himself, he'll know whether any of the other brothelkeepers does."

"Good enough." Sostratos knew of Simaristos' place. When he got to the urge, he visited less expensive establishments. Even if the women at those places weren't quite so pretty, what you did with them or what you had them do for you felt just as good. And going home with more silver felt good, too.

Or he could just take Threissa to bed again. Most masters wouldn't stop because she didn't care for it. Her resentment might even have excited some men more. But he wasn't one of those men. He wanted a willing partner, even if she was willing only because of money.

He said his farewells and started home, to pass the news to his kin. He hoped Ptolemaios prevailed, not only because that would be good for Rhodes but also because Egypt's newly proclaimed king thought well of him. That mattered little in the grand scheme of things, but it did to him.

XVIII

GOING TO THE HARBOR EVERY DAY AFTER NEWS of the fight between Antigonos and Demetrios on the one hand and Ptolemaios on the other gave Menedemos an excuse to get out of his father's house. Philodemos didn't even bark at him when he left, though, the way he did when Menedemos headed for a tavern or a brothel.

Just because he went after news, though, didn't mean he got any. It was late in the sailing season now, more than a month and a half past the equinox. He wouldn't have wanted to sail from Egypt to Cyprus or Rhodes today. The risk of storms grew high after the cranes flew south.

So sometimes his walks to the harbor turned into walks to other places after he saw no new ships tied up at the quays. Sometimes he came home after drinking too much. "You're turning into a Thracian," his father grumbled. "Have you forgotten you're supposed to water your wine?"

"When you drink to forget, you do better when you forget to water it." Drunk, Menedemos thought that was the height of wit. His father only snorted and stalked away.

Next morning, with a pounding headache and a mouth that tasted as if someone had emptied a chamber pot into it, Menedemos didn't think he'd been so very clever, either. He munched raw cabbage to try to dull the aftereffects of his binge. It worked less well than he wished it would have. He drank some more wine, then. Philodemos would have been pleased at how carefully he watered it. And it actually did some good.

He didn't go to the harbor that day, though. It might have been autumn, but it was bright and sunny, too much so for comfort. He sat in the andron, reading a book of the *Iliad*. It was the second book, the dullest in the poem, but it suited his mood. *The Catalogue of Ships* listed every town in Hellas that had joined Agamemnon to attack Troy, and told how many ships it had contributed.

Having worked his way through that, though, he wondered how many ships there were all told, and how many strong-greaved Akhaians manned them. He went through the second half of the scroll again, flicking pebbles on a counting board whenever he came to a new listing. He totaled up 1,186 ships. Then, just to make sure, he did it again. He felt proud of himself when he got the same answer twice running.

That was a lot of ships, far more than Demetrios and Ptolemaios put together had had when they fought each other off Salamis. They would have been smaller ships, though, than the monsters that met there. Any vessels bigger than a trireme dated to very recent times; he knew the Athenians and their foes hadn't had any when they fought a century before. For that matter, even triremes would have been news to Homer. So how many men *would* the Akhaians have brought along?

Menedemos went back through the listings—yes, surely the most tedious part of the *Iliad*—once more. The Boiotians, he found, had had a hundred twenty men in each of their fifty ships. By contrast, the chieftains Methone, Thaumakie, Meliboia, and Olizon had commanded a total of seven ships with fifty men apiece.

"Split the difference," Menedemos muttered. Halfway between fifty and a hundred twenty was ... some more pebble work told him it was eighty-five. So if each ship carried about eighty-five men and there were 1,186 ships ....

Back and forth went the pebbles in their grooves. He hardly needed to look at his fingers as he flicked the tablet. The answer came to just over ten myriads: ten ten thousands. That was a lot of warriors, more than any modern general was likely to put in the field. And, to oppose them, Priamos and shining Hektor would have had about as many fighting men, or the war wouldn't have lasted anything like ten years.

Knowing something like that made Menedemos want to tell it to somebody. His father would have been interested—he'd got his own love for the *Iliad* from Philodemos—but he wanted as little to do with his father as he could manage. Instead, he walked across the street to his father's brother's house. Luck was with him; Sostratos answered the door when he knocked.

"Hail," his cousin said. "What can we do for you?"

"Do you know how many soldiers Agamemnon lord of men led against Troy?"

"Not offhand, my dear, no, but why do I think you're about to tell me? Why don't you come in before you do?"

When they were settled in the andron, Menedemos said, "You think so because I am. He commanded eight hundred ten above ten myriads, more or less."

"And how do you know this so precisely, O sage of the age?"

Not without pride, Menedemos explained his method. His cousin listened attentively; that, at least, Menedemos had been sure he would do. Menedemos finished, "And so, you see, I've reckoned it up exactly."

"You have if everything Homer says is true, anyhow," Sostratos replied.

He shocked Menedemos. "It's *Homer!*" he exclaimed. To him, that said everything that needed saying. All that made Hellenes what they were sprang from the *Iliad* and *Odyssey*.

But his cousin said, "He was a great poet, O best one, but he was a human being. He made mistakes. Doesn't a Trojan named Khromios get killed three different times in the *Iliad*?"

"How do you know there weren't three separate Trojans named Khromios?" Menedemos said. They both laughed, but nervously. They were treading on dangerous ground, ground that might give way under their feet and pitch them headlong into a real quarrel.

"Well, maybe." Sostratos picked his words with care as he went on, "What truly makes me wonder about the epics is that hundreds of years went by between the fall of Troy and Homer's time. You won't disagree with me there, I hope?"

"No," Menedemos replied, oddly reluctant to admit it for fear of walking into a trap. "Why does that matter, though?"

"Herodotos wrote about the Persian Wars less than a lifetime after they happened. Where he could see things for himself, he did very well—I found that out in Egypt. Where he could question men about exactly what happened and compare stories, he was also good. Where he couldn't do either, where he had to listen to old tales, he wasn't investigating anymore. Thoukydides criticized him because of it."

"I thought you liked Herodotos better than Thoukydides, though," Menedemos said.

Sostratos blinked in surprise, then grinned enormously. "By the gods, my dear, you've spent all these years *listening* to me! Who would have dreamt it? I *do* like Herodotos better. History needs to be interesting, or who'll want to read it? But Thoukydides was right here. Once you get past what the people you're talking with can remember, exaggerations creep in and you can't be sure you're rid of them all."

"Homer wouldn't make silly mistakes like that, though," Menedemos said. "He *is* Homer, you know."

"The point is, he wouldn't know he was making mistakes, because he wouldn't be able to question anyone who knew the truth," his cousin replied. "Think, why don't you? You've been all over Hellas. Is it really likely the Akhaians could have raised ten myriads of men and sent them off to besiege Troy for ten years without everybody back home starving to death because no one was left to work the fields?"

"Well ... no," Menedemos admitted reluctantly. "But if you can't trust Homer, you can't trust anybody."

"You know, my dear, you can enjoy him as a poet without enjoying him as a historian. They're different trades, like carpenter and potter," Sostratos said.

"But ... but ..." Menedemos felt himself floundering. "Think of all the other poets and playwrights who've borrowed from him since his day."

"That's poetry, too. Were the gods and goddesses truly on the windy plains of Troy, helping first one side and then the other, depending on who was friendly with whom on any particular day? That *is* poetry, not the real world. How many gods are running around loose these days?"

"People say the Alexander was one. The Athenians say Demetrios and Antigonos are two more."

Sostratos made a face at him. He knew why, too. Hellenes often spoke of a very talented man, or one who had done a lot, as divine. They might make offerings to his memory, or to him if he was still alive. That didn't mean they thought he was a match for Zeus or Apollo or Ares. There were questions of degree.

As if plucking that thought from inside his head, his cousin said, "Not everybody thinks the way we do about these things. As far as the Ioudaioi are concerned, there's only one god who does everything. They'd fight if we tried to make them give kings divine honors."

Menedemos sniffed. "Who cares what a little tribe of barbarians off in the middle of nowhere thinks? You don't see their god doing things these days, either, do you?"

"Certainly not," Sostratos replied, as if he were one of the men Sokrates so enjoyed questioning.

"There you are, then," Menedemos said.

"Here we all are," Sostratos said. "We are, but what about the gods? For all we know, they've gone on holiday together: ours, and the invisible one the Ioudaioi worship even if he doesn't do anything, and the Egyptians' falcon and jackal-head and I don't know what all else, and the Persians' good god and his wicked foe, and all the others, too. They're all at an inn somewhere, drinking neat wine and eating fried tunny and baby squid and trying to sweet-talk each other into bed. And the world they made can cursed well take care of itself."

Menedemos laughed, more uneasily than he'd thought he would. "You know, my dear, that sounds a lot likelier than I wish it did."

"I was just spinning a yarn, but the same thing went through my mind, too," Sostratos said. "It would explain quite a bit, wouldn't it?"

"Too much," Menedemos answered. "Much too much." Sostratos got off his couch, walked over, and solemnly set a hand on his shoulder.

Like everyone else on the island of Rhodes, Sostratos wondered when fresh news of Antigonos and Demetrios' invasion of Egypt would come in. He wondered all the more after the first storm of the season dropped rain on the polis. His house had a new cistern, to catch and save as much water as possible in case the two new kings, victorious over Ptolemaios or not, besieged Rhodes next.

His cousin's house across the street had a new cistern, too, nicely lined in stone and brick to retain as much water as possible. Many people who could afford such precautions took them. Maybe the brickmakers and stonemasons made extra silver because men needlessly feared a war that might not come. Sostratos didn't think so, though. He hoped some of the artisans spent some of their profits building cisterns of their own.

For a while, he wondered whether news of the fighting in Egypt would stay hidden till spring. Bad weather on the Inner Sea curtailed sailing. But then he realized this news would also travel by land, up through Palestine, Phoenicia, and Syria into Antigonos and Demetrios' Anatolian heartland. And a rowboat could get to Rhodes from a town like Loryma. It was only 150 stadia, maybe a few more, across the strait separating the island from the Karian mainland.

So he kept up his new habit of haunting the harbor. He often saw Menedemos there, too. He worried that Menedemos might be squabbling with his father again. Uncle Philodemos, it seemed to him, often squabbled for the sport of it. They didn't quarrel loudly enough for him to hear them shouting from across the street, but that proved nothing. Quiet quarrels were often the deadliest.

He wanted to ask his cousin if everything was all right, but remembered too well how cold and silent Menedemos had gone when he tried that before. So he greeted him whenever he saw him and talked about things like how Antigonos and Demetrios' war against Ptolemaios was likely to be going. Since they had no facts yet, they could guess to their hearts' content.

"It's awfully late in the year to try a naval campaign. I mean, it's *awfully* late. I wouldn't care to do it myself, by the gods. You're just asking for shipwreck if you put to sea now, especially in a place where you don't have any friendly harbors close by," Menedemos said.

He was a skipper himself, of course. By the standards of older men, he was a bold one, too, putting to sea earlier in springtime and staying out later in the fall than they might. If he said he didn't care to go sailing this far past the autumnal equinox, that carried weight.

But Sostratos had about as much seafaring experience as his cousin, even if he hadn't held command. And simply agreeing with Menedemos would have cut the conversation short, which he didn't want to do. So he said, "I don't know, my dear. If you were talking about the waters around here, I'd have to say you were right. But Egypt is a different world—we saw as much for ourselves. The seas and the winds in those parts may stay calm enough to let Demetrios do whatever his father needs him to."

"There *are* storms on that coast after the setting of the Pleiades, and Demetrios couldn't very well have moved before then," Menedemos replied. "Hellenes have known about them for as long as we've been going into that part of the world. Are you pretending to be ignorant, O marvelous one? That's not like you."

The epithet made Sostratos' ears burn. It sounded flattering; it was anything but. Sokrates had used it to tag people who he thought were marvelously stupid.

Sostratos did his best to hold his own: "Don't you think the chance to seize Egypt is worth running a few risks for? How many times were you lucky to come back alive after you slept with somebody's wife?"

"That wasn't at sea," Menedemos said. "At sea, you have more than yourself to worry about."

"Well, all right." Sostratos left it there. He didn't really feel like arguing. And Menedemos was better about looking out for others and not thinking so much about himself and his restless prong than he had been a few years before. *The river of time wears away even the hardest stone*, Sostratos thought.

The sun slid down the sky towards its low point at the winter solstice. The twelve hours of daylight each felt short and cramped, while those of the night stretched like warm wax. The difference between winter and summer was more pronounced in northerly Macedonia, as it was less so down in Alexandria.

If one could work out how much the hours changed in different seasons at different places, one might learn something interesting, or so it seemed to Sostratos. He pulled out a wooden sphere with which he'd studied geometry when he was younger, but soon put it away again. He didn't remember enough to work out exactly what he wanted to calculate.

And then he forgot spheres and geometry and the sun's motions, for news from the edges of Egypt finally did start trickling into Rhodes. The next time he saw Menedemos heading down to the harbor, he hailed him and said, "By the gods, my dear, are you sure you're not Teiresias in disguise?"

"I don't *think* I am." Menedemos looked down at himself. "Of course, the old seer was a man of parts, and some of the parts were pretty strange. Didn't he spend seven years as a woman?"

"So they say. They aren't around for me to question now, so I can't be sure. But if he could be a woman, he shouldn't find being a Rhodian too far beneath him. And you were a seer yourself when you said Demetrios' fleet would run into trouble off the coast east of the Delta."

"I didn't need to be a seer for that, only a seafaring man," Menedemos said. "I'd bet Demetrios' captains tried to warn him but he didn't want to listen to them. His loss, and his father's."

"Antigonos didn't cover himself with glory coming at Egypt by land, either," Sostratos said. "He didn't move fast enough—I don't suppose he could have, in that desert country—and Ptolemaios had all the approaches to the Delta well garrisoned before the invaders got to them."

"Ptolemaios had more than soldiers fighting for him, too," Menedemos said. "Have you heard how much he was offering Antigonos' soldiers to go over to him?"

"No. Tell me!"

"Two minai of silver a head for ordinary fighting men, and a whole talent apiece for commanders."

"By the dog!" Sostratos said softly. "Egypt is so rich, the Ptolemaios can spend money as if he shat it into his chamber pot every morning. After all, it worked with us, didn't it?"

His cousin looked sour as wine that had gone over to vinegar. "Too right, it did. But what choice did I have? If I'd told him no when he wanted to hire the *Aphrodite*, he would have taken it anyway and we'd still be stuck in Alexandria—if he didn't knock us over the head and toss us into a canal for the crocodiles to get rid of."

"I wasn't criticizing. You did what you had to do, no question about it," Sostratos said. "And just in case there were any doubts, putting a crown on your head and calling yourself a king doesn't turn you into a kind man."

"I didn't have any doubts, but why do you put it that way? Ptolemaios wasn't officially a king yet when he made us go along with him," Menedemos said.

"True. I wasn't thinking of that just then. I was thinking of the old Cyclops when soldiers started slipping out of his camp and heading for Ptolemaios' forts so they could collect their ... their ...."

"Desertion bonus?" Menedemos suggested.

"*Euge!* Desertion bonus, that's perfect!" Sostratos dipped his head in agreement and admiration. "Antigonos put loyal men out between his lines and Ptolemaios', and they caught some of the would-be deserters and brought them back for judgment, I suppose you'd call it."

"I don't like the sound of that, my dear," Menedemos said. "Even among the Macedonians, the Antigonos doesn't have a name for being a gentle fellow."

Sostratos dipped his head again. "There are reasons he doesn't, too. He assembled his army, then brought the deserters out before the men and turned his torturers loose on them."

"That must have given the rest something to think about," Menedemos observed.

"Antigonos hoped it would, anyhow. But his soldiers kept sneaking away, he couldn't get past Ptolemaios' strongpoints and into the Delta, and Demetrios' fleet was having too much trouble with the weather to be any help. So he gave up in Egypt. The men he has left are marching up through Phoenicia and Syria now, probably on their way back to Anatolia. The fleet is going that way, too," Sostratos said.

"Let me guess," Menedemos said. "As soon as spring gets here, it's our turn. We saw all this coming a while ago."

"We did. What we didn't see was any way to stop it. If Antigonos and Demetrios had both died trying to grab Egypt, that might have done the trick, but they didn't. Our turn, sure enough. Either we bend the knee or we fight for our lives—that's how it looks to me."

"It looks the same way to me. I wish it didn't, but it does. Aren't these grand times to live in?" his cousin said.

"If we win, the poets will sing about our brave deeds the same way they sing about the fight for Troy. People hundreds of years from now will know Rhodes by her greatest hour."

"How about if we lose?"

"If we lose, some historian will write, 'Although Antigonos and Demetrios could not seize Egypt from Ptolemaios, they subjected Rhodes in the following year.' And that little bit will be as boring as the rest of his work. No one will want to listen to it. The scribes won't make new copies. And pretty soon mice will nibble holes in the papyrus of the last one left, and no one will know what he wrote anymore."

Menedemos sent him a sly look. "You could do a better job than that with the story, my dear."

"Maybe I could, but I wouldn't want to write about Rhodes losing. Even if I did want to, chances are I'd get killed in the fighting or captured and sold as a slave. Hard to write history if that kind of thing happens to you."

"I suppose it might be," Menedemos admitted. "But wasn't Aisop a slave?"

"So they say. For one thing, though, there are almost as many different stories about him as there are about Homer. For another, you don't need to investigate and to travel and to ask questions of lots of important men to weigh all their answers to write stories about talking animals."

"You don't think your master—if you had a master, I mean—would trust you to go around the Inner Sea asking your questions when he didn't need you, knowing you'd come back after you got done?"

Every once in a while, Sostratos found standing a couple of palms taller than his cousin a useful thing. As he looked down his nose at Menedemos now, he realized this was one of those times. "Don't be more foolish than you can help, my dear. How far do you trust your family's slaves not to run off?"

"Not very. And Rhodes is an island. They can't go far unless they sail in a ship or steal a boat. They still want to be free, though."

"They do," Sostratos agreed. "It makes you wonder whether Aristoteles knew what he was talking about when he said some men were slaves by nature. Would they try so hard to escape if they were?"

"I don't think so. But I also don't think we'd get the work that needs doing done unless we made somebody do it. If we had to do all that ourselves, we wouldn't have time to be proper men."

"Something to that, I'm sure. You aren't just talking about work around a household or in a shop or on a farm, either," Sostratos said. "Can you imagine the Athenians sending free men to work the silver mines at Laureion?"

"Not unless you mean free men they wanted to get rid of," his cousin replied. "How long does your ordinary slave last when he gets sent to the mines? A few months?"

"A few ten-days, more likely," Sostratos said. "But that silver was important to Athens. The polis spent it to build the fleet that built the Persians at Salamis. Without it, without the triremes it paid for, there might be a Persian governor there right now. We might have one here, too."

"So we might. That's the other Salamis, of course, the one by Athens."

"Yes, of course. That sea-fight has had almost two centuries of fame by now. I wonder whether, two centuries from now, our sea-fight at Cypriot Salamis will be remembered ahead of it."

Menedemos winked. "I tell you what, my dear. If I'm around two hundred years from now, I'll write you a note with the answer."

"That means you think I'll be around two centuries from now, too. Generous of you."

"When it comes to words, I'm generosity itself," Menedemos said.

"Many men are," Sostratos said. But he couldn't help laughing, no matter how much he wanted to. "I wonder how generous we'll have to be for Rhodes in the coming year. Our silver, our lives …. If the polis needs them, how can we say no?"

"I'm better with spear and shield and sword than I was when I was a youth," Menedemos said. "Those exercises were just for show then. Now they're liable to keep me alive. Knowing that makes me work harder."

"It's the same with me. I still keep hoping we won't need to use what we've practiced, but I don't believe it anymore."

"There's a baby in my house, too," Menedemos said. "He can't keep himself safe yet. We've got to do it for him."

"Your half-brother," Sostratos said. Menedemos dipped his head. Something went across his face as he did, but it was gone too fast for Sostratos to read it, so he went on as he would have anyhow: "My cousin. As you say, we'll do what we can. That's all we're able to do."

One of the things Menedemos hadn't understood about babies was how fast they grew and changed. When he came home from Alexandria, Diodoros had been a little lump of a thing, unable to roll over or smile or do anything but nurse, make messes, and yowl. He'd had a perpetually startled expression. And why not? The world was very new to him.

Now he was almost half a year old. He could laugh and smile. He looked interested all the time, not amazed. He'd figured out how to roll over. He reached for things and stuck them in his mouth when his hand actually got them, which it sometimes did. He'd swallowed a tiny crawling beetle before Baukis could extract it. It didn't seem to have done him any lasting harm.

He still cried when he was unhappy or wanted something, but he made more intriguing noises, too. They weren't words yet, but some of them were starting to sound like things that could turn into words. In the same way, you could tell that he would turn into a person.

Baukis brought him down to the courtyard more often. In the coolness of winter, she didn't need to worry about him baking. The plants in the little garden fascinated him. And she could put an old blanket on the ground and let him roll around on it. He enjoyed that.

Menedemos enjoyed seeing Baukis out and about, even if she did have Lyke or another slave woman with her. He enjoyed the little boy more than he'd dreamt he would, too. When he scooped Diodoros off the blanket and into the crook of his elbow, the baby would laugh. Or, looking up at Menedemos, he'd smile a wide, almost toothless smile, recognizing him as a familiar, acceptable person.

"He likes you!" Baukis exclaimed whenever she saw him do it.

"No accounting for taste," Menedemos answered the first time she said that. A few paces away, Lyke snorted softly. Baukis didn't even notice what he said. When Diodoros found something he liked, that made her happy.

How much attention she gave the baby left Menedemos frustrated. He wanted her to notice other things—him, for instance. He had wondered if she would go again to the women's religious festival after which they might have started Diodoros the year before. He'd hoped she would: it was the only chance he was likely to get to see her alone. But she'd stayed in. Even with the slaves to help her, taking care of the baby left her exhausted all the time.

And Diodoros was a healthy baby, for which Menedemos joined his father and stepmother in praising the gods. One of Xanthos' kinswomen—Menedemos wasn't sure if she was a niece or a grandniece—had had a boy about the time Baukis gave birth. She called him Xanthiades, perhaps to curry favor with her rich relative.

But he never thrived. He was skinny and sickly and often shat green, which even Menedemos knew to be a bad sign. And, just about the time when word of Antigonos and Demetrios' failure at the edge of Egypt got back to Rhodes, little Xanthiades died.

Xanthos sadly went on about it at great length, the way he went on about everything. Menedemos' father didn't tell him to shove a stopper in it. They'd been friends for years, and even Menedemos understood that talking grief out helped lessen it. But after a while, his father's patience started to show. Sooner or later, Xanthos always went off to inflict himself on someone else. Menedemos did wonder why it couldn't have been sooner that time.

His thoughts snapped back to the courtyard when the slave woman stepped away for something she needed or wanted to do. Alone with Baukis! Alone in public, and with him holding her son, but alone. He opened his mouth to say something witty and charming, something that would make her remember why she'd given herself to him the year before.

Before he could speak, she stepped toward him. In a low, urgent voice, she demanded, "How bad will it be come spring?"

He started to give her some reassuring lie. A look at her blazing eyes and set mouth told him that would be a mistake. "Well, I don't think it will be good," he said, and waited to see what happened next.

"How bad will it be?" she persisted. "Men never want to tell women anything, curse them. All I know is bits and scraps I've overheard. But women and babies pay the price when the men who run things are stupid, don't they?"

"We're as ready as we can be to defend Rhodes," Menedemos said slowly. "Demetrios is a good general, though. We may not win."

"Can't we just give him whatever he wants?"

"He wants us to ally with his father and him against the Ptolemaios. Egypt trades through Rhodes, and we get a lot of our grain there, too. Besides, it would cost us our freedom. He'd surely put a garrison in the polis to make sure we didn't go back on our promises."

She tossed her head. "That's not losing your freedom. Losing your freedom is being sold for a slave. Losing your freedom is watching them do to your son what they did to Astyanax in *The Trojan Women*."

A man wouldn't think that way. A man would think being forced into an alliance with a stronger power was the same as slavery. Men took care of themselves no matter what. Women, especially women with small children, couldn't. "You feel we ought to yield, then?" he asked.

"Of course, if the only other choice is standing siege till we're overrun."

"That isn't *of course*. If Demetrios attacks us, we do have a chance to hold him out of the polis."

"How good a chance?"

"Good enough that it may be worth trying, anyhow." Menedemos hesitated, then asked, "Why does my father say to you about it?"

Baukis' nostrils flared angrily. "Nothing much. He thinks I'm a child who doesn't understand anything, the same way most men think about women." She eyed him. "You don't think of me like that, do you?" *You'd better not!* was written all over her face.

"Not for a moment," Menedemos assured her. Whether or not he was telling the truth … he could worry about some other time, when it might matter. As long as she was his father's wife, it wouldn't, or not very much.

Diodoros started to fuss. "Give him to me," Baukis said. He did. They touched for a moment. It felt like fire to him. She didn't seem to notice at all. She jogged him up and down and patted him on the back. He went right on fussing.

"Let me try," Menedemos said. He wanted to feel her touch again, and he did, though again she paid the brief, accidental contact no mind. He hoisted his half-brother (his son?) onto his shoulder and patted the baby's back the way she had.

"Don't do it so hard!" Baukis said.

At almost the same instant, Diodoros let out a belch so loud, a fat old opsophagos would have been proud of it at a feast. As soon as he did, he went back to being happy. "There you go!" Menedemos told him. "You had that in there all the time, didn't you?" He lowered the baby to the crook of his elbow. Diodoros stared up at him and started to laugh. Yes, they had a family look, all right. Well, they were family, one way or the other.

"He likes you," Baukis said.

"I told you before, he's too little to know better," Menedemos said. She made a face at him. She liked him in that moment, if only because her son did, too. *You take what you can get*, he thought.

"I want him to grow up to see the kind of man you are," she said. "He'll learn from you, the same as he'll learn from your father." She didn't talk about which of them had sired Diodoros. She would have been madly foolish to do that where anyone might overhear. And she wouldn't know for certain, either, any more than Menedemos did.

"I want him to grow up free and safe. As long as he does that, everything will be fine," Menedemos said. *I just want him to grow up*, went through his mind. Along with all the sicknesses that could cut short the thread of a child's life, the Fates also had to steer it past war and famine … if they meant to, of course.

"Tell me it will be all right," Baukis whispered.

"It will be all right." Menedemos sounded as sincere as he did when he was seducing other men's wives in far-off poleis. But Baukis was here not just in Rhodes but in his house. And Demetrios and Antigonos, while not here yet, were bound to be on their way. Spring …. Spring might be very bad.

The slave woman came back. She knew all about what Menedemos and Baukis and the rest of the free folk of Rhodes only feared. Day by day, she got through. All Menedemos could do was pray he'd never have to.

HISTORICAL NOTE

Salamis is set in 306 BC. As the story notes, this sea battle was by the Salamis in eastern Cyprus, not by the one near Athens. It was the second sea-fight off the Cypriot city, the earlier one having taken place almost fifty years before. All the people of Rhodes could do in this year was nervously watch the thunderous war on land and sea between Antigonos and Demetrios on the one hand and Ptolemaios on the other.

Menedemos is (just barely) a historical figure, though everyone else in his family is fictitious. Other historical figures who appear in *Salamis* are Demetrios, Ptolemaios, and Ptolemaios' henchmen Argaios and Kallikrates. Historical figures who are mentioned but have no direct role include Demetrios' father Antigonos; Demetrios' late brother Philippos; Demetrios' admiral Antisthenes; Ptolemaios' brother Menelaos; the rival warlords Seleukos, Kassandros, and Lysimakhos; and Demetrios of Phaleron, who had ruled Athens for Kassandros till Demetrios Antigonos' son ousted him the year before our story takes place.

In one way, doing the research for this book showed me how much things have changed in the past twenty years. If, at the end of the twentieth century, I wanted to see pictures of amphorai from different places around the Greek world, I would have had to drive down to the UCLA research library and dig until I found the particular book (more likely, books) I needed … if no one else had checked out the critical one. In this modern world, I went to Google Images on my tablet, typed in "amphora" and whatever place names I needed, and had lots of color images at my disposal. Beats working.

267

In another way, things haven't changed at all. Menedemos could very well have used the method he did to work out how many Akahaians went to Troy to fight. I used that method myself when I was writing an undergrad paper for a course on the history of ancient Greece in 1969. After I'd added up all the ships mentioned in Book II of the *Iliad*, I went to an encyclopedia (print, of course—no Wikipedia in those dark days) to make sure I'd done it right. The encyclopedia said something like "Agamemnon took 1,186 ships and approximately 100,000 men to Troy." I stared at that, realizing that whoever had written the article I was checking had done exactly the same thing I had: taken the average of the two figures for men per ship Homer gives and multiplied it by the number of ships (which I had right, by the way). It was the very first time I ever actually felt like a historian.

I've transliterated most Greek personal and place names straight into English, with no detour through Latin. In *Salamis*, you'll see Demetrios, not Demetrius; Platon, not Plato; and Kition, not Citium. I've made exceptions where places have a very familiar name in English, such as Athens, Crete, and Cyprus. I've also left the names of Alexander the Great and his father, Philip of Macedon, in their conventional forms. The other Alexandros and Philippos who appear in the story do so under names that would have been more familiar to their contemporaries. Transliteration never makes anyone perfectly happy. All writers can do is their best.

END